HE CAUGHT HER MOUTH
WITH HIS OWN . . .

She felt as if it were happening to someone else. Or as if she had stepped out of her body for the moment, while this thing was happening to it. So how could she resist? His tongue filled her mouth and sensations shot through her that seemed to belong more to her fantasies than her real life. Was it she, Elizabeth Rogers, who was here half-standing, half-melting, in the overpowering arms of this man?

His hands pulled downward suddenly, and her robe parted . . .

MISTRESS
OF THE
WESTERN WIND

A TORRENT OF DESIRE,
A STORM OF ADVENTURE!

Also by Jessica Richards
from Jove

TULAROSA

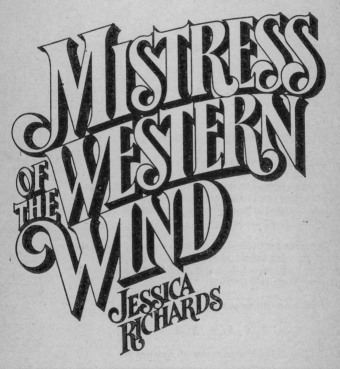

MISTRESS OF THE WESTERN WIND

JESSICA RICHARDS

A JOVE BOOK

First Jove edition published May 1980

10 9 8 7 6 5 4 3 2 1

Printed in the United States of America

Jove books are published by Jove Publications, Inc.,
200 Madison Avenue, New York, NY 10016

Text designed by Michael Serrian

BOOK ONE

∾Chapter One

IN 1852, DURING HER SECOND YEAR OF
marriage to ship's master David Creighton, of Stonington,
Connecticut, Charlotte Creighton became pregnant with
their first child.

Captain Creighton was pleased. He had married late, at
forty, and he had always imagined himself the father of a
son.

He'd take the lad to sea with him. He'd give him sea legs
as a toddler, have him climbing the rigging as soon as he
could walk. The boy could learn his letters on shipboard,
and learn the stars and the tides and the currents as well.
When he got old enough, he'd be his father's cabin boy,
then a seaman, and one day . . . captain of the finest clipper ship ever to sail round the Horn! For Captain Creighton, there was no life but the sea.

Charlotte Creighton wanted a girl, though she never
voiced the desire aloud. But more than that—though she
never voiced this aloud either, nor so much as hinted at it
to Captain Creighton—she was grateful simply to be pregnant.

It meant that she would not have to go to sea anymore.

7

Charlotte Burr was from the inland village of Washington, Connecticut. At twenty-four, she was still unmarried, still living at home with her father. She taught music to young boys at the Reed School, a private seminary named after its founder, an Episcopal minister and former missionary.

Dr. Reed had been a missionary to the Hawaiian Islands before opening his school. He had known Captain David Creighton from those days. Captain Creighton commanded a clipper in the China trade. When Dr. Reed moved to Connecticut, he had invited Captain Creighton to come up and visit his school, and during a layover in Stonington Creighton accepted his invitation.

Charlotte and her father were invited to the dinner reception for Captain Creighton. The elder Burr declined. He was not given to social pursuits other than grouse hunting and drinking, both of which he mostly did alone.

Charlotte accepted, even though she was not at all sure how she felt about it. She always felt out of place, a spinster at a dinner party, disrupting people's table arrangements. She never knew what to say to anyone, and never enjoyed any of the small talk she did manage to make. She had nothing in common with any of the ladies—and, of course, nothing to say to the gentlemen. If one didn't learn that at age sixteen or seventeen, when it counted, there was no chance of ever learning it.

And besides, she looked like what she was—an old-maid schoolteacher. She had to admit it, as she stood before the mirror on her way out to the Reeds' house. The high, stern cheekbones, the sharp gray eyes that could make her face turn as icy and forbidding as she wanted it to. It was a good face for terrorizing unruly twelve-year-old boys, or for putting fools in their place. She was afraid it was not much good for anything beyond that.

She had not known that Captain Creighton was unmarried, or that she would be seated next to him at the dinner table. And she had not expected the dour, wizened old Dr. Reed to have an acquaintance who looked like the captain. If she had formed a mental picture of him at all, before meeting him, it was something like Dr. Reed—short in stature, with dried-up skin and bearing, small eyes, and a

8

turned-down mouth. Perhaps coarser and more vulgar, from having followed the sea instead of a godly, academic life.

What she encountered, instead, was a huge man, weathered, direct, and powerful. His dark beard was square-cut, and shaved clean over his upper lip. It intensified the shape of his naturally broad, square face. His lips were broad, firm, and purposeful, and when they turned up into a smile, it was not a smile that one would forget quickly. His eyebrows were bushy. His nose was unexpectedly small and regular, throwing his face into a sudden and striking handsomeness. The squared corners of his beard were graying, like the tips of a leaf beginning to turn after the first cold night of October.

When he looked at her, he must have seen something more than she saw when she met her own eyes in the mirror. Who knows what a man sees who keeps his feelings to himself? Perhaps he saw the soft, voluptuous, full-busted figure that not even her severe clothing and stiff posture could disguise. And perhaps he noticed that when she talked to him, her gray eyes softened, and her cheekbones seemed not stern and angular, but strong and handsome, setting off a face of rare beauty. All Charlotte knew was that she felt different when he looked at her.

Captain Creighton talked to Charlotte throughout the dinner. He talked about the sea, but not at length. He talked more about his house in Stonington, where he had been spending the last few months. His mother had died during his last sea voyage, and he had been setting the house's affairs in order, and taking care of her effects.

"I'm very sorry for your misfortune," Charlotte said.

"Yes, I shall miss coming home to her," the captain said. "But she had a long life, and she suffered very little at the end, they tell me. So my stay at the old house has been more prolonged than usual."

"How sad and ironic that it should be so, now that you have no one to share it with."

"Yes, isn't it? And ironic, too, how loss increases our capacity to value what we have. I find I appreciate the beauty and tranquility of the old house more than I have in years—perhaps ever."

"Oh, do tell me what it's like!" said Charlotte.

9

Captain Creighton puffed out his cheeks as though blowing smoke through an imaginary pipe.

"My grandfather built it," he said. "The first Creighton to ship out from Stonington as master of a Yankee vessel. It's a fine house, made of brick, and the hand carvings over the doorways were done by my grandfather himself."

"Your grandfather did wood carving . . . as well as being a sailor?"

"Oh, yes. A ship's captain gets to be master of many trades, and there's time aplenty at sea."

"Tell me more about the house."

"Well, it's on a hill, overlooking the village, and the sea. Behind it, there's a garden, and a trellised rose arbor. . . ."

"Who will take care of the rose garden, while you're away at sea?"

"I shall have to hire a gardener. Of course, it won't be the same as it was under my mother's tending. But things never do stay the same on land, do they?"

That night, and for many nights to come, Charlotte Burr saw the big house in Stonington before she fell off to sleep, and in her dreams. She saw the fan-shaped white shutters on the windows, the white gate and stone walk up to the great front door, the treasures from far-flung lands brought back by three generations of sea captains: Persian rugs and Chinese tapestries, damask tablecloths and East Indian china, tables from India whose legs were intricately carved ebony elephants and whose tops were etched brass. She saw the rose garden, and beds of chrysanthemums, and herbs outside the kitchen window.

She saw the captain, too, in her mind's eye, and when he came into her thoughts, her body seemed to lose the tight discipline she had always kept over it. Her muscles relaxed, and part of her felt flushed, warm and moist. She was slower in undressing and putting on her nightgown in the evening than she had ever been before. When she accidentally brushed any part of her body lightly, with her hand or with the bedclothes, it made her tingle all over.

Charlotte had never told anyone how much she hated her life. She hated teaching at the Reed School. She hated the noise and the lack of a life of her own. She hated standing up in front of a classroom in front of a pack of awk-

10

ward, gawking, adolescent boys. There was nothing, and no one, in Washington who meant anything to her.

Charlotte decided that if Captain Creighton were to come back, and if he were to propose marriage to her, she would accept.

Six months later, Captain David Creighton returned from a voyage to Europe, paid another visit to Washington, and asked Charlotte to be his bride. He showed her an artist's rendering of the brick house in Stonington. He disclosed to her his assets at the present time as well as his expectations as a ship's master. He told her of his esteem and affection for her.

It was not the most romantic of proposals, but it was all the romance that Charlotte needed or wanted. She considered all the thoughts she had weighed in Creighton's absence. She looked at him, and felt the same stirring that she had felt before. She told him that she accepted his proposal.

They were married in Washington, in the stone church on the village green, which was also the school chapel. Dr. Reed had arranged that a few of the senior boys be present as representatives of the school, though Charlotte would have preferred that they not be. Charlotte's father gave the bride away. Mrs. Reed, who disliked Charlotte intensely— even more entensely than the Hawaiian maidens she had lived among, who were heathens, and could not be expected to know that the Lord hated women with small waists and firm bosoms—stood up with her, and also played the organ for the ceremony.

They went to Stonington that afternoon, and Charlotte saw the house that she was to be mistress of. Her first home, the house that had been waiting for her to come and take over, to give it that imprint of herself that had for so long lain dormant in her hope chest.

The house—her house—made her feel serene. And that serenity helped her to deal with the warm, moist, excited feelings that had come over her during those nights alone when the captain had entered her thoughts. The feelings were even stronger and more confusing, now, when she was about to enter his bed.

11

She had been better able to accept them when she was alone. She knew that did not make sense—after all, her husband was the cause of the feelings—but it was true, nonetheless. Charlotte was a private person. She was not used to sharing her feelings, and she found it hard.

She undressed behind a screen. The buttons and stays in her garments seemed harder to unfasten than they ever had, as if her clothes had a mind of their own and wanted to stay on her body. Her fingers trembled and fumbled faster, as if, disloyally, they could not wait to lay her body bare.

Finally, it was done. The last bow untied, and her shift on the floor at her feet. Charlotte was tall, with a long, tapering waist and firm round breasts that she brushed with her arm as she reached up for her nightgown, which hung over the top of the screen. The feeling startled her, and she dropped her hands to her sides. She was paralyzed; but she had to fight it. She could not just go on standing there naked, growing ever more intensely aware of her nakedness. Even the cool breezes that played through the room seemed to be finding their way to the private parts of her body, stirring them to more trembling and sensation. She reached forward again, pulled down her nightgown, and put it on quickly.

She came out from behind the screen. She stood beside the bed, not daring to get into it; and when her husband came into the room, dressed in a long nightshirt, he stood at the opposite side and they looked across at each other.

For the space of several heartbeats, neither of them moved. Then Captain Creighton reached over and turned down the bedclothes on Charlotte's side. She could put it off no longer. She got into bed.

The captain turned down the sheets on his side as Charlotte was turning them back up on hers, and swung in beside her. He sat up straight and stretched his upper body over the bedside table to blow out the light.

She was alone in bed with her new husband. In the dark. Her mingled fear and anticipation grew stronger, and she waited for him to do something to allay it.

She knew, in general, what it was that he would do. But she was not quite sure how it would work, or how it was that it would calm the feelings that began in that part of her body, and made her want to squirm and move her hips and legs in ways that she knew a lady must never, never do.

Clenching her fists, tightening her shoulders and her jaw and the muscles of her neck, she lay perfectly still. She could not tighten the lower part of her body at all, anymore. A sound came out of her mouth, from somewhere deep in her throat, surprising her.

"Did you say something, my dear?" asked her husband.

"No, nothing, David, I . . ."

And then he was on top of her.

He wrapped his left arm around her, and held her close to him, while his right hand lifted the front of her nightgown. She wanted to throw her arms around him and return his embrace, but she could not bring herself to. Her upper body remained rigid, while her lower body seemed to be detached from the rest of her, doing something that it knew how to do, that she would never have dreamed of doing. Her thighs parted. Her pelvis, like a wave, seemed to swell up toward him, as she felt his flesh against hers, and something hard and blunt poking against her, and then no longer against her, but actually inside.

Her head swam. It was all she could do to remember not to cry out, not to wrap her arms—even her legs!—around him. She lay still, and the feelings swirled around her and filled her up. And then ended. Abruptly. Her husband rolled off her, and lay next to her on the bed with his back to her. And nothing had been allayed. The feelings had been resolved. She heard the rumbling, regular breathing of her husband's sleep next to her, and she got up, went into the antechamber, and cried.

❧Chapter Two

DAVID CREIGHTON LEFT THE NEXT MORNING for New York, to check on the progress of the repairs to his ship, the *Union Flyer*. He would also arrange for a cargo, and discuss the prospects for the next voyage with the *Union Flyer*'s owners. Messrs. Arbour and Brooke.

He told Charlotte to expect him back in a week. In his absence, Charlotte set up housekeeping. She felt calmer, and more at home, with him gone.

She visited the local tradesmen, and began to know the community. The women of Stonington were a strange group. They were tight-knit, and yet they were all loners. Their thoughts and their fears were always with the sea, with husbands and sons who were on it and might never come back from it. When three married women met on the street, they could look at each other and know that the next time they met, one of them would very likely be a widow.

Charlotte knew that there were widows aplenty in Stonington. But what struck her even more immediately was the lack of hospitality to a newcomer that these women showed. It seemed that their fatalism could encompass the prospect of losing their men to a fall from the rigging during a gale at sea, or the slap of a whale's giant fin, against a small boat, or the treacherous rip tides of the Sound carry-

15

ing off a fisherman as he went out to haul lobster pots, far better than it could accept the prospect of losing a man to a woman who was not one of them.

Charlotte did not mind the cold reception of her fellow sea wives. Solitude had never been a problem to her. For her, the real shock came about a week after she moved to Stonington, when a neighbor, Mrs. Conacher, engaged her in a rare conversation at the butcher's.

"You're one o' the lucky ones," Mrs. Conacher had said. "At least, your man's a ship's master, so ye'll be goin' with him when he puts out to sea."

Charlotte was stunned, but she managed to recover herself enough not to show it.

"Is that the custom?" she asked. "I mean . . . that only the captain's wife is allowed to accompany her husband on a voyage."

Mrs. Conacher took Charlotte's attempt to cover up her ignorance as an expression of sympathy, and continued a little more warmly.

"Yes, it seems unfair, doesn't it? If a ship's not carrying its full quota of passengers, and there's cabins left over, you'd think they'd be after lettin' the mate's missus have the use o' the space, wouldn't ye? Well, I just have to wait for my man to get his own ship, someday. The Lord knows, he deserves it. Lucky for you, to go straight into marriage with a captain. Most of us here married young."

Her husband came home the next day, and Charlotte confronted him with the question immediately.

"David, is it your plan that I sail with you when you put out to sea again?"

"What? Of course it's my plan! I've just been informing Arbour and Brooke of my nuptials, and the arrangements have all been made for your convenience. You don't think I'd sail for Manila without you, surely, when it's possible to bring you along?"

"I . . . would not object, David. The house is comfortable, and I have just been getting used to it. There is more than enough here for me to occupy my time with—"

"Nonsense!" he cut her off. "I want you with me, and I mean to have it that way. All the shipping companies are making provision for captains' wives these days, and I mean to avail myself of that privilege. We sail together."

16

She tried again, hoping to make herself plainer.

"David. I married you in the expectation that our mutual bond would expressly not interfere with the conduct of our individual daily lives—"

"Then you were a damned fool, and it behooves you now not to compound your foolishness by dragging this discussion out any further," he said. "You'll sail with me as my wife, and there's nothing more to be said on the subject."

Charlotte had never been in New York before. She should have been excited. Captain Creighton took her to Delmonico's for dinner, and down Fifth Avenue. He was enjoying showing her the city, and he was fairly humming with excitement as the time for sailing drew nearer. She could not share in either emotion. She felt cold and dead inside.

On the morning of their departure, they went down to Canal Street, to the musty, oak-paneled offices of Arbour and Brooke, Inc. Her husband introduced her to both men, and they bowed and shook hands with her. Arthur Brooke was a youngish man, with fluffy hair and muttonchop sideburns; Edward Arbour was the senior partner, tall and stooped, hook-nosed and solemn. They told Mrs. Creighton what a fine ship the *Union Flyer* was, and they seemed to take it for granted that she should feel both honored and fortunate to be making this voyage aboard such a fine vessel.

Charlotte had never felt so alone in her life.

Boarding the ship was even worse. They drove to the waterfront in a hansom. The ship had been brought from its loading berth to anchor at Castle Garden, at the foot of Manhattan, and it was there that they were to board it. Charlotte looked about her, and she had never seen anything so ugly or brutish, nor imagined that there could be anything like it in the world. It was all the awfulness she had seen in the worst boys at the Reed School, but without Mr. and Mrs. Reed to keep it under control, and put into the huge, sloppy forms of grown men who were more like animals.

The waterfront stank of fish and liquor and filth. The air

17

exploded with curses and the sounds of violence. But as shocking as the sights, sounds, and smells of the waterfront were to Charlotte, what shocked her even more was the casual acceptance of such squalor by her three companions, all apparently gentlemen on the outside. Arbour and Brooke seemed completely at ease, not thinking to apologize to her for the conditions they were dragging her through, even exchanging conversation with some of the waterfront creatures they passed, and showing no apparent distaste over it.

And her husband just seemed to grow more and more animated and invigorated, as if the foul air had some sort of tonic in it.

They reached the ship. Drunken, unshaven louts staggered up the gangplank, carrying sea chests on their shoulders or under their arms. There were women with greasy hair and slatternly clothes, standing in postures she had never imagined she would see a female human being strike. There was a man on his hands and knees next to the foot of the gangplank, vomiting into the fetid water of the harbor.

"Well, there she is," said Arthur Brooke. "Isn't she a beauty?"

Brooke and Arbour joined Captain and Mrs. Creighton in the captain's cabin, aboard ship, for a glass of sherry and a few final words with the captain. Then they went ashore, and the ship weighed anchor and, pulled by a harbor tugboat, began to move away from the dock, headed for Sandy Hook and the open sea.

Charlotte stood on deck, looking back at the dock, although there was no one standing there whom she knew or cared to wave good-bye to. There was just the land, and the memory of her home, the house on the hill in Stonington, where she had lived for less than a month, and which she would not now see again for more than a year, if ever.

Captain Creighton stayed out on deck, too. Arbour and Brooke were down at pierside, watching the ship move out, with the late-afternoon sun burnishing her sails; and there was a flock of sightseers, as well, to whom the launching of a great clipper ship was a sight well worth turning out for.

Captain Creighton stood on the poopdeck for as long as

18

the ship was still in sight of land, an imposing figure in his elegant black cutaway suit, bow tie, and high stovepipe hat. The mates handled the work on deck, and sailors, or those who were sober enough to understand orders, climbed aloft to the yards and began to put up sail.

When the ship was finally out of sight of land, Captain Creighton went below. Charlotte stood a while longer in the same spot, watching nothing but the unfamiliar and endless expanse of sea, foam, and grey evening sky, immobilized with dread and the realization that, no matter how tightly she gripped the ship's rail, she could not stop the deck from undulating beneath her.

When she did snap out of her trance and look around, she beheld her husband, coming back up on deck, as she had never seen him before. He was out of his shore clothes and into his seaman's outfit—striped woolen jersey and loose-fitting pajamas, China-side straw slippers on his feet.

Charlotte unconsciously shrank back against the rail. Her husband seemed to have disappeared, and been replaced by a monstrous figure, foreign to her in every particular. His burly, barrel-chested form, which had managed to appear portly and distinguished in his dignified, conservatively tailored shore clothes, was now revealed as menacing and animalistic. His body bulged with the muscles of a navvy, powerful and uncouth. She realized for the first time how big his hands were. It was suddenly hard for her to believe that those immense, bearlike paws, with their thick fingers and splayed knuckles, had ever touched her, had ever held her own hands in their grasp. The sounds that seemed to erupt out of him, from deep in his throat, as he shouted out orders to the crew, were like the howling and baying of some wild animal in the jungle.

Charlotte went below decks, to her cabin. She looked around at the bare walls, with no samplers, no curtains, nothing breaking the bleakness but a picture of a clipper ship, a map of the Western Hemisphere, and a round window out of which she could see only the same dark sky and endlessly moving sea that she had seen from the deck.

What was she supposed to do on this ship? What would she occupy her time with? Who would she talk to, with no other women around? What was expected of her? Her husband had explained nothing. She felt a mounting terror rising up inside her, and she threw herself down on a chair and sobbed uncontrollably.

Eventually, her sobbing subsided, but her fear did not. She changed into her nightgown, brushed out her hair, and got into bed. She turned her face to the wall, and tried to sleep.

She was still awake when her husband came into the room, but she pretended unconsciousness, and did not acknowledge his presence.

Captain Creighton did not come to bed for quite a while. Charlotte could hear him in the cabin not far away from her, rustling papers and muttering to himself.

Once, she pretended to roll over in her sleep, and opened one eye a crack to look at him. He was sitting at his desk, going over his charts and making notations in his logbook. As he swiveled around in his chair, Charlotte could see see his naked chest swing in and out of her field of vision.

Although they had shared the same bed, and the act of marriage, they had always been properly modest and respectful about revealing themselves to each other, and she had never seen his chest before. A tremor of revulsion passed through her body.

Her husband's chest was covered with coarse, black, matted hair, thick and tufted across his breast, sparser and wiry down his rib cage, then obscenely heavy again on his stomach. As she watched, he scratched his hairy stomach, grunted, and frowned at the chart in front of him.

Charlotte rolled back over again, and shut her eyes tightly. It was a nightmare beyond her wildest imagining. First, to have the home that she waited so many years for offered to her, then snatched away. Then, the very earth taken out from under her feet. Then, set down amid a bunch of drunken, fiendish brutes—and finally, her husband turning into an animal right before her eyes!

She lay rigid, and did not open her eyes. Finally, she heard him stand up, roll up his charts, and close his logbook. There were a few other sounds, and, moments later, he lay in bed beside her.

She felt a little bit more secure when she realized he had covered his nakedness with a nightshirt. But then she felt a heavy hand on her shoulder, and suddenly all her terror,

20

revulsion—and something else—were concentrated in the same place.

She tried to resist his pressure and pretend that she was sound asleep, at the same time. It was no use. He was too strong for her. And he had his rights as a husband on his side. Inexorably, she was rolled over onto her back.

When the other heavy hand began pulling her nightgown up, her eyes flew open, and she started to plead with him from the depths of her terror.

"No! . . . David, no! . . . I can't . . . you mustn't . . . don't make me . . ."

He was not looking back down at her, and all she could see of his face was his thick black beard, curling down his neck and meeting with the mass of hair now hidden under his nightshirt. She pictured, again, his hairy chest and stomach, and she struggled to get loose.

Her lower parts were exposed now, and his big hand pressed down on her hip, holding her flat. She could feel his thumb brushing against the hairs that grew near her most private part. She could feel his male member, hard and insistently there, lying against her thigh.

It disturbed her deeply. It was just touching her, not doing anything that she had to permit as a wife. Just *there*, impossible to ignore. She felt like reaching down and moving it away, but there was no way that she could, and the thought of holding it in her hand made her tremble all over.

She felt herself growing weak again, and she tried pleading once more.

"David, no . . ." she said. "What if . . . ? David, we are going to be at sea for over a year! What if . . . I were to conceive? . . . David, I'm afraid! Have pity on me . . ."

His heavy body rolled over on her, and she thought again of the hair on his chest and stomach as he entered her, and she thought of the pressure—she could still feel it—of that hard, blunt, hot, disturbing presence against her thigh. Her body shook and trembled in a way that was completely new to her, and she experienced sensations that she had never felt before, out of control this time, making her cry out loud and press her body closer to the feeling, whether to cut it off or get more of it, she did not know.

21

And this time, she was not left with the edgy, unresolved feeling she had always experienced before. She was spent. She felt as though she had been swept through a long tunnel, and out the other side. She was not sure she liked it. The edgy, unresolved feeling was more in keeping with her nature.

In the middle of the night, Charlotte woke up sweating. Her body felt as if it had been turned inside out. Her stomach was churning. Her whole system felt as if it had been altered, the feeling was in the center of her body.

It's happened, she thought, panic-stricken. I *am* with child.

She lifted herself up on her elbows, and looked over at her husband. He lay deep in sleep, his damp, rumpled nightshirt covering his body, his beard in disarray, his mouth open, snoring heavily. At that moment, she hated him beyond all reason. But she wanted to wake him up, cling to him, and beg him to help her.

Then, after another moment, she realized what the feeling in her stomach really was.

She thought you were supposed to go up on deck and lean over the side, but she was afraid to go alone, and she was not dressed. Nobody had told her what to do. Nobody had told her anything. There was a water closet connected to the captain's cabin, but she forgot about it in her panic. And in another moment, it was too late. For the second time that night, her body heaved and shuddered, and she threw up on her husband.

⌘Chapter Three

THE BABY WAS A GIRL. CAPTAIN CREIGHTON was away at sea when she was born. Charlotte named the baby Elizabeth, after her mother. She was glad that her husband was away for the birth. He would be away for another seven months, at least, which meant seven whole months for the baby to go on being a girl without his even knowing about it.

Elizabeth had not been conceived until the homeward voyage. Charlotte had managed to remain seasick and unapproachable for over two months, or until after the ship had rounded Cape Horn. The Cape Horn passage was so unspeakable that after it was over, and she had survived it, the day-to-day motion of the boat no longer affected her.

She began to settle into a daily search for ways to occupy her time on board ship. She read, or worked at her sewing in her cabin. She spent many hours playing the piano in the ship's saloon. Sometimes, on pleasant days, she would take her sewing up on deck, and sit out in a deck chair. But she preferred having walls around her to the endless, unbroken expanse of sea; and she could never get used to the sight of sailors climbing up the rigging, or out along the masts, a hundred feet or more above the deck. Occasionally a dot of land would be sighted, an island in the distance, and she would come up to look at it. The

23

distant dots of land were her friends, because she could imagine them as looking like New England. If they passed close enough to make out any of their foreign, unfamiliar details, the islands seemed as threatening and hostile to her as the sea.

She had been able to use her sickness to fend off Captain Creighton's advances, but after the Horn, she had to submit to him once again. Then, after seeing—and loathing—the Orient, and setting sail from San Francisco Bay for New York harbor, she had begun to feel sick to her stomach again, in the morning. This time, she knew the cause of the feeling.

During the last months of her pregnancy, she moved with slow and stately steps around the house in Stonington, like a queen. Her face was serene, with the familiar glow of expectant motherhood. The weight inside her was like an anchor: an anchor keeping her safe and secure in her snug harbor, far away from the high seas.

When Captain Creighton next appeared in the doorway, with his sea chest over his shoulder, Elizabeth could sit up to eat her cereal, if Charlotte or Mrs. Perkins, the nurse, propped her up against a cushion. She had cereal once a day by then, in addition to the nourishment she got from Charlotte's breast. The doctor said she needed it to become stronger and more robust. Charlotte thought that she was quite robust enough for a girl, already, but the doctor was quite firm about it, and Mrs. Perkins thought that babies should be fed as much as possible.

Charlotte had been denied the pleasure of informing the captain that he was the father of a girl. The news had already traveled from Stonington to the offices of Arbour and Brooke in New York. So if Captain Creighton had been disappointed when he first heard the news, Charlotte never knew about it. And certainly, there was no evidence of disappointment as he burst into the house.

"Where's my daughter?" he roared.

"Be quiet, Captain! She's sleeping," said Charlotte sternly. Fat Mrs. Perkins moved protectively in front of the cradle, as if using her bulk to hide little Elizabeth from the invader.

Captain Creighton strode across the room with china-rattling steps. Mrs. Perkins stood her ground until he was almost upon her, then retreated, looking over at Charlotte for support.

Charlotte just stood back, wringing her hands helplessly. But there was a curious half-smile on her face, a smile that spoke of the secret understandings between women and babies, and the final revenge against husbands who renege on their promises.

Little Elizabeth's eyes were open. The commotion had wakened her, but she had not yet started to cry, as she usually did the minute she woke up. Captain Creighton loomed over her, smiling broadly through his big black beard.

Elizabeth beamed back at him.

His great hands scooped her up out of her cradle, like a black bear scooping a trout out of a stream.

"No! . . ." gasped Charlotte.

Captain Creighton tossed the baby in the air, and caught her over his head.

"No!" said Charlotte again, this time with greater urgency and severity. "You must be careful with her, Captain Creighton. She is a delicate child, and she must be handled delicately—and not overfrequently. It harms her digestion. You'll injure her."

Elizabeth was gurgling happily.

"Ah, yes, you know your Papa, don't ye, Lizzie?" the captain boomed. "Aye, we'll have some high times together, Lizzie and Papa, won't we, hum hum?"

"Her name is Elizabeth, not Lizzie, and I'll thank you to call her by her proper Christian name," said Charlotte. "Now put her down. She's had enough excitement for one day."

"Not a bit of it," said the captain. "She's loving every minute of it, as any fool can see. There, listen to her laugh."

Charlotte walked over to confront her husband. She stood braced firmly before the towering bulk of the sea captain.

"Well, she's delicate, nevertheless, as you'll do nothing but prove to all our sorrow if you keep up this behavior."

Captain Creighton scarcely seemed to notice her. He

went on cooing to his daughter, chucking her under the chin, tickling her, and making funny faces at her.

Charlotte knew at that moment that the hopes that she had pinned on a girl child were to be dashed. She would be spared another trip, and maybe one more after that, while Elizabeth was an infant; but she would be going back to sea again, and her daughter with her. There was no escaping it—it was as certain as the ebb and flow of the tides.

She came to live every day at home as though it were her last. She lingered, dewy-eyed, in the doorway to look at the lilacs whenever she went in or out. She became given to deep sighs, as she sat before the fireplace reading in the evenings. Sometimes, she would not leave the house at all for days. She would stay at home with the baby, and let Mrs. Perkins go out and do the shopping for the household.

Home had very quickly come to have a particular meaning for Charlotte. It was the house in Stonington *without* Captain Creighton in it. It was not home anymore, when he returned from the sea and usurped it. When he walked in, loud and callous and disrespectful, he trampled down the buds of tranquility and civilization that she worked so tirelessly to preserve and nurture during his absence.

And always while he was there—and for a long time after he left—it was no use even trying to set an example for Elizabeth of the quiet, homely virtues. It was all too clear that Elizabeth welcomed the intruder with open arms, and the agitating influence he had on her lingered for weeks after he left to go back to sea.

"Madam," said Captain Creighton when Elizabeth was five years old, "I propose that yourself and our daughter come aboard ship with me, when the *Western Wind* sails for the Orient next month."

"I am not sure, Captain Creighton, that such a proposal is best for either the safety or the upbringing of a young girl," Charlotte replied. But there was little hope or conviction in her voice.

"Nonsense, madam. There is no finer, healthier life than the sea. And Elizabeth is the daughter of a ship's master."

Charlotte was suddenly hysterical: "Captain Creighton—Captain Creighton, I beg you! Take me with you, and spare the child! Leave her alone. She can be sent to live with relatives—your relatives—and brought up as a young lady should be. I am your wife. It's my duty to go with you, as you desire, to spend the rest of my life in a ship's cabin, if need be, but spare—"

"Madam!" Captain Creighton thundered. "Control yourself."

In the nursery, Elizabeth cried out in her sleep. Mrs. Perkins was there, but Charlotte went in herself, to cover up the child. As she tucked her back into her bed, and stroked her forehead, she felt an aching surge of tenderness and protectiveness in her breast. But she knew, deep down, that it was useless. Elizabeth, the moment she heard that they were going to sea with Papa, would respond with a squeal of absolute delight, and from then on there would be no checking her impatience until the moment they left.

✤Chapter Four

THREE DAYS LATER, THEY HEADED DOWN TO New York City and Castle Garden, where the ship was waiting for them. Elizabeth had never seen anything so beautiful. It was copper-colored on the sides, almost all the way up to the top. Around the deck level, there was a gold-painted band that went all the way along the sides, and around to the front. Above the deck line, the sides of the ship were also painted jet black, and they had brightly polished brass rails at the top. And right on the front, there was a figurehead—statue of a lady with a billowing white dress on, who was there to represent the western wind. The hem of her dress was done in gold leaf and her hair was painted jet black.

Elizabeth gasped when she saw it. Charlotte looked stony-faced, and Mrs. Perkins frowned and shook her head.

Captain Creighton was already there. He had come earlier with the ship's owners. Elizabeth was brought into the captain's cabin to meet Mr. Brooke and Mr. Arbour, then shown by the steward to the cabin that she and Mrs. Perkins were to share. It was in the back part of the ship— below the poop deck, the steward told them. Elizabeth wanted to explore the whole ship, but they told her to sit and mind her manners like a proper little lady, while Mrs. Perkins unpacked.

She was permitted to go up on deck when Mr. Brooke and Mr. Arbour left the ship, and then her father asked the steward, Mr. Chase, to show her around the poop accommodations, as a special treat, since it was her first sail.

Most beautiful of all was the saloon, which had beautiful walls of smooth, highly polished wood. There were two different kinds of wood used in the paneling, one light-colored and the other dark, and the effect was striking. There was a table in the middle of the room, with benches on either side, and padded backrests on the benches. There was a horsehair sofa against one wall, and an upright piano, its wooden bench bolted to the floor in front of it.

There was a large, handsome potbellied stove, with its filigreed brasswork polished and gleaming, and a sideboard cupboard with beautiful elaborate woodworking on the edges. It was built to fit the curve of the ship, and it contained plates, wineglasses, bottles, and the like.

There was a pantry next to the captain's cabin, and on the other side of it was the first mate's cabin, and then a cabin which the ship's second and third officers shared. Mr. Chase had a tiny cabin of his own, and their were four other cabins for passengers. No passengers were making this voyage, and Elizabeth and Mrs. Perkins had been given one of those cabins.

There was another small room which Mr. Chase did not show her, and Elizabeth guessed that it must be the bathroom and water closet for the ship's officers and passengers. She and Mrs. Perkins were supposed to use the captain's private bathroom and water closet.

Her own cabin was painted a bright, cheery white, and had a large round window with a brass frame. There were bunk beds in it, the top one for her, the lower one for Mrs. Perkins. There was a little ladder so she could climb up to it.

By the second day out to sea, Charlotte was seasick again. So was Mrs. Perkins, but not Elizabeth. The rocking of the ship on the ocean only seemed to exhilarate her, and make her livelier than ever.

Twice a day, once in the morning and once in the afternoon, one of the women—whichever was least incapacitated—would struggle up on deck and take Elizabeth for a short walk.

Charlotte or Mrs. Perkins, whoever's turn it was, would totter feebly for a few weak steps around the center of the deck, staying close to the deck house, clutching with a death grip the hand of the struggling, straining, five-year-old girl.

"I want to run," Elizabeth would say.

"Well, you can't," would come the cross reply. "It's too dangerous."

"I want to go see Papa."

"Papa's busy, running the ship."

"I want to look over the railing."

"Well, you can't—and stop pulling at my arm like that! If you're going to be a horrid, ungrateful child every time I take you for a nice walk, we'll just go right back to the cabin."

And the rapidly weakening woman, welcoming any excuse to cut short the torture she was going through, fearful that at any moment the child would pull free from her grasp and run headlong over the side of the ship, would turn around, stagger back to the hatch and descend again to the safety of below decks, pushing the child along in front of her.

The best walks for Elizabeth were the ones on which she saw her father. But she liked to watch the sailors, too, the helmsman at the helm, the men climbing the rigging, scrubbing the decks until the wood was faded to almost white, except for the dark, teakwood borders that always gleamed with their dark luster. The whole of the poop deck was planked with that same beautiful teakwood, and there were thin, elegant pinstripes of white putty running between the planks. Other sailors polished the brass, and others hauled on huge ropes as their muscles strained and they sang rhythmic songs of the sea.

And on top of the ship, there was always a sailor on lookout in the crow's nest. He was so far up, sometimes Elizabeth could see him and sometimes she could not.

But her father was the captain of them all. Elizabeth thought his stiped sweater and rough pajamas were thrilling, and she loved his captain's hat. Whenever he was on deck and she came out for one of her walks, he would smile and wave to her. If he was not too busy, he would come over and talk to her. Once, he even picked her up on his shoulder and carried her over to the rail with him, and she squealed with delight.

"Well, how do you like the ocean?" he asked.

"Oh, Papa, it's beautiful!"

"And the clouds?" He pointed upward, and her eyes followed his finger. "They're telling us we're going to have good weather, but you can see they're not moving—that means good weather for little girls, but not for big sailing ships. But what breeze there is, we'll find. Look over there—" His finger arced across the sky, and pointed at a speck near the horizon. Elizabeth could see that it was another sailing vessel. "They're up ahead of us now, but your Papa's found the bit of breeze they haven't, and in another two hours we'll be even with 'em, and then by 'em."

Elizabeth did not get to stay on deck long enough to watch her father's prediction come true, but she asked Mr. Chase later, and sure enough, they had passed the other ship.

In the evening, when Captain Creighton was off watch, Elizabeth would sometimes be allowed into his cabin for a few moments just before her bedtime, and he would tell her all about the day's events: how far they had come, what the nearest land was, what kind of sailing they could expect for the next day.

He told her about the engraving on his wall, the framed picture of a majestic clipper ship.

"That's a picture of the *Flying Cloud*, Lizzie. She's the fastest clipper ship ever to sail round the Horn to San Francisco. Eighty-nine days, Lizzie. Think of it. Eighty-nine days!"

"How fast will we go, Papa?"

"Oh, it'll take us upward of a hundred days, to Frisco. A hundred and fifteen, twenty, maybe."

"Could you make the *Union Flyer* go as fast as the *Flying Cloud*, Papa?"

"Bless me, no!" Captain Creighton tousled his daughter's dark hair. "The *Union Flyer* isn't built for that kind of speed. The *Flying Cloud* is an extreme clipper."

"What's an extreme clipper, Papa?"

32

"An extreme clipper is a beautiful ship, Lizzie," said the captain. "Look at the picture. You can see how majestic she is. Her mainmast is over two hundred feet tall, and she carries thirty-five sails."

"We only have twenty-five," said Elizabeth.

"Bless me, if you aren't just exactly right? You remembered," chuckled her father. "You've a natural seaman's head, my firl."

"You would have done better if you'd been captain of the *Flying Cloud*, Papa," Elizabeth said.

"By God, I'll bet I could have, at that," her father replied.

"Captain Creighton, attend to your language in front of your daughter," Charlotte said. 'She had intended icy reproof, but she was far too seasick to bring it off; her words came out as a tortured moan. Captain Creighton ignored her as he went on talking to Lizzie. The glint of a long-cherished dream was kindled in his eyes.

"Someday I will, Lizzie," he told her. "If I ever get command of a ship that's built for that kind of speed, and the strength to take the merciless poundings of the Cape run as she'd have to for such a venture, I'll do it. Eighty-nine days, eleven hours, New York to Frisco. We'll do it in eighty-eight, won't we, sweetheart?"

Elizabeth glowed. Her father picked her up in his arms and kissed her on the nose, then lofted her high in the air, brought her back down, and hugged her.

"Bedtime for you, now. Go along with Mrs. Perkins and get ready. Papa's got work to do."

Ten days out of New York, on the high seas due east of Cuba, the *Union Flyer* hit its first bad weather, a tropical squall our of the Caribbean. The storm hit at night, and the boat began pitching wildly. Captain Creighton was off watch when the storm hit, but he was ready for it. He was sleeping in his clothes, and he quickly put on his slicker and high boots, and hurried up on deck.

Elizabeth woke up too, as did Mrs. Perkins. A few minutes later Charlotte came into their cabin, wearing her dressing gown.

"It's just a storm at sea," said Charlotte. Her voice was

strained and tense as a mast ready to snap in the wind. There was no reassurance in it.

Mrs. Perkins just went down on her knees and started praying. She prayed out loud, and then her voice grew weak and shaky, and she had to leave her knees to run for the basin and be sick in it.

Elizabeth was not in need of reassurance, anyway. She was excited by the storm. She stood on tiptoe to look out of the porthole, spreading her arms along the wall for balance, and watched the flying spume and the towering, crashing waves in the darkness, until her mother ordered her back to bed.

By morning, the storm had barely abated. Captain Creighton had been on deck all night. He came back to his cabin for an hour's rest, shortly after daybreak.

On his way, he stopped in at Elizabeth's cabin to reassure the women. He was drenched through, and droplets of salt water ran off his beard. He looked like the Old Man of the Sea.

"Storm won't break till late today, maybe tomorrow, if I'm any judge," he said. "We'll weather it, though. It's not such a bad one."

"Pray God I never see worse," moaned Mrs. Perkins, but the captain had already closed the door behind him and gone.

The bosun came to wake him in an hour, as he had been instructed. Elizabeth, who was wide awake, could hear the footsteps out in the saloon, the rapping on the captain's door, and the seaman's guttural voice calling out her father's name.

A moment later she heard her father's footsteps, and knew he had gone back on deck to take over again. She got up and went over to the porthole, and stared out.

"Are we going to take a walk on deck today, Mrs. Perkins?" she asked.

"Heavens, no, child! Let's just pray we'll survive down here," said Mrs. Perkins. She rolled over and doubled up with another attack of nausea.

The cabin fell silent. It was silent for a long time. Then Charlotte sat up, raised her head, and looked around.

"Where's Elizabeth?" she demanded.

Mrs. Perkins sat up, also alarmed.

34

"Perhaps she's gone to the W.C.," she suggested.

"She's supposed to tell—" said Charlotte, rushing out across the saloon to the captain's cabin, knocking on the door of the water closet, and calling out Elizabeth's name.

There was no reply.

Charlotte ran up the hatchway and opened the outer door of the deckhouse. Wind, rain, and salt spray lashed at her face as she leaned halfway out, clutching the doorpost with both hands, and screaming for help.

An able seaman saw or heard her, and came over.

"What is it, ma'am?" he asked, shouting into her face to make himself heard over the sound of the gale.

"My baby's gone!" she shouted back, and then repeated the statement, as if saying the words once had set in motion some reflex within her that could only be satisfied by shouting them over and over again: "My baby! My baby's gone!"

Elizabeth was not afraid of the storm, and she wanted her walk. As she stood by the porthole, watching the wind and the waves, she saw an occasional sailor go by, half-sliding, half-lurching, gripping ropes and railings for support, body braced against the wind. She felt rebellious and angry. It wasn't fair that she couldn't go out in the storm like the sailors.

Elizabeth had a little slicker and boots, too, in the closet of the stateroom. Papa had bought them for her to use on the ship—but what good were they if every time it rained, she had to stay in the cabin with Mama and Mrs. Perkins?

She tiptoed over to the closet and got out her miniature foul-weather gear. She put the boots on quietly, sitting down on the floor in front of the closet and struggling with the rubber that caught and tugged on the heels of her shoes. She slipped into the slicker, and tied the rain hat tightly to her head. Neither of the women had looked up and noticed her.

The clothes felt fun to wear, not like her stuffy dresses and starched petticoats. The clicker was crinkly when she moved, and the boots made her take big steps. She strode across the room with her sailor outfit on, pretending she was an able seaman climbing the rigging, or a helmsman holding the ship on course.

At the door, she looked back at her mother and Mrs. Perkins. She expected them to stop her, to tell her to put those dreadful things back in the closet. But neither of them looked up.

Elizabeth stood and watched them for a moment. She had never really expected that she was going to do it. But no one had told her no, and a prickly, excited feeling filled her. Finally, she could resist no longer. She opened the door a crack, and slipped out.

No one noticed Elizabeth as she climbed up the companionway and stepped out onto the poop deck. The decks were in an uproar. They were awash with water, and the ship was tilted incredibly over the starboard side. Elizabeth slid several feet before she could stop herself, and she let out a scream that no one heard. But she was not too frightened to continue. She felt wildly exhilarated, and the stab of fear that coursed through her when she slid across the deck only made it more exciting.

She had come out on the forward part of the poop deck, away from the helmsman. She wanted to go back and watch him, but she was afraid that she would be seen and sent below, so she decided to move forward instead.

She began to make her way slowly across the port, climbing up the wide expanse of tilted deck. Waves were crashing up against the side of the ship broadside as it rode high out of the water to port. They sent heavy torrents of water flying across the deck into Elizabeth's face, and she had to duck her head and gasp for air because the water pried open her mouth and left a salt taste inside.

She quickly learned that she had to turn her head sideways and duck whenever she saw a wave break against the ship. Then, after the water pelted over her shoulder and the back of her head, she could open her eyes again.

They sky was a swirling, impenetrable gray. The rain slanted down as though it were being thrown, in bursts that were sometimes almost as powerful as the waves.

The ship was still sailing under about a quarter sail, running with the storm. Elizabeth could see two sailors not far from where she stood, struggling to unfurl one more sail. They did not notice her, intent as they were on their work. Elizabeth knew that Papa must have ordered them to do it, and she looked around to see if she could spot him, but he was nowhere in sight. But there were the sailors to watch, and Elizabeth stared at them, fascinated. She knew that if they were putting on more sail, it meant that they were beating the storm.

Elizabeth wanted the storm never to end. It was too exciting, and being out in it was the most exciting thing she had ever done. Her tiny muscles were strained as she braced her light body against the wind, and the water pelted her from above and from all around, but she felt invincible. She felt like her papa, standing her ground out on deck, and she shouted commands into the teeth of the gale, to imaginary sailors: "Reef those sails, men! Haul in the yards! Bring her about!" She wasn't sure what the words meant, but she had heard her father call them out, and she knew they were captain's orders.

She ran across to the forward railing of the poop deck, holding her arms out in front of her to grab hold of the breastrail when she reached it.

She peered down through the railing, clutching it with both hands, and looked over the main deck and onto the fo'c'sle, where the sailors lived. She saw men, staggering, looking exhausted, going down the fo'c'sle hatch, and others, grim-faced, coming out. Elizabeth knew that her papa had been on deck for longer than any of those sailors, but she was sure that he could not possibly look so exhuasted and beaten down.

He was probably back at the stern of the ship, telling the helmsman what to do. Or perhaps he was at the helm, holding the ship on course. Anyway, he was wherever it was most important for him to be.

Suddenly she heard a roaring on the port side of the ship. She turned toward it, then put her hand to her mouth and stared numbly.

A giant wall of water was approaching the ship, more immense than anything she had ever seen, bigger than she could ever have imagined. She screamed, clutched the breastrail with both hands, and closed her eyes.

She heard a crash like thunder as the wave broke against the side of the ship, and then she was surrounded by the swirling water. Even with her head turned away from it, the water filled her nose and mouth and eyes, and made her choke. It tore at her frail fingers and arms, and pulled

37

at her body until she let go her grip on the rail. She was spun, swirled, and dragged; she no longer had any sense of which way was up, or down.

And then it was past her. She did not know where she was, but the water no longer surrounded her, and she could breathe again.

Sze opened her eyes, and fought to clear the stinging salt out of them so she could try to figure out where she was and what had happened to her.

She was still on board ship. The water had thrown her against the breastrail, and wedged her body into the narrow space between two posts. Or perhaps she had instinctively thrown herself there, for protection. She could not be sure. But the post had saved her life.

Her eyes still burned and stung from the salt water. Her hat had been ripped from her head by the force of the wave, and her hair hung limp and wet and stringy, plastered to her head.

She was soaked clear through to the skin, and starting to feel chilled. Her back and chest were bruised from the buffeting against the railing posts. There were welts and bleeding scrapes on her fingers and hands, and a cut on her forehead where it had been banged hard against the railing. Her head hurt from the bump, and the salt water in all her wounds stung mightily. Her ears were ringing. As soon as she had recovered breath enough, Elizabeth started to cry. She screamed out with pain and anguish and fear, and the hot salty tears streamed down her face mingled with the freezing salt water of the angry ocean.

And, as suddenly, she stopped. Once again, she was much too interested in what was going on to bother with crying. She was save, in her little cubbyhole. The big wave had gone over her, and nothing had happened to her. The ship was straightening out again, coming back to an even keel.

Elizabeth started picturing the wave again in her mind. It had been as big as a house, and had made a noise like giants roaring when it hit the ship. Mrs. Perkins would never believe it.

Elizabeth began to laugh delightedly.

She started singing, in a high-pitched, childish voice, snatches of a sea chanty she had heard the men singing as they worked the decks: "Heave away! Haul away! Heave away! Haul away!"

She could not remember any of the rest of the song, but she crowed out those words over and over, still jammed in between the posts of the breastrail.

She could see all the way forward from where she sat. The ship would nose down into tremendous hollows, with huge waves towering over it. They looked as if they were going to crash down on the front of the ship the way Elizabeth's wave had on her, but each time, the vessel would nose up again, and Elizabeth's spirits would surge with the ship. She squealed and sang and shouted as if she were helping to lift the bow of the ship up over the waves.

That was how they found her, about fifteen minutes later, during a lull in the storm: singing happily, her song punctuated with squeals of delight, overseeing the sailors as they scurried about the main deck, beginning the task of repairing the damage that Elizabeth's great wave had caused. A crewman heard her voice over the wind and looked up, thinking he had heard one of the officers up on the poop shouting an order.

"Well, I'll be blowed," he said.

Elizabeth waved at him delightedly.

Captian Creighton was summoned, and he picked her up in his arms.

"Did you see the big wave, Papa? she asked. "Wasn't it exciting? Did you see what a clever place I found to hide? I don't think most little girls would think of anything so clever, do you? I think I must be a born sailor, Papa, don't you? Did you see . . . ?"

Elizabeth did not, at least for the next several hours, have to answer to her mother's hysteria. By the time she reached the cabin, she was fast asleep in her father's arms.

ᴗChapter Five

AFTER THAT TERRIBLE DAY OF HE STORM, Charlotte lost her daughter completely. Elizabeth became a legend among the sailors of the *Union Flyer*, on that voyage and for every voyage thereafter. She could go anywhere on the ship, except into the fo'c'sle where the men lived. The officers all kept an eye on her, and let her tag along wherever they went. All the sailors knew her and she knew what all their tasks were, and what purpose each task served in making the ship run. Everyone admired the way she could climb ropes, and that she knew how a hand-lever windlass was operated, and could identify all the sails, by name, on a full-rigged ship—all this and much more, by the time she was eight.

In her gingham dresses, starched collars, and petticoats, she would clamber up the rigging, follow the bosun back and forth from poop to bowsprit, peer over the mate's shoulder as he boxed the compass, or the helmsman's as he stood at the wheel. The lookout would call down and tell her if he spotted whales or porpoises, or other full-rigged ships traveling the same route. The bosun taught her how to tie sheepshanks and running bowlines, and told her stories about famous shipwrecks and the Northern Lights and St. Elmo's Fire, the glowing ball of light that would sometimes appear on the peak of a mast or the tip of a yard during a storm, and which the sailors regarded as a powerful omen.

Charlotte taught Elizabeth her lessons, what there were of them. She taught her how to read and write and do household arithmetic. The lessons she got from her father and from Mr. Bridewell, the first mate, were more to Elizabeth's liking. From them she learned how to tell where you were by the stars, and how to predict the weather from the clouds. She learned how to sew from the sailmaker, and he made a little sailor's cap for her.

She would not permit her mother to teach her how to play the upright piano in the saloon. She dismissed that as a woman's pastime.

The only times that she had to spend whole days on end with her mother or Mrs. Perkins was when they were in port. Then her father would be busy with customs officials, and dock officials, and cargo inspectors, and the man who was buying the cargo that the *Union Flyer* was carrying, or the man who would be consigning a new cargo to the ship—all the shore people.

In San Francisco or London, sometimes they would go shopping. In Hong Kong or Tokyo or Bombay or Manila they hardly ever left the ship at all; but sometimes Elizabeth's father would bring back some beautiful silk cloth, or a tiny carved ivory statue.

He would bring back beautiful skeins of brightly colored yarn, too, and show them to Elizabeth. They were for himself—for his needlepoint, which he often did to relax in the evening on shipboard. It was painstaking but soothing work for him, and Elizabeth would sit with him sometimes as he worked on it.

Needlepoint was man's work, to Elizabeth. Many of the captains did it, or knot tying, or delicate carved scrimshaw. She could not have imagined her mother's nervous hands doing anything so patient, or Mrs. Perkins' fat fingers doing anything so fine.

"Papa, what are the stores in India like?" Elizabeth asked.

"Oh, crowded and noisy and full of everything you could imagine, Lizzie. The stores are all out in the street, little nigger men with baskets and pushcarts and all shouting at the same time, and you have to bargain with them for everything—that's the fun of it. And the streets are full of snake charmers and magicians—"

"When I get bigger I'll go shopping in Bombay by myself," said Elizabeth. She glared defiantly over her shoulder at her mother, and her body inclined backward in the direction of her father.

"When you get older, God willing, you'll understand why Mrs. Perkins and I have kept you from places that are not safe or fit for little girls and proper young ladies," said Charlotte. Her voice quivered with an icy passion which swept over Elizabeth and fixed on Captain Creighton.

Elizabeth's eight-year-old defiance crumbled before Charlotte's stare. She could not look up. Her body was no longer tilted toward her father; now she was hunched forward over the ivory elephants she had been playing with on the floor. She knew, without looking, that her father would frown and grow rigid, then avert his eyes and look down at his charts. He acted that way every time her mother talked about her growing up.

Charlotte felt bitter victory at such moments; and those little victories were all she had left. She had no home anymore, and no future. The only thing that sustained her was a sense of herself as a Cassandra, foreseeing the awful destruction of her family and powerless to do anything but stand by and watch it happen before her eyes.

She felt a kind of sixth sense about disaster, just as she had developed a kind of sixth sense about sex—or maybe they were the same thing. Her sixth sense about sex told her when Captain Creighton was going to demand it before he ever made a move toward her. It gave her a kind of fatalistic satisfaction about the whole experience that, in its way, replaced the satisfaction she would never have dreamed of taking from the act itself.

Mrs. Perkins was Charlotte's only friend, but there was a world of difference between the two women. Mrs. Perkins, in her years of shorebound marriage to a seagoing man, had learned to put the sea in the back of her thoughts. It was always there, as it was always there to all sea wives and mothers—a looming, unfathomable backdrop against which her life was played, and within which her husband's had finally been lost. But Mrs. Perkins belonged to the land, and when she left Charlotte's employ she would go back to it. For Charlotte, the backdrop had become the whole texture of her life, and whatever morbid satisfaction she had in her life was drawn from it.

The only time Charlotte came into her own as a mother was when Elizabeth's clothes were off.

Charlotte had an absolute terror of undressing her daughter on board a ship full of men, an she took elaborate precautions to safeguard Elizabeth's modesty—and to make sure that Elizabeth knew she was doing it. The child was always bathed in a large basin on the floor of her stateroom—never in the bathroom that was reserved for the use of passengers and the ship's officers, not even the private one in Captain Creighton's quarters.

The ritual was as follows. First, Charlotte would draw dark drapes over both the cabin's portholes. Then, she and Mrs. Perkins would bring the hot water to the cabin themselves. Charlotte did not want a male steward or cabin boy to know that a bath was being prepared for her daughter behind those closed doors. When the water was ready, Elizabeth would be ushered behind a screen—away from the covered portholes—to undress. And while she was actually in the tub, Mrs. Perkins would stand guard first by one porthole, then the other, alert for even the slightest sign of a spy outside.

Every time Charlotte sponged and lathered Elizabeth, she examined her daughter's lithe, wiry body for telltale signs of female softness, like a specialist checking a patient for symptoms of a rare disease. She scrubbed Elizabeth's skin with a fierceness that made the child wince, and sometimes even cry out. Charlotte did not mean to hurt Elizabeth. But it gave her a kind of motherly satisfaction to see her daughter acting like a little girl instead of a hardcase sailor.

When the *Union Flyer* came home from yet another voyage, in the summer of Elizabeth's twelfth year, a rumor waited for them at the docks: Captain Creighton was to be given a new ship!

Elizabeth heard it as she waited on the dock with her

mother and Mrs. Perkins, for their trunks to be unloaded. As Mr. Johnson, the tall, potbellied bosun with the sad, walrus face came down the gangplank, she broke away from Mrs. Perkins' grasp and ran over to him.

"Is it true, Mr. Johnson? Is my father getting a new ship?"

"That's what I hear, Miss Lizzie," he answered. A smile creased his walrus face as he looked down at her, and his pink cheeks stuck out like knobs.

"Come back here at once, Elizabeth!" Charlotte snapped.

"Don't know any more'n what I've heard," the bosun answered. "But you can bet she'll be a beauty."

Mrs. Perkins marched up behind Elizabeth, seized her hard by the shoulder, and pulled her away. The bosun shrugged, and walked on.

Captain Creighton was gone all that day, as usual, making his report to Arbour and Brooke, while Charlotte took Elizabeth uptown to the hotel they always stayed at while in New York and Mrs. Perkins went back to Connecticut.

The captain arrived at the hotel late in the evening, after Elizabeth was in bed. She got up when she heard him come in, wrapped her robe tightly around herself, put on her slippers, and came out into the sitting room. He had just finished unrolling a large scroll on the table.

Elizabeth ran over to him. Charlotte, relieved of the responsibility of being his sole audience, did not order her daughter back to bed. Instead, she made way for Elizabeth, and went over to sit in a chair on the other side of the room.

"Papa! It's your new ship!"

Her father beamed. "The *Spirit of the Waves*, extreme clipper, at present nearing completion at the McKay Shipyards in Boston," he said. "These are the plans for her. And—" he unrolled a smaller scroll, and placed it on top of the large one "—there's what she'll look like."

Elizabeth gasped. It was an artist's rendering of a magnificent full-rigged ship, the most beautiful ship that she had ever see, even more magnificent than the picture of the *Flying Cloud* that had always hung on the wall of her father's cabin aboard the *Union Flyer*.

"And you'll be the master of it?" Charlotte asked, from the other side of the room.

"That I will," said Captain Creighton.

"When will it be ready to put to sea?" asked Charlotte.

"In approximately three months. I'll be going up to Boston, to see it at the shipyards and consult with McKay on the design."

"In that case," said Charlotte, "Elizabeth and I will start for home tomorrow morning. You'll go back to bed now, Elizabeth. Immediately."

"Oh, Papa," said Elizabeth. "You'll beat the *Flying Cloud*'s record now—I know you will."

Charlotte had never expected to spend three months in Stonington again. Four or five weeks had been the maximum between voyages—just long enough to start getting used to the house again, and then the heartbreak of leaving it for yet another time. It had become a routine for her.

Elizabeth went to spend the afternoon with her Grandmother Creighton, and Charlotte spent the day dusting and cleaning. She always cleaned her first day home, but this time she put an extra effort into it. The house in Stonington was to be her home now for three, four, maybe six months. She polished all the pewter, not just the main pieces, but everything. And she started setting out some of the things they had accumulated in their travels but which had remained crated and stored, waiting for the day that Captain Creighton should retire.

She pushed the furniture aside in the parlor, and laid out the Persian rug on the floor. It was hard going, and she thought of calling in a neighbor boy giving him a nickel to help, but she liked working by herself too much to allow anyone else to share it with her. She set out the ornate silver candlesticks from South America, and the Chinese jade horses, and a large mirror in a beautiful hand-carved Oriental frame.

She studied herself in the mirror, something she never did at sea, and decided that she was still a presentable woman. There were lines in her face, but her skin had not suffered too much damage from the sea air—perhaps the salt had even preserved it. She was a little surprised at her own solitary vanity, but she went on looking at herself in

46

the mirror. She was plumper than she had once been, from the starchy seagoing diet, but then she was older than she had once been, too.

What a backward life she had! Most women anxiously awaited the return of their husbands' ships to port, so that they could once again share their conjugal beds. For Charlotte, her husband's being in port meant that, at last, she could escape from his bed. And while other women might be primping for their husbands, here she was, primping before a mirror as she prepared for three months alone.

But in the end, she had to acknowledge the bitterest disappointment of all: that this was her home no longer. That after a few weeks, no matter how carefully she straightened the antimacassars, how brightly she stepped over to the kitchen window in the morning to look at the roses and the grass and the trees, and the white picket fences around houses that always stayed in the same place, no matter what she said to neighbor women about how good it was to be home and how nice it was to talk to another woman again—it was all a sham. It was not really her life.

At first she was furious. She could have killed Captain David Creighton for what he had done to her.

But after a few weeks, she began to realize that she missed Captain Creighton, too. The luxury of sleeping alone had begun to wear thin.

She actually found herself daydreaming of nights they had spent together, on board the *Union Flyer*. She conjured up the picture of herself in the stateroom aboard ship, lying motionless in her flannel nightgown.

She has retired first, and he is sitting in his chair, reading, or studying his charts, or doing his needlepoint. Finally he gets up, blows out the lamp. He changes into his nightshirt in the bathroom, and walks toward the bed.

Is it something in his step, or a sixth sense in Charlotte that makes her know? But she does know: the pulsing and fluttering in her thighs tell her that he is going to want her tonight. She closes her eyes, but does not roll over away from him.

She is aware of him in stages. His shadow, first. Even with her eyes closed, even with the lamp out, she knows when he is looming over her; she feels the deeper darkness

47

on her lowered eyelids. Next it is his smell, salt air and pipe tobacco.

As he climbs into bed beside her, and she feels the knobby hardness of his knee against the softness of her thigh. It is the first part of him that touches her, and she feels that imprint of her thigh, even after it is withdrawn.

Because he does not touch her again right away. He settles himself on his back, burrowing with his shoulder blades, grumbling and rumbling. Why is he making such a fuss about getting comfortable on his back? She wonders. She knows he is not going to stay in that position.

She knows every move he is going to make, before he makes it: whether it will be just more shifting and fidgeting, or a move toward her. He raises his arm, now . . . but only to rub the back of his hand across his brow. But the next move he makes . . . he will stretch his arm across the breadth of his body without moving off his back, and across her body also; he will clutch her waist. His fingers will dig into her as he pulls himself over, and even through the flannel nightgown she will be able to feel the imprint of each finger along the hollow of her waist and the swelling rise of her hip.

She moves just a little, the better to adjust to the weight of his body on her. He is heavy as he half-covers her, but she knows from experience how to make herself comfortable beneath him. Now she tenses, draws in her breath, as his weight is eased from her. But just for a moment, just long enough for him to lift the skirts of his nightshirt, of her nightgown. Then the awesome awareness of flesh touching flesh, and—as startling and overwhelming, still, as it had been twelve years ago—the sensation of being entered, and her body becoming something she does not understand.

Charlotte never knew, through all the years that she was married to David Creighton, that she was the one who had the passionate nature, that she, not her husband, was the one for whom sexual couplings were a transcendent, self-displacing experience. She never knew that if her repressive, Puritan morality had not held her back, she would have overpowered her husband with the intensity of her desire.

48

Charlotte continued to try to instill in Elizabeth on appreciation for the virtues of shore life. She firmly believed that the natural and proper instincts of a young lady were to want a settled, peaceful life, with a little cottage of her own; and she hoped that, somehow, it might not be too late for those instincts to flower in Elizabeth—and that this long shore period might be the time they took firm root.

But she was only setting herself up for further disappointment. Elizabeth lived only for the day that they would go back to sea in the new ship; and while she waited for that, she lived for those occasional days when her father would come home with news of its progress.

Her father was hardly ever home during those three months, which stretched to four, then four and a half. He was either in Boston, at the McKay Shipyards, or in New York with Arbour and Brooke. He only stopped in Stonington as he passed on his way from one city to the other, but each time Elizabeth could see the mounting glow of excitement on his face, as his beautiful new ship drew ever nearer to completion.

Even when he stayed for a few days in Stonington, Captain Creighton was immersed in the plans for his new ship. He carried with him a copy of the *Flying Cloud*'s logbook for her record-breaking voyage, and he studied it until he knew it by heart.

It did not leave him much time for talking with Elizabeth, but when he did talk to her, he talked about the upcoming voyage. That was fine with Elizabeth. She was thrilled to be a part of it all.

It was fine with Charlotte, too. She was finding something strange about those rare nights that Captain Creighton spent at home: that after the tension of waiting in bed for him to make his marital demands, and dutifully acquiescing to them, she slept better and woke up feeling rested and refreshed.

During this period a retired naval officer came to visit Captain Creighton in Stonington. His name was Commander Matthew F. Maury, and he was America's leading authority on winds and currents, and author of two Bibles for ship's masters, *Sailing Directions* and *Wind and Current Charts*.

Commander Maury had a red face with white eyebrows,

and no interest in children at all, not even special little girls who knew all about ships and the sea, so Elizabeth stood at a respectful distance and watched as the two men sat together in the evening and pored over maps and charts and tables. There was so much to learn!

Elizabeth wanted more than anything else in the world to go up to Boston and see the great McKay Shipyards where the *Spirit of the Waves* was being built, but Charlotte clung to her fraying convictions and would not be budged from the house in Stonington.

And, of course, her father would not take her up to Boston alone, as much as she longed for it. She knew it was out of the question, but she did not quite understand why, and no one would explain it to her. She was fairly certain that it had something to do with the way that her mother covered all the portholes and bolted the door and looked at her so strangely when she bathed. Her mother only did that on shipboard, and Boston was on land, but somehow it seemed to be the same thing.

The *Spirit of the Waves* was towed down to New York Harbor from Boston, and it was there that Elizabeth first saw it, at Pier 19, down at the foot of Fletcher Street, just as she had first seen the *Union Flyer*.

By now, though, the New York waterfront was a familiar sight to her—it felt like a homecoming, after the months of exile in Stonington.

And the ship itself was everything she had expected it to be. Masts reaching to the sky, yards squared in perfect symmetry. Lines long and sleek and sharp and beautiful, everything freshly painted and coppered and smelling of new wood and tar.

On the prow of the ship was an incredibly, striking, larger-than-life figurehead. It was a statue of a woman, straining forward, her eyes uplifted toward the horizon. And she was not wearing anything.

She was dressed in a flowing robe, also carved out of wood, that draped around her legs and stomach, with one corner of it clutched to her chest. And on her chest, on either side of the cloth, were round globes that looked to Elizabeth for all the world like sailors' wool caps, except that they were part of the woman's body.

50

Once she boarded the ship, the figurehead was lost to her sight beneath the bowsprit; she would not see it again until they disembarked at San Francisco. But she wondered about it often; it was carved into her memory.

The *Spirit of the Waves* left New York Harbor on November 11, 1865, the winds were right, and the ship moved under them just as McKay had said it would; McKay had built the *Flying Cloud*, and he had told Captain Creighton that the new ship was every inch her equal. He came on board with the owners before the *Spirit of the Waves* weighed anchor: a short man, with a businessman's dress and manner, but a workingman's hands. He had a firm mouth and a jaw as sharp and square as any yardarm, but a poet's curly hair, and vague, faraway look in his eyes. Excitement swelled the ship in the way a strong trade wind fills the sails. Everyone on board knew they were going for the record. Captain Creighton had offered the crew a bonus if they made it.

∾Chapter Six

CAPTAIN CREIGHTON LET ELIZABETH MARK
the ship's daily progress on the big map in his cabin. It
was Elizabeth's first navigation lesson. Her father read her
the latitude and longitude numbers from his ship's log at
the end of each day's run. Then Elizabeth marked the spot
on the map with in a pin and stretched a piece of black
yarn between it and the previous day's pin. Every fifth day
was represented by a blue pin, every tenth day by a red
pin. At the start of the voyage, she had marked the route
and the daily progress of the *Flying Cloud* on the map,
using pins and white yarn.

The first week and a half out of port they sailed east-
southeast, out into the North Atlantic. They were on a
course to pick up the trade winds out of the northeast that
would give them the fastest southerly speed. The *Spirit of
the Waves* caught the wind on her seventh day out of port,
and began her southward run a good two days ahead, and
some 125 miles west, of the route of the *Flying Cloud*.

Elizabeth was ecstatic. But the steadiness of the wind
proved to be illusory, and by the tenth day the *Spirit of the
Waves* was crawling along on becalmed seas, and Elizabeth's heart sank as they slowed to seventy or eighty miles
a day over waters through which the *Flying Cloud*, after

waiting longer to seize a favorable wind and current, had logged close to two hundred miles a day.

On the evening of the eleventh day, Elizabeth stood next to the big map, waiting as her father figured the coordinates and made his logbook entry.

"Latitude 28°, 36′ North, longitude 39°, 14′ West," he said. With the pin between her fingers, Elizabeth traced the coordinates on the map. She found the spot, but hesitated before she pushed in the pin.

"Can you tell me that again, Papa?"

"Latitude 28°, 36′ North, longitude 39°, 14′ West," said her father brusquely. He did not like having to repeat himself when he gave an order.

Elizabeth knew she had heard right and counted right the first time, but even so, she checked the coordinates again, reading down the side of the map to the latitude line, and then in to the correct longitude.

For the first time since they had started, the pin had crossed over to the right of the white thread.

"But, Papa, we've drifted out farther east than the *Flying Cloud*," she said.

"That's right, Lizzie," her father said. "We've got to range a little farther out into the Atlantic, now, and pick up a fresh wind."

"But I thought that we were going to be gaining all that time on them," she persisted. "Now we're even farther off in the wrong direction than they were."

Captain Creighton came over to stand beside her at the map. He patted her head.

"Don't you worry about it, Lizzie," he said. "It's just one of those gambles that a seaman's got to make. You go with the winds and the currents as you find them, then look for better. That was the course I chose, and it worked well enough to get us here. Now we'll map out another one."

"Do you figure out your course every night, from all those charts and books that you look at and the things you write down?"

"Heavens, no—those are just figures. Anyone could do that job, if they took the time and the trouble to learn how to do it. Why, aboard the *Flying Cloud*, Captain Cressy's wife did all the navigation. A real seaman's work is up on deck, and that's where I'll be the moment I decide to bring the ship about and head south for the equator again, not down here. The charts are just a guide."

"Could I learn how to navigate for you, Papa? Like Mrs. Cressy?"

"Oh, well, first you'd have to learn to use a sextant, sweetheart—which means first you'd have to be big enough to lift one and hold it steady. Then you'd have to learn your numbers a whole lot more."

"I'm big enough to hold a sextant steady, Papa," said Elizabeth. "Really I am."

"What about your numbers?"

"Oh, I'm really good at numbers," said Elizabeth enthusiastically. "I can add and subtract and I know most of my times tables—"

"You'd have to know a lot more than that, I'm afraid," said her father. "Just for a start, you'd have to work logarithms. Which would mean you'd have to learn algebra, and square roots, and . . ."

Elizabeth began to realize that she was in over her head.

"Well, someday I'll know all that," she said. "Then I'll be your navigator, and I'll stay down here in your cabin and do all your charts and tables while you're up on deck running the ship."

Captain Creighton chuckled. "You'll be long grown up and gone by then," he said. "Well, it's your bedtime now. Give us a kiss, and go on in and let your mother get you ready for bed."

It was Elizabeth's bath night. Charlotte had altered the bath routine slightly, now that Elizabeth was thirteen. She scrubbed herself now, and the screen was set up in front of the tub, for the sake of "privacy" and "modesty," as Charlotte said.

Elizabeth did not see that it made any difference to her privacy and modesty; at some point during every bath, her mother always found some reason to come behind the screen, and she almost always ended up by taking the washcloth out of Elizabeth's hands and poking it in her ears, or scrubbing her neck and back with it—while, as always, subjecting Elizabeth's smooth, wiry, hairless body to the most merciless scrutiny.

Tonight was no exception. As usual, Elizabeth undressed behind the curtain, and started her bath by herself.

"I want to learn how to do logarithms," she announced to her mother as she bathed.

"What? Nonsense—you've no need to clutter your mind with such things. Household arithmetic is all a lady needs," said her mother, appearing at the side of the screen to glare down at Elizabeth.

"Well, I'm not going to be a lady," Elizabeth retorted hotly. "I'm going to learn logarithms and help Papa. I'm going to be his navigator, and I'm never going to grow up."

"Such nonsense! Of course you're going to grow up. Now give me that washcloth—you're just dabbing at yourself. How do you expect to get clean that way?"

"Well, I don't care, I'm not going to, anyway.

"And I can't scrub any harder—I'm sore. My chest hurts."

Charlotte's hand froze in its descent toward the back of Elizabeth's neck. A curiously triumphant gleam came into her eyes, and she fixed her daughter's chest with a piercing stare.

Elizabeth looked down, startled, wondering what it was that her mother was looking at. She saw nothing unusual, but after a moment she felt odd and uneasy and her eyes slid away from both her own body and her mother's strange, piercing glare, to fasten on the pattern of Chinese bridges and strange, crooked trees on the screen in front of the tub.

She made her mind wander away from where she was, and suddenly she thought of the figurehead on the bowsprit of the *Spirit of the Waves*. She would have liked to ask her mother something, but she was not quite sure what. And her mother never liked to answer questions anyway. All she really liked to do was look strange and talk in scary riddles when Elizabeth asked her a question.

On the fourteenth day of the voyage, for the first time Elizabeth put a pin in the map behind the *Flying Cloud*'s pin for the same day, and her lip trembled.

"They're going so fast," she said. "And so straight! See, for the last three days they've been running right down the fortieth meridian." She had begun to think of the *Flying Cloud* as if it were running along beside them, as if each

56

one of its pins and white thread were going down the map at the same time that Elizabeth put in the pins and the black thread for the *Spirit of the Waves*.

"Don't you worry about that," said her father. "If they keep going down the fortieth meridian, they'll end up bumping right into Brazil." He broke into a deep, rumbling laugh, and Elizabeth laughed too, but it still ate at her insides to be behind the *Flying Cloud*.

The next day she put a blue pin right next to the plain silver pin that marked the *Flying Cloud*'s fourteenth day. They were a full day behind!

"Oh, Papa," she wailed. "We should never have taken that shortcut! Now we'll never catch them."

Her father's face darkened. He half-rose out of his seat and scowled at her. She shrank back and wished she could swallow her words.

"Don't ever look at a bunch of pins on a wall and think you can tell me how to run my ship!" he thundered.

"But, Papa," Elizabeth whimpered. "I didn't mean . . ."

His wrath subsided as quickly as it had arisen; but Elizabeth still trembled. It was the most terrifying thing she had ever experienced.

"Only the captain can make those decisions for a ship, Lizzie," he said. "Only the captain, right or wrong, and he'd better be right a lot more than he's wrong. And he makes 'em as he has to, on the quarterdeck, using everything he's read in the charts and everything he knows in his heart and his head about the sea. And after that . . . it's in the hands o' God."

Elizabeth could not imagine why she had said what she had said. She knew that there was no finer captain on any ship at sea than her father; and if they were falling behind the *Flying Cloud*, it could not be his fault. She wished she could have cut her tongue out. She felt a surge of guilt—perhaps it was her fault for not helping more. Or her mother's fault—if she were like Captain Cressy's wife, she would be helping her husband run the ship.

Captain Creighton came over to the map, and laid his hand gently on Elizabeth's shoulder. "We're only a short way out," he told her. "There's a long voyage ahead of us. They sailed in June, we sailed in November, so all weather

57

patterns will be different. We'll pass them again, and they'll pass us back more than once before we reach San Francisco."

Elizabeth felt silly, and a little embarrassed. But she still resented her mother for not helping more, and she still wished she were big enough to do the job.

"Look up here ahead," said her father. He pointed down on the chart. "That's where the *Flying Cloud* ran into trouble, in the Horse Latitudes. Dead calm and an occasional head wind, and she had to beat for three days."

Elizabeth looked where he was pointing. It was true. She had been so caught up in her game of racing alongside the *Flying Cloud* that she had not even thought of looking ahead at its subsequent progress. But only a few days along—on the seventeenth day of her journey—the *Flying Cloud* had drifted westward, toward Venezuela, making virtually no forward progress at all. On the eighteenth day, she came back eastward on course, but was scarcely farther south at the end of the day than she had been at the beginning of the seventeenth; and the pins for the nineteenth and twentieth days were almost on top of each other.

"That's where we'll catch 'em," said Captain Creighton. "By the time we pass the equator, we'll be right up even with 'em again."

They continued to fall back for a couple of days, but then, just as the captain had predicted, on the seventeenth day out from New York they started to gain again. With a good southeasterly breeze at their backs, they crossed the equator on the evening of the twenty-third day, just a half a day behind the *Flying Cloud*, and so they continued down the South American coast.

Elizabeth grinned now, every time she put up another pin. They were pulling steadily ahead of the *Flying Cloud's* pace almost every day.

∽Chapter Seven

ELIZABETH HAD BEGUN TO WATCH HER BODY AS closely as her mother did. It was beginning to frighten her. Her chest—it still felt sore, not all the time, but often enough. Was there any swelling? Sometimes Elizabeth thought so, and sometimes not. She could not be sure. There was no black-and-blue mark, as from a bruise, but it felt tender all the time.

She noticed something else, though, that struck her as strange.

She was beginning to grow hair, first between her legs, and then under her arms.

Elizabeth pondered long and often about what that meant. Would it grow longer and thicker? Would it spread? Her father had hair on the backs of his hands, thick black hair. So did Mr. Penning, the bosun, and Mr. Wolven, the sailmaker. Maybe she would get it, too. Maybe it would start under her arms and grow all the way down them, as she'd seen on Mr. Wolven's arms when he had his sleeves rolled up. Maybe it would start at the top of her legs and grow down, as she'd seen on the sailors' legs when they rolled up their bell-botton pants to swab the decks. Maybe all that would happen instead of anything happening to her chest, and she would grow up to be a man instead of a lady, and go to sea instead of having to get married and learn household arithmetic.

"How do they know whether you're going to grow up to be a man or a lady?" she asked her mother.

"Boys grow up to be men, girls grow up to be ladies," answered Charlotte.

"Yes, but how do they know . . . ?"

"You're too old to be bothering me with ridiculous questions like that," said her mother.

"How's my princess this morning?" her father asked when she came up on deck the next morning. She shrank from him in abject terror, and spent the rest of the day in her room.

She did not know if her mother knew about the hair under her arms. She kept her arms down at her sides as much as possible. She wanted to keep it a secret for as long as she could.

On Christmas Eve, the *Spirit of the Waves* was only a few days' sail from Cape Horn. It was midsummer in the southern latitudes, but they were already starting to feel the rough, icy, polar winds.

Captain Creighton led a religious service for the crew, and then another for the officers and his family. He gave Elizabeth a present for Christmas, a little looking glass in a frame he had carved himself. Elizabeth loved the hand-carved frame, but she did not know what use she had for a looking glass. She wished it had been another tiny carved ivory elephant.

Forty-seven days out of New York—four days ahead of the *Flying Cloud*—they sighted land, the tip of Tierra del Fuego.

Now it was daylight almost all around the clock. The Antarctic midsummer was mild, so Captain Creighton took advantage of both the favorable winds and the long hours of visibility to drive the *Spirit of the Waves* around the Cape.

Elizabeth still had to go to bed at her normal hour, but she could not sleep. She stole over to the porthole when she was sure that Mrs. Perkins was asleep, and looked out. She could see the desolate spit of land out of the porthole, like an unreal other world with its hazily defined rocky crags and green, ghostlike moss and tufts of saw grass. Sea birds floated above it or perched in small groups on the rocks. It was thrilling to watch how quickly it slipped by.

Captain Creighton drove himself for sixteen to twenty hours at a stretch. He hated to leave the bridge. He would only relinquish command to the mate, Mr. Bridewell, for the time it took him to do his navigational charts and write in his logbook, then grab the shortest of catnaps and a hurried bite of food and coffee before he came out on deck.

He never seemed tired or haggard, though: his eyes glittered, and he pounded his fist in his palm to let off energy as he came down the companionway into the saloon to go through to his quarters. He exulted with Elizabeth over the time they were making around the Horn, and shook his head with wonder over the times the *Flying Cloud* had made over the same stetch.

"By God, that was a great ship, Lizzie!" he told her. "She passed these straits in July—in the dead of winter, and she kept pace with us. Oh, she had luck on her side, too, but she was dead game and as trim a deepwater ship as was ever built!"

Elizabeth did not like to hear good things said about the *Flying Cloud*. Her eyes went to the engraving of the rival ship on the wall, the picture she had looked at so often during the voyage. When it had been on the wall of her father's cabin on the *Union Flyer*, she had loved to look at it. Now she hated it. She wanted her father to beat it more than anything in the world.

It seemed as if the only person on board who was not excited was Charlotte. She had taken to playing the upright piano in the saloon for hours on end, even through the Antarctic passage. She played Mendelssohn, and Chopin nocturnes, and Scottish airs, glaring over her shoulder at her husband for making a racket when he strode through the room. Elizabeth hated her mother for it. Whenever she thought about how her mother would not help her father, Elizabeth felt so angry she wanted to break things.

Up on deck, Elizabeth bundled up against the weather, and then felt too hot and restricted, and wanted to throw off all her heavy outer garments in order to run and climb freely. Many of the sailors were in their shirt-sleeves, even

61

though Elizabeth could see their breath in little clouds before their faces as they panted from the exertion.

But Elizabeth pulsed with excitement. All through the long, bright, eerie twilights while she lay in bed trying not to fidget and disturb Mrs. Perkins, all the times that she glided secretively to the porthole and then scampered back to bed at the first hint of a moaning or stirring from the old governess, the excitement seemed to run all through her. She watched the curious, flat, lustrous gleam on the surface of the swell as it rose and fell outside her porthole, looking almost solid, as though she could reach out and stroke it.

When she did sleep, she had strange, disturbing, exciting dreams—some of them when she was not even asleep, or not sure that she was. She felt, at those times, as if she were awake; she was dimly aware of the shiny sea through her porthole, of her hands and tender chest and other parts of her body she had no name for. And it felt as if she were thinking, not dreaming, the scenes and images and stories that filled her mind: but at the same time, as in a dream, she seemed to have no control over what happened in them.

They are coming around the western tip of Tierra del Fuego. There have been a couple of hours of darkness, not enough for the crew to get the glare out of their eyes, and now a gray glow is developing behind them in the east, another Antarctic sunrise. Elizabeth awakes with the first rays of dawn, and goes over to her porthole.

She sees a ship emerge from a rocky inlet, and sail on a sharp collision course toward the Spirit of the Waves. It is a pirate vessel, waiting at the edge of Cape Horn to pick off weary and unsuspecting merchant ships. Elizabeth can see the black flag with the skull and bones as it bears down on them.

No one else has seen the pirate ship yet. Elizabeth runs up on deck, but her father is not there. She calls to the mate, and points out the ship to him. He is stunned, too shocked to act. The pirate ship is running under full sail, and there seems to be no hope of escape.

"Put out more sail!" Elizabeth shouts. "Helmsman, bring her about—five degrees south! Bosun, pipe all hands on deck!"

The mate pulls himself together, as the sailors spring to carry out Elizabeth's orders. She runs back down to the after deckhouse to wake her father.

She stands for a moment in front of her parents' door. She has never entered her parents' bedchamber before while they were in bed, but this is an emergency. She has to summon her father on deck.

She flings the door open, but he has heard the commotion already. He is dressed, and ready to follow her up on deck. Across the room she sees her mother, still cowering in bed.

She explains the situation to her father as they hurry up to the bridge, but they are too late. The pirates have taken over the ship, and all around them their faithful crew is being slaughtered. The decks run red with blood.

Elizabeth and her father are seized by the pirates. Elizabeth puts up a tremendous fight, but at last she is overcome by the pirate captain, who is tall, strong, and cruel-looking. The pirates go below and bring up her mother and Mrs. Perkins, still clad in their nightdresses.

The pirate captain eyes them contemptuously. "The plank," he says.

"No! No!" screams Elizabeth's mother, sobbing hysterically.

Elizabeth will not give the pirate captain the satisfaction of seeing her break down. She holds her head high. Captain Creighton's face begins to grow pale. Elizabeth squeezes his hand encouragingly.

But there is nothing they can do to save the two hapless women. First Mrs. Perkins is forced to walk the plank, then Elizabeth's mother. Sharks circle hungrily in the water below the plank.

"T-take care of your father, Elizabeth!" are her mother's last, tearful words, before the point of a pirate sword forces her over the side.

Now the pirate captain looks down at Elizabeth. She glares back at him without blinking, and she can see that his face is as handsome as it is cruel, and that he has an evil gleam in his eyes.

"And what shall we do with you, my little spitfire?" he asks.

"No!" Elizabeth shrieks. She ducks away from the pir-

ate, and runs for the mainmast rigging. She starts climbing. She is up to the main topgallantyard, and the pirate is right behind her, chasing her.

She cannot climb any farther. She turns to wait for him, to fight him if necessary, with the last ounce of strength in her body. He keeps coming. She can see him grinning at her, with that same evil glint in his flashing dark eyes.

Suddenly, a great, glowing, whirling ball of light appears at the end of the yardarm. Elizabeth knows what it is: St. Elmo's Fire! In a second, it has skimmed down the length of the yard, and surrounded Elizabeth.

Her body lights up with the unworldly glow. She is consumed by it, but not burned. Her body tingles all over; she is warm and cool at the same time. Sparks hiss and snap all around her, and her hair stands out from her head.

The pirate captain is only a few feet away from her. He stops and gazes at her, with an expression of awe on his face.

His mate, guarding her father, looks up too. Quick as a flash, her father knocks down the mate, and takes his gun. He aims, fires. The pirate captain makes a last lunge for Elizabeth. His fingers fasten around her thigh, still electrically charged from the heavenly phenomenon. His body twitches as the charge runs through him, too; then a bullet pierces his heart. His hand trails down the length of Elizabeth's leg, and he falls from the yardarm, to plunge far below into the icy waters of Cape Horn.

Elizabeth bundled up tightly under the covers, shivering from the excitement of her fantasy. Her knees were curled up against her chest, her hands were tucked between her legs

She began to feel hot and uncomfortable, and the covers were all bunched and tangled around her. It made her feel funny to stay in one place for too long She leaped up again, and stole over to the porthole.

With their leader killed, the rest of the pirates run back to their ship and sail away. Only Elizabeth and her father are left to bring in the Spirit of the Waves.

Her father is disconsolate. He leans over the taffrail, his head in his hands.

"We're finished, Lizzie. We're licked. I'll have to keep out what sail we've got on now, hope for no change in the weather, and try to signal a passing ship or make it into Valparaiso."

Elizabeth comes over to him, puts her arm around him. "Don't worry, Papa. We can still break the record. I'll help."

Captain Creighton looks up, surprised. "You, Lizzie? But how?"

"You'll see, Papa. I can do anything for you. Now, look! We've left the Cape behind. We're coming out into the South Pacific, with the wind at our backs. Let's put out all the sail we've got—I'll climb up in the rigging! We're bound for San Francisco!"

She is off in a twinkling, down to the main deck, and single-handedly hoisting the heavy sails. Her father watches with amazement. Then, slowly, a broad smile spreads over his face.

"By God, Lizzie, we'll do it! I never thought it would be possible for one person to crew a whole full-rigged ship, but you're doing it! I know we'll break that record now."

"Is that you over by the window, dear?" asked Mrs. Perkins sleepily. "Come on back to bed, now. You'll never get to sleep standing over there."

By the fiftieth day out of port, they were around Cape Horn, and Elizabeth glowed with satisfaction as she put the red pin out in the open ocean.

She pinned the *Spirit of the Waves* to the equator on January 21st. They were dead even with the *Flying Cloud*—seventy-one days to zero latitude. But they were over seven hundred miles east of the *Flying Cloud*'s wide-swinging route. They'd run up the coast from the Cape along the same line until about four days ago, when they began to veer eastwardly, while the *Cloud*'s path turned farther out into the Pacific.

"There's no need," Captain Creighton told Elizabeth. "Maury showed me how we can find just as good sailing closer in. The currents are there. He and I, we figured that if I could catch the trades just right, I could shoot up right inside the 110th meridian. There's little danger, by Maury's reckoning, of cutting her too close till we're off California. Till then, the direct route is there if we can find it. And by God, Lizzie, we've caught it!"

Elizabeth stood on the poop deck beside her father on the morning of the twenty-first as they neared the equator. It was a blistering hot, cloudless day, and the sea was sluggish.

Elizabeth felt sluggish, too, hot and uncomfortable. She had felt that way all day. And she had been uncharacteristically clinging, and childish. She had not wanted to leave her father's side, not to walk amidships with Mr. Penning, the bosun, or to stand up at the bowsprit posing like a figurehead, feeling the cool salt spray in her face and watching the prow of the ship cut through the water. She had stayed right beside her father, often reaching out to touch him for reassurance, like a five-year-old.

She was clumsy, too, and slow in reacting. Several times her father almost tripped over her, and finally he got quite cross and snapped at her to watch where she was going. She ran down to her room and dissolved into tears.

The next day there was something wrong with her. She was not sure what it was, at first, but by midmorning she was absolutely sure that it was something drastic.

She was frightened. She did not know what it meant.

She wondered if she should talk to her mother about it. She was not quite sure why, but she had a feeling that it was something she should tell her mother.

But she resisted the feeling defiantly. She never told her mother anything, and she did not plan to start now. Her mother never knew anything, never understood anything.

And worse than that—she had an awful feeling that if she yielded, and went to her mother now, she might always have to go to her mother from now on.

She went back up on deck. Her mind strayed, for a moment, to the fantasy of St. Elmo's Fire: aflame but not burning, like magic, an omen . . .

"Papa," she said, "I'm bleeding between my legs and it won't stop. But I'm not cut."

Her father stiffened, and took a step backward. He would not look at her.

"Papa . . ."

66

"It is a female matter. Go talk to your mother." Captain Creighton's voice was distant and final. He turned on his heel and walked away.

Elizabeth went down to the stateroom, where her mother and Mrs. Perkins were sitting. But she was so scared and upset by her father's reaction to what she had told him, she was unable to get the words out, but could only stammer and hang her head.

To her surprise, her mother seemed to know exactly what the trouble was, without Elizabeth's even having to tell her. It even seemed she had been expecting it. She was very solicitous. She barred the door and covered the port-holes, brought water for Elizabeth to wash her legs in, and gave Mrs. Perkins Elizabeth's bloody undergarments to rinse out. Then she gave Elizabeth some rags and showed her how to fold them between her legs and fasten them to a sash around her waist.

Then she made Elizabeth sit down, and took a seat across from her.

"You'll have to change those three times a day until the bleeding stops," she said. "More often, if it's hard. But it won't be, most likely, not for the next few years."

"The . . . next few years?" Elizabeth stammered in terror. "Will it . . . ?"

"No, it will stop in four or five days. But this will happen to you every month for the rest of your life, because you're a woman now, like me. And you must never let a man touch you there."

She nodded her head vigorously several times. Elizabeth did not know what she meant, but she was afraid to ask.

"Do you understand?" asked Charlotte.

"Oh, er, yes," said Elizabeth.

"You'll have to stay in your room until it's past," said Charlotte. "No more running around like a deckhand."

"I . . . I feel all right," said Elizabeth, too frightened to know whether she did or not.

"No arguments. Your father will agree with me, so there's no point in your sneaking around and asking him behind my back."

"Y-yes, Mama." Elizabeth was fervently sure that she

would not be sneaking out to her father behind her mother's back.

As soon as she was alone, Elizabeth lay down on the bed and sobbed as she had never sobbed before. It helped; it loosened, a little, the knot that was forming inside her. She did not understand what her mother had told her, but she had gotten one thing out of it: this bleeding was somehow indisputable proof that she was a woman for sure, in spite of the hair that was now beginning to cluster and form a patch down between her legs.

Curiously, she felt a tremendous sense of relief, to know at last. And a terrible sense of loss.

She did not know how far they traveled that day. It seemed as though the wind had died away completely, and they were crawling along, but she could not be sure from inside her cabin

After the next day, she got used to the feeling. She felt that she was ready to go back out on deck, but she did not dare to disobey.

By the third day, the bleeding had stopped, and she told her mother.

"You're sure?" asked Charlotte.

"Oh, yes," said Elizabeth. "Quite sure."

"That's because it's your first one," said her mother. "Next time, it will be worse."

"Yes, ma'am."

"I think you'd better stay below one more day. I'll speak to your father this evening, and tomorrow we'll see."

Elizabeth did not like the idea that her mother should have to talk to her father for her. Besides, it was all over now. She felt fine. All day she chafed at being cooped up below decks. She hated it when she was alone; she felt caged and trapped. She prowled from one porthole to another, but the narrow view from the little round windows was unsatisfying. It was even worse when her mother or Mrs. Perkins was there. They read aloud to her, or tried to keep up a conversation, but all that meant was that she could not even stalk around and look out the windows.

That evening, she was allowed to go and visit her father in the captain's room. He was solicitous about her health, as if she had just gotten over an attack of influenza. And there was a note of forced gentleness in his tone that had never been there before, and that set her teeth on edge.

She looked at the map on the wall. It had not been kept up while she had been away from it, and her father smiled and cleared his throat when he saw her looking at it.

"I left it for you, Lizzie, till you were feeling better," he said. "We'll fill it in tonight."

Elizabeth was pleased, but at the same time she felt let down. She did not think for a minute that her little strings and pins were necessary for the running of the ship, but she could not help feeling piqued that the *Spirit of the Waves* had gone on quite well for four days without them.

She smiled at her father shyly. "Thank you, Papa. Let's do it now. If you have time." She got out her pins and yarn as her father thumbed backward in his log book.

"January 22, 1865. Seventy-two days at sea. Light, baffling air from ENE to NE. Clear and hot. Latitude 1° 20' North. Longitude 110° 24' West. Made ninety-four miles, sailed ninety-four miles."

Elizabeth found the coordinates, and pressed in the pin.

It was a poor day's run, but not bad with the wind against them. The *Cloud* had done better, but not that much better. It was still a close race.

Elizabeth was beginning to feel like her old self again. Her father read off the next day's coordinates. Now, that was more like it! The ship was moving through the tropics at a fair rate. The *Flying Cloud*, seven hundred miles farther out to sea, had done no better. Elizabeth's heart leaped, and she tied the thread in place with a flourish.

"And the next day, Papa?"

It was like racing along with the wind. In the space of a couple of minutes they had covered four days and hundreds of miles. They were traveling in a steady north-northwesterly direction now, and they would keep to that course until they were above the 36th parallel, due west of San Francisco and about five hundred miles offshore. It was thrilling to come back and make up all that time in a rush. Four days . . . and then she remembered what her mother had said. Every month for the rest of her life.

"Elizabeth," said her father, closing his logbook. He paused after he had said her name, and his tone of voice had changed abruptly. Now he sounded stern and hesitant at the same time.

"Yes, Papa?"

"I don't think you should . . . run as freely about the ship as you have in the past. You're growing up, now, and it is time that you started to behave more circumspectly, like a young lady."

"But, Papa, I . . ."

"Elizabeth, this is for your own good. And I want you to obey me."

"Yes, Papa."

Why had he said that? There had never been any question of her not obeying him. Everybody obeyed her papa aboard ship. To disobey would be mutiny.

Elizabeth had the feeling that everyone aboard ship was looking at her differently now. She felt shy, and did not want to go anywhere. She was embarrassed next to Mr. Bridewell or Mr. Penning, and no longer ran along with them when they walked forward. She spent much of her time shadowing her father. And she found herself going below in the middle of the day, without anyone even telling her to. She had never done that before.

They continued up the Pacific coast of the Americas. On the eighty-first day, they were due west of Baja California, and Elizabeth felt so close to San Francisco that she could almost reach out and touch it. Baja California—it was almost the same as California, wasn't it? Just another week to San Francisco and the record.

The next morning Elizabeth was on deck early. The sky was gray and angry, and her father was preoccupied, conferring with Mr. Bridewell. Elizabeth suddenly felt cooped up on the poop deck. There was no one around for her to walk with, and she was now forbidden to walk forward by herself. But she didn't care. She wanted to walk forward, and she wanted to be by herself anyway.

Swinging around ropes and climbing over lifeboats, she made her way forward along the starboard rail of the ship.

She lay sprawled on top of one of the lifeboats, craning her neck to look fore and aft, when she heard voices up ahead of her. She crept closer to listen to the sailors.

There were three of them, crouched down for concealment behind the lifeboat, sneaking a rest from their duties. Elizabeth felt a sense of outrage at their shirking, but she shared a common cause with them of hoping that the bosun would not happen by, since she, too, was not where she should be.

"What's the name o' that ship we're supposed to be beatin', again?" asked one of them, a small, rat-faced young sailor with an accent that marked him as off the streets of New York.

"The *Flyin' Cloud*," said a burly, bearded older man, with a bandana wrapped around his head.

" 'Flyin' Fuck' is more like it," said the third man, another old sailor, balding and jowly. "That's what I give for makin' Frisco in any goddam record."

"There's that bonus," said the young man.

"Bonus!" snorted the burly sailor. "Ten dollars a man. What's it mean? One more whore in Frisco, one more night drunk."

"Hey, that ain't so bad," said the young man.

"It's bullshit. The first gash you stick it in, first night you hit port, that's sweeter than honey. After that, it's all the same."

"Hey, look, I'll take all I can get," the young man replied.

"I'll give you a little lesson, Sanderson, me lad," said the burly man, patting the front of his dungarees. "There's only one thing you have to know about every woman in the fuckin' universe. They all have cunts. An' it ain't true about Chinese women bein' different, 'cause I'm here to tell ye, I've tipped a few of 'em over, and they're straight up an' down as any white-assed bitch. And you ain't never gonna stick yer dick in every one o' those holes, so there ain't no use tryin'. Ye bust yer hump for four months at sea, thinkin' o' nothin' but that nice, warm, hairy wet nooky so bad ye can taste it. Then ye get into port, draw yer pay, tip over the first whore you see and ram it between her legs, and yer in fuckin' hooker heaven. Three weeks later yer on another fuckin' ship, dreamin' o' nooky again, and fucked if ye can remember how many o' the little ladies ye've had."

Elizabeth was hearing a language she had never heard before. It frightened her, and it fascinated her—so much that she completely forgot her indignation at the sailors for not being properly respectful of her father's record. She couldn't understand very much of what the burly sailor was talking about, except that it was about women. But *ram it between her legs*—that was a clue. *Warm, hairy, wet nooky*—between *her* legs, it was hairy now. That was part of being a woman. And sometimes it felt warm and wet, when she had her daydreams. She couldn't understand why, but it was starting to feel that way now. She squirmed forward on her stomach along the top of the lifeboat to listen more closely.

"Yer pretty horny, ain'tcha, Zanussi?"

"Fuckin' right I am. Hey, that's the only good reason for breakin' the fuckin' record. Goddam sooner we get into Frisco, goddam sooner I'll be dippin' the ol' wick, eh? Shit, all this talkin' about it don't help none, you can bet yer ass on that. It's gettin' me so fuckin' horny, if we ain't blowin' into port in another week, I'll dive overboard an' swim the rest of the way. Or else stick it into the captain's daughter."

Elizabeth gasped. By this time, she was almost at the edge of the lifeboat, and the three men looked up and saw her.

The man called Zanussi looked startled for a moment; then, with nothing more to lose, he regained the momentum of his hostility. An evil smile spread over his face.

"So, listenin', were ye, me little pretty?" he croaked. "Hear enough, did ye?"

Elizabeth could neither move nor reply.

"Heard enough? Mebbe you'd like some more, eh? Has yer mama told ye about what a man can do for a woman, yet? Has she told ye about this?"

Zanussi hooked his thumbs into the waistband of his trousers, and with a sudden, brutal flourish, he pulled them down over his hips.

Between his legs, there was a wild, grizzled bush of hair, and a thick, white, ropelike part of his body that was beyond belief to Elizabeth. The other two sailors fell back in amazement, but then snickered as Zanussi held it up in his hand and shook it at her.

"How about it, missy? Like to sit on it?"

It seemed to be growing larger as he held it, and pointing straight at her. Elizabeth backed down the length of the lifeboat on her hands and knees, then climbed down to the deck and ran as fast as she could for the after deckhouse.

She was shivering and pale as she entered the cabin. Mrs. Perkins looked at her with concern.

"What happened to you, dear?" she asked.

"N-nothing. I was up on deck, and I . . . I guess I stayed out too long. I g-got cold."

"You look like you've seen a ghost," Mrs. Perkins said. "Did anything else happen to you?"

"N-no," said Elizabeth. She was fervently glad that her mother was not there.

"Are you sure? You weren't wandering around forward again, were you?"

"No. Nothing happened. I just got cold and I don't feel well."

Mrs. Perkins looked hard at her. Finally, she turned away.

"I'll have the steward get you some tea," she said.

Elizabeth did not go up on deck again that day, or the next. A squall came up overnight, and she stayed in her bed, thinking and trying not to think.

The squall blew them somewhat off course. The day's progress was east-northeast—"still in the same current pattern," Captain Creighton said optimistically. "Just that much less of a run when we get ready to bring her in." They held to their north-northwest course again, through choppy seas, for the next four days.

Mrs. Perkins had talked to her mother about what happened. Her mother did not ask prying questions, but sometimes she looked at Elizabeth in a way that made her feel that her mother was looking right through her, as if she just *knew*, without being told, the way she had known about Elizabeth's bleeding. Elizabeth was sure, by now, that her mother had some mysterious way of knowing everything that happened to her.

She wondered if her mother had said anything to her father about it. She prayed not. It would be so unfair; her father had so much on his mind already. Commander Maury's currents, the bad weather he had been fighting for the last three days. With no sun to shoot, he had been forced to fix their position by dead reckoning. They were closer to shore at the end of eighty-six days than the *Cloud* had been, but his calculations might be misleading. And they

73

still had to sail north for another day and a half before they turned east toward San Francisco Bay. And if, on top of all that, Elizabeth's mother had been burdening him with a lot of unnecessary problems about her . . .

At a time like this, a wife should be helping her husband, not adding to his difficulties.

Eighty-seven days out of New York, 350 miles southwest of San Francisco, the *Spirit of the Waves* pointed her figurehead of the lady with the flowing robes straight at San Francisco, and took off on her last sprint at the record.

Two days later, Elizabeth's pin crowded the coast of California.

The *Flying Cloud* had begun its eighty-ninth day 240 miles off shore, and made the last day's run in twenty-one hours. The *Spirit of the Waves* was only one hundred miles offshore.

But Commander Maury's warning about approaching from the southwest proved to be well-founded. The current ran against them, and the wind came out dead ahead. The ship had to beat all day, making no forward progress at all, while Captain Creighton raged, and Elizabeth cringed and died inwardly.

Charlotte played the piano in the saloon below. She was playing when Elizabeth came below, exhausted, desolate, choking back her tears.

Seeing her mother was more than she could bear, and her passion exploded. "How can you?" she cried. "You don't care anything about all that Papa's worked for. You don't care about him being the best captain in the world! If you'd been a proper wife like Mrs. Cressy we would have made it! If you'd helped . . ."

"Elizabeth!" Charlotte voice cut sharply into her daughter's tirade.

Charlotte's eyes softened and clouded just a little, but her voice was still stern and icy as she continued: "Go to your room and go directly to bed. We'll have no more of your disrespect."

"Yes, ma'am." Elizabeth walked on sullenly, her head bowed.

"And Elizabeth—"

"Yes, ma'am."

"Don't judge what you cannot understand."

"Yes, ma'am."

Elizabeth was asleep in her bed when the eighty-nine-day, twenty-one-hour mark was passed. She awoke to find the *Spirit of the Waves* still at sea, still making little or no progress. She had plenty of time to sulk and nurse her resentment at her mother before the ship finally stumbled into San Francisco almost a full twenty-four hours too late.

Elizabeth's parents informed her before they began the trip back that it would be her last voyage. She was now of an age, they said, to be ashore for proper schooling, and to learn the graces of a young lady. She was to be sent to live with an aunt and uncle.

Elizabeth tried to enjoy her last voyage, but she could not, knowing how it would end. She would be going ashore. The *Spirit of the Waves* had failed to write Arbour and Brooke into the history books with a record-breaking performance, and the shipping concern had decided to sell her. Elizabeth would never see the ship that her father and mother would next be putting out to sea in.

The sailor Zanussi did not sign on for the return passage. The afternoon she had spied on him was a nightmare she tried to put out of her mind, but it was not as easy as that. And the *Spirit* made a sluggish homeward passage—137 days, San Francisco to New York.

When Elizabeth's time of the month to start bleeding came next—and every time after that—it was accompanied by terrible cramps and sickness that made her take to her bed the first day, and sometimes the second day, too.

Not much that her body did surprised her anymore. It was just a depressing reminder to her of how her life had fallen apart. The hair under her arms did not spread. The hair between her legs grew thicker. And she no longer had to worry about the tenderness in her chest, or wonder about the breasts on the figurehead of the ship. She was growing them too, round and pointed, just like the statue's. But hers were pointing her toward shore. On board ship, breasts were only for figureheads.

❧Chapter Eight

UNCLE JAMES CREIGHTON WAS THE MOST boring man Elizabeth had ever seen. He had a bald spot on the top of his head, and he wore the same boring dark suit of clothes every day as he left the house for work.

Elizabeth never even knew what he did! Not that she cared, but it was nevertheless strange to her, after being accustomed to men whose work and life were one, and were carried on in the same place, to see this uncle, her father's brother, disappear every morning and come back again every evening to a house where he did nothing, except occasionally receive another gentlman who would always be as dull-looking as Uncle James himself, and whom he would take into the study, where they would smoke cigars and talk.

The first few months that Elizabeth lived at Uncle James's house, he had addressed an occasional remark to her at the dinner table, and Elizabeth had tried to make sure that she answered "Yes, sir" or "No, sir" correctly, as Uncle James was given to asking questions like:

"I'll wager a winter at sea can have its moments, but you won't find snowdrifts like this in the Atlantic—fine sleigh-riding, eh?"

But after a few months, he seemed to feel that he had

discharged his obligation to make her feel at home. To Elizabeth's relief, he rarely spoke again.

Living in Uncle James's house was easier when he wasn't there. When there were only women at home, everything was much more relaxed.

During her first year ashore, she went to school during the winter, but after that she stayed home where Aunt Eleanor could teach her the womanly arts of running a household—in which, except for mending, she had no experience at all.

Elizabeth took to the household routine sullenly and rebelliously. Aunt Eleanor was patient with her. Captain David Creighton was no blood relative to her, and she neither knew him very well nor liked him very much. She wished that she had gotten Elizabeth a few years earlier, when she could have done more with the girl; but there was no helping that, so she settled it in her mind by accepting Elizabeth as one accepts a slightly retarded child. She did her best, and did not blame herself for any shortcomings in Elizabeth.

Elizabeth did not really have any personal animosity toward Aunt Eleanor, either, though she knew perfectly well that she acted as though she did. She was sullen, hostile, rude, and angry. She would not learn how to run a household. She did her chores badly, or not at all, and she would not move or talk like a lady, or learn the things she was supposed to have conversations about.

Aunt Eleanor probably deserved a nicer ward than Elizabeth. Elizabeth could not really blame her, or Uncle James, for her exile ashore, and she knew it. But she was not overly concerned with fairness, not after the monstrous unfairness that had been inflicted on her.

If there was blame to be placed, it belonged on her body. But she could not hate or resent her body. In fact, she had become quite fascinated with it. Between the ages of thirteen, when she had first been sent ashore, and seventeen, her body had changed drastically, and she had observed it closely every step of the way.

The patch of hair at the base of her belly had now completely covered the once smooth, rounded mound, but all around it, new soft, smooth curves had developed. Her stomach was curved now, very slightly like the gentle swell of a becalmed ocean, between the hard triangle of her rib cage and the soft triangle between her thighs. Her waist narrowed in and her hips widened out, dramatically; and her buttocks, too, had become firm and round. Most dramatic of all, the flat, boyish chest, on which breasts had just begun to bud when she had left her father's ship, was now full and womanly. By seventeen, her breasts were large, round, heavy and sensual. Her nipples were dark, and stood out from the white curve of her breasts.

She had learned a lot about her body. She had had to teach herself, but she had learned. She had learned, by touching herself all over, what parts of her body felt especially good when she touched them. She found different ways of touching herself—scratching, with her fingernails; lightly, with the faintest brush of her fingertips; kneading, with the flat of her hand.

She slept in the nude. It was shocking, unheard of, immodest; but she did it. Every night, she got ready for bed in the conventional way, put on her nightgown, said her prayers under the supervision of Aunt Eleanor, and got into bed with her hands outside the covers, as she had been taught. She waited, clutching the blanket up around her chin, hands trembling with anticipation, as she listened to Aunt Eleanor going down the stairs. When the sound of footsteps had died away completely, she waited a few moments longer, and then began to push the blankets down little by little, tantalizing herself with the gradualness of her own movements. Finally, she slid her feet down over onto the floor, stood up, and peeled off her nightgown.

The first time she stood naked in her bedroom, when she was just fifteen she stood looking down at herself, rooted in one place and trembling, but not from the cold. She ran her hands down the sides of her body and over her hips. Her own touch left goosebumps, and she could hardly keep from squealing with excitement. Then she scampered, naked, back into her bed, and up early the next morning to put her nightgown back on.

Another night, with the light of the full moon streaming in her window, she got up the courage to look at herself in the full-length mirror. It was the first time in her life that she had ever seen herself naked, straight ahead. She knew it was something a girl was never supposed to do. She half expected that the mirror would break—or that it would retain her image, and her shame and wantonness would still be reflected there in the morning when Aunt Eleanor came in. She scarcely saw her reflection at all.

But she had done it. She thrilled that night to her own bravery, and to her relief that nothing terrible had happened to her. The next time, she looked at herself. She looked into her own eyes, and she looked directly at her full breasts, and up and down her body.

At seventeen, she was completely at ease, in her own room, with her nakedness. She danced lightly around the room, whirling and posing before the mirror, spinning across the floor—making sure to avoid the creaking boards which she knew by heart, so as not to awaken her aunt and uncle. She stood at the window, and looked out at the empty streets of town in the moonlight. She had fantasies of someone passing by and seeing her, but she stepped back quickly whenever she saw anyone approaching in the distance.

And in the warm weather, she lay with the sheets and covers thrown off her, and let the breezes blow over her body.

And still, her body held new surprises for her. One warm summer night, she lay awake very late, edgy and unable to sleep. There seemed to be something in the air, something electric and urgent. Whatever it was, it would not let her relax.

With nervous fingers, she touched and probed her body, especially the place between her thighs where it felt best of all. It was wet and slippery down there, and the slipperiness made her finger slide easier, and she felt better and better.

But this time, the rubbing seemed to increase her tension. She felt hot all over, and she could not tell whether the warmth was inside her or outside. It became hard for her to breathe: her lungs, even her heartbeat felt suspended, waiting for something to happen. What? She was afraid, but she could not stop.

And then she began to feel something from deep inside

her, like nothing she had ever felt before. She wondered if she was going to die; but even if she were, she would not stop now. The sensation was like a whirlpool in reverse, starting from a single point at her center, and spinning, churning outward, always from the same source, all through her body. She cried out, and went limp.

She lay absolutely still and silent. Partly, she was afraid that she had woken someone up, and she would be discovered. But more than that, she was silent out of a great sense of reverence for her own body, and for what had happened to her. And later that night, before she went to sleep, she did it again. And knowing what to expect this time, she found that it was even better.

And the next morning, she was discovered by Aunt Eleanor. She did not wake up early in the morning to put her nightgown back on and rearrange her bedding. She slept soundly, and stirred only at the sound of her bedroom door slamming shut.

The room was empty when she opened her eyes and looked up. She knew instantly what that meant. Her aunt had walked in and, too shocked to stay, had immediately retreated and closed the door behind her.

In another moment, she heard her aunt's voice from outside the door. "Elizabeth. Make yourself . . . decent this instant, and then come and let me in."

Elizabeth did as she was told. But she was surprised to find that she did not feel the least bit frightened or ashamed. She felt strong and defiant. She had a sense of power and invincibility that she knew must stem from the source she had tapped in herself the night before.

Aunt Eleanor was the one who was nervous, though she tried to hide it behind a show of sternness and moral outrage.

"Elizabeth, I want you to promise me that I will never again find you in that disgraceful state."

Elizabeth's smile, with just the corners of her mouth, had the devil in it.

"Of course, Aunt. I promise."

There was more that her aunt wanted to say. Her face darkened with it, but for a long time, no words came out.

"Elizabeth . . . you don't . . . touch yourself down there, do you?"

"Down where, Aunt? What do you mean?"

Aunt Eleanor exhaled sharply, turned abruptly, and walked out of the room.

✎Chapter Nine

ELIZABETH KNEW THAT AUNT ELEANOR
would never walk into her room again and she knew that
Aunt Eleanor was afraid of her.

Aunt Eleanor wanted Elizabeth out of the house, and at
the same time she was afraid to let her go out of the house.
She wanted Elizabeth married, and she was afraid to let
her near a man. She treated Elizabeth like a vial of nitro-
glycerine, unstable and capable of going off at any time.

Actually, in spite of all her exploration of her own sexuality, Elizabeth had never really thought much about
men, or about having a man touch her. The possibilities of
her body were quite absorbing enough for her.

And the young men that Aunt Eleanor invited to the
house for tea or social evenings did nothing to divert Elizabeth from that self-absorption. They were all as dull as Uncle James. None of them knew anything about the sea,
which was the one subject Elizabeth really cared to talk
about. Being New Englanders, they knew about shipping—
about cargoes, and accounts, and such matters. But it was
not the same, not at all.

Elizabeth was ruled more and more by her passions. She
had no time for being nice to people who did not interest
her. She had no time for mending fences with her aunt—no

time to do the things around the house that would mollify Aunt Eleanor.

She spent time in her room, and she spent time taking long walks. The long walks were always to places overlooking the sea. The time in her room was for touching herself, exploring her body—or for reading. There was a bunch of old books in Uncle James's house that her father had left there years ago, before he had a home of his own, and Elizabeth read them in the evenings. There were books by old sea captains, like *Voyage in the Ship Perseverance*, by Captain Amasa Delano. There was an early edition of Commander Maury's famous book. There were books on astronomy, and books on higher mathematics that were terribly difficult, but Elizabeth read them through, studying the theories tenaciously until she understood them and then applying them to work out the problems exercises.

She knew that Aunt Eleanor did not think much of her reading those books, but there was not a great deal that she could say against it. After all, they were Elizabeth's father's own books, and there was certainly nothing sinful about them—compared to the other things that Aunt Eleanor imagined Elizabeth to be doing, they were quite harmless.

Aunt Eleanor could, and did, venture sharp comments about the number of better things there were for a young girl to be occupying her time with than musty old books, frequently listing them in detail in case Elizabeth had forgotten.

"Well, I don't care!" Elizabeth snapped back on one of these occasions. "I am going to marry a ship's captain, and then I shall have far more use for knowledge of the stars and the tides than for all your dusting and flower arranging and playing 'Silver Threads Among the Gold' on the piano!"

To which Aunt Eleanor replied, "You'll marry who'll have you, my dear. And even a ship's captain appreciates a wife who has the social graces."

Elizabeth sniffed. Aunt Eleanor turned and fixed her with a cold, direct stare. "*If* anyone will have you," she said. Her voice was filled with such provocative contempt that Elizabeth could not hold herself back from rising to the bait.

"What do you mean by that?" she asked.

"You know what I mean by it, young lady. You're no kin to me, and it's for the respect to the sainted woman that was your grandmother that your Uncle James and I have kept you under our roof, not for that father of yours, or for anything you've done since you've been here to show yourself worthy of the Christian welcome we've given you. But remember—and remember well—that sailors are no different from any other men, and for all their whoring and fornicating around the fleshpots of sin all over the world, they want a wife who is pure and ladylike. Men won't take soiled goods into their houses—or onto their ships. Do you understand me?"

Elizabeth thought she did, although she was not quite sure. But she answered back with a confident air.

"Don't you worry about me. I know how to take care of myself, and I shall have any man I want."

"I warn you, young lady—" Aunt Eleanor took two steps closer to Elizabeth, and thrust her chin forward so that their faces were only inches apart. "I warn you . . . and listen to me well. In spite of any promise that my husband made to your father . . . if you so much as bring any hint of scandal or disgrace on this household, you will be sent packing. If you want to live out your life in some waterfront brothel in Boston . . . it's no responsibility of mine."

The effort of saying the words had left Aunt Eleanor emotionally exhausted. Elizabeth knew it, and knew that she was stronger than her aunt. She giggled in Aunt Eleanor's face.

Elizabeth's favorite place to walk was an old cemetery, the final resting place of generations of Connecticut seafarers—those who had lived long enough to die on land. Elizabeth felt at home there, among the departed souls of exiles from the sea.

One corner of the graveyard—Elizabeth's favorite— had fallen into neglect. Overlooking the harbor, it was wild and untended, with high grasses growing up around the shrubs and vines climbing over them. Elizabeth could sit hidden among the tall grasses and watch the sloops and the whaling vessels, the inevitable, ugly, smoke-belching steamers, and the occasional full-rigged ships, as well as the countless small fishing boats that went in and out of the harbor every day.

She was beginning to think more about men. She often daydreamed about marrying a ship's captain. She took it as a sign that she was growing up. When she had first come to live on shore, back when she was thirteen and fourteen, she had daydreamed only of going back to sea with her father, but now she was outgrowing that. She would be eighteen in just a few more months, and she was close to being ready to marry.

She worried more about what her aunt said than she admitted.

She had met an older man, a handsome ship's master of twenty-nine. His name was William Dwyer, and he had just returned from his first voyage at the helm of his own ship, the *Northern Lights*, owned by his great uncle, Hamish McNab of Stonington. Captain Dwyer came to Stonington to report on the voyage, and stayed to visit for a month while the ship was in dry dock.

Mr. and Mrs. McNab gave a party to introduce the bachelor Captain Dwyer to the young people of Stonington, and Elizabeth met him there. Not for the first time, though. Captain Dwyer had been Second Mate Dwyer on her father's ship, when she had been only nine years old. Would he remember her?

Of course. "You were such a fine little sailor, then. We used to joke that I was the third mate of the ship and Mr. Penning the second, because you were really the first mate. But now—look at you! You've become a lovely young woman."

Elizabeth was about to tell him that she was still a good sailor, and that ever since she had been ashore she had been reading about navigation and astronomy and even shipbuilding. But at the last second, she changed her mind and said:

"And I remember always thinking, back then, that you were the handsomest young officer on any of my papa's crews."

Actually, she remembered no such thing, but she could hardly begin their acquaintanceship by telling him that she thought him handsome now.

He told her about his first voyage as a captain, about the

difficulties he had encountered and the places he had been. Elizabeth listened raptly. There were a couple of difficulties that he described that seemed to her as if they could have been handled with a little more skill and a quicker wit, but she kept that opinion to herself. She did not want to interrupt the flow of his stories. It had been a long time since anyone had talked to her about sea voyages and foreign ports. The stories that she had told her acquaintances about her own experiences had long since begun to sound stale, even to her.

The first time they danced, Mr. Dwyer put his hand around her waist and she felt a rush of warmth. It was nothing like the overpowering sensation she got when she touched herself, but on the carriage ride back to her uncle's house, she relived the touch of his hand, and saw, over and over again, the smile on his lips so close to hers that it would have been a simple matter for them to lean together and kiss . . . but of course, they had not.

And it was different that night, too—she found herself imagining, without willing it, that it was his hand touching her. She blushed, she felt ashamed, even though she was all alone; then she felt suddenly bold, though at the moment of climax there was no thought in her head but the sensation.

She decided she must be in love wtih Mr. Dwyer. She wondered how long it would be before she could marry him and they could sleep together in the big captain's bed aboard the *Northern Lights*.

She went the next day to the cemetery to look out at Stonington Harbor, wishing that the *Northern Lights* was there so she could see her future home—but, of course, it was up in Boston in dry dock. Even so, she tingled all over with a new kind of excitement as she perched on a headstone and looked out on the blue sky and darker blue water, the swooping gulls and towering mastheads. She hugged herself, and rocked gently on the stone.

"Here, you! Wotcha think yer doin' here?" a harsh voice suddenly boomed out from behind her. She turned, startled, and beheld a burly young man with a sea bag over his shoulder, not fifteen paces from her.

"Who are you?"

"Who are you, is more like it," said the man. "And wotcher doin' with yer arse in me old man's face?"

"*What?*" Elizabeth could not tell whether the man was angry, or mocking her. He had a fleshy, handsome face, with full lips that seemed to curl naturally into a sensual sneer. His eyes had the perpetual squint of a seagoing man, so it was hard to read the expression in them.

"That's me dad's tombstone yer settin' on," he said. "That's what I'm doin' here. Come up to see the ol' bugger, first time in ten years."

Elizabeth could tell now that he was drunk. She had gotten up from the tombstone, and now she moved around behind it, keeping it between her and the sailor. But she did not feel scared. Not very scared, anyway.

"My name's Jack Murphy," he said. "That's me da's name, too. See?" His eyes squinted down to even narrower slits, and he pointed at the chiseled letters on the tombstone. "Jack Murphy, died 1862. I were two years at sea, then. Shipped out when I 'uz twelve years old, on a steamer, and ain't set foot in Stonington since."

"I'm Elizabeth Creighton," said Elizabeth, and then she could not resist adding: "And I lived on a clipper ship when I was twelve years old. How can you work on one of those awful smelly steamships?"

"Well, now, to each his own," Murphy said with a shrug. "Or her own, I reckon. Pleased ta meetcha, Lizzie. And me old dad thanks ye fer keepin' his face warm so nice, like."

"I . . . I wasn't really, you know," she answered. "I was just sitting on top of his headstone. That's not the same as his head."

"Rum go if it was," giggled Murphy. "Wrong shape fer his head, though. Too long an' flat. What about if it 'uz his tongue, stickin' up through the ground, an' you perched on th' end of it. That'd tickle yer fancy, eh wot?"

"What do you mean?" Elizabeth drew back, and tried to act outraged, but she could not sustain it. She giggled, too, and then their eyes met. She was defenseless against her obvious enjoyment of his banter.

"Don't you know that's no way to talk to a lady?" she said.

"Sure, and wot kinder lady is it as perches 'er bunghole on me da's tongue, now?" he said. "I don't rightly know

88

much about ladies, though. Wot I mostly sees is t'other kind."

"What other kind?" teased Elizabeth.

"What other kind, indeed?" said Murphy philosophically. He sat down at the foot of his father's gravesite, reached into his sea bag, and pulled out a bottle of rum—a quart, nearly full. He uncorked it, took a large gulp, and waved the bottle at Elizabeth. "Want some?"

"No, thank you."

"Your loss." He took another gulp. "What other kind, indeed? I 'uz ree . . . fererrin' to th' whores an' lowlife wot hangs around th' docks. But wot th' hell . . . mebbe it's all th' same. You ever have a tongue up yer pussy before?"

"No . . ."

"Well, ye have now. It's all the same. Yer a whore too. A whore t' me dead da, here's to ye, God love ye." He took another drink of rum.

. . . Whoring and fornicating in the fleshpots of sin all over the world, Elizabeth thought. She had looked up "fornicating" in the dictionary, but she had not been able to find "whoring" at all. "Do I look like a whore to you?" she asked with open curiosity.

"Mmm . . . mebbe. It's hard to tell."

"What does a whore look like? Why is it hard to tell?"

"Well, fer one thing, ye c'n see a lot more o' them. Here, have a shot o' this."

"Oh, no thank you, I . . . maybe I will." Elizabeth stayed behind the tombstone, but she leaned forward and stretched out her hand. Murphy passed her the bottle. She held it in one hand, squeezing the neck as though she wanted to choke off the liquor before it reached her mouth. She squared her shoulders, tipped the bottle up partway, and let a small stream of liquid trickle past her lips, across her tongue, and down her throat. It burned, and the smell was so strong it made her take a step backward, but it went down easily. She took a larger swig, and collapsed in a fit of choking and sputtering.

"Hey—don't drop th' bottle!" said Murphy.

"Don't . . . don't . . . ah . . . don't worry about me," managed Elizabeth, recovering herself, holding the bottle up in front of her. "I can handle it." To prove her point, she drank again, this time a little more cautiously, and got it all down.

She leaned over the tombstone and handed the bottle back to Murphy. "What do you mean, you can see a lot more of them?"

"Well, now, them whores, y'see, they wear dresses like—" Murphy took another drink and handed the bottle back to Elizabeth "—like *this*."

Elizabeth giggled. "No they don't. You're making it up."

"They do. An' I'll tell ye somethin' else. They . . . say, Lizzie . . . wot're you wearin'?"

"You're silly. You can see what I'm wearing."

"No, no, I mean what else . . . wot're ye wearin' underneath?"

"Why, I'm not going to tell you that!"

"No, no, c'mon . . . friends, right? I'm tellin' ye all sorts o' good stuff . . . I'm sharin' my rum with ye, right?"

He grinned at her. She smiled back, and took another swallow of rum.

"Well, a hoop, you know . . . a hoop with a bustle attachment, to give it the new shape . . ." Murphy snickered, and Elizabeth flushed a fiery red. "And a corset . . ."

"Wot's it made of?"

"Well, wire, you know, and twill tape. And the corset is whalebone . . . the stays, anyway . . ."

"Purty stiff."

"Were you ever on a whaler?"

"Never min' me. What about the rest? Y' got t' tell me everythin'. I'm tellin' ye lots o' good stuff . . . ye want me t' tell ye 'bout whores, right?"

"Yes."

"Y' want me t' tell ye whether ye'd make a good whore, right?"

"Right!"

"Then y' gotta tell me . . . 's'all there is to it. Wot else ye wearin'?"

"A petticoat . . . that's over the hoop . . . an' a pair of pantaloons . . ."

"That's over yer ass an' yer pussy."

Elizabeth dissolved in giggles. "No, silly. That's over my chemise. That's over . . . over my ass and my pussy."

"An' yer titties, too." Murphy's eyes bored into her chest.

"An' my titties."

"Well, them whores, now—sometimes they don't wear nothin' under their dresses."

"*Nothing?*"

"That's right . . . not a blessed thing."

"Oh, my."

They passed the bottle back and forth one more time. Elizabeth was feeling quite lightheaded by this time, dizzy and prickly and very warm. All the clothes that she was wearing were beginning to feel tight and constricting on her.

As Murphy went on, talking about brothels and dance halls and waterfront gambling casinos, she tried to imagine what it would be like to be a whore and walk around in a low-cut dress with nothing on under it, right out in the open where everyone could see you. With her head full of rum and her body hot and chafing under her ladylike attire, it sounded fun and exciting.

Murphy lurched to his feet, and peered down into the now-empty bottle. "Hey, I 'uz gonna come up here an' drink a round wi' me ol' dad," he said plaintively. "Drink one fer me, an' then pour a little on his grave. But it looks like we drunk it all. Well, I guess Dad won't mind if I give him his share passed through me kidneys, eh?"

He tossed the bottle over his shoulder, and it smashed against a tombstone behind him. Swaying unsteadily, he anchored both hands on his hips and struggled to hold his balance. Then, as Elizabeth's eyes bulged, he took out his penis and began to urinate in front of her.

Elizabeth leaned forward, wide-eyed. She rested her chin on the tombstone and stared. When he was finished, he shook the last few drops off the end, pulled the foreskin forward again over the tip of his penis, and looked up at her. He cupped the organ in his hand, and pointed it at her.

"Purty good, hey? Like that, do ye?"

He buttoned himself back up again. "Ever see anythin' like that before, Lizzie?"

Elizabeth thought with a shudder of the sailor on board the *Spirit of the Waves*, and did not answer his question.

But even that awful memory did not seem so frightening now. She stood up, took a step backward, and said, "I don't have to wear this old hoop all the time, either."

She turned around, reached up under her dress, and undid the buckle at her waist. The hoop fell flat on the ground at her feet. She turned around to face Murphy.

"Do I look more like a whore, now?"

"What about the pantaloons?"

"Oh, you can't see them." But she removed them, too, again turning away as she did it. "Now?"

"I dunno. D' ye feel like a whore?"

"I don't know. What does a whore feel like?"

"Hey, come around here and I'll tell ye."

"Oh, no. You stay on that side of the . . . of your father, and I'll stay on this side." But she came up and knelt up against the tombstone again, leaning over it with her chin and her hands. "Tell me, Jack. Tell me . . . what does a whore do?"

A flicker of surprise passed over Murphy's face, and was quickly replaced by a sly, pleased smile. He knelt on the other side of the tombstone, his face only inches from hers.

"Gi' us a kiss and I'll tell ye all about it."

"Why, Mr. Murphy!"

"C'mon. See, I'll stay over here on my side, and jes' lean over . . ."

Elizabeth felt too good not to. She leaned forward to meet him, and they kissed. She felt his lips press against hers, and she liked it. She tilted her head to the side so they could press closer. And suddenly it was not like touching anymore, not like any touching she had ever known before, anyway. His lips, his tongue, seemed to have become a part of her, and she could feel him all the way through her. The wetness, the softness, the fullness of it drew her in, closer and closer to him.

Then she felt his hand close tightly around her upper arm, and he was jerking around from behind the tombstone. With lightning instinct, she pulled away and rolled backward to come up crouching a few yards away from him. She looked up into his face: flushed, excited, full of the lust of the chase. She realized that she felt the same way. He sprang at her, and she darted behind a large headstone. Breathing heavily, she faced him, her hands resting on the stone; she shifted her weight back and forth from one foot to the other, waiting for him to make the first move so that she could run in the other direction.

"Yer a sly vixen, but ye won't be able to outrun me with that long skirt hobblin' up yer ankles," he said.

"Then I'll take it off." Her heart pumping, she unfastened the button at her waist. As the skirt fell to her feet, he rushed at her around the left side of the tombstone, and she bounded out of the circle of cotton cloth at her feet and skipped away to the right, her long legs flashing in the sunlight.

Her one remaining outer garment, the long polonaise jacket and overskirt, still covered most of her thighs, but did not restrict her movement. She had never felt so free, so light on her feet, so daring. She danced ahead of him, flitting from one tombstone to the next, laughing as he stumbled. His face was bright red now, but still handsome, and it glowed with sweat from his exertion. There was a glint of determination in his eyes. At the center of his trousers, there was a huge bulge that looked even larger than the organ he had taken out and showed her before.

She led him in a circle around the graveyard, in and out between the stones, until at last, out of breath, she came to a huge piece of granite, with a life-sized statue of a winged female figure—an angel—atop it, carved from a dark, almost black stone.

She leaned against the pedestal to rest. She was completely hidden from him now, and he from her. She heard his voice, not too far away:

"They used t' say, if a virgin lies with a man under that statue, th' angel will turn white."

She looked up at the angel and wondered if it were true.

"You'll never catch me, anyway," she called back.

She would not know from which side he was coming at her until the last second, and then it might be too late for her to run. She would have to think of something different, some new trick to outwit him, but that was fine—she was getting bored with this phase of the game, and it was time to increase the stakes, anyway. Quickly and quietly, she unbuttoned the front of her jacket, slipped out of it, and rolled it up into a ball in her hands.

She could sense that he was close, creeping up around

one side or the other of the pedestal. She listened for his breathing, but she could hear nothing. Still, she knew he was there.

With a rush, he was around the side of the pedestal, lunging at her with both arms outstretched; and she tossed the rolled-up jacket into his hands.

The trick worked. He stopped, confused, and caught it, while she skipped away, now wearing nothing but her chemise, which fluttered as she ran to give him a peekaboo glimpse of her naked bottom. And as she looked over her shoulder, she could see from the expression on his face that while she might have escaped him, she had also inflamed him, and there would be no holding him back now.

She ran as fast as she could, zigzagging and weaving through the headstones, but he ran faster—and whether by instinct or by some primal, unconscious signal she was giving him, her feints and maneuverings no longer seemed to have any effect. Whatever she did, he stayed right on her trail, and kept gaining steadily.

They had come back full circle, to the senior Murphy's headstone, and she was only a few steps ahead of him. She ducked behind the stone and turned to face him, ready again to circle around it and keep him at bay. But he never hesitated. He came straight on, vaulted right over the top of the tombstone, and tackled her around the waist.

They fell to the ground together. Elizabeth landed on her back, with her chemise up around her navel, and Murphy landed half on top of her, with his face pressed right up against her thighs.

She was pinned. She beat at his back and shoulders with her fists, but there was no escape—nor did she want one, though she kept struggling.

"Let me go!" she breathed.

"Not much," he grunted. "Ye want it too much. I can smell it."

He pressed his face against her thighs, and they parted. Elizabeth could smell it then, too, commingling with the smells of rum and earth and grass—the rich, heady aroma of sexual excitement—the musk of her own womanhood, and she recognized it as surely as if it had been put in a sachet and labeled.

The young sailor pushed further. Elizabeth felt a sudden

thrill that began between her legs and went winging through her entire nervous system, and her eyes widened with amazement as she realized that he had put his tongue inside her.

Her head fell back, and she looked up at the fleecy white clouds that appeared to be spinning, whirling through the heavens. Her thighs spread wide for him.

He stood up, straddling her. She saw his face silhouetted against the sky, the clouds ringing his head, and only his eyes, hot and hungry, showed clearly.

"Guess ye'll stay put while I gets rid o' me trousers, eh?" he said in a hoarse voice.

"Yes, but quickly . . . please . . ."

He was quick; he was very quick. Her body trembled, waiting for him, and then, in just a few seconds, he was on her, inside her, exploding in her with a burst of pain; then past the pain, and building quickly, very, very quickly, to a moment that was like the ones she had brought herself to, but infinitely more intense. Her eyes were tight shut; her ripe breasts flattened against his chest and bulged out on either side; her forearms locked across his back and twitched convulsively with each tremor of pleasure that passed through her.

Then it was over, and he had rolled off her. Once out of her sight, and no longer touching her, he was out of her thoughts. She lay on her back for a long time, looking up at the sky, and thinking only about herself, about her body and what wonders it was capable of. She turned her head and looked over at the black angel. It was still black. Perhaps she had not been close enough; or perhaps it knew something.

Finally, she rolled over and looked up at Murphy. He was sitting on a stone, and he had put his dungarees back on. He looked different, now. More ordinary. A young sailor. She raised herself up to her knees, straightened her shift down over her hips, and sat back on her heels. Her hands were folded in her lap, and a reserved smile was on her lips.

"You've done yourself proud, my lad, for an able seaman. I happen to be a captain's daughter."

"Shucks, I don't hold it against ye," said Murphy with an easy smile. "Yer right good as any whore."

◈Chapter Ten

ELIZABETH ARRIVED AT HOME IN THE EARLY
evening and went straight to her room, pleading her monthly
sickness. She fell immediately into a sound sleep, and
awoke the next morning with a monstrous hangover—a
headache and nausea which she did not know whether to
attribute to the drinking or the fornication. The hangover
lasted through most of that day, but her fears and worries
lasted longer than that.

It disturbed her particularly that, by the second day, she
could no longer remember exactly what the sailor looked
like. She had taken so much pleasure from the experience,
and yet the man who had given her that pleasure meant
nothing to her. Did that mean that, in fact, she was a
whore? She did not think she really wanted to be a whore.

She resolved to change her life completely. She would
get married. She would fall in love with Captain Dwyer
and marry him, and he would take her back to the healthy,
morally bracing life of the sea.

Captain Dwyer came for dinner the next week. He was
stiffer, more wooden than Elizabeth remembered him, but
she was still prepared to fall in love with him, if that
proved to be a workable solution to her dilemma. They still
had the sea in common.

Captain Dwyer talked expansively about the sea that night at dinner, and about his experiences as second mate on the *Union Flyer*.

"You know," he said, "what really made those voyages a treat for all of us sailors—as much of a treat as any sea voyage can be, you understand—and I've heard others who shipped out with your father say the very same words—was your mother. Mrs. Creighton—now there was a lady. No matter what kind of difficulty we ran up against, no matter what mishaps befell the ship, or what the weather, she kept to her chosen routine, and she kept her dignity. Hearing her play that piano, even in the roughest of times—well, it just made us all think of home."

"A good woman," Aunt Eleanor agreed.

"And you know," Captain Dwyer continued, "she was sick in her cabin the first few days out of port on every voyage. We all felt for her, every man jack of us—and a lot of the men came to think of it as a good-luck omen for the voyage, so it just gave us all the more affection for her. And admiration, too, that she'd come on every voyage with the captain, even being sick that way. Yes, a remarkably fine lady, Mrs. Creighton was. And the present Mrs. Creighton, too, I'm sure," he finished, smiling politely at Aunt Eleanor.

Elizabeth began to find Captain Dwyer tiresome, and very soon made it clear that she was no longer particularly interested in his coming around. Calf love, Aunt Eleanor called it. A young girl's fickle fancy.

Only a few months later, her parents returned from another voyage. The James Creightons got a letter from them in New York: her mother had become infirm. The last passage had been a particularly rough one for her, and she was going to have to stop traveling. Her father, also, had decided to retire.

It was the greatest shock Elizabeth had ever received, greater even than being sent ashore herself. She could not imagine her father retired from the sea. She could not fathom how her mother could have inveigled him into such a decision. She knew that he could perfectly well continue at sea without her mother accompanying him: she was no help at all aboard ship, and not much for company either, whatever superstitious good-luck charm the sailors made out of her seasickness.

Elizabeth was invited to go and spend a few days with them in New York. She took the New York–New Haven railroad into town. It was a good day's journey, and she had plenty of time to think.

She thought about it all the way into New York, and by the time she got there she had made up her mind what had to be done. If her father needed someone to go along with him and keep him company when he went back to sea, why then, she would volunteer to go with him, even if it meant that she would never meet a young captain of her own and never get married.

And, if her father was retiring because someone had to stay home and take care of her mother, then she would volunteer to do that. She would move into the big brick house with her mother, and take care of her. Whatever it took to save her father, Elizabeth was willing to do.

Elizabeth planned the whole conversation out, many times over. She would get her father alone, for a private talk. It could not be too difficult, especially if her mother was not well. She would certainly want to stay in her room and rest at some point, while Elizabeth and her father went out for a walk together.

Her father and mother both came to meet her at the station. Charlotte Creighton had new lines of strain in her face, and she looked thinner and older, but otherwise she seemed well and in good spirits. There was some color in her cheeks, and her eyes were bright. Elizabeth felt better when she saw her, as if she had been holding her breath for a long time, and was finally able to let it out. She had not realized how much she had been worrying about her mother's health.

Mostly, though, she was eaten by impatience. She wanted to talk to her father alone so she could tell him of her plan, and seeing him only made it seem more urgent.

They went to her parents' hotel first, so that she could freshen up after the journey. They had taken a suite with a private room for Elizabeth.

It was her mother, not her father, with whom Elizabeth found herself alone.

99

"My, you've become such a young lady," said her mother. "Do you have any special beaux yet?"

"No, Mama."

"Ah, but you will. It's your time, now."

"That may have to wait on its own time," said Elizabeth. "It's not for me to say when I'll be wanted—if ever. Or what duties I'll be called upon to perform in this life."

"Yes, duty is important, surely," said her mother. "But your duties at home, with Aunt Eleanor, are just to prepare you for your duty to your husband, and that is the most important."

Elizabeth was beginning to feel uncomfortable. What was all this talk about husbands, anyway?

"The Bible says, 'Honor thy father,'" she said. "'And mother.'"

"And it says, 'Therefore shall a man leave his father and his mother, and cleave unto his wife: and they shall be one flesh,'" her mother replied.

They met Captain Creighton downstairs, and the three of them got into a hansom and went to a restaurant for dinner.

For all of her impatience about her mission, Elizabeth could not help but be impressed. Just as this was the first time she had been given her own private room in a hotel suite, so it was the first time she had been allowed to eat with her parents in a fancy restaurant. When, as a child, she had stayed overnight in New York, she had taken all her meals upstairs in the room with Mrs. Perkins. It gave her confidence.

"It's wonderful, Papa," she said. "Thank you so much. I love New York."

"Tomorrow we'll have a real holiday, Lizzie," her father promised. "We'll go to the theater in the evening."

"Oh, thank you, Papa."

Then Captain Creighton turned to his wife.

"Madam, I am pleased to say that I was able to settle all the financial details of the transaction. We shall set out in three days' time."

"I am very happy to hear that, Captain Creighton," said Charlotte.

"Then it's not true, Papa? You are going back to sea again, after all?" asked Elizabeth.

"No, Lizzie, nothing like that," said her father, with one of his heartiest laughs. "Bless me, no. We're retiring, right enough, and high time. We've bought a piece of farmland in eastern Connecticut near Washington, where your mother's family comes from. We're selling the house in Stonington, and we thought to spend our last years far away from the sound of the ocean. Otherwise, the old salt might get lured back by a mermaid beckoning on a sea breeze, eh, madam?"

This last remark was directed, with an affectionate chuckle, at Charlotte—in a tone of voice Elizabeth had never heard her father use toward her mother before. Elizabeth was beside herself. She could not keep from bursting out:

"But Papa, you *can't*!" She was close to tears as she went on, "You can't let yourself be taken off to a farm! You belong—"

"*Elizabeth!*"

The sharp rebuke came not from her mother, usually the custodian of her manners, but from her father. Charlotte Creighton sat very quiet. Elizabeth stopped, but her face was still flushed, and she trembled a little.

Captain Creighton began the conversation again after a few moments.

"Washington is a lovely village, an historic old community," he said. "It has a flavor all its own. When the nation's capital was incorporated back at the turn of the century, the town elders of Washington, Connecticut, sent a message to the federal government protesting the usurpation of their name."

"Father . . ." Elizabeth began haltingly, "will I . . . ?"

"Of course you'll be coming to live with us, dear," said her mother, "as soon as our new house is built—in about six months or so. In the meantime, you'll be staying on with Uncle and Aunt Creighton. You are quite a part of their household, now."

"Yes, Mother," said Elizabeth in a quiet voice.

"You can finish your education in Washington, get your certification, and perhaps teach there, if some young fellow doesn't marry you first. They have fine schools there. Your mother was teaching in one of them, when I met her."

Elizabeth did not trust her voice to answer. She concentrated as hard as she could on not letting her face do anything disgraceful.

"You're not eating, Lizzie," her father said. "New York restaurant fare too rich for you?"

"I . . . maybe," said Elizabeth. "That must be it. I feel a little faint. Perhaps it would be better if I just rested this evening, and went straight back to Stonington in the morning."

"Nonsense," said Captain Creighton. "We've a holiday tomorrow, and the theater. Look at your mother—she never let a little upset stop her from doing anything. Now, I don't want to hear another word about it."

"All right, Papa," said Elizabeth. "I'll just go back to the hotel and lie down for the rest of this evening, and be fine tomorrow, I promise."

The note read:

Dear Papa and Mama,
I have decided to go straight back to Uncle and Aunt's house in Stonington. I am afraid I won't be feeling well for a few more days—Mama will understand why—and I don't want to ruin your vacation. I will visit you in Washington soon. Your loving daughter,

Elizabeth.

Once again, the curse of Eve was working for her. Elizabeth propped the note up against her pillow and hurried out into the night. She did not know exactly where she was going, but she was sure that she would find what she was looking for along New York's waterfront.

∽Chapter Eleven

THE WOMEN WERE ALL AGES—LINED, LUMPY, unattractive old crones; slim-hipped girls, no older than she was, with long stringy hair that hung straight down to their shoulders; attractive women with puffy, tired eyes. They were in doorways, leaning out of windows, on street corners. She heard their voices, mixed with the men's, from inside the buildings with the brightly lit exteriors that Elizabeth did not dare to enter. They were saloons, and dance halls, and gambling casinos.

The street life itself was awesome enough, even without going into any of the buildings. It was frightening and thrilling, exhilarating and intimidating. At first it was too much for Elizabeth. She walked quickly through the streets—Water Street, South Street, Peck Slip—her head down, not daring to see too much. She was torn and confused—drawn to the light for safety, to the shadows for anonymity. She did not stop or look up when men whistled after her, or shouted out lewd suggestions.

Afraid as she was, though, she felt very brave for daring to venture out into this dangerous world at all. And her appreciation of her own courage made her feel braver still, so that gradually she slowed her pace a little, raised her eyes a little, and began to look around her.

And gradually she began to feel more and more that she had been right after all, that she had come to the right place. She looked at the faces of the women. She could not meet their eyes, but looked at them with quick, darting glances. They looked hot, and hard: the way she felt, behind her own eyes. She was one of them.

And beneath her outer garments, she was naked. The shape she exposed to the world seemed strange to her, with no hoop, no bustle, no corset, but she liked it. There was nothing revealing about the conventional, dark-colored, conservatively tailored broadcloth outfit that she was wearing, but those who looked at her would know, or could guess, that there was nothing but Elizabeth under it. The skirt and jacket hung strangely. They rubbed against her loosely and made her feel very conscious of her body.

She stopped near a corner. There were two women standing on the corner, under the street lamp. Elizabeth stood in the shadows near the wall of a frame building, and watched them. One was plump and dark, with a square face and round, ample breasts. She wore a black dress of some thin material that stretched tightly across her wide hips. The other had red hair, and a broad face with a wide, heavily painted mouth and a strong jaw. She wore a dress of deep crimson and black, cut low in front. There was an air of authority and arrogance about her.

As Elizabeth stood in the shadows and watched, a bearded man came by, and the red-haired woman stepped out in front of him. "Like to have some fun, handsome?" she said to him in a hoarse voice, grating but provocative.

Elizabeth gasped, and put her hand up to her face. When she looked again, seconds later, the red-haired prostitute and the bearded sailor were walking off together. Elizabeth hurried on, in the opposite direction.

Three blocks later, she slowed down. She found herself at an empty street corner, under the pale glow of a gas lamp. When she looked up and saw the lamp, she realized that she had actually stopped, and been standing under it for several moments, her mind a blank. She also became aware of how much she must look like the two whores on the other corner, but she still continued to stand there.

A short, swarthy man was walking rapidly down the block. He was abreast of her before she could get her wits about her and react, but just before he passed by she took one step out toward him and said, as much like the red-haired woman as she could: "Like to have some fun, handsome?"

Her voice cracked. The short man walked right past her without even acknowledging her presence. Elizabeth pivoted and watched him recede into the gloom, still striding purposefully toward a destination he would not be swayed from—not, at any rate, by Elizabeth Creighton.

She did not know whether to feel crushed or relieved. But she knew that she felt out of place. She did not belong out here, after all, and she could not imagine how she could ever have thought she did.

She knew that she had to get home, somehow; she was no longer sure that she knew the way. She turned a corner that she thought must be the right way, and immediately found herself hopelessly lost, on a street that she had never seen before.

She had never seen anything like it, either. There were men walking up and down, not looking at each other. They were looking at the women who stood in the windows of the houses, dirty-looking women leaning over filthy, cracked, rotting windowsills. The windows were open and curtainless. The women leaned out and called invitations to the men, in obscene, explicit language that both repelled and excited Elizabeth.

She stopped to stare at a large, square-jawed, square-shouldered woman with black hair. The woman was naked from the waist up. Her breasts were immense and chunky, like two huge sacks of flour attached to her chest, and she held her arms folded under them, pushing them out so they looked even bigger and seemed to be squared off at the bottom. Elizabeth could not have imagined that a woman's breasts could be that big.

Mrs. Perkins must look like that without her clothes on, she thought. But instead of making her giggle, as it might have at another time, the idea filled her with awe. *All women are like that,* she thought. *Even Mrs. Perkins, even me, everybody. All women have breasts, no matter what they hide them behind, with nipples that get hard when you touch them. And hair between our legs, and a slit there that opens and gets wet and causes feelings that we can't ignore or walk away from.*

She did not have the simple words to say it to herself:

we are all sexual creatures. So the thought played itself out in her mind, expanding as it did. *Under her dress, Mrs. Perkins is the same as this whore in the window. They lie to you, and tell you it's not the same. They tell you we're different from this kind of woman, but that isn't true.*

She remembered what her mother had said: *You're a woman now, like me. This will happen to you every month, for the rest of your life. And you must never let a man touch you there.* Her mother, too! Could it be . . . ?

"Hey, bitch, wotcha starin' at?"

The strident, ugly, female voice split the air, and shocked Elizabeth out of her reverie. She put her head down in shame and embarrassment.

"Go on, get outta here!" shouted the whore. "Before I have my mack rearrange yer hoity-toity face."

Elizabeth hurried on. But as she moved down the block, she looked back quickly over her shoulder. The woman had stood up, and was leaning out the window now, calling after a passerby. She had thighs the size of Elizabeth's waist, and a huge bush of black hair that Elizabeth guessed she could hide her whole hand in. The thought of how much sexuality there was in that immense triangle made Elizabeth shudder.

She stopped again, by another window, to look at a smaller prostitute, a young woman with a thin, sad face and wiry blond curls. The woman's fragile but full-breasted body reminded Elizabeth of her own, and she could see a curious reflection of herself in the woman's sad eyes, too.

The blond prostitute was wearing a thin, frayed robe that hung open in the front—two straight lines of faded purple framing a strip of pale body, with the half-arcs of two full breasts at each side of the frame.

"Try me for a dollar, sailor?" she called out in a surprisingly sweet, plaintive soprano. "Try me for a dollar? How about it, sailor? For a big cock like yours—seventy-five cents."

The man whose eye she had caught nodded, and turned in. Elizabeth watched the woman leave the window, and go over to the door. The sailor whose back Elizabeth had seen on the street a minute earlier, was suddenly visible from the front, indoors, as he entered the prostitute's dingy room.

Elizabeth realized that she had been waiting for the curtain to close, for the scene to end. But there was no curtain, no privacy on this street of women without shame. The sailor followed the girl over to the bed. She lay down, still in her open robe. Her legs were spread apart, her knees bent slightly.

The sailor knelt between her thighs. Elizabeth held her breath as the girl sat up and undid the rope belt around his waist. Then, with a hand at each side of his waistband, she pulled his trousers down around his thighs.

In silhouette, Elizabeth saw the sailor's penis rising, slowly and gracefully, like the staysail at the fore of a schooner being unfurled. It grew bigger and longer as it rose, and as it reached the apex of its arc, the prostitute caught it in both hands, and held it.

Her left hand cupped the shaft from underneath, its long, skinny fingers reaching forward to scratch gently along the underside of his scrotum. With her right hand, she pushed back the fold of skin that extended over the head of his penis. Then she put her fingers to her mouth, wet them, and rubbed the knobby head that had come forth like the tightly curled bud of a flower.

She looked up and said something to the sailor; Elizabeth could not tell what. The sailor nodded his head.

The blond prostitute placed her right palm flat against the sailor's pelvis, flush against the base of his penis. Then she leaned forward, and took the head of his penis in her mouth.

Elizabeth could not believe it. Her knees would hardly support her as she watched. She leaned up against a lamp post and gripped it tightly for support. All around her in the street, men were passing by, paying her little or no mind as they looked over the whores in the windows, giving no more than a passing glance to the incredible scene that Elizabeth watched, transfixed.

The blond prostitute's head moved backward and forward, as the sailor's penis went deep inside her mouth, deeper than Elizabeth could have believed possible, then out again so only the head was still hidden from Elizabeth's sight. The girl's cheeks were sucked in, and Elizabeth could not read the expression on her face. She did not notice the man's face. She wondered what it could possibly be like, to have a man's penis inside her mouth. Would it make her sick? She wanted to try it. She wished that she were the blond prostitute with the thin body and sad eyes. She wished that she were the prostitute with the massive breasts and thighs, and great black mound of pubic hair. She wished that she could turn and run, but she was rooted to the spot.

The girl lay on her back again. Her robe fell open, revealing her ripe breasts. The nipples were not erect. The sailor bent over her, and the prostitute took his penis in his in his right hand and guided it down into her vagina.

Elizabeth watched the expression on the girl's face, half sad smile and half grimace. She watched the girl's hand guiding the man's penis until their bodies were so close that she could not see any more, and there was no room for the girl's hand. It had been withdrawn now; it lay by her side, clenched into a fist.

The fist tightened into a hard knot, and the girl's shoulder twitched. Elizabeth knew that meant that the prositute's body had been entered by the sailor. She wrenched herself free from the lamppost, and ran all the way to the end of the block.

She caught the lamp post on the corner, to steady her nerves. She realized that there were tears in her eyes, and she fought to regain control. She breathed in and out, regularly, and the tears and near-hysteria receded.

She turned around to take one last look down the block full of women in the windows, of men who did not look at each other. Then she turned to continue on in the direction she had been running.

As she did, she was aware that she was in shadow: something was blocking out the light from the gas lamp. And as she turned, she ran smack into the barrel chest of a giant.

He stood at least six feet five inches, and every part of his body was huge, from fingers the size of her wrists to his tangled, bushy, salt-and-pepper beard and outsized, crooked teeth that protruded from a mouth that was curled open in a hard leer.

108

His sailor's pea coat hung loosely open over a stomach that was broad, but looked hard as a rock. His dungarees were baggy and looked slept in, but they could not disguise a bulge that looked huge, even in proportion to the rest of him. Elizabeth looked up at him, rooted in terror where she stood.

She tried to speak, and as she did, she amazed herself with the words that came out of her mouth, and with the other feeling that battled her terror.

"Hey, there, sailor," she said, in a tone of voice she had never used before in her life. "How about it? Want to have a little fun?"

"I might," came the answer. "How much?"

She did not know what he meant. She looked at him blankly, and he repeated the question: "How much d'yer charge?"

She still did not understand; and then she did. Her courage and her mania left her again, and she trembled in confusion and doubt. She did not know what to say.

" 'Smatter, cat gotcher tongue?" growled the giant. "Look, woman, ya gotta place to go?"

She shook her head.

"C'mon, then, we'll go down ta the barges." He grabbed her by the arm and pulled her along behind him.

Elizabeth followed him, half-dragged, half-running to keep up, down the dark, dirty, narrow streets of lower New York. Her wrist hurt from where he was squeezing it in his crushing, giant grip, and her fingers were beginning to feel numb. The streets were full of unconcerned people, engaged in or looking for violence and lust of their own; there was no one who would have responded if Elizabeth had screamed. And she was not going to scream, anyway: she had gotten herself into this on her own, and she would see it through.

As he strode ahead of her, Elizabeth could not see his face—only his shoulders, broad as a yardarm; his back, bulging with muscles; his rump, flat and square and hard; his powerful legs, moving like pistons.

They came to a low fence that marked the end of the last roadway and the beginning of the docks. There he jerked her forward and let go of her wrist, sending her crashing

109

and spinning into the fence. He motioned for her to climb it.

She flexed her hand, first, to make sure she could still use it, feeling the soreness of her wrist and the tingle as feeling began to creep back into her fingers. It was not unlike the tingle that she had felt between her legs earlier, but that had long since been surpassed by a knot of feeling that was of such intensity she could no longer tell whether it was pain or pleasure.

She gathered up her skirts, and determinedly swung over the fence at a single bound. She was not going to let this brute see her stumble. She waited on the other side until he stepped over.

"Over there," he said. He pointed into the darkness, then took her by the elbow this time, and marched her beside him until they came to the water's edge, and a barge tied with great thick ropes to a stanchion on the pier. He pushed her, and she half-fell, half-leaped down onto the straw that filled the barge.

The straw stank, and its saw-toothed edges cut her. She landed on her side, but rolled over onto her back to look up at him, her eyes smoldering with challenge. If she was afraid, she did not show it. Her fear had been overwhelmed by her excitement, and by the hard, unbending desire that she had not long ago been unaware of, but which now drove her beyond all passion or reason. He glared back at her.

"Let's see it," he said.

She knew what he meant. With a gesture that was angry defiance of all who had let her down as much as it was the lust of the moment, she drew up her skirts, laying bare her sex to the sailor's eyes.

The giant grunted his approval. Then he loosened his belt, and jumped down from the dock onto the barge.

He wasted no time in preliminaries. He entered her suddenly, deeply, and brutally. She felt as if she were being split in half; but her pelvis surged up to meet him, and her wail carried over the docks like the cry of some eerie, supernatural being from the primal depths of the sea.

* * *

It was over in an instant, and the giant was gone. The last view she had of him was, once again, of his massive back, disappearing into the waterfront alleyways.

She lay for some moments, unable to move. When she finally stirred, she found that he had left two dollars on her stomach.

Two dollars! She had earned it as only a woman could, and she was grimly proud. She stood up gingerly, and climbed off the barge with difficulty.

The two dollars was tucked into the waistband of her skirt. The saloons of Water Street were still as garish, as loud, as strong-smelling and unfamiliar as they had been before, but she had had her baptism now, and was not afraid to enter one. She chose the biggest, brightest, most raucous of them all, and walked into it. She had the feeling that all eyes must be on her, judging her, sizing her up, from the moment she walked into the place, but she made her way directly over to the bar and asked for a glass of rum.

The bartender served her.

A sailor at her side nodded to the bartender, who reached over to pick up a nickel from the sailor's pile of coins, but Elizabeth stopped him.

"No, I'm paying for myself," she said. "I've got money."

"Oh, hoity-toity," snarled the sailor. "Think yez're too good to drink with the likes o' me, is it?"

Elizabeth looked at him, not certain of what to reply. The sailor went on, "Yeah, you wit' them fancy clothes. Pretty fancy dame, eh? Think yez're better than the rest, is it now?"

Elizabeth looked at him, and then her eyes swept around the room. The men were sloppy and drunk, most of them. And the women looked tired, dirty, and ugly, either old or worn out before their time. Their clothing was lurid and sexually revealing compared to Elizabeth's, and many of their faces were painted, but they were not attractive, and they seemed to know it. They exposed too much of themselves. She saw naked breasts spilled out of dirty bodices, she saw women clinging desperately to the arms of men who would let them, but sho paid them no mind. *Yes*, she thought. *I* am *better than the rest.*

111

"Well, yez ain't in here, Miss Fancy," said the sailor. "One whore's like another in here, and that's a fact." A crowd of men had begun to gather around, drawn by the sailor's angry, belligerent tone. The sailor looked over his shoulder for reinforcement. "Am I right, lads?"

"Right!" growled a chorus of male voices.

Elizabeth shrank backward, but there was no place to go.

"Le's break her in," said one sailor. "Every new whore needs to be broke in, right?"

"Le's see what she looks like!" cackled another, and with bony fingers he reached forward and pulled at the front of Elizabeth's jacket. The threads that held the buttons strained and snapped, and the jacket fell open, exposing Elizabeth's full breasts to the howling delight of the drunken mob of both men and women.

"Plump, ain't they?" said a henna-haired, whiskey-breathed slut, stepping up and pinching Elizabeth's nipple cruelly and painfully.

Now there was nothing left to Elizabeth but her panic. She turned, and tried to run; but she was hemmed in on all sides. A man, two men, grabbed at her; another hit her hard with his open hand, and sent her careening toward the floor.

She landed on her head with a crash. She saw a burst of white light, and hoped that she would lose consciousness, but that was not to be. With her eyes screwed tight shut, she felt her skirt being pulled up to her waist, and a rough, callused hand on her thigh.

Then, as suddenly, she felt the hand pulled away from her thigh. She heard the noise of a brief struggle, and a voice barking out the command: *"All right, belay it, you fucking swabs!"*

She opened her eyes.

A tall man was standing next to her. She was aware, in the same instant, of the flashing anger in his blue eyes, the grim set to his jaw, and the pistol in his right hand, which was covering the mob that had now shrunk back several paces from where Elizabeth lay.

As he realized she was looking up at him, he cast a quick glance down at her on the floor. His attention did not waver from the grumbling sailors whom he still covered with his revolver, but Elizabeth could tell that he had taken her in completely with that glance. She felt suddenly modest, and covered her bosom with her arm."

"You don't belong here, do you?" he asked her.

"N-no," she said.

"Well, don't ever start thinking that you do," he said tersely. "Now we're leaving."

"B-but . . ." she gestured down at the torn jacket which she was now holding closed with her right hand. He nodded.

"We'll need a cloak." One was produced, instantly.

"And we'll need the lady's buttons back. You lubbers, down on your hands and knees and find them—all of them. *Now!*"

He made a short, sharp gesture with the gun. But it was more than the gun that sent a dozen strong men down on their knees, searching among the sawdust and spilled beer, spit and sweat and tobacco juice for the small mother-of-pearl buttons from the front of Elizabeth's jacket. It was the note of command in his voice, that brooked not even the possibility of disobedience.

The buttons were found, and given to the man with the gun. He put them in his pocket, then beckoned Elizabeth toward the door. Only after she had walked out, the commandeered cloak wrapped around her, did he follow. Once outside, he put the gun back in his waistband, but kept his coat loose so that he could reach it again, quickly, if need be.

"Let's go where we can get a carriage," he said.

They went to his lodgings, a clean furnished room on a street off lower Broadway. The landlady woke up when they came in, and started to say something to him, but he silenced her with a few whispered words, and sent her off to bed.

"What did you say to her?" asked Elizabeth.

"That you'd had an accident with a runaway carriage, and you needed a place to rest and see to your cuts and bruises before continuing your journey in the morning."

"You're very gallant." She was angry at him, but she did not know why. Now that the terror was wearing off, she supposed that she should be expressing her gratitude; but what she felt was anger, and she was finding it hard to hold back. She knew that she quite likely owed her life to him, and she knew, also, that it was somehow his fault that she felt these surges of anger at him.

He motioned her over to the chair in the corner of his sparsely furnished room, then took off his coat and hung it on the wooden coat tree in the corner. Elizabeth sat back in the chair, with the unfamiliar cloak still wrapped around her, and took a good look at him for the first time. He was not so much older than she—twenty-one, perhaps. His skin was cracked and crinkled around his eyes, but from weather, not from worry or age. His eyes were blue, a deep blue against a weather-tanned face and black hair. He was over six feet tall, and his shirt-sleeved upper body was slender but powerful, with arms like whipcords. On his chin was what must have been a first growth of beard, full enough and neatly shaped, but soft and downy. It invited stroking, like a kitten, though the rest of his features were craggy and toughened. It was cut in the sailor's fashion, just beard and no mustache.

He was an odd, irritating combination of toughness and softness. He had seemed so stern, so commanding, so able to take charge in the saloon—it was that force of his presence that had saved her. Yet looking at him now, Elizabeth knew that there coexisted with that hardness a gentleness, a vulnerability that both warmed her and irritated her. She could not help thinking, *I could get the better of him.*

"What are you going to do with me?" she asked, steeling herself to be prepared for anything.

"Give you this, for a start." He dug into his sea chest, and came out with a sewing kit. He handed it to Elizabeth, along with her buttons from his pocket.

"Thank you," she said, and took them. "I'd better . . ." her voice trailed off, and she turned her upper body around so that she pointed her shoulders and the back of her head toward him, while she shucked off her coat under the cloak. Then she bowed her head, sat primly on the edge of the chair, and set to work on the first button.

"Where do you come from?" he asked her.

"Stonington."

"Then we'll see about getting you back there in the morning. Finish that up now, and get some sleep." He

114

pulled off his boots, and lay down on the bed, fully clothed, with his face to the wall. Elizabeth felt abandoned.

"Wait a minute!" she said. "What about me?"

"You have to sew your buttons back on, and then get some sleep. You've had a long night of it."

"And just where do you think I'm supposed to sleep? Just because I wandered into that awful place by accident, you don't think I'm . . ."

He sighed. "If there is one thing you can count on, miss, it's that I'll be sound asleep long before you're finished with your handiwork. So if I did have any designs on you, which I think it should be apparent by now that I haven't, I'd hardly be in a position to act on them anyway. I don't think we need to stand on ceremony, for this evening anyway, but I do think we both need to get some rest and forget about what's happened, as best we can. All right?"

She did not answer him. Instead, she continued to stare at him accusingly, her jaw set and her expression obdurate. The sailor sighed again.

"Doesn't matter to me. I can sleep anywhere." He took a blanket, spread it on the floor in a corner, and settled himself again. It was not long before she heard the regular breathing that told her he was asleep.

She went on sewing. Only her hands protruded from under the itchy cloak, and her breasts rubbing against her forearms made her feel clumsy, not sensual. She hated to sew buttons, and though she knew how much she owed the stranger, she resented his sleeping while she worked. She was very tired and very sore, and her emotions were so jumbled she felt like crying.

It was only a few hours before dawn, that time of night when even safe at home, in one's own bed, things can seem unreal. Here in this stranger's furnished room, nothing seemed real to Elizabeth, least of all her feelings.

She was sore, scared, and lonely. She missed the company of the stranger who had gone to sleep and left her alone, the man who had saved her life and whose personality she found so appealing and yet so grating. She was cold, through to her bones, and she wished she had not banished him to the floor, so that she might burrow in next to him for warmth. And yet, seeing him down there where she had banished him, she felt a hot, mean sense of triumph, and a kind of contempt for him, for letting himself be ordered about like that.

She arrived home the next day. She took a carriage from the railway depot to Aunt Eleanor's house, and, sobbing, told the story of the runaway carriage that the sailor had invented for his landlady, with her own embellishments: the accident, barely escaping death, losing consciousness, the kindly old woman who had taken her in and tended her until she could travel again. Aunt Eleanor questioned her: what was the kindly old woman's name, so they could write and thank her? But Elizabeth hid behind her hysteria. She had been much too upset to remember. She did not want to talk about it. She had to go to her room.

And in the end, it was easier, as always, for Aunt Eleanor to accept the story than to go through the disturbing process of trying to imagine what really happened. Elizabeth's mother and father were notified that their daughter was safe and sound.

Elizabeth was sure of one thing: it could never be allowed to happen again. She would reform completely. She was at an age when she could easily be turned out of the house if Aunt Eleanor's suspicions were given any more fuel. And she was afraid. Afraid of herself, afraid of what might happen to her.

She kept the memory of the terror she had felt that night in the saloon, and she kept the memory of how those women had looked. Those would have been enough to scare her into a chaste life, but there was another memory that frightened her even more: the memory of a lightning bolt filling and splitting her body, of a moment when she was not herself and nothing else mattered in the universe but this total possession by an overpowering force, by an unknown and faceless man. She knew that she could never, ever, allow herself an opportunity to repeat that moment, because she knew she would sacrifice everything else in life for that moment.

She kept to herself almost all the time. She did not want to go to social events, she did not want to meet young men. She did not want to go for walks anymore, to the cemetery or anywhere else. She had decided on what she would do

116

for the rest of her life. She would go up to Washington, Connecticut, as soon as her parents sent for her, and she would become a schoolteacher. She would live with her parents, but she would never bother them. She would be a shadow. They would hardly know that she was there. She began to concentrate on forgetting everything that had ever happened to her, including the young man who had saved her and then slept on the floor. She had never even known his name.

✂Chapter Twelve

FALL TURNED INTO WINTER, AND WORK ON THE
new Creighton house in Washington was stopped with the
first snowfall. Elizabeth stayed on in Stonington, and continued living her secluded life. Aunt Eleanor consoled her,
and told her not to worry, that the house would be finished
in the spring, and that meanwhile she was as welcome as
she always had been. But secretly, the older woman cursed
her brother-in-law for the delay. She had been happy at
first that her niece had become subdued. She did not miss
the rebelliousness, or the worry about what Elizabeth was
up to.

But she knew something had upset the girl badly, and
she felt sorry for her. Perhaps an argument with her parents when she had visited them in New York. Maybe she
no longer wanted to live with her parents, although whenever the subject was raised, Elizabeth would dutifully express her enthusiasm.

Aunt Eleanor knew, of course, how much the sea figured
in Elizabeth's daydreams, and she wondered if it was the
prospect of moving inland that troubled the girl so.

But most of all, Aunt Eleanor began to be concerned by
the thought that, somehow, Elizabeth would never leave.
She knew that the plans had all been made, but until the
house was finished and Elizabeth packed and gone,

Eleanor was hard put to count on it. She could not shake the vision of Elizabeth remaining indefinitely, a morose figure haunting the parlor and the upstairs bedroom, a solitary spinster becoming a permanent fixture in their household. For all the trouble she had been, Aunt Eleanor was still fond of Elizabeth; but that prospect was simply too much.

Where she had previously stressed the merits of young merchants, curates, and members of the professions to Elizabeth, Aunt Eleanor now tried to invite young ship's officers to meet her niece, hoping to strike some spark of interest. But Elizabeth was interested in nothing, and nobody. Aunt Eleanor's apprehension mounted.

Elizabeth's parents came down for Thanksgiving, without effecting any change in her mood. They were due again for Christmas.

Elizabeth was not looking forward to seeing them. Her father looked older to her, since he had retired. Even though it had only been a few months, she saw the signs. He looked weaker, less alert, less commanding. She had made up her mind to go up to Washington and spend the rest of her life in safety and quiet, teaching schoolboys, but she did not have to like it. And she was beginning to feel more restless than she suspected, or cared to admit.

Aunt Eleanor had run out of optimism, but she felt a surge of hope when she answered the young man's knock at the door. And Elizabeth had not deviated from her pessimism, but she could not deny a spark of interest when Aunt Eleanor knocked at her door, and said: "There's a gentleman here to call on you, dear."

"Oh, Aunt, I can't see anyone today," said Elizabeth. "Tell him I'm ill, please. Who is it?"

"It's a Mr. Wales Rogers. He says he's an acquaintance of your father's and he met you in New York at a social gathering."

"What? I didn't meet any—" She stopped short. "What does he look like?"

"Tall, dark, bearded, handsome-looking if you care for the type," said Aunt Eleanor. "Which is, I should say, a nautical type, if you know what I mean."

"I . . . I'll come down," Elizabeth said, suddenly flustered.

She did not know why she should be so disconcerted. It could not possibly be him. And if it were, why should she be excited, anyway? Besides, if there were any chance that it was him, she would not see him anyway. But since it couldn't be . . .

She took her time in preparing to come down. She changed into her best Sunday dress, and made her toilette with painstaking care, so that when she finally descended the staircase, she was as proper as a minister's daughter and as immaculate as a banker's daughter.

She felt confident that she could handle herself with poise, whoever this Mr. Wales Rogers turned out to be.

A moment later, she was standing in the entranceway to the parlor, and realizing how completely unprepared she was. And yet, she understood in the same instant, she had known all along that it could be no one else but him. The blue eyes that looked straight at her were the same ones she had avoided when he had put her on the train for Stonington five months ago, said an awkward good-bye, and strode off down the platform. They were the eyes that had flashed a challenge the very first time she saw them, the night before, as he stood over her with a revolver in his hand, protecting her from her attackers.

She had never expected to look into them again. And certainly not here, in her aunt's living room.

She could not suppress a gasp, as his eyes caught hers and held them with his particular intensity. For a moment, she could not remember his name.

"Mr. . . . Rogers, what a pleasant surprise? What brings you to Stonington?"

"A few errands," he said. "Not the least of which was the prospect of making your acquaintance again."

She almost giggled at the contrast of his formality with the situation of their last meeting, but she controlled herself and was as formally polite in return.

"How fortunate for me. You've met my aunt, of course. Mr. Rogers . . . Mrs. Creighton."

"Of course . . . when Mr. Rogers arrived. But I've work to do. You'll have to entertain the young gentleman, Elizabeth. You'll stay to dinner, Mr. Rogers?"

121

"I think not, Mrs. Creighton. Another time."

Aunt Eleanor left the parlor. Elizabeth faced Wales Rogers. She was still uncertain, but some of her confidence was returning. She had detected, behind the politeness, the faintest edge of nervousness in his voice, and it made her feel more assured. She remembered the flash of insight that had come to her when they had first met: *I could get the better of him.*

"What are you doing here?" she asked him. "How did you find me? How did you find out who I was? And why?"

"Get your wrap and come for a ride with me," he said. "I've got a horse and sleigh outside, and we can talk more freely."

"I'm not sure I want to talk more freely with you." But she was going. She realized with a trace of annoyance that every time she was sure she had him under control, it turned out that she did not, not quite. And the prospect of finding out what he was all about intrigued her too much.

As they moved beyond the village and into the farmland, the snow was hard-packed on the ground and the sleigh moved along swiftly, past trees hung with icicles and drifts piled up against snow fences. Large clouds of steam came from the horse's nostrils with each breath, and smaller ones from the two riders in the sleigh. Elizabeth felt the cold through her coat, bonnet, scarf, and muff, but she kept her distance from Wales Rogers on the seat of the sleigh anyway.

"Now, how did you find me out?"

"Well, there's no point in saying it was an accident. I looked for you. You weren't hard to track down—and don't worry, I didn't ask anything that might end up by casting suspicion on your reputation."

"Most gentlemanly of you," Elizabeth said coldly. "And did it take you all this time?"

He chuckled. "No, the search was a matter of days. The time was in deciding to do it. But what about you? Are you all right?"

"What do you mean?" Elizabeth snapped. "Have I learned my lesson? Have I realized the error of my ways?"

"Not that," he said. "I was wondering how you felt now,

122

and if you'd found whatever it is that you were looking for."

"What makes you think I was looking for anything?"

"Perhaps you weren't," he said mildly.

He gave his attention to the road, and they drove in silence for a while. He had a steady hand on the rein, and kept the horse moving at a swift but not overtaxing clip. Elizabeth expected him to change the subject, now that she had closed him off, and make small talk. But he did not, and he did not seem uncomfortable about the silence, either. She tried to come up with a subject for small talk, but she could not, for the life of her, think of a thing.

"What do you think I was looking for?"

"I didn't think about it. I wouldn't presume to guess. I'm content to concern myself with what I'm looking for."

"Oh? And what is that?"

"I'll let you know when I'm sure I've found it."

She barely had time to reflect on the implications of that last remark, when he abruptly changed the subject. "I haven't actually met your father, of course. That was just a story for your aunt. But I've admired him tremendously. I've read about his San Francisco run in the *Spirit of the Waves*, when he fell just short of breaking the *Flying Cloud*'s record."

"I was on that voyage!" said Elizabeth excitedly, turning toward him and placing her fingertips on his sleeve for just a moment. He turned to look at her, with matching enthusiasm.

"No! Really!"

"Yes. I grew up on shipboard, actually. That voyage on the *Spirit of the Waves* was my last before they sent me ashore to make a lady out of me."

She smiled impishly, and drew an appreciative chuckle from him. "Well, they certainly didn't succeed in taking all the spirit out of you. And a good thing, too."

"But you haven't told me anything about yourself!" Suddenly the mood had lightened, and they were like any other young couple getting to know each other. "What is your ship? And what do you do on it."

"I'm first officer on the clipper *Wild Wave*, out of New York," he said.

123

"First officer! That's wonderful. And you're so young, too."

"I'm twenty-two," he said. "There's men my age who are captains on the clipper ships, and I mean to be, too, within the next two years. It's a young man's vessel, built for speed and daring."

Elizabeth thought of her father. "I know," she said.

That night, Elizabeth's thoughts were not so different from what her mother's had been, nineteen years before. Wales Rogers had gone back to New York. She did not know when she would see him again, or what it would be like when she did.

But her depression left her, and was replaced by a period of bewildering mood shifts. She would be cheerful and co-operative as Aunt Eleanor had never seen her before, then angry and rebellious, or suddenly plunged into self-doubt. She would burst into tears or song for no reason at all.

There was no one whom she could talk to about her feelings. She had never been close enough to Aunt Eleanor to use her as a confidante, and perhaps that was just as well. Because what could she have said, but: "I can't stand this waiting for something to happen! Why can't my life be my own?" And what would her aunt have replied, but: "It's a woman's lot in life, my dear."

But if she thought about taking her destiny into her own hands, she had to think about that night in New York, and then she was left afraid, and wondering if perhaps it *was* something a woman could not do. And she was plunged back into her maelstrom of emotions.

And then she had to think about Wales Rogers again, and the way she had met him. What did he think of her? And why had he come to see her? Could he possibly be considering courting her, after that?

And, inevitably, when she thought about that night, she could never feel as single-mindedly contrite as she thought she ought to. Because a part of her could not help but wonder if she would ever experience anything so exciting again.

All of this confusion and indecision lasted for no more than a week. Because at the end of that week, Wales reappeared in her aunt's parlor.

"I sail in two weeks, so I won't beat about the bush," he said. "I want you to marry me."

And she was taken completely by surprise. And she was unstrung—so much so that she forgot to be subtle or tactful, but said the first thing that came into her mind.

"Even after seeing me that night on the waterfront? What did you . . . what could you think of me after that?"

"All I could think then was that you were like no one I'd ever met," he said seriously. "And that stayed with me, until I finally had to come up here and see if my first impression was right. And it was."

"You could tell so quickly?"

"Yes."

"I don't . . . know if I can."

"Then think about it," he said. "I'll take a room in town and stay the night. We'll talk about it tomorrow."

"Are you sure? I mean . . . are you sure that's what you want? And you'll come back tomorrow?"

He smiled at her, and shrugged. "Have a pleasant evening." He said his good-byes to Aunt Eleanor, apologized again for not staying to dinner, and left. Then Aunt Eleanor came out into the parlor, where Elizabeth still stood, staring at the wall in front of her.

"My goodness! What did the young man say to you?" she asked.

"What? Oh, nothing," said Elizabeth. "I think I'll lie down, if you don't mind, Aunt. I have a terrible headache."

"Yes, I imagine you do," said her aunt. "Well, see that you don't decide anything that makes it worse." And she, too, was out of the room in an instant, leaving Elizabeth feeling that everyone in the world knew more about what was going on than she did.

Elizabeth was left to think it through. He wanted her . . . she guessed that meant he loved her. And she . . . how did she feel about Wales Rogers? Every time she had seen him, every time she thought about him, she was maddened by not knowing the answer to that question. He was not like anyone she had ever met. He intrigued her—but she was not sure that he excited her. If he was so bent on

125

marrying her, then why hadn't he just insisted on it, instead of leaving it up to her like this? At least, he could have given her an ultimatum—decide by tomorrow, or goodbye. Elizabeth hated being told what to do my anyone, but she found that she was even less satisfied with being given so many options.

But she certainly could not dismiss him from her mind. And he would be a captain soon, master of a clipper ship. And she would be going back to sea with him.

∾Chapter Thirteen

ELIZABETH'S SEXUAL ADVENTURES HAD LEFT her no more prepared for marriage than if she had been a sheltered, virgin bride. And when her aunt took her aside to explain to her about a woman's duties in marriage, what was described to her was so different from anything she had experienced on her own, that she felt like a virgin.

Aunt Eleanor told her that it was her duty to love her husband, and therefore, it was her duty to submit to his demands—the demands of the flesh that all men felt.

Did she love her husband-to-be? She had decided in her mind that she did, when she decided that she would marry him; but she only felt it for the first time a few evenings later, when she broached to him a subject that was very private and close to her heart. She was uncharacteristically shy and hesitant. She had never voiced these dreams to a living soul since Aunt Eleanor had so angrily rejected them. Elizabeth did not know what she would do if Wales became angry at her, or worse, laughed at her. She felt as if she were putting her soul in his hands.

"I've been . . . studying for a long time to be a captain's wife, Wales."

"What do you mean?"

"I mean real studying. In books. I've read about trigonometry, and astronomy, and geography. I could be a real help on board ship."

"Why, that's capital!" She could feel Wales's enthusiasm leap out to meet hers, and she was buoyed up by it, as excited as if they had embraced physically.

"Have you read Selden's *Popular Astronomy*?" he asked her.

"Oh, yes! And Mr. W. Lansing Brown's astronomy texts, and Commander Maury's *Sailing Directions* and *Wind and Current Charts*."

"Oh, but this is marvelous. You must keep on reading while I keep on sailing, and when I . . . when *we* get a ship of our own, what a team we'll make!"

"Then you must tell me what to read."

She had never had anyone to guide her studies before. Wales gave her a list: hydrography, marine hydrostatics, navigation and geography and marine biology, shipbuilding and naval architecture. She got a pen and paper and wrote it all down.

Wales never talked to her about the night they had met, on the waterfront, and he seemed painfully, unnaturally shy about any sort of intimacy with her. It was as if, in his mind, she had become the most sacrosanct of virgins. Even clasping her hand between his had become an exercise in boldness that was almost more than he could manage.

Elizabeth could always tell when he started to think of touching her. He would be sitting on the sofa next to her, talking about how to use a sextant, and his body would pivot a few degrees in her direction. His glance would dart down to measure the distance to her hand, or over to calculate the angle of her shoulders, and—and she could feel the pressure rising inside him as he tried to keep up a conversation while waiting for what he considered the right moment to touch her.

She would do nothing to help him. Something made her hold back, though she grew fonder of him every day and she knew that she could perfectly well put an end to all this nonsense by just taking the initiative herself, leaning over and kissing him. But she would not.

And it was nonsense, for certain. She had already agreed to marry him, after all. How could he think that she would not let him touch her?

But between Wales's putting her on a pedestal and her aunt's cautionary advice, she was coming to think of herself more and more as pure, somewhat fragile, a creature to be handled delicately, and protected from defilement. Her two wild adventures began to seem more and more like fantasies, or dreams, or stories about events that had happened to someone else.

Captain and Mrs. Creighton were to arrive in Stonington on December 17, three days before the wedding. Elizabeth, by December 17, had given herself a horrible case of nerves. The weather had been bad for two days, and Aunt Eleanor had told her not to count too much on her parents' arriving just on time. When night fell, and another day and evening passed, Elizabeth grew more and more restive, until finally she leaped up from her chair in front of the parlor fire, ran upstairs to her cold bedroom, and threw herself down on top of the quilt, sobbing uncontrollably.

Aunt Eleanor followed her, and tried to console her, but she wanted only to be left alone and would not be consoled.

How could she have been? No one knew the reason why she was crying, and there was no one to whom she could have said it out loud: she did not want her parents to come to the wedding. She never wanted to see them again. She did not need them anymore; and for all of her, they could stay up in Washington, Connecticut, for the rest of their lives and never bother her again.

∾Chapter Fourteen

ELIZABETH WOULD NOT EVEN COME DOWN-
stairs to see Wales off in the morning when he left for
New York, and his new ship. She pleaded the sickness she
had been having, but they both knew that was not the real
reason. True, she had thrown up again that morning, but
she was not too sick to come down and wish Wales good-
bye and a safe voyage, is she had wanted to. She was not
too sick to tell him how proud of him she was, now that he
was finally about to embark on his first command, if she
had wanted to.

But she did not want to. She was sick and angry and
heavy with spite. She had waited three years for this day.
She had gone on living with Aunt Eleanor and Uncle
James, in the expectation that it would be just a little
longer. Just a little longer until they built a home of their
own. Just a little longer, especially, until he got his captain's papers, and a ship of his own. But it had stretched
out for three years, three years of Wales going off to sea as
first officer, three years of Elizabeth staying home with
Aunt Eleanor, reading and mending and doing housework.
And now that the day was finally here, she could not share
it with him in the way she had planned to, and she would
not share it with him any other way.

Elizabeth Rogers was pregnant.

* * *

Wales put his sea chest in the back of the buggy that was to take him to the railroad station, and came around to climb up next to the driver. He paused for a moment, and looked back up at Elizabeth's window.

Elizabeth was sitting on her bed, far enough back from the window so that Wales could not see her, although she was able to see out to where he stood. She felt a hot stab of triumph when she saw him turn around and look, but she would have wished, to make her triumph complete, that his glance could have been furtive, over one shoulder. Instead, he turned completely around, with one foot propped up on the runner of the buggy and his arm draped over its side. Unashamed, he gazed up at her empty window for several minutes.

She could not make out his expression from her position on the bed, and she did not dare get up and move closer to the window, for fear of being seen. Still he stood there, and finally her curiosity got the better of her. She slipped down from the bed and began to tiptoe, in a wide arc, toward the corner of the window. She peered around the sash, but at the same moment Wales wheeled and swung up into the buggy. The driver clucked at the horse, and Wales rode off without looking back again.

She did not come downstairs for some time after he left. She was supposed to be sick, after all, and she did not want to destroy the illusion. Besides, that would have meant facing Aunt Eleanor, and she did not want to do that right away. Aunt Eleanor did not much approve of the way she was acting these days, any more than she had approved of the way she had behaved as a single girl. Elizabeth did not care a great deal about Aunt Eleanor's views on the way wives should behave toward their husbands, any more than she had cared about her views on the comportment of young ladies. And in the heat of an argument, she was not at all shy about letting Aunt Eleanor know how little she cared. But she did not feel up to it this morning. She was too miserable.

Wales had shipped out on the *Richard M. Himsvark* right after their wedding, and been gone for ten months. He had been home for two months after that, then it was

132

off to sea for another ten months, as first mate once again. After that voyage, there was talk by the owners of the *Richard M. Himsvark* of giving him a command, but before the talk had proceeded very far, they went bankrupt. It was a bad time for the sailing ship trade. Steam was becoming more and more popular. The transcontinental railroad had been completed in 1869, the year before Elizabeth and Wales's wedding, and no new ships were being outfitted. The *Glory of the Seas*, built by Donald McKay in 1869, had been the last clipper ship to be constructed. McKay had gone bankrupt on the ship, and it was not likely that a clipper would ever be built again. Wales might get his master's papers, but there were more captains these days than there were ships. Elizabeth had begun to resign herself to the possibility that the man she had married might never have command of a vessel of his own.

Then, when she had almost given up hope, it happened. The captain of the *Western Wind*, owned by Sears and Nickerson of New York, was retiring, and he recommended Wales to Mr. J. Henry Sears. Wales went to New York to talk to Sears and wrote back the good news—which Elizabeth received just as she was becoming sure that her unvoiced suspicions were correct, and that she was, in fact, pregnant.

Pregnant.

Well, she was a woman, and it was what she had been born for, or so she had always been told, so she supposed that she wanted it. But not now. Not when what she wanted more than anything else in the world was finally within her grasp, and would be hers right now, if she had not become pregnant.

Aunt Eleanor, in telling her about the responsibilities of a woman to submit to her husband in marriage, had used, among other vague phrases to describe sex, that it was the part of the marriage that was "for the man." It was the part that young girls were ordered sharply away from watching when dogs or goats or horses did it—although girls were allowed to be present and watch—even help—for the other half of the process, the birth of the puppies, or the kid, or the colt. That was the part of marriage that was for the woman.

There was something in the whole idea that Elizabeth

could not understand, just as she could not understand why, when a couple was courting, it was such a munificent favor when a girl let a young man squeeze her hand, or put his arm around her waist, or kiss her, but after they were married, he had a right to her body anytime he wanted. And, even more confusing, those little pecks and hugs, if the girl decided to allow it, were supposed to be thrilling and pleasurable for her; but afterward, sex was supposed to be a pleasure only for him, and a duty for her.

Elizabeth knew that she liked many things that only men were supposed to like, like trigonometry and celestial navigation and a life at sea. And she knew, also, how she had responded to the touch of a man, to the searing thrust of a man inside her—but she knew that that was different from the act of marriage.

It must be different. Because the act of marriage seemed to be what everyone said it was—a duty, not a pleasure. It was not the most exciting part of her marriage to Wales.

Maybe the man's part was better. But unlike her studies, this was an area in which there was no way in the world that she could do the man's part. And there was nothing for her to do—nothing that was proper, anyway—while he was doing it.

Worse than that, she could not even talk to him about it. Wales was the most understanding man alive—sometimes too understanding for his own good—but there was no way she could even begin to talk to him about her sexual dissatisfactions in marriage, and expect him to understand.

It seemed so unfair to Elizabeth. Marriage was supposed to bring two people closer, and yet the greatest symbol of it, the marriage bed, only made them more separate.

She loved Wales, she was sure enough of that—she had decided on it. What was wrong with her, then, that it was so hard for her to lie back and accept his taking pleasure? Millions of other women had done it before her. Could it be that she did not love him enough?

Well, if not, it was probably his fault, for not being a captain, so that he left her at home when he went off to his adventures. Sometimes at night, when he was home, and he took his pleasure with her, Elizabeth's mind would wander back to when she was a little girl, running around the poop deck of her father's ship. She had been everybody's favorite, then—everybody thought that she was such a special little thing. Now she was just another young married woman, living with her family while her husband went off to sea. Now she would never be special to anyone, except Wales.

And sometimes she wondered if she had *ever* been special to anyone. She thought of how she had lost the run of her father's ship, and finally been sent ashore. Could any woman ever be special in a man's world, or did her role have to be defined, inevitably, by what they could do to her?

The best part of being a married woman, when Wales was away, was not having to listen to her Aunt Eleanor's notions of how a young lady should spend her time improving herself with the social graces. She could throw herself, instead, into the passionate study of her books. When she had finished with all the ones that her father had left, she borrowed more from Mr. MacNab and other Stonington shipowners.

She was amazed at how much there was to know. Even her father had never done this much reading. He had not had too, of course; he had learned his seamanship by experience, which was by far the best way, but this was the closest substitute she could get.

At first she thought of her studies that way—as a substitute for the real thing, as a way to mark time until she could actually go to sea. But gradually, she came to love studying. The books became her passion. Her excitement was in understanding their concepts, remembering facts and tables, putting different elements together, comparing one author's theory with another. She spent every free minute in reading.

She came to be regarded as a little strange around Stonington. Old Mr. MacNab, with his Scots tolerance of eccentricity, smiled and bantered with her every time she came to borrow another book. He was the friendliest—but even he offered no more than good-natured teasing about her enthusiasm. He never talked to her about what she was reading.

Her studies cut her off from most regular social life, because there was simply no one to talk to about what she was most interested in. The women did not know anything about it, and the men who did, like Mr. MacNab, were not to be bothered discussing such subjects with a woman—especially a woman who was likely to know more than they did.

Wales was the only person she could talk to about it all. When he was home, they would sit and talk for hours, and he would supplement her new-found knowledge with his experience, or with his own reading; he would suggest new lines of study to her. When they talked like that, she felt a closeness to Wales that she treasured. It was the best part of being married.

The worst part of being married, now, was being pregnant. And the worst part of being pregnant was that she did not have to be. If she had known, for sure, that Wales was going to get his command, she could have hardened herself and put him off the whole time that he was at home.

That was another thing she had learned—duty or no, the reality of married life with Wales was that she did not have to let him make love to her. He would be hurt—sometimes she could tell that he was terribly hurt—but he would not force her. He would not assert his right to her.

She felt guilty about knowing. She felt it was a secret that she was not supposed to have found out, and that it was wrong. But when he looked hurt, it made something wicked happen inside her, so that she felt driven to go on hurting him.

She did not really want to hurt him. But all too often, when it came to a choice between hurting and just lying back and doing nothing, she would hurt him.

The *Western Wind* sailed for South America with a cargo of manufactured goods, then on to the Orient to load up with tea, and then back home again. Wales would be gone for over a year. That meant that the baby would be at least eight months old when his father saw him for the first time—and, more important to Elizabeth's reckoning, he would be old enough to take on board for the next voyage.

She tried to tell herself that one more voyage was not so long to wait. But it seemed an eternity. As she grew larger

136

and larger with child, she found herself less and less able to concentrate on her reading, until finally she gave it up altogether.

Aunt Eleanor thought that this was entirely proper. In her eyes, making baby clothes was a considerable sight more important for Elizabeth at this stage than reading books on subjects she already knew far more about than she would ever need. But it was mixed satisfaction for the older woman, because the same impulses that turned Elizabeth away from her books also made her increasingly cranky and irritable, until by the end of the seventh month she was virtually impossible to live with.

"Why didn't you just go ahead and have the baby at sea, if nothing else will satisfy you?" Aunt Eleanor snapped at her one morning, after a particularly grating series of complaints by her niece. "Other women have, you know. Your second cousin James Gillingham was born at sea. So was Mr. MacNab's son."

"Wales would never have allowed it," replied Elizabeth in a surly monotone.

"So, now, all of a sudden, when it suits her, she thinks of what Wales would or would not have allowed! Go along with you. How would you know—you never even asked him."

"What makes you think I didn't?" asked Elizabeth, but Aunt Eleanor only sniffed, with the superior air of an older woman who of course knows everything.

"Those were women who were got with child on shipboard, not women who were four months along when the ship left port," Elizabeth said.

"Go along with you!" Aunt Eleanor said again. "You were afraid, that's all."

"Well, it's easy for you to talk!" Elizabeth blazed. "You're not the one who's carrying the child. There's much that can happen in giving birth, and I see nothing wrong with wanting safe surroundings, and a midwife, and if needs be a doctor who's had some experience with a woman's condition. Yes, and what if the baby's stillborn, as your two were?"

Aunt Eleanor gasped, but Elizabeth overrode her. "It can happen, the Lord forbid. Wouldn't you want to make sure it had a decent shore burial?"

Suddenly Elizabeth was crying, and in her aunt's arms. Eleanor held her tightly, and felt a rush of compassion for the young mother-to-be who had grown up under her roof.

"There, dear, you're safe here," she said, as Elizabeth burrowed close into her shoulder and gave herself over to unrestrained sobbing. "There've been times between us, sure enough, in all these years, but I couldn't love you more if you were my own daughter. You know that, don't you? Of course you do. I know how you feel. Your old aunt'll see that no harm comes to you or your baby. It's all right now. You go ahead and cry if you want to."

Elizabeth did not reply, but she clung to her aunt and cried until she had cried herself out.

∾Chapter Fifteen

MRS. BEST, THE MIDWIFE, CAME TO STAY IN THE house a week before the baby was due. Elizabeth liked her. She was a tall woman in her forties, with thinning red hair, powerful forearms, and a decisive, no-nonsense manner. She had shepherded countless babies into the world, and she knew what she was about. Elizabeth felt helpless and lost in the grip of an experience about which she knew nothing, and she was glad to let Mrs. Best take over.

Elizabeth spent that week in bed. They put an extra heating stove into her room to make it warm enough, and brought her light meals to her on a tray. She was not feeling well. She had pains, and cramps. Mrs. Best did not seem alarmed, but she had Elizabeth describe the pain in detail. She felt Elizabeth's stomach through her nightdress, and even raised it to press directly on Elizabeth's distended skin, right over the live, palpable, moving form of the baby, and at the source of Elizabeth's pain. Her hands were warm, broad, dry, and strong. Her touch was reassuring, but Elizabeth was still frightened.

"Do you think you should call the doctor?" she asked.

"Let's not worry until we have to. The doctor will be here if he's needed. Just tell me where it hurts."

* * *

But the pain did not go away. It got worse, and Elizabeth became feverish.

"It's not just labor pains, is it?" she asked Mrs. Best.

"No, dear," said Mrs. Best. "I'm afraid you're having some problems."

"Am I going to lose my baby?"

"Not necessarily. I don't think so. We'll just take one step at a time," Mrs. Best said.

"Am I . . . am I going to be all right?"

"I'm sure you will. We're doing everything we can. I've sent for the doctor. Now don't talk. Just try to relax as much as you can."

The pain just went on. A couple of times Elizabeth passed out from its intensity, but Mrs. Best gently brought her to consciousness, patting her hand and bathing her face with cold water. Once she used just the faintest whiff of smelling salts. Elizabeth had to be awake for the delivery, if the time ever came. Aunt Eleanor stood by the door, ready to get anything Mrs. Best asked for, ready to go down and let the doctor in as soon as he arrived, ready to do whatever Elizabeth needed.

Elizabeth was in labor now. She was feeling the contractions, the rhythmic pain that was coming about every twelve minutes, as Mrs. Best timed it. Those pains were not the same as the pain, the pain which never left her and only got worse. She struggled to stay awake, as Mrs. Best told her to, but she could not quite remember why. As the torment grew worse, she could not even quite remember who Mrs. Best was.

Elizabeth heard the sound of a buggy pulling up outside, and the rap of the brass door knocker, as if it were from another world. Mrs. Best drifted away, fading into that other world as well. Then she was back, wavering on the edge of Elizabeth's consciousness, and Aunt Eleanor was besdie her.

"That'll be the doctor," Aunt Elanor said. "I'll go down and let him in." She faded away again.

"I'll have to talk to him, too," Mrs. Best said.

"No . . . please don't leave me," whimpered Elizabeth.

"I'll be right back," said Mrs. Best.

Elizabeth had no idea how long Mrs. Best was gone. The

only time that she had any awareness of was *now*, not a few seconds ago or a few seconds to come. And the only faces she could even remember were faces she could actually see looking down at her. By the time Mrs. Best said *I'll be right back* and left, she had already forgotten her aunt. And after Mrs. Best, too, went out of focus in the hazy distance of the other side of the room and then disappeared altogether behind the closed door, all that existed in her world was the aloneness, the pain, the discolorations on the ceiling, and the enlarged pores on her cold, pale hands and wrists that lay above the patchwork comforter.

But she forgot that, too. When she was alone, it seemed as if she had always been alone, and would be alone forever; but when the door opened and Mrs. Best's rangy form swam back into her field of vision, that seemed perfectly natural, too.

"I've brought the doctor," Mrs. Best said. "And someone else."

There were two blurry forms behind the midwife, or perhaps two blurry halves of the same form; but then one half detached itself and floated out of the haze toward Elizabeth's bedside.

It was Wales.

Wales . . . of course. She never questioned for an instant what he was doing there, when he was supposed to be halfway around the world. It just seemed the most natural thing that he should be with her now, when she needed him so much. She reached out and took his hand, and clung to it with both of hers.

"Wales . . ." she said in a small voice.

"There, it's all right, dearest," he said. "You're going to come through this. I'll be right here with you . . . don't worry."

His voice was so steady and gentle that it was hard to be exactly sure when he had finished talking. His reassuring words seemed to roll on through her consciousness. Steady and dependable . . . just like Wales himself. He sat by the head of her bed all night, holding her hand. At one point the doctor told him grumpily that since he was here, there were things he could be doing to make himself useful.

"I believe that I'm the most use I can be, staying right

here where I am," he replied firmly, and would not leave her side.

He was right; Elizabeth would not let him swim off out of her pain-racked consciousness, now that he was here. And she clung to him harder, with a surge of gratitude that he had known what she needed most, even without being told.

The labor pains were coming closer together now.

"It's not going to come out right," the doctor told her. "It's not placed right. We'll do the best we can." She would have asked him for more of an explanation, or for some reassurance, but she could not find the words or her voice, and he had already turned away from her to talk to the midwife.

He did not speak to her again. He talked to Wales. He told Wales that he could wait in the next room, but she would not let go of Wales's hand, and he said no, he would stay. Finally, the doctor disengaged her fingers from Wales's, he spoke to Wales sharply but inaudibly, and Wales left the room.

They told her afterward that she had not passed out during the birth of the baby, but she was sure that she must have, because she could not remember it. Almost, but not quite. She had a little girl, a daughter. She lost consciousness after the delivery, and did not regain it for a long time. Afterward they told her it had been three days and three nights. And after she was better, they told her that she had hovered between life and death. But she guessed that, even when she did not know whether she was conscious or unconscious, or how many hours or days and nights had passed.

She thought she remembered, when she woke up, that Wales had been with her, but that did not seem possible. Mrs. Best was the one sitting by her bedside when she opened her eyes.

"Wales . . . ?" she said in a bewildered tone, the word coming out like a croak from dry lips and a dry throat.

"Yes, he's here," said Mrs. Best, smiling. "He's just taking a little nap on the couch. We've been sitting up with you in shifts."

"But how . . . how can he be? How many . . . how many years have I been . . . what about my baby?"

Mrs. Best soothed her rising panic with a strong hand on her shoulder and a warm smile.

"No, it's only been a few days, and your baby's fine. Your husband's back early, that's all—and a lucky thing for you, dear. I'll call him in for a minute, and then you rest some more."

Wales came in. He stood over the bed, looking taller and stronger, even, than Elizabeth remembered, and his face glowing with thankfulness that she was all right. She reached up and took his hand, surprised at how sore her arm felt, and realizing for the first time, to her greater surprise, how much her whole body hurt.

"The baby . . . ?"

"She's fine," said Wales. "Mrs. Best will bring her in . . ."

But Elizabeth was asleep again before Mrs. Best got back. She slept through the night, and woke up in the morning still hurting but refreshed.

She learned then why Wales was in Stonington: a hurricane at sea, a near shipwreck, extensive damage, the ship forced to limp back to New York. A few days later, when she was feeling stronger, she heard more of the details. There had been a violent tropical storm in the Caribbean. It had come up without warning. The ship had been forced way off course, almost run aground on a reef. The main- and mizzenmast had snapped, two sailors had been lost overboard, several others seriously injured. The hull had been half stove in, much of the cargo destroyed. Emergency repairs had made the ship strong enough to get back to its home port, but not strong enough to take the chance of continuing.

Elizabeth thanked her lucky stars that she had not insisted on making the trip with him—and that he was alive.

She thought of little else except the baby, and getting her strength back, for the next few weeks. The baby was named Anne Creighton Rogers, after Elizabeth's father's mother.

Elizabeth was confined to her bed, recuperating, and Anne was brought in to her for feeding. She was a beautiful, funny-looking thing, with a thatch of black hair and little red fists and toes that curled up so that they almost

143

looked like another pair of fists. Elizabeth was glad that she'd had her. She liked being a mother, and she loved little Anne.

Wales was around, all during that time. He stayed in Stonington, and every morning and evening he would come in and sit with Elizabeth, rock the baby, talk with her, and keep her spirits up. It was a great comfort to her when she was sickly, but as she began to get stronger, she began to worry more about him, and their future.

Wales had failed in his first command. He had brought the ship back to port in ruins, a scant few months after he had taken it to sea. In times like these, with business bad and fewer and fewer sailing ships on the sea, what were the chances that he would ever get another?

She brooded on it a great deal. He was being so good to her, and she had needed so much when her condition was desperate, that she did not want to be cruel to him now— but the fact was, she was terribly afraid that he had let everything they both wanted slip through his fingers. And she could not help but wonder if it had happened simply because Wales was not capable of handling command of a ship.

She tried not to be too harsh. Not everyone could command a ship, she reminded herself. Not every man was like her father. Many people had to compromise on their dreams. At least she had the baby, little Anne, and if she was never go to to sea again, that would be some consolation. Wales, meanwhile, was talking to Mr. MacNab about a position as dispatcher in his office.

"I could ship out on one of his ships—not as captain, but as supercargo," he told Elizabeth. "But I don't want to leave you and the baby right now—not for a job like that, certainly. And besides, I know I'll get another ship of my own."

Elizabeth wished that she shared his confidence. She was glad he was staying, and not glad at the same time. He was still a comfort to her, but having him around as a reminder of his failure made her uncomfortable.

She thought of her parents up on their farm, and of the years they had spent at sea together. Why did all the luck go to those who didn't appreciate it, like her mother?

* * *

There was an inquiry into the circumstances surrounding the wreck of the *Western Wind*, and Wales went into New York for it, but did not talk a great deal about it when he returned. But not long after, there came a letter from Sears and Nickerson.

Wales read it first, nodding his head a couple of times, but otherwise betraying no emotion. Elizabeth waited impatiently.

"What do they say?" she asked finally.

He handed her the letter, and she read it. She was surprised—and ashamed at her surprise—to find that the owners had words of high praise for Wales's handling of the ship: "Without your skill and cool head, the *Western Wind* might well have been wrecked, and the lives of all its crewmen forfeited . . . in fact, much of the cargo, more than we had anticipated, was saved.

"As regards the *Western Wind*, she may well be reparable, as you recommend, but we have decided not to undertake the enterprise. We are putting the vessel up for sale. However . . ." Elizabeth's hands trembled with excitement as she read this part, and her voice went up. "However, Captain Benson of the *Trident* has informed us that he plans to retire after his next voyage, and we would be honored if you would assume command of that ship for us."

Elizabeth felt like jumping up and down. She bounced in the bed, where she was seated. "Wales, that's wonderful! You'll be back at sea, with a new ship of your own, in a year or less. I'm so proud of you!"

Wales took the letter and folded it, a little half-smile on his face. "Perhaps," he said.

"Perhaps? What do you mean? You're not going to turn down the *Trident*, are you?"

"I don't have to answer them for a few days. There's another possibility I want to explore," he said.

"Another possibility? What do you mean? I thought this was the news you'd been waiting to hear."

"It is, but in a different way. You remember John Rosenfeld, who owned the *Richard M. Himsvark*? He's formed a new partnership with two other businessmen, and I may go in with him. They may buy the *Western Wind*.

I'd be joining them in the business end of it—I'd be a part-owner."

Elizabeth was apprehensive. "Do you really think that's a good idea, Wales? It seems like such a risk."

"A seafaring career is one risk after another, Elizabeth."

"Yes, I know. But those are the risks of the sea—pitting your knowledge and skill against the wind and the tides, while this is . . . different. Suppose you can't raise the money? Suppose you can't make her seaworthy again?"

"We'll make her seaworthy again," said Wales with determination. "She's a good ship, and I know it. And who should know better than I what it will take to set her right? And I told Sears, when they brought her in, that I thought they should keep her and repair her, so my conscience is clear on that score."

"But all the business, the financing of it! That's not a sailor's concern. It's all so humdrum and complicated! I just don't know—maybe you should stay with Sears and Nickerson, and let them worry about all that."

Wales laughed. "My dear, you know as much as any man about marine science and celestial navigation, not to mention a half-dozen other deepwater subjects I could name off the top of my head, but you have a very strange idea of the job of a ship's master! What do you think your father spent his time doing in overseas ports—wining and dining the local ladies? He was buying and selling cargoes, checking inventories and replenishing ship's supplies, taking care of the payroll. A ship is a business."

Elizabeth frowned. She did not like being informed of her ignorance, especially when her father was the subject under discussion.

"Of course," Wales went on, "it was a fine run your father made to try and break the *Flying Cloud*'s record, but speed's only the half of it. It wouldn't have counted for much if he hadn't been able to get a good price for his cargo once he got there. Your father was part-owner of the *Spirit of the Waves*, you know, and then of the *Orion*, the ship he finished his years at sea aboard."

"Yes, I knew that, of course," said Elizabeth, who had not. "It just never seemed all that important to me."

"You can count on it that it was important to him," said Wales. "And not for security—there's precious little secu-

146

rity in owning a deepwater ship, and that's a fact. A man's best security is in his own skill and his good name. No, it's important because a man needs to be his own master in all ways, not just on the quarterdeck."

"All right, then, Captain Rogers," sighed Elizabeth. "If you think it best, go ahead with your partnership, then. And if it fails, there's always Mr. MacNab's countinghouse for you, and a little cottage in Stonington for myself and the baby."

"As to that, it'll be the countinghouse for me, anyway," said Wales with a cheerful grin. "At least for a while. There's money to be raised and spent, and months of rebuilding, before the *Western Wind* is seaworthy again."

And in fact, in spite of all her reservations about the project, Elizabeth soon came to be spending nearly as much time supervising the reconstruction of the *Western Wind* as Wales did. As soon as she was back on her feet, there were household responsibilities to get back to, and the new responsibilities of baby care, but the doctor had ordered her to take it easy at first, and get plenty of fresh air, so she was able to go and sit above the shipyard and watch.

It was easy to fall in love with the *Western Wind*. She was a huge, beautiful square-rigger. Her bow had a bold, dashing rake to it, with lines that were lightly concave below the waterline but convex above, and her stern was curvilinear and finely formed. She was a full 250 feet long, longer than most clippers, and her mainmast measured a towering 188 feet. As soon as Elizabeth laid eyes on her, she could well understand why Wales wanted this beautiful eagle of the seas to be his own. She felt the same way herself.

When Wales was not there Elizabeth kept a respectful distance, on the edge of the shipyard, but when he came to the yard at the same time that she did, she would walk with him as he paced around the ship, or talked with Samuel Rosenfeld about what still needed to be done, and what work could be put off for a foreign port, where workmen and materials would come cheaper. Wales wanted the lifeboats repositioned, a new deckhouse built, and a seventeen-foot flying gangway installed that would span the distance

147

from the aftercabin top to the boat gallows—hinged, so it could be hoisted to clear the mizzen hatchway when cargo was being discharged. Rosenfeld argued that it was unnecessary, but finally gave in, with a compromise: the additions would be made, but later, out of the U.S. Wales got his return compromise: that a small donkey boiler and engine be installed in the *Wind*'s forward house immediately, by American mechanics and with an American engine.

Rosenfeld disagreed. He was a pudgy young man of thirty-three, with sandy hair, impeccably styled clothing that always seemed to have a shirttail out or a collar askew, and an amiable, owlish manner that allowed him always to appear good-natured even when he was trying not to be: for instance, when he was arguing a point that Wales was unalterably opposed to. Wales, with his remarkable evenness of disposition, never seemed to be getting upset—even when he raised his voice and became animated, it somehow did not show. So the two of them could be at crossed swords over some point of design or question of budget, and unless one were watching them as closely as Elizabeth, it would not show.

Elizabeth loved to watch them ambling up and down the length of the shipyard—her husband, with his quiet, commanding presence and long-legged, rolling seaman's gait; Rosenfeld, his short legs moving like pistons to keep up, his face all breathless amiability. Then, after an hour ro so, they would return, with Rosenfeld still smiling, and panting, "Well, Mrs. Rogers—that husband of yours is determined to drive me either to the poorhouse or the madhouse, but I'm blessed if I can figure out which!"

But it was the *Wind* itself that she most loved to watch. Here was her reading come to life—a chance to get to know a great ship from the inside out, with all the smells, the sounds, the bulk and weight and strain and pride of workmanship. The damaged hull was the subject of the heaviest repairs. After the broken timbering had been replaced, and salt packed between all the timbers to prevent rot, the entire hull was stripped and recaulked, and then tar and sheets of felt were applied up to her twenty-two-foot draft mark. Then she was ready to be resheathed with the alloy of copper and zinc known in the shipyards simply as "yellow metal." The plates—over 3,500 of them, each one

148

weighing six and a half pounds and measuring 14 by 48 inches—were delivered from New York, with nail holes already punched in them by a firm on South Street that had a special machine for process, so that when they reached the Stonington shipyards they were ready to be applied to the *Wind*'s hull. The hull, alone, took over two months to repair, but it was finally done, and then, at last, the whole ship was seaworthy again.

Wales gave notice at MacNab's, and left for New York to negotiate for a cargo. In less than a month, they were ready to sail for England. This time Elizabeth, still too weak to sail herself and with a baby too young yet for the rigors of sea life, was nevertheless in high spirits. She felt herself a part of the ship after having seen it through its refitting, and she was content to wait for the promised next voyage, when she and little Anne would be on board. And the following spring, she watched from the bridge, beside her husband, as the *Western Wind* sailed out of New York Harbor, bound for Cape Horn, San Francisco, and the Orient.

BOOK TWO

❧Chapter Sixteen

THE SHIP FELT GOOD. SHE HAD BEEN TESTED ON her first deepwater run to London and back, and Wales knew she was ready for the pounding of Cape Horn, and a good run across the Pacific. She was fast and she was sturdy and she was in good trim.

He had a new crew, and new officers. Only Ronald Whiteurs, his old bosun, was back with him, and he was glad of at least that blessing—Whiteurs was the best bosun he had ever shipped with. He was a tough, taciturn, black man of indeterminate age, but certainly not young. He had been a slave in his youth, and a seaman before the mast for over twenty years. He could not read from books or write his name, but he could read the winds and the evening skies, and he was smart enough, and tough enough, to command the respect and obedience of any crew member, however racially bigoted he might be at the outset.

The second mate was a boy of eighteen named Ben Harris, the nephew of Rosenfeld's partner. He was a goodlooking, agreeable lad, but short on both experience and ambition. He would never have been Wales's choice for a second officer, but at least he'd cause no dissension. He was one of the compromises Wales had been forced to make in order to get some of the modifications he'd wanted for the Flyer. Wales had suggested that the lad be taken along as supercargo, with no other responsibilities assigned to him than supervision of the commercial details of the freight consignment, but he had finally accepted the partner's nephew as second mate. Wales had made sure all the arguments about young Harris had taken place behind closed doors, and that the boy himself had no knowledge of them. *Trouble enough bringing a green lad like that along to be a working officer, without getting him nervous and having him think I don't trust him,* Wales reasoned. *And worse than that, if the crew should get an inkling of lack of respect . . .*

By way of balance for Harris's inexperience, there was the first officer, Mr. Thomas Dowling. Wales had sized him up as being tough—ruthless, even—cool as ice, quick, and experienced. He had other impressions of Dowling, too. He did not like the man, and his instinct was that the first mate was not a man whom he could ever like or trust in the realm of personal dealings. Not that there was anything shifty about Dowling—it was just the reverse, a fierce directness, a barely leashed savagery. Wales's guess was that Dowling was not a man whose desires were likely to be tempered by moral or philosophical restraints.

Dowling had cold blue eyes, and straight blond hair that swept back in sleek, even lines, and curled slightly at the nape of the neck. His thin lips had little trouble in forming an amused, cynical smile. He was not tall, but his bearing made the clear statement that height did not matter. His dry voice demanded to be heard, and could cut through a howling wind to shout commands over a storm at sea.

He had the air of a man with a past, and the rumors were that there was more to his background than he talked about—smuggler, skipper of an opium clipper in the China seas. He was thirty years old and a fine seaman, yet he had no command of his own—and no master's papers, though he clearly had the knowledge and experience to have gotten them.

It was all one to Wales, as long as Dowling did his job. And he was clearly the most capable man for it, of all the prospective mates that Wales had interviewed.

And on this voyage, there was more to occupy Wales's concern than the men on the ship's payroll. There was his baby daughter, about to embard on a life that would set her apart from other children her age, as his wife had been set apart in her day. Would it be good for her? Was it fair to her? There was Jennie Speaker, the baby's nurse, a warm, open young girl, already devoted to little Anne, but inexperienced and a little frightened of shipboard life. Jennie was pretty, with soft, auburn hair, and a face and figure that were just growing out of adolescence and into young womanhood. Wales had wondered if a romance might be kindled between her and young Harris, but so far Jennie seemed to have evinced no interest whatever in the young second mate.

And finally, there was Elizabeth, his wife of four years, the love of his life. How would the voyage be for her, and how would it be for their marriage?

Wales knew that the marriage had not been perfect, and that Elizabeth had never been completely happy in it. He knew, too, how much she had always wanted to go back to sea. He knew how much of a strain being landlocked had put on her, and on her feelings about him. Well, now he had given her what she wanted: a ship of their own, and Elizabeth making her first voyage with him.

As always happened when he thought of her, a slow smile spread across Wales's face, and hung there for several moments, until he noticed it. Then he recomposed his features into the stern mask that was appropriate for a captain on the bridge.

But the thoughts remained. Elizabeth . . . how he enjoyed her! She was so full of life. It overflowed from her in whatever she did—in her enthusiasms, her ambition, her energy, even her pettiness.

His mind went back to the first night he had set eyes on her. Yes, she had a demon in her, a demon to draw her down to the seamy and violent waterfront, so far out of her depth, a sheltered child of seventeen. Maybe that destructive demon and the spark of life that so attracted him were two sides of the same coin. It had been there, that night, blazing in her eyes through the terror.

Wales was glad he had been there that night; it remained one of the most satisfying memories of his life, as was being at her bedside through the pain and danger of giving birth. But in a way, that moment in the waterfront dive, when he as yet wanted nothing from her and so could experience, undiluted, his appreciation of her, was the closest to her that he had ever felt.

Sometimes Wales felt guilty for enjoying Elizabeth so much—for enjoying her more than perhaps she enjoyed him. Nevertheless, that was the way he felt. Even when things were tense between them, and he could see her dissatisfaction, he still took pleasure in her presence.

They would be together, now, every day for more than a year, for the duration of the voyage. And for many more voyages to come.

And they would be together every night. Once more, Wales could not suppress a smile as his memory felt their bodies pressed together, and the indent of her full breasts upon his chest.

Dowling, Harris, Jennie Speaker, and Captain and Mrs. Rogers all took their evening meal together in the ship's saloon, served by Ritter, the German steward. It was an awkward mix of people, and conversation was generally sparse and strained. Wales often experienced something that was between annoyance and jealousy—he would have preferred to have had that time with Elizabeth alone, but tradition dictated this ritual.

But they had the evenings after dinner, when Wales was not on watch. And as they had planned, Elizabeth was doing the navigational chores.

She sat at the wide captain's desk, swiveling back and forth to consult tables, then reached over and jotted down notes. Wales, who had just come in from above decks, watched her sway, entranced by the sweep of her limbs, the flow of her body. His eyes gradually focused on the nape of her neck, and almost without thinking, he crossed the room with large steps and pressed his lips to it, wrapping his arms around her from behind.

"Wales! I'm still working."

"Well, be quick about it," he said playfully.

"I can't be quick about it if I'm going to do it right," she said. "You don't want the ship going off course and getting lost, now, do you?"

"It wouldn't," he said, continuing to fondle her. "I wouldn't let it." His arms circled her waist, his right hand rubbed her belly gently and suggestively, his face burrowed

156

into her neck. She spun around suddenly in the captain's chair, pulling herself out of his grasp.

"So, then what I'm doing is just playing a game? The gallant captain will take care of everything, with no charts, no navigational tables? Just head south until you run into an iceberg, then head north? Thank you very much, sir!"

"Oh, hang it all, Elizabeth, I didn't mean it like that! I only meant . . . oh, you know. Obviously what you're doing is important. I don't have to tell you that. I'm . . . you finish it up, I'm going to take another turn up on deck and make sure everything's shipshape before I turn in."

"Don't wear your nightgown tonight," he said.

Elizabeth hesitated for a moment. "All right." She was undressing behind the screen. She slipped on her robe, walked across the cabin to the bed, got under the covers, and then took it off.

Wales was already in bed. He was naked, too. He hung back from her for just a split second of anticipation, then gathered her in his arms. His body was hard and muscular; his sex was hard, too, and pressed against her thigh like a club. They lay on their sides, close against each other. Wales's arms were tight around Elizabeth; his fingers kneaded up and down her back. He pressed kisses against her cheek, her neck, her forehead, her mouth.

Her arm rested across his back, but he knew that when he rolled over on top of her, it would fall, as it always did, to her side, and there it would stay. She never put her arms around him and held him when they made love. But, as always, her passivity only increased his ardor, and he caressed her body with his hands and his mouth. His touch was fervent but delicate, constantly on the alert for her response, ready to concentrate on whatever gave her the most pleasure.

Tonight, he felt that he was succeeding. Her body moved under his; her breath came heavier. Drawing his own excitement from hers, he cupped her breast in a hand beginning to tremble, and stroked her erect nipple with his thumb. Her head moved from side to side. *Now*, he thought, while her interest was still at a peak, before she began to lose patience. He entered her.

He felt the rush of excitement that he always felt at that

moment. Then it was over too quickly, almost before he realized it, and they lay side by side on the double bed, not quite touching.

"Wales," said Elizabeth, "if we put on full sail tomorrow and head easy-southeast, we'll pick up the Gulf stream almost a full day sooner, and be on a perfect course to head down into the trades.

"We'll stay closer to the continent and pick up the Gulf Stream around the 31st parallel," said Wales. "I think it'll be best in the long run. I don't know about the sail. We'll have to wait on tomorrow's weather, and it doesn't promise to be the best.

Elizabeth did not reply, not right away. She lay silent, not looking at him. Wales reached over and laid a hand on her hip. Her body seemed stiff and unyielding, and after a moment his fingers seemed to curl back, cold and rebuffed. He withdrew his hand.

She sat up in bed and reached for her robe. She held it against her chest first, then put it on. Each action was quick and curt, but there were long, distant pauses between them.

"I'm cold," she said. She got up, went over behind the screen, and put on her nightdress.

There was another long pause after she returned to bed.

"My father would have put on full sail and headed for the Gulf Stream," she said before she turned over and closed her eyes.

∾Chapter Seventeen

JENNIE SPEAKER COOED TO LITTLE ANNE AS SHE
began to dress her. "Yes, my darling, hold your arm up
like that, while I tuck it in the sleeve . . . there! We're
going for our walk out on deck today, I guess you've
missed that, haven't you? Yes, I know, we've been down
here in the tiny old cabin for three days, haven't we, but
it's nice weather again now. We're going up on deck with
the big sailors, like your papa . . . and we're fine little
sailors, too, aren't we? Not seasick a day, neither of us, and
a whole month at sea, too . . . Now the other arm, that's
my darling . . . I'll bet it's not every two young ladies
aboard ship for the first time could say that, but we're special, aren't we, you and I?"

The sound of her own words struck Jennie as a bit too
prideful to make her comfortable, even as a bit of nonsense
to coo at a baby, so she amended: "Well, you're special
anyway, my little love. The littlest sailor of them all. *You*
weren't scared through that big storm we had the last two
days and nights, were you, now? I was, though. But Captain Rogers brought us through. Yes, and Captain Rogers
is your papa, my little sweetheart—and he brought us
through to safety, didn't he? Yes, he did, yes, he did!" she
crooned, tickling the baby, who lay on her back laughing
with delight. "Yes, he did, oh, yes, he did!"

Mrs. Rogers came into the cabin. "Is the baby ready for her walk, Jennie?"

"Yes, ma'am, all ready."

"Good. Let's go, then."

"Yes, ma'am. Just a moment." Leaving Anne on the bed, Jennie picked up her hairbrush and began a hurried attempt at her own toilet, brushing her thick auburn hair with choppy strokes.

"Oh, for heaven's sake, Jennie, just put a bonnet on," said Mrs. Rogers. "You'll be blown every which way in the wind on deck, anyhow."

"Yes, ma'am," said Jennie. "It is a beautiful day, isn't it? I'm so glad we came through that storm safely. I was so scared. But Captain Rog—"

"That was nothing, Jennie," Mrs. Rogers told her. "Just a little blow. But you wait—we'll be going through some real storms."

"That was real enough for me. But I guess you've seen lots worse?"

Mrs. Rogers smiled, and Jennie could see that old memories were passing before her eyes.

"Well, I certainly hope we don't encounter anything a lot worse. I didn't even think there could ever be a storm *that* bad."

"My father would have run with that wind," said Elizabeth. "He would have been putting on more sail, not striking sail."

"I suppose so, ma'am," said Jennie.

The baby was dressed warmly, and Jennie put on her heavy cloak, too. The weather was getting chillier every day as they went down the coast of South America, closer and closer to what Mrs. Rogers, like the sailors, called "Cape Stiff," but Jennie still thought of as the "Cape Horn" of the maps and geography books, with the formality that she would have felt toward a famous man whom everyone else knew but she had yet to meet. She had heard of the storms around Cape Horn, and the tales made her shudder. She was glad that Captain Rogers was in command of the *Western Wind*.

Mrs. Rogers only wore a light cloak. The cool air did not seem to be bothering her, yet, and the storm of the past forty-eight hours had hardly ruffled her at all. While Jennie

160

had simply cowered in her cabin, rocking the baby and trying to calm it—and herself—Mrs. Rogers had been as active and nimble as if they had been floating in a calm, landlocked lagoon. And while Jennie had sat on her bed with one arm crooked around the bedpost to hold her back from being flung across the room each time the ship lurched violently, Mrs. Rogers had negotiated the steeply pitched decks as lightly as a dancer, even helping the steward carry hot coffee to the officers when they came below for a breather.

She had even offered to take coffee forward to the crew, but Captain Rogers had forgidden that. Jennie had heard the exchange when she had slipped out to the saloon for a few moments, her fear of being alone overcoming, for the moment, her fear of moving.

". . . My father always made sure the men were fortified well for hazardous work."

Captain Rogers' jaw was clenched, as Jennie had seen it before when Mrs. Rogers brought her father into an argument, as she seemed to do more and more often; and, as usual, the captain did not reply directly.

"The men on this ship know how to do their work in a squall," he said. "Have you seen to Anne lately?"

"Yes," she snapped.

"Oh, yes, sir, that's true," said Jennie from the doorway. "Mrs. Rogers has been there every time I needed her. She's come by every ten or fifteen minutes, and she holds little Anne and calms her down every time she needs it, where she won't do anything but cry and scream for me—and she's always so good for me, too. I guess it's that she senses how frightened I am, and how calm Mrs. Rogers is."

The captain and his wife looked up, surprised, at the voice. Mrs. Rogers walked over and put her arms around her.

"I'm sorry, Mrs. Rogers . . . I am so frightened," said Jennie, sobbing.

"It's all right, Jennie," said Mrs. Rogers. "You've been doing wonderfully. Come on, we'll go back to the cabin, and I'll sit with you for a while."

Jennie had never been so impressed by Mrs. Rogers as she was during that storm. She wondered if it were really possible that the weather at sea could get as bad as Mrs.

Rogers said, so bad that the storm she had been through would seem mild by comparison. And she wondered if it were true that Mrs. Rogers' father would have sailed through the storm as if it were nothing more than a good stiff wind.

Jennie felt hurt whenever she heard Mrs. Rogers talking to Captain Rogers about what her father would have done. She knew it pained him, though he never responded in his own defense. Jennie thought that Mr. Rogers must be a very fine captain. He kept the ship looking trim and moving sharply. He was strong and forceful with the men and the other officers, but he always seemed fair. And he always had a smile and a kind word for her, whenever he saw her on deck with the baby, or when he joined them at mealtimes. But Mrs. Rogers, all too often, just did not seem to see it that way.

Elizabeth had never felt so strong or healthy. The fatigue that had lingered after her difficult childbirth was all gone. She felt better than she had before the baby was conceived. The creaking of the decks, the screech of straining ropes, the flopping and whistling of sail in the wind quickened her steps like march music. The salt spray put sparkle back in her hair, and the sea air filled her lungs like sails.

She had almost started to fear, at twenty-one, that she was growing old. But now she felt youthful again. She was ready for anything the sea had to offer, and when the squall came up, she greeted it with gusto.

It had come on suddenly, from the southeast; they were sailing into it as fast as it was coming up to meet them. Elizabeth was sitting up on deck, sewing, with Jennie and the boby, while Jennie watched Anne toddle around from one side of the deck to the other. Elizabeth kept watch out of the corner of her eye, amused at Jennie's protectiveness. Jennie made sure that she was always between Anne and the nearest rail. Anne's footing became surer and steadier with each passing day. She was getting her sea legs as quickly as she was learning to walk.

Elizabeth noticed the storm first. She scooped Anne up in her arms.

"Come on, Jennie," she said. "Help me get our things together and let's get below."

"Ma'am?"

"There's a storm coming up."

"Are you sure?" Jennie asked nervously. "But wouldn't the officers come and tell us . . . ?"

"I'm telling you," snapped Elizabeth. "And we haven't that much time, so get to it."

Jennie did as she was told, and they were at the stairwell before pink-cheeked Second Mate Harris arrived to warn them.

"I guess you don't need any help," he said, slightly flustered and blushing as he always was in the presence of the ladies.

"No, you look to the ship, Mr. Harris," said Elizabeth. "And tell Captain Rogers that I can manage without taking up the time of an officer."

"Yes, ma'am."

Elizabeth got Anne and Jennie settled in their cabin, told Jennie what to do, told her not to worry—he would be close at hand if any emergency came up. Then she put on her foul-weather gear and went back up on deck.

The storm was already on them. Sailors were reefing sail, securing lines. The hatches were battened. Wales was on the bridge, giving a running stream of orders to the helmsman, and sending Dowling forward with orders to the crew. The ship was moving well, under sharply reduced sail, at a tangent to the path of the storm. Everything seemed to be under control, although Elizabeth had the uneasy feeling that Wales had missed a few beats in beginning to prepare for the weather, and that he was lucky not to have been caught off guard—especially since, with her handling the navigational duties, he had nothing to occupy his time but bridge command.

There was nothing exactly wrong. Elizabeth watched the sailors aloft, clutching the yards as they fastened the upper topstails against the winds that threatened to pry their very fingers loose from the rigging; she watched the sailors on deck, bracing against the waves that crashed over the rails and through the shrouds, the foaming water that swept and eddied across the decks, pulling and twisting at their heavy-booted feet. Everyone was pulling together, and the ship was running a strong course—a course that she would soon be recharting. She'd be needed down at the navigator's desk as they ran through this one.

But she was still a little uneasy. She did not have the feeling of security she had always felt on her father's ships.

She did not sleep, throughout the two days and nights of the storm. There was too much to do, too much to worry about, too much excitement.

Wales did. On the morning of the second day, he came below during Dowling's watch. Elizabeth was working her tables when he came in, and she saw him out of the corner of her eye. He took off his slicker and sou'wester and hung them, dripping, on a peg. He sat down on the end of the bed and pulled off his boots, and left them standing, pointed outward, at the foot of the bed. He did not interrupt Elizabeth, and she did not break from her work to speak to him. He lay down, fully clothed, on top of the bed, and pulled a coverlet over his frame. Within seconds, he was asleep.

He slept for three hours, and was awakened by the steward to go back on deck again. Elizabeth was gone by then, up on deck for a few minutes where Dowling stalked the bridge like a cat, then down to tend the baby and reassure Jennie.

The same nervous energy was still carrying her along when she walked the baby on deck with Jennie, the morning after the storm broke. Then, everyone else had returned to the steady pace of shipboard life. The sailors off watch were asleep in the fo'c'sle, those on watch were making repairs, scrubbing and cleaning, settling the ship back to normal. But she was still moving too fast; she was out of step, and she knew it. It made her irritable. She did not see why Wales should be going out of his way to be polite to Jennie, or so solicitous after little Anne, when he should be keeping his mind on the ship. She had kept hers on her responsibilities for the last forty-eight hours—even while he slept!

She had begun to run down, though, by evening. Mr. Harris was on watch, and Wales and Mr. Dowling joined her and Jennie at supper.

"Isn't it wonderful that the weather got nice again?" said

Jennie. "Do you suppose it will stay this way for a while? I hope so."

"This is just a lull," said Dowling. "We won't see much good weather between here now and the Pacific."

Jennie's face clouded. "I suppose it will get worse, too. Mrs. Rogers says this wasn't a bad storm at all."

"Compared to some," Elizabeth interjected.

"Mrs. Rogers should know," said Wales. "She practically cut her first teeth on a gale."

Jennie looked curiously at Wales. So did Dowling.

"Hadn't you heard that tale?" said Wales to Dowling. "If you'd spent more time on Yankee ships you'd certainly have come across it before—it's near legendary." He turned to Jennie again. "Yes, when Mrs. Rogers was not much older than little Anne in there, she rode out a nor'-easter from the poop deck of a clipper ship—a gale that would have made our squall look like water bubbling in a saucepan by comparison."

He smiled over at Elizabeth, who tried to return his smile appreciatively through eyes that could barely stay open.

Jennie gasped in amazement, and stared at Elizabeth as though she were a figure from a book come to life.

"Somebody was asleep at the helm, letting her above decks in the first place," said Dowling, cool and unimpressed. "Whose ship was that, anyway?"

"My father's!" said Elizabeth, without the scathing anger that she would have mustered had she been less tired.

"It's hard to fault Captain Creighton, either as skipper or father," said Wales gallantly. "He made the second fastest run ever from New York to San Francisco, *and* raised Mrs. Rogers."

The weather did get worse. As they drew down near the 40th parallel, the seas began to be choppy all the time. The skies were overcast, and they were pelted with sudden, driving rains. Many days the sun did not break through at all, and Wales had to establish a position by dead reckoning. That meant all the more work for Elizabeth, when he was finally able to establish a sextant reading, because the course had to be constantly monitored and readjusted.

That was fine. Actually, it gave them a relatively safe

avenue for communication. In most ways, the tension between them was growing. Elizabeth knew full well, though Wales had never said so directly, how grating it was on him to have her constantly talking about what her father would have done. But the longer she was at sea, and the more her familiarity and confidence returned, the clearer a sense she had of what she would do—and what her father would have done. It was hard to hold back from giving him her observations and advice, especially when she knew that they were valid. She took her share of the responsibility. Wales was lucky to have her, and not some frightened, confused little landlubber like Jennie Speaker.

And if he didn't want her suggestions, he could always tell her so directly.

Her thoughts ran along these currents as she sat at her desk unable to concentrate, in the middle of the afternoon. Her body felt stiff and dissatisfied. She had a cramp in her left thigh, just below her buttock, from sitting too long, and she stood up to try to knead away the tightness. Rubbing her leg, she walked over and stood next to the porthole.

It was a hazy-sunny day, but the wind was erratic and the seas ran high. The ship seemed to be moving in an unpredictable, twitchy fashion, which only served to increase Elizabeth's tension.

Something flashed before her eyes, suddenly, incongruously. It was gone before she could quite believe what she had seen, but then it reappeared again in the water. The white, thrashing soles of a pair of bare feet; the dark legs of a pair of sailor's pajama trousers. Then an arm and hand with open, vainly stretching fingers, and finally a bearded face. The sailor's mouth was closed against the lung-crushing force of the waves; his screaming was all in his wide, terror-filled eyes, but no one would have heard him, anyway. Elizabeth fancied that his eyes met hers, in a last, desperate appeal for help, but she could not be sure.

She ran up on deck, barefooted, and shouting in her own sea-practiced voice that could be heard half the length of the ship: "Man overboard! Man overboard!"

Dowling reached her first, his hawklike face grim and hard. His eyes met hers quickly, and went on in the direction of her pointing finger. "Where?"

166

"Saw him from the starboard porthole—fell from a yard," Elizabeth said crisply. "He'll be drifting on that course." She held her pointing finger steady, and Dowling sighted down her arm, touching her shoulder as he squinted into the distance. Wales was beside them now. As he sprinted over, he had already barked out the command to ready a small boat, and it was being done now under the direction of Whiteurs, the bosun.

"Mr. Dowling, take the boat out," Wales ordered. He looked astern through his telescope.

"Aye, aye, sir," said Dowling.

"Nothing," said Wales. "He collapsed the telescope, and strode to the breastrail. "Slack sail!" he commanded. And to the helmsman: "Bring her about west a full turn."

The ship came about off wind, and rode in the water as the small boat grew smaller in the distance. Elizabeth watched it go, frowning. Still frowning, she went below, and back to her desk and her books.

Three anxious hours later, just before dusk, the boat returned. Elizabeth came to the bridge, beside Wales, to hear Dowling's terse report. "No sign."

"He's gone, then," said Wales. "No chance of his lasting through the night."

"Wales . . ." Elizabeth touched his arm, and spoke quietly, so no one would hear her calling him by his first name instead of his title on the bridge, "I've been doing some figuring. Calculating the wind and the drift in this part of the Atlantic . . ."

She showed him her figures with trembling fingers. "I think I'm right." She had never been so unsure of herself. Wales did not say a word while she talked, but he looked intently at the sheet of foolscap she had put in front of him. When she finished, her heart was pounding, and she could hardly breathe.

Wales did not hesitate a second. "Mr. Dowling, take the boat out again. Mr. Whiteurs, ready a second boat. I'll take it out. You come with me, and three men."

The sunset that night was eerily, frighteningly beautiful. The low clouds on the horizon refracted the light and sent long fingers of deep red, bright orange, and mystical violet across the heavens. Elizabeth's knuckles were a pale white as she gripped the taffrail fiercely.

"Red sky at night," she whispered. "Sailor's delight."

Young Mr. Harris, now the officer in charge, stood next to her, as if for reassurance. He swallowed, nodded his head, and looked solemn.

Elizabeth could not leave the bridge, not even to kiss Anne goodnight. Not even to get a warm cloak. She had not noticed the cold until Jennie brought her cloak up to her; then she realized she was trembling, and wrapped it around her shoulders gratefully.

"They'll find him, won't they?" asked Jennie. "I mean, with your directions . . . ?"

"I hope so," muttered Elizabeth. "I hope they all come back safely. . . ."

As the last rays of sunset were withdrawing from the sky, she saw the two small boats in the distance. The lookout called it out, and the crew jammed the rails to witness their approach. And they saw, when the boats got close enough, the sailors on them raising their oars to wave in triumph. They had found him!

A cheer went up from the men at the rails, wild, raucous, joyful, chaotic.

Then, above the rest, a second cheer:

"Hurray for Mrs. Rogers!"

And in an instant, all the men had picked it up: "Hurray for Mrs. Rogers! Hurray for Mrs. Rogers! Hurray for Mrs. Rogers!"

Elizabeth felt weak. She tried to turn and face the cheering sailors, but instead she burst into tears, and ran below to her cabin.

ᴅᴠChapter Eighteen

THEY PUT THE SAILOR IN ONE OF THE EMPTY passengers' cabins in the after deckhouse, unconscious. Mr. Whiteurs told Elizabeth a little about him. His name was Alexander Mapp, and he was from Boston. And he was a Negro, to Elizabeth's surprise.

"But the first thing I saw was . . . the bottoms of his feet looked so white!" she said to Whiteurs.

"They are," he said. "You most likely never saw the soles of a colored man's feet before."

"And then I saw his face, and I never noticed—never even thought about the color," she said. "Only how terrified he was. And I was, too. And I guess the only thing I was thinking of then was what I could do to help."

"You done good," said Whiteurs.

"Do you know him well, Mr. Whiteurs?"

"I've shipped with him, on and off, maybe ten years," said the bosun. "I've laid over with him in tough ports like Maracaibo and Manila . . . and Savannah, and I can tell you he's as tough as they come. Yeah, and a good man to have on your side if there's trouble, on sea or land."

"He's your friend, then."

The black bosun ducked his head and methodically filled his pipe. Elizabeth knew the man was not going to be rushed into any statement about his feelings, and she waited.

"Yeah," Whiteurs finally said crisply. He paused again, puffed thoughtfully on his pipe, and then continued. "If it matters no more. Looks like Mapp's done hauled anchor this time. Tough as he be, I don't know as he'll pull through this one."

Elizabeth touched Whiteurs' gnarled hand, and spoke with controlled emotions.

"I'll take care of him, Mr. Whiteurs. We'll see him through."

Mapp was near dead from exposure, and from the water he had taken in. Elizabeth nursed him day and night for eight days. Jennie helped, too, but Elizabeth was never far away. She felt an almost mystical personal responsibility for Mapp's welfare.

She would not neglect her other work, either, even though Wales told her he would take it over for her, for as long as Mapp needed intensive care.

"No," she said. "I can handle it."

"You're getting overtired, dear," Wales said solicitously.

"There's many on this ship that are tired," she said grimly. "But they do their duty."

"Yes, but you're not a sailor, Elizabeth," Wales said. "You're not on the ship's payroll. You're my wife, and the mother of my child. I appreciate your help, but you don't have to kill yourself. The ship will run without you."

"I wish I could be sure of that!" she snapped at him.

"Oh, for God's sake!" he answered. "Let's not start in on that. Do the navigation. My aim is to keep this ship on course and on schedule. All I care about is that the navigation is accurate. And if you're too tired—"

"It will be."

Mapp recovered consciousness on the third day. Elizabeth was with him when he opened his eyes. She strained to hold him up, and managed to help him drink a few mouthfuls of broth. When he lay down again, she changed the cold compress that was on his forehead for the fever.

"Feel better?" she asked.

He grunted. He looked up at her, and opened and closed

his mouth a few times, as though to prime it for speaking after long disuse.

"You an angel," he said.

"You had a close call, but you're going to be all right now," she said.

"I remembers . . . but not everything. I remembers bein' out in the ocean for a *long* time. I thought I was a dead man, for sure."

"Well, you're alive, and you're going to stay that way. But you're not very strong yet. Have some more broth, and then get some rest."

She lifted him to a semi-upright position again. He was a big, heavy man, and still too weak to support himself, but she got him propped up enough to be able to drink, and then braced him with her shoulder while she raised the cup to his lips. He spattered and choked, and hot broth ran down his beard and onto his chest, but he did get some of it down.

"How does that feel?" she asked him.

"Better. Thank you."

He woke up again a few hours later, and this time he talked for several minutes. He remembered more, now: hanging onto a piece of flotsam with numb fingers, seeing the sharks circling around him.

"If it hadn't 'a been for my skin, I be a dead man, now," he said. "Sharks don't like to go after black skin like they likes to go after white, you know that? Sharks loves that white meat. Sharks, they likes white things, shiny bright things."

"It's a good thing they didn't see the soles of your feet," Elizabeth could not resist saying.

Mapp's eyes widened in surprise, and he grinned up at her, his first smile since regaining consciousness. "How you know that? But I was just about to let go, and give up on livin' no more in this world, when I seed that boat with the cap'n and Mr. Whiteurs. Ol' bosun and Cap'n Rogers, they done saved my life."

"You saved my life," Mapp said the next time he saw Elizabeth.

171

"Who's been telling you that?" asked Elizabeth.

"Miss Speaker . . . Mr. Whiteurs . . . every one I see," said the sailor. They tells me the whole story. You some fine lady, Mrs. Rogers. And I ain't gonna forget."

Mapp was moved to the fo'c'sle, rested another day, and went back to work. It was just in time—the *Western Wind* was coming around the coast of Argentina, and would be entering the fierce passage of Cape Horn. They would need every man available to them, and all the skill and concentration that they could muster.

Elizabeth went out on deck at high noon with the heavy Dent sextant held in both hands, to sight the sun. She knew without looking that every member of the crew who was on watch turned for an instant from whatever job he was doing, to look up at her, and she could hear, without hearing, the whispers and hoarse words of appreciation: "There she is! There's Mrs. Rogers!"

She spent the rest of the day below, with little Anne. She read aloud to the baby, and sang her songs, and played games, and told her stories about heroic seamen and great passages. Anne fell asleep in her lap that evening, and Elizabeth cradled her, rocked her, and hugged her, before tucking her gently in bed.

✎Chapter Nineteen

Wednesday, February 24, 1875, fifty-five days at sea

First part—light, baffling airs. Cloudy, misty weather and a falling barometer. Midnight—it commenced blowing heavy and increased to a heavy gale from SSE. Trimmed sail, still made good progress, considering conditions. Helmsman M. Cakars injured but not seriously. If things don't get worse we should come through fine and make good time.

Wales copied down the page full of figures that were Elizabeth's logarithmic calculations, feeling an odd but unmistakable tension as he did, and the final accounting: "Made seventy-one miles."

It had been a brutal night. Both watches were piped on deck at midnight when the squall hit, and they worked throughout the night. The wind whipped through rigging, and tore loose stays, pins, ratlines. Sailors worked feverishly to keep the decks cleared, under Whiteurs' direction. Harris stood by the helmsman, transmitting steering commands from Wales and seeing that they were carried out. His pink cheeks were red from the lashing of the weather, and crusted with salt. Dowling paced the main deck, barking out orders, sending the most sure-handed and sure-footed seamen aloft, as Wales stood on the bridge.

He was watching the masts carefully. They were straining, but they were holding and they could still take more strain if the wind increased. The *Wind* was fighting the gale, and holding her own; she could still make time through it. The topgallant sails were reefed, but the topsails were all still out, and the ship was still running. He signaled to Harris to take her off wind a little, and then a little more. The winds were still baffling, and it was necessary to make constant adjustments to hold to a course that the ship could sail to.

The seas rose and fell in giant, sudden eruptions, and the *Wind* went from peaks to troughs with dizzying suddenness. A thirty-foot wave loomed high over the stern of the ship, and broke over it. It smashed into the helmsman's back with the force of a load of bricks, and drove him forward into the wheel. When the wave had cleared, the ship's stern still rode above the water, but the helmsman lay unconscious, his jaw broken, the wheel spinning back and forth, crazily, out of control.

Harris, who had also been knocked off his feet by the wave, and several yards across the deck, pulled himself back up and raced over to the wheel. He stood in front of it for a moment, trying to gauge the speed and force of its thrashing, then grabbed it.

"Careful!" Wales shouted. "Don't break your arm off!" But the mate wrestled the wheel back under control.

"Good lad!" Wales called back to him. "Now hard a-port! Hard a-port!"

Harris could not restrain a fleeting grin at his captain's approval; then his face was all strain again, as he carried out the order.

"Reef the upper topsails!"

"Reef the upper topsails, you swabs!" shouted Dowling, and men leaped to the ratlines to carry out the order. Harris straddled the unconscious helmsman, pressing the man from both sides with his boots to keep him from being washed overboard, and struggled with the wheel. Gradually, he brought the ship about, as the masts bent and groaned under the strain, and waves crashed over the side.

"Hold her steady! Steady as she goes!"

"Steady as she goes, sir!" Harris's voice was strong and proud.

"Get a man up here to help! We've got an injured man here!"

But the sailor with the broken jaw was stirring. Moaning, he rose to his feet.

"Take the wheel, sailor!" shouted Wales. The sailor nodded in acknowledgment, unable to talk, and resumed his post.

"Put out those upper topsails! Main topsail . . . fore topsail!" Wales shouted down to Dowling.

"Main topsail—fore topsail, sir!" called out Dowling, and set to it.

"No!"

Wales turned around, startled. Elizabeth was standing next to him on the bridge.

"My God, what are you doing here?" he asked in surprise. "You should be below."

"I'm all right, Wales. But it's too soon—you can't be crowding sail now. If the wind comes out steadier behind us, you'd have a chance, but this—"

"Elizabeth, I haven't time! I think you should go below."

Elizabeth was silent, and Wales turned his attention back to the wind and the waves. But Elizabeth stayed up on deck.

She felt she belonged. At the same time, she felt the thrill of doing something forbidden, something she had never done before. Certainly never on her father's ships—he would never have stood for such a thing. But on her father's ships she had been a child. Now she was a grown woman—"our ship" Wales had said when they began the voyage—and her judgment was as good as anyone's could be.

She decided not to think about the thrill, and forced herself instead to concentrate on the plight of the ship. It was serious, she told herself, perhaps more serious than Wales realized. He should be concerned with riding out the storm in one piece, not making time and distance—not at a moment as precarious as this.

The wind and water pried with cold, wet fingers inside the flaps of Elizabeth's foul-weather gear, leaving her wet and freezing all over, so that her bones ached. She stood

175

with her back pressed against the wall of the deckhouse, for what little protection it gave her against the howling wind and crashing sea. She was back out of Wales's way—and out of his field of vision. She was not sure if he knew she was still on deck. But, after all, he had not *ordered* her below.

Her hands were wrapped into fists, her fingers holding onto each other for dear life—she knew how many sailors had lost fingers to frostbite and gangrene around the Horn.

"Put out the mizzen topsail!"

"Put out the mizzen topsail, sir!"

"Oh, my God, no!"

She did not know if Wales had heard her exclamation. He seemed to stiffen, and half-turn in her direction. But then he continued shouting his orders down to the deck, and did not look around.

Ritter, the steward, brought hot coffee to the saloon. There was a momentary lull in the storm. Wales drank his coffee standing up, afraid of giving way to fatigue if he sat down. The hot steam of the black coffee softened his frozen beard and eyebrows, and made his face sting as the numbness began to leave it.

"Anything to eat, sir? Some soup?" asked Ritter, his guttural German voice low and solicitous.

"No . . . nothing," muttered Wales distractedly.

"You should keep up your strength, sir," said Ritter.

"Don't worry about my strength," said Wales. "My strength is all right."

"Yes, sir. And you, Mrs. Rogers? Some soup?"

Ritter's voice was solicitous to her, too, but it was different. There was an overtone that Elizabeth could not at first identify, it was so long since she had heard it—especially since the rescue of Alexander Mapp.

But then she recognized it for what it was. It was disapproval. Ritter was not saying the words aloud, but he clearly did not feel that Elizabeth had any place on deck in a gale.

Elizabeth felt strange, now that she was back below decks. Suddenly it seemed crazy to have been up there, standing on the bridge in the teeth of a gale . . . for what? She had gone above without thinking; it had seemed so

176

natural and so important while she was there, as though it were something she did all the time, as though it was expected of her.

She had followed Wales down. He had not even had to order her—there was no question of her staying up on deck without him. And because of that, she felt less strong, less independent, and much less sure of her right. She stood close to the wall, holding her steaming, bitter black coffee, and wishing that Ritter had not called attention to her.

"Mrs. Rogers?"

"No . . . no, thank you, Ritter," she said.

"Elizabeth, you can't come back up on the bridge till this storm blows over," Wales said to her.

"I can take care of myself, Wales," she said. "Really I can. I've done it before, you know."

"I know, I know. Of course. When you were three years old. Everybody knows that story. But you shouldn't have then, and you can't now. Besides, what about the baby? What about taking care of Anne? Don't you care about making sure that she's well cared for?"

"Of course I care! But she has Jennie."

"And the ship has me!"

Elizabeth's eyes widened at Wales's sudden vehemence.

"But, Wales," she said, the words rushing out of her before she had time to think or stop them, "I should be able to help. I have a right. I know a lot about running a ship. You ought to listen to me. There's a time for crowding sail and a time for holding back, believe me! And there are things that I can sense before they happen! I can tell you things! My father—"

"Elizabeth, that's enough! There's only room for one captain on a bridge, and on this ship, for better or worse, that's me. Not you, and *not your father!* I'm not going to argue with you anymore. Now please stay down here, and don't bother me on deck. You're only one more thing that I have to worry about. And get some rest—you need it."

He drained the rest of his coffee in one gulp and strode back to the companionway without looking around. Elizabeth stayed leaning against the wall, feeling chastised, angry, and ashamed.

"Will you want more coffee, Mrs. Rogers?" asked Ritter. She did not answer him, and he cleared away the big metal pot. Elizabeth went back into the captain's stateroom and took off her mackintosh and boots.

Her clothes were soaking wet, and she removed them, too, putting them to dry in front of the coal stove that Ritter had stoked up. She was still shivering with cold, and she still felt wet all over. There were goose bumps all over her body.

She took a large, rough towel, and rubbed her body vigorously, drying herself and restoring her circulation.

She was suddenly very conscious of her body. *Strange*, she thought, it was the first time she had been so aware of her nakedness since her teenage years. She touched her breast. *Soft*. A woman's body, still, under those heavy high boots, and the India rubber mackintosh that sailors wore. She began to cry. At first it was tears rolling down her cheeks, apparently no different from the salt spray that had covered them just a few minutes earlier. Then there followed soft cries, and then deep, racking sobs. She did not know why she was crying. She decided to get dressed, and go visit her daughter.

Anne, by now used to the noises and movement of the sea, was sleeping through the storm. Jennie Speaker was not. She would not even put on her nightdress, for fear that disaster might force her to flee the cabin at any moment. She lay fully dressed, curled up in a tight knot on her bed.

When the great, rumbling noise came from somewhere below her, deep in that part of the ship that she never thought of, she sat straight up in her bed, filled with a nameless terror. She did not think she could move if her life depended on it. But when the cabin floor suddenly tilted at a sharp, crazy angle, she threw herself out of bed to catch little Anne and save her from being flung out of her trundle bed and across the room. When she held the toddler in her arms, she looked around her and saw that the cabin was now practically on its side. She did not know what was happening, and she screamed, "Mrs. Rogers! Mrs. Rogers!"

Thomas Dowling heard the noise, and knew what it was. He grabbed a rope, cursing and preparing grimly for the starboard list that he knew would follow, thinking ahead to the hellish task that waited to be performed, if the ship survived at all.

The cargo was shifting! The merciless pounding of the waves against the port side had affected its balance, and the center of gravity of the heavy manufactured goods that had lain stable and centered in the hold, was now sliding over to starboard, and the ship with it. Wales tried to come about, but there was no way to check the momentum. There was nothing to do. Nothing that Wales could do but wait for the slide to end, and pray that the heavy crates would not stave a hole in the side of the ship.

Elizabeth, buttoning up her dress, was flung bodily across the cabin. She hit heavily against the wall, and sank to her knees, clutching her shoulder.

The throbbing pain she felt was superceded by outrage. Her mind was racing. She had a sense that she was thinking very clearly, though she could not have said exactly what the thoughts were. She only knew that something had to be done. Fighting off the pain, she found her boots and mackintosh where the impact had hurled them, and struggled into them once again.

The lantern in the saloon danced and rattled and went out as she came out of her stateroom, leaving the outer room in darkness. But instinctively, in the gloom and the crazy pitch of the flooring, she headed straight for the companionway.

The iron door of the small heating stove in Jennie's cabin sprang open, and three glowing coals rolled out. Jennie watched with stupefied fascination as they rolled across the floor like wheels on some Satanic pull toy, and came to rest at the edge of Anne's trundle bed. Jennie stumbled, fell, and scrambled around to the edge of the bed. She batted at a red-hot coal with her open hand. It bounced away, and rolled right back again, leaving Jennie with searing pain and blackened, blistered fingers.

Desperate, she unlaced her boot and pulled it off, ignoring the pain in her hand that grew more intense with every tug on the bootlace. The coals were resting against the sheet that hung over the side of the bed, and they had already eaten a large, smoking hole out of it. Jennie's mind was riveted on the coals. She did not think of moving the sheet away from them, only of getting them away from the sheet. She batted at them with the heel of her boot, and they sprang away, only to roll back, still glowing red-hot as they were fanned by the constant movement.

Anne cowered at the head of the bed, crying, "Mama! Mama!" Jennie screamed too, as she batted wildly, over and over again, as though she were playing a game that had gone hysterically out of control and could not be stopped.

Finally, one coal skittered sideways, past the bed, and rolled to rest in the downward corner of the room, near the door. Then a second was cleared. There was only one coal left, and Jennie could push this one with the heel of her boot, over to the corner of the bed, where it could roll free to the wall like the others.

But it was too late. With a flourish, the sheet went up in flames.

And Anne was still on the bed! She was flattening herself against the wall, trying to keep as far away as she could from the fire that spread toward her, lapping up the sheet as it came, building a wall of flame between her and the despairing eyes and reaching arms of Jennie.

"Jennie!"

"I'm coming, darling!" Jennie ran around the corner of the flames, reached over, and scooped up the terrified child. Together, they fell to the floor in the corner of the room, with Anne clinging to Jennie's neck.

"I want my mama," Anne sobbed.

"We'll find her," said Jennie. "We've got to . . . get out of here." She suddenly felt too weak to move. She put her hand to the floor to push herself up, and now the pain was too much. Her arm crumpled beneath her.

And the fire seemed to be closer to her than the bed.

She looked down, and saw the hem of her dress smoldering. She was sitting up against the coals that she had knocked into the corner!

Jennie screamed. With her good hand, she stretched up for the doorknob, but just as her hand closed around it, the door opened from outside, and the bulky figure of Ritter appeared in the doorway.

Jennie thrust Anne into his arms, and started to scramble to her feet.

"No—don't move," he said, putting a hand on her shoulder. He swung Anne around, and set her down outside the cabin. "Don't worry, dear one," he said to her. "And wait right here."

Anne did not stir. She stood in the doorway, in the very spot where Ritter had placed her. The steward kept his restraining hand on Jennie's shoulder as he stomped out the smoldering edge of her dress.

"Now go," he told her when it was out. "Or can you help?"

Jennie opened and closed her mouth, but no words came out, only a squeak. She shook her head.

"All right. You've done well. See to the baby," said Ritter. He ran to the head of the bed, flipped the mattress over upside down on the floor, and smothered the fire, stomping out the tongues of flame that came up around the edges. When it was subdued, he moved on, panting, to the stove, and got the door closed and latched.

Face blackened, eyebrows singed, the steward looked around the room. It was safe, now—safe from fire, anyway. He stepped back out into the passageway, to see to the little girl and the young woman who cared for her.

Jennie had fainted dead away. Anne sat next to her, stroking her temple and saying plaintively, "Wake up, Jennie. Wake up, Jennie, please."

"Don't worry, dear one," said Ritter, picking up Anne and holding her against his soot-stained cheek. "She's all right. Everything will be all right."

The rumble of the ship was louder and more menacing than the roar of the wind by the time Elizabeth came up on deck. The ship was settling slowly over onto its side, and the yards dipped so low they were almost in the water. The sailors who were still aloft were no longer high in the air, but almost at eye level with the bridge, and far out over the ocean. They were scrambling back down the masts now, as the yards were far too precarious to risk any more work.

A wave reached up and took the foretop and topgallant yards, snapping them as though they were icicles. Elizabeth slipped and slid across the deck, finally reaching Wales's side on her hands and knees. She pulled herself up and hung onto the railing next to him.

"Do something!" she hissed at him.

"There's nothing to do," he said.

The ship tipped farther. The yards were touching the water now, and the vessel was almost completely on its side, the deck virtually perpendicular to the ocean.

"Cut the masts!" Elizabeth said. "It'll work—it's our only chance! Their weight is carrying us down. They're going to drag us under!"

"I don't think so," said Wales wearily.

"You don't think so!" Elizabeth pounded the rail with her fist. The ship lurched and she almost slid down into Wales, but she clutched the railing tightly and kept her distance from him. "What kind of man are you? Are you just going to stand there and let the ship go down? This is no time for indecision—we've got to do something!"

Wales turned away from her.

"Mr. Harris!"

Harris made his way over to the rail. "Yes, sir?"

"Take Mrs. Rogers down to her cabin. She's to remain there for the duration of the Cape Horn passage."

Elizabeth stared at him. "You're putting me under cabin arrest?"

"If you want to look at it that way, yes." He did not flinch from the accusation. Harris stood by, looking as though he would rather be anywhere else in the world, even out at the end of the mast, than where he was.

"Mr. Harris," said Wales.

"Never mind, Mr. Harris," said Elizabeth. "I'll go myself. I know better than to take an officer away from his post during an emergency."

Harris looked at Wales, who nodded. Elizabeth started for the companionway on her own.

"If we ever get around Cape Horn, and I ever see you again, I'll never forgive you for this," she called back to Wales. "But with you in command, we'll never make it."

❧Chapter Twenty

DOWLING SAW THE CAPTAIN ORDER HIS WIFE off the bridge. He saw Harris cross over, and stand facing the two of them. He saw the captain's wife shake her head, motion Harris away, and start to leave the bridge by herself. He was sure that he could imagine accurately what had been going on between them.

Son of a bitch, he thought. *Looks like the old man finally told her off. I didn't know the bugger had it in him.*

He kept watching, out of the corner of his eye, as she turned and shouted a parting shot back at the captain. He could not hear her words or even the inflection of her voice from his distance, above the roar of the storm and the ship, but he could recognize the flash of her eyes. *He can't keep her down*, thought Dowling. *He doesn't have what she needs. But if we live long enough . . .*

There was no guarantee of that. The ship lay virtually on its side. But it had stopped tilting. The rumble of shifting cargo was heard no more, and even though the winds still howled, the air seemed almost silent. And, gradually the storm was blowing itself out.

They were still afloat, but immobilized. Unless they could right the ship, they could do nothing but drift aimlessly, and wait to be skewered and split apart by an iceberg, or blown to pieces by the next burst of fury from the storm.

"Mr. Dowling!" called the captain.

Dowling had been expecting it. He knew what had to be done, and he knew it would end up on his shoulders. Well, what the hell. He was the toughest sea dog on this voyage, and no mistake. He'd see it done right.

"Yes, sir."

"Take a detail of men down in the hold."

"Aye, aye, sir."

Dowling ran quickly over the men in his watch. He'd have to use the biggest, toughest sailors of the lot for this job, and none other. They would have to go down into the hold and shift back every barrel and crate, until the ship was back on an even keel. They were huge, heavy, bulky things—sewing machines, Scotch whiskey, varnish, wagon tongues, apple cider from New England, bags of cement from Rosendale, New York. There were, Dowling remembered with grim humor, twenty-three crates full of silver-handled caskets. Well, they'd not be needing them. Burial at sea would be their fate, every man jack of them. Together now, or separately, someday.

"I'll take Gallatin, Clifton, Hergesheimer, Lewicki, Naulls, Fontinato, Braun," he snarled. "I've got some fun for you swabs. We're going to get out of the weather for a while. We're going below."

They had all worked cargo often enough before, yet never had the sea seemed so close to them. The planking underneath them felt more like a thin membrane than the sturdy wall of a ship. They worked silently, no sea chantey to set the rhythm as there would have been up on deck, no talking to each other, only a few muttered curses that became hollow, muffled echoes which seemed to mock and curse back at them. The only voice they heard was Dowling's, harsh and driving, yet precise as a surgeon in his orders. The crates had to be moved by degrees, stacked securely and then moved on, gradually shifting the center of gravity back to the center of the ship. They worked by flickering lantern light, fortunate at least that there was nothing flammable or explosive in the hold.

Dowling drove them, and himself, relentlessly. But as he

184

worked in the gloom and must at the center of the ship, as his eyes measured the cargo, the space, the danger, as his voice kept a cadence of cursing and reviling and commands, another part of his mind worked independently. That part conjured up a glistening, wet face, with tendrils of ash-brown hair clinging to smooth, strong cheeks and a delicate brow. And the vision—clear even from halfway across the ship—of a flash like lightning shooting from eyes the gray-green color of the turbulent sea.

The men were sailors. They were no strangers to the hold, but they hated it. They were at home in the rigging, on the main deck, open to the elements and under the sky. Too much time in the hold was making them claustrophobic, but there was no relief. Both watches were on constant duty until the emergency was passed, and there was no time to be lost.

They could feel the ship moving imperceptibly under their feet, shifting back to a slightly less radical angle. But the hole still slanted crazily under their feet, the waves still pounded near them, and the thudding boxes still crashed around them in the airless gloom.

It was Karl Braun, the biggest man of the crew, a six-foot, four-inch German, who felt the strain most. Dowling knew it, and he was ready when Braun finally snapped. When the German's head began to twitch on his thick neck, and his hands began to tremble, Dowling was in front of him.

Braun dropped the crate he was lifting. He made a move to run, and discovered that the first mate was right there. Braun stopped. His whole body was trembling now. Dowling caught his eye with a look that pierced his hysteria like a beacon.

"Pick it up, Braun," he said. "And get back to work. There'll be no slacking here."

A wordless wail came from Braun's throat. His body stopped trembling and coalesced into a weapon of rage as he hurled himself at Dowling.

The mate's left fist traveled no more than nine inches. It caught the German in the solar plexus, and Braun's fearsome drive spattered, his arms flying out from his side, fingers open. Dowling's second punch built fluidly from the first. His right arm swung in an arc powered by his body's momentum, and smashed full into Braun's jaw, sending him down in a heap away from the boxes.

The seaman lay inert for a long moment. As he started to stir, Dowling picked him up by the top of his shirt, held him against the wall, and slapped him three or four times in quick succession across the face.

"Ready to get back to work, Braun?" he said.

"*Ja*," said the sailor thickly.

"Then get to it. And that goes for the rest of you fuckers, too. Break's over."

Ritter met Elizabeth at the foot of the companionway.

"Your daughter and Miss Speaker are waiting for you in the captain's cabin, Mrs. Rogers," he said in his most formal tone.

"I can't go in there," she said.

"Madam?"

"I said I can't go in there. I'm under arrest. Cabin arrest. I'll be in the first passengers' stateroom. Please bring my personal belongings in there for me, Ritter."

The steward's face betrayed no surprise. He was completely impassive. "Yes, madam."

"Why are Miss Speaker and the baby in the captain's cabin, anyway?" asked Elizabeth, the strangeness of the situation finally hitting her.

Ritter told her in an emotionless monotone, as though he were reciting a lesson in front of a class at school. Elizabeth understood the point: not that Ritter felt no concern, but that he would not believe that she did, and would not share his with her.

"I see," said Elizabeth. "Well, tell them to come and join me in the passengers' stateroom. I'm sure that Captain Rogers will not forbid me to have visitors, though you can clear it with him if you think it necessary."

"I am quite certain it will not be necessary, madam," replied Ritter stiffly.

"I'm afraid it's not working, sir."

"Frightened, aren't you, lad?" Wales looked with sympathy into the eyes of the second mate, whose ashen face looked haggard and old, and impossibly young, at the same time.

"I'm scared to death, sir," admitted Ben Harris. "I'm afraid we're done for."

Ten hours after the job had been started, the ship seemed as far over on its side as it had ever been. Wales was still on the bridge, holding onto the breastrail. Whiteurs was beside him; Harris had just joined them.

"The barometer?"

"Falling again, sir."

Wales pursed his lips and made no reply.

"Shouldn't we send someone below to check up on Mr. Dowling's crew, sir?" Harris asked. "They might be in trouble. They might all be dead."

"And doing nothing?" Wales asked. "You feel nothing? You hear nothing?"

Harris shook his head sadly.

"They're working," said Wales. He was silent, then, straining forward with the attitude of a man listening for something, although no sounds carried from the hold. He shifted his weight, as though testing for something: first to one leg, then the other, then back to an equal balance. He stayed alert with all his senses, though Harris could still not detect a thing.

"We'll get through, Mr. Harris," he said at last. "I believe you'll even live long enough to become a sailor. You've done well."

"Thank you, sir," said Harris. "But . . ."

"You still don't feel anything."

"N-no, sir."

"And you, Mr. Whiteurs?"

Whiteurs nodded his head. "Lighter," he said.

Harris looked back and forth from one to the other—the young, steel-visaged captain, the ageless Negro with heavy-lidded eyes that were a veil, behind which lay more knowledge of the sea than the boy could imagine—with wonder and disbelief.

"Mr. Whiteurs, go down below and warn Mr. Dowling," said Wales. "Mr. Harris, give the order to raise the upper main topsail and main topgallant."

"Sir?"

"Look sharp, Mr. Harris!" Wales's voice was brusque and commanding again. "Give the order!"

* * *

The sail caught the wind, and the ship sprang forward with a lurch. Rudderless, she began to move in an arc, like a giant gear beginning to turn; but as the sail filled, the mast seemed to surge up to meet the wind. The rumble came again from the hold—the cargo was sliding back into place, and the ship was standing upright again!

Wales took the helm himself, and as soon as the rudder dipped back into the water, he brought the ship about before the wind, and held her on course as she began her strange and majestic roll upright.

"Hold on, you lubbers! We're going to ride her back," commanded Dowling. He and his crew crouched on top of the outer edge of the pile of crates, resting on their hands and the balls of their feet, ready to spring away. They felt the tug of the ship, and watched as the boxes beneath them, which they had labored ten hours to bring to the lip of success, began to slide the rest of the way under their own momentum.

As the slide began, they cheered, but their cheers were drowned out in the rumble of the moving crates. The sound reverberated throughout the closed-in hold, and as they scrambled for safety, no other sound could be heard above it for several moments.

Then, as the rumble faded, another sound began: a scream. A huge crate had fallen sideways, and able seaman Lewicki was pinned under it. The box lay across his thigh, just above the knee, and his leg had certainly been crushed.

Dowling vaulted over the cargo to the side of the screaming crewman. He lifted the box and held it six inches off Lewicki's leg.

Dowling had moved so quickly that it seemed an eternity in which he stood, holding up the side of the crate, before the others caught up with him and dragged the man to safety.

The strain of holding it was so great that he had not even been able to curse, but once Lewicki was freed and he had set the crate back down, he began. In even tones, like a steady rainfall that can keep falling all day and night, he defamed the ancestry of every member of the work gang, their possible unspeakable sexual practices with each other, with their close relatives, with each other's close relatives, with donkeys and trees and the bungholes of the ship's water casks; he ascribed to them obscene and estraordinary anatomical characteristics, and he threw in several vile but astounding irrelevancies. In the same breath, he ordered them back to work.

"Stack those crates that fell back in place, and fasten the lot down! And if I don't like the job you've done, I'll manacle every mother-swiving one of you to the side of a crate, and see what happens to your scurvy bones the next time the cargo shifts."

Lewicki moaned, too agonized to talk.

"You've got a broken leg, sailor," said Dowling. "Don't worry, it'll stay broke till we get out of here. Now let's get this job done, you monkey-assed sons of bitches!"

He paused for a moment, and looked at the crate he had pulled off Lewicki's leg. "Six silver-handled, oak caskets," he read. "Too good for you, sailor. Braun, Gallatin, Hergesheimer—let's lift this fucker up and get it out of here."

❦Chapter Twenty-one

THE FARTHER AWAY SHE WAS FROM PEOPLE, the easier it seemed to be for them to appreciate her. Elizabeth was a heroine in the fo'c'sle. The story of her rescue of Mapp had become legend overnight. It was the kind of story that spreads as if by magic—carried on the wind, on the wings of gulls, by the spirits of the deep, so that by the time she reached San Francisco, she would somehow already be legendary there: people would be pointing and whispering as she disembarked, and men would be lifting their glasses in toasts to her valor in sailors' bars all along the Barbary Coast. The men of the *Western Wind*, meanwhile, were telling and retelling their versions of the stories of Mrs. Rogers and the giant wave, Mrs. Rogers and the *Spirit of the Waves'* assault on the *Flying Cloud*'s record. They were almost as fanciful as the stories that Elizabeth had invented for herself at one time, but the sailors repeated them as gospel. The fo'c'slemen worshipped her.

Not so the people she saw every day. She knew that Ritter, for one, hated her. She had been forced to see him six times a day, throughout the week that it had taken them to complete the Cape Horn run—the week of her imprisonment. He brought her meals to her cabin, and took the trays away. He was always completely formal. There was never a hint of sympathy in his manner, and his disapproval was so obvious that there was not even any need for him to express it. He seemed to be saying by his demeanor that this was the condition she deserved. Ritter was her jailer, and she hated him with the steady, implacable hatred that is reserved only for jailers.

Jennie came in to visit her every day, and brought the baby. Jennie tactfully never referred to the fact that Mrs. Rogers was confined to her quarters, and whenever she made an accidental allusion to it, she became so embarrassed and flustered that she could not go on at all. And at those times Elizabeth, though she felt guilty about it, would sullenly and willfully withhold any reassurance from the girl.

Jennie had looked up to Elizabeth at one time, practically idolized her. Now . . . now Jennie treated her in the same way, with the same outward respect; but it was not the same.

Jennie idolized Wales. Whenever she visited with Elizabeth in her cabin, throughout the Cape Horn passage, she would go on and on about Wales—what a great captain he was, what command he had over the ship, how it responded to him. Elizabeth could never quite believe that Jennie did not know how darkly, vengefully angry those accounts made her. But then, Elizabeth herself never realized just why Jennie's devotion caused the resentment that ate away at her as deeply and insidiously as it did: Jennie felt the same reverence for Wales that Elizabeth Creighton had felt for her father.

Anne always seemed to look forward to visiting her mother. Elizabeth was afraid that her daughter would resent her for not being there when the fire broke out. Ritter had told her, with smug satisfaction, how Anne had cried out, "Mama! Mama!" in vain. But there was no sign of resentment or holding back from the child. She climbed into Elizabeth's lap, she threw her arms around her mother's neck. She told her long stories of things she had learned about the ship. She told Elizabeth all about her dolls' adventures on shipboard: "Dolly's not a good sailor, like you and me. But I scold her. I tell her if she doesn't learn how to behave aboard ship, she'll have to be sent home."

Anne never asked why her mama was no longer living in

her papa's cabin, or why she never came to see her in the nursery, and Elizabeth never brought it up, either. Wales had, in fact, sent word below that Elizabeth should be permitted complete freedom to leave her cabin to go and visit in Anne and Jennie's cabin, but Elizabeth had sent word back that she chose not to do so. She was a woman of honor, she said, even when her honor had been called into question by others. She would not violate the terms of her arrest.

"Terms of her arrest!" exploded Wales when Ritter brought him the message. "The hell with her, then. Let her stay there and rot, for all I care."

Ritter nodded, and disappeared below. Wales almost followed. His heart ached for Elizabeth, and he wanted to go talk to her, and explain to her what he had meant. He wanted to hold her in his arms, and reassure her that he still thought she was special, that he still loved her, that he still wanted her as his partner on this voyage. But there was no time.

There was no time for thirty hours. Wales was on the bridge, battling through the new gale which had blown up, trying to keep the ship on an even keel with half his yards on one side destroyed. He took an hour and a half for sleep in the middle of those thirty, and that was all. Jennie served him coffee before he went back up on deck—Ritter was sleeping and Wales had decided not to wake him. He had been about to go to the galley and get it himself, when Jennie appeared at the door of her stateroom. She was wearing a long dressing gown and bedroom slippers, and her auburn hair was loose, falling around her shoulders and halfway down her back.

"Oh, Captain Rogers," she said. "I'm sorry . . . I know I don't look very proper."

"Don't be silly, Jennie, you're perfectly presentable," said Wales blearily. "This is a ship's saloon, not a Boston parlor, and it's the middle of the night. Besides, I still can't see straight anyway. I'm just going to get some coffee and go back up on deck."

"You sit down. I'll get the coffee," Jennie said. "No, I mean it." As Wales put up his hand to decline her offer, and took another lurching step toward the kitchen, Jennie ran around in front of him. She put her hands on his chest to stop him, then lowered them immediately, and stood before him, blushing, tugging her robe even more tightly around her body. "I mean it," she said. "I'm up anyway, so there. I'll get your coffee. It'll just take a minute. I'll be glad to do it. I can get to the galley and back. You sit down. You need it. I'll be back. You sit here. I'll be back."

She bobbed back and forth as she talked and repeated herself, starting out of the room, then stopping for another breathless sentence. Finally, she broke off completely, looked at the captain's face for a moment, then whirled and ran.

It was only after she had dashed into the pantry that Wales permitted himself a smile, and then a weary chuckle.

Jennie was back in a few minutes, with a large pot of coffee and two mugs. "I guess I'll have some, too," she said apologetically. "Since it's here. I'm a little cold. I need to get warmed up."

"Of course," said Wales.

They sat opposite each other and drank their coffee in silence. Wales, preoccupied with the ship's problems, was vaguely aware that Jennie wanted to say something to him, but he did not have the time or inclination to give it much concern. Whatever it was, she did not say it.

All that she did say, as Wales was draining the last of his mug, was: "I never drank black coffee before I went to sea, but now I—"

"Yes, it's a life with little room for the shore luxuries," said Wales.

"—but now I really like it like this. I doubt if I could drink it with cream and sugar anymore."

Wales smiled at her again. "Oh, don't say that, now, Jennie," he teased. "You don't want to start liking this sea life too much. Thank you for the coffee." He stood up, now fully alert, and headed back up on deck. Jennie watched him go, then picked up the mugs and pot and carried them back out to the pantry.

Wales woke up from five hours' sleep, the most he had allowed himself since the Cape Horn passage had begun. He washed, trimmed the ends of his beard, and put on a clean pair of East Indian pajama trousers and a woolen

194

jersey. He told himself that there was nothing unusual in this. After all, the gale had blown over, the emergency was past. He had finally taken himself off watch—why not clean up a little, if it would make him feel fresher and more comfortable? He'd work better for it.

He had never bothered, with such niceties while going around the Horn before.

He knocked at the door of Elizabeth's cabin.

"Who is it?"

"Wales."

"You can come in," she said. "How could I stop you? The door's not locked—not from the inside, anyway."

Wales pushed the door open, and stood in the doorway. The stateroom had one chair and a small table, both fastened to the floor, and an austere, narrow bed in the corner. It had been designed as a passenger's cabin, and a few homey touches had been added to it—a sampler on the wall, a flowered spread on the bed. All these had been removed by Elizabeth. The room was bare and Spartan now, Wales noted, like a monk's cell. Like a cell. Elizabeth sat in the chair. She was dressed formally, and her ash-brown hair was tied primly in a bun at the back of her head. Wales closed the door behind him and took three strides into the room. He stood stiff-legged, with his hands behind his back, back to the wall, and cleared his throat. He looked like a schoolmaster and like a schoolboy at the same time, and when he spoke, his voice managed to be both stern and nervous.

"Elizabeth, I . . . I hope you understand why I had to do what I did."

"You are the captain," said Elizabeth. "Your word is law aboard this ship. I understand that well enough. This is not my first shipboard experience, if you remember."

"I know, but I'm also your husband, and—"

"It seems it's impossible for you to be both." Elizabeth's voice was cold, forbidding and final. She looked straight at Wales, with an expression that seemed to say there was not enough between them that was personal to make her feel uncomfortable looking into his eyes. She was saying he was not worth her turning her head away. Wales felt it, and desperation welled up in him.

"Elizabeth, for God's sake, of course I can be both! It's

not turning away from you if I'm concerned with saving the ship."

"From me? Saving the ship from me?"

"Oh, no, of course not, that's not what I meant."

"But that's what you did, isn't it?"

"If that's what it seemed like, I apologize."

"There's no need for apologies. In fact, it's hardly proper for a man in your position to be going around offering apologies, is it? That seems somehow distasteful to me. I believe that if a man—especially a man who wants to think of himself as captain of a deepwater vessel—makes a decision, he should be prepared to stand by it."

Wales was too confounded to reply. Elizabeth gauged his confusion, and the moment before he was ready to answer her coherently, she began again.

"I assume, now, that I am still under arrest. Or have we rounded the Horn?" She got up, went over to the porthole, and looked out. "No, it still looks like the Cape passage. Bleak, isn't it? And yet it has a majesty all its own. You couldn't call it beauty, exactly. A land God forgot. But it is compelling. Once seen, one would never forget it. I never have. I have never seen it from quite this vantage point before. But then, I was never a prisoner on my father's ship."

Before he could speak, she whirled from the porthole to face him, dark anger in her eyes. "Haven't you something better to do, *Captain*? Shouldn't you be up on deck? Or is the ship running so well that it can get by without either of us for the remainder of the Cape run?"

"I had hoped you wouldn't be so vindictive," said Wales. She smiled sweetly. "*I'm* not being vindictive," she said.

"I have to go back up on deck," said Wales.

"Go then," replied Elizabeth.

Wales started to say something more, thought better of it, nodded stiffly, and went out.

Elizabeth felt nothing after Wales had left. After a while it began to seem odd to her that she felt nothing, when she realized that she had been standing in front of the porthole, not looking out, for a long time. She did not know how long she had been standing there, or what she had been looking at, or what, if anything, had been on her mind.

❧Chapter Twenty-two

WHEN THE SHIP ENTERED THE SOUTH PACIFIC
Ocean, Elizabeth came out of her cabin and went up on
deck. She did not talk to Wales, or acknowledge his presence on the bridge. She walked over to the taffrail and
looked out astern, putting her hand to her forehead and
squinting off into the distance, as if trying to retrace the
Cape Horn passage with her eyes. She walked forward,
onto the main deck, smiling and waving at the several
nearby sailors. She acknowledged the greetings, the good-
will of the fo'c'slemen. Then she went below, back to her
adopted cabin.

She continued taking her meals there, not joining Wales
and the other officers at their mess. She took a perverse
satisfaction out of the arrangement. She liked the idea of
being conspicuous by her absence. And she liked the idea
that the one person on ship with whom she had the most
contact—outside of her daughter—was the man who disliked her most. Ritter still brought her all her meals, and
took away the trays. He was Wales's man, and she made
him interchangeable with Wales in her mind. She allowed
herself to think of Ritter's dislike and disapproval as a
proxy for Wales's feelings, and that made it all the easier
for her to keep alive her smoldering resentment.

Wales never tried to talk to her on deck. He was afraid

to, she reasoned. If he were to try to approach her on deck, and she were to snub him openly, it would destroy his credibility with the crew, and undermine his authority beyond repair. *She* was the hero of the *Western Wind*, not he; she was the force to be reckoned with.

She had thought about it, and made up her mind what she would do if Wales did make a public overture to her on deck. She would be polite. She would speak to him as though there were nothing wrong between them. She would not be the one to humiliate him in public.

But she would not make any move herself, nor would she let him know her mind. Let him take the chance of making a move. If he dared.

She did not go back to doing the navigation for Wales, either. They never talked about it. He did not ask her to, or tell her not to. But Elizabeth was no longer seen sighting through the large Dent sextant on the poop deck each noon. So the crew knew, through no action of hers, that things were not the same.

Wales came to see her one night. It was late, near midnight, and she was already in bed, in the narrow cot up against the far wall of her cabin. She was half asleep. He knocked, but did not wait for an answer. He walked right in.

She was wide awake the instant she saw him, but she feigned grogginess. "What time is it?" she asked. "What do you want?"

"I just wanted to talk," he said. "I know it's late, but . . . I just wanted to talk."

"Well, it must be important, for you to be waking me up at this hour," she said. "Oh, all right, since I'm awake, what is it? I hope we discuss it quickly, and get it finished. I'm very tired."

"It's . . . it's . . . oh, I don't know, Elizabeth. I just wanted to see how you were . . . if you were all right, you know."

Elizabeth was looking at the tension in Wales's body. It was a though he were pushing up against an invisible shield that was pushing back at him, holding his arms from reaching forward, holding his body from leaning over her. She could feel his tension touching her, and it was clumsier, heavier than any sort of physical touch with his hand or body could ever have been.

If he was a real man, and he wanted me so much, he'd just take me, she thought.

"I'm all right," she said dully.

The pressure was still there. It was menacing and boring at the same time. Nothing was happening! *What is the matter with him?* she thought. *Doesn't he know that he's my husband? I couldn't refuse him. I could hate him for the rest of my life, but I couldn't refuse him.*

"Well, I'm glad you're all right," he said at last, thickly. "If there's . . . if there's anything you need, just let me know."

"I'm sure everything will go on being all right," she said. "But what I really need now is mysleep. Good night, Wales."

Wales had never visited the ship's nursery more than occasionally. He was too busy to become heavily involved in domestic matters. Now, however, his visits became a little more regular. Anne had become his only real family, or at least the only member of his family who accepted him. Wales and Elizabeth instinctively timed their visits so that neither would show up while the other one was there, and gradually they began to evolve a rough schedule.

Wales could relax in the nursery, as nowhere else on shipboard. Not that it was the job of a ship's master to relax; but this voyage was more tense than most, what with all the sailors wondering what had happened to Mrs. Rogers, the "Sailors' Angel," and grumbling that it had been a good-luck charm to see her up on the poop deck with sextant in hand, every noontime. "It'll mean bad luck," they muttered, but the superstitions of sailors are not always well-founded, and the *Western Wind* was to make it to San Francisco, the first leg of its passage, with no further serious mishaps.

The bad luck all belonged to Wales, and playing with his daughter was a welcome escape from it. He loved it when she crawled up into his lap, put her arms around his neck, and presented her fat cheeks to be kissed. Jennie relaxed him, too. She always had a kind word for him, and she seemed genuinely solicitous of his welfare.

Elizabeth, on the other hand, found that Jennie's solicitousness made her nervous. Perhaps the girl was just naturally kind-hearted, but Elizabeth had difficulty believing it. She was much more comfortable with the open hostility of Ritter. She could never quite believe that Jennie did not feel the same way about her, and she found that her visits to the nursery, though she still went every day, were becoming shorter and more formal.

Sometimes she took little Anne up on deck with her, alone, and that was easier. They went in the evening, when the weather was good. She would hold Anne up in her arms, and they would watch the sun setting over the Pacific together. Then Jennie would come up and get Anne, and take her below to bed.

After that, Elizabeth lingered in the dusk, listening to the slap of the waves against the side of the ship. It was a sound that was always there, but one only heard it in rare moments of tranquility. It was like a heartbeat. A heart kept beating every second of one's life, but how difficult it was to stay still and listen to it!

In those quiet moments, Elizabeth could almost imagine herself away from all the strain of the present, and off in another time, another place, another ship. Her father's ship. The *Union Flyer*, rugged and bold, strong and sturdy, able to carry her anywhere; the *Spirit of the Waves*, swift and dashing, with yards that scraped the horizons and a moonraker that danced with angels in a fair wind. Ships where she had been happy, where everyone had known who she was.

The ocean was the same. The gentle roll under her feet of a ship's deck on a calm tropic night was the same, soothing and sensual, like being in the arms of a lover. The moon, which shaped the changing tides and the changing hearts of men, would always be the same. And on those nights, if she kept her gaze fixed outward, far beyond the rail, she could feel that she, too, would always be the same.

The rest of the time, calm was not her natural state. Tension was. The tension of the antagonism she felt when Ritter knocked, waited for an answer, and then came into her cabin silently to leave or pick up a tray. The tension of resentment she felt when she happened to catch sight of Wales from a distance, or encounter him in a passageway.

The tension she felt about First Officer Dowling. What was that all about? He, of all people aboard the *Western Wind*, was an enigma to her. She could not tell which side he was on. Often she noticed him looking at her. His eyes were cool and ironic, but challenging. They were probing, judging; but they were detached. Did he want something from her? Did he admire her? Did he hold her in contempt? Did he think she was pretty?

Other times, she caught herself looking at him. What was she thinking? She could never be sure, because her thoughts scattered in a panic when she surprised them. Or maybe there were no thoughts. Perhaps there was just the impression of sea-swept blond hair, piercing, ice-blue eyes, a hard line of a mouth, and a hard, whiplike body. Perhaps there was no more and no less than a vision of broad, flat shoulders, a narrow waist, long, straight legs, and a bulge that was round but not soft-looking in the front of his dungaree trousers.

She met him unexpectedly one night, in the pantry off the main saloon. He was pouring himself a cup of coffee, and his back was to her. The first thing she noticed was his shoulders, and then his hips. They were poised from force of habit: alert, ready to whirl, to coil into a defensive crouch, to strike if necessary. She could imagine him with a knife in his hand. He had heard her coming before she saw him, and he had already determined who she was. He knew that no threat loomed behind him, but he was ready for anything anyway, on instinct.

His shoulders were flexed and powerful; their power took her breath away. His hips were lithe and sinuous, and their fluid grace made her feel almost dizzy. She stopped where she was, afraid to go farther, unable to turn back. He spun around slowly, languidly. He scarcely seemed to be moving, so it came as an unexpected shock that his ice-blue eyes were suddenly locked into her own.

She waited for him to be polite. She wanted him to offer her a cup of coffee, and break this sudden, gripping spell.

She stood and waited. He stood, his body poised, his mouth straight and inscrutable, the upper lip slightly flared. His gaze was bold, and he did not turn his eyes from hers. She felt that if she stood there another second, she would faint, or else just melt.

She opened her mouth, but she was afraid of what might come out of it, unbidden. She closed it, then tried again.

"Mr. Dowling, I'd love a cup of coffee too, if you wouldn't mind. I've been restless—couldn't sleep—decided I'd get up and sit for a while."

Dowling's eyes cut into her, and his lip curled back farther into a faint, ironic smile. "One of the benefits of sleeping alone, eh?" he said.

Elizabeth blushed, confused as to what he meant or what her response should be. "Yes, I . . . I suppose so," she said.

Dowling continued to regard her with the same sardonic smile. *All right*, he seemed to be saying. *Now what is it you really want?*

Elizabeth felt a sudden, rapid twitching, like a nervous tic, between her thighs. She wanted to reach down with her hand and quiet it, but she knew she could not do that. Dowling walked out of the pantry to sit at the table. He motioned with his head for her to follow him, and she did. She sat across from him. She ground her bottom, hard, into the wooden bench, but it did not still the quickening, moist sensation she felt there. It only made the feeling grow, and spread out through her body.

Elizabeth had been excited from the moment, just before she saw him, when her instinct had told her Dowling was just around the corner, but now she was starting to like the excitement. She wanted more of it. She had a strong impulse to tease him, although—or perhaps because—she knew it was a dangerous game.

"How do you like the *Wind*, Mr. Dowling?" she asked.

The question seemed to amuse him, but he answered it laconically. "She's a good ship. Trim. She carries sail well."

"Is she different from the vessels you've been used to?"

"And what kind of vessels have I been used to?"

"Well, the stories are," said Elizabeth, relishing the words, "that you have a past that one doesn't ask too many questions about."

"And there are those who'd tell you that that's the kind of warning a sensible young woman would heed."

There was a tinge of menace in his voice, but it only served to excite her further. And she knew full well that it was intended to.

"Perhaps they'd be right," she said, and paused for just a breath before asking, archly, "are the stories true?"

"What else do the stories say?"

"Well, I've heard that you spent the past several years in the China Seas."

"There are good ships in the China Seas. Fast. Maneuverable. They have to be."

"And I've heard you were the master of an opium clipper."

"You did, did you?"

His eyebrows raised slightly. Elizabeth found her center of balance shifting, making her body tilt forward toward him. Her lips were pursed out.

She came to her senses and straightened up. She hoped he had not noticed. But she knew that he had.

"Well, it is getting late, isn't it?" she said. "I imagine I could probably sleep now. Coffee doesn't affect my nerves at all. It's a good thing, too. It's nice to be able to get up . . . have a cup . . . talk a little . . . and then go off to sleep without having it affect you, isn't it?"

She was trying to decide, rationally, whether she was feeling calm or agitated. She had pictured herself casually getting up as she spoke, and clearing away her coffee cup; but she found that though she had carried out the entire action in her head, she was still sitting at the table across from him.

"Oh, to be sure," said Dowling.

"Well, it has been a pleasure. Even though you never did tell me very much about your adventures."

"What adventures?"

"Oh, go on with you! You can't expect me to believe you haven't had adventures, skippering an opium clipper in the China Seas. But, of course, you haven't admitted as much to me yet, have you?"

Dowling rose, and held up one finger toward her as a signal for her to wait. "I'll be right back," he said.

He disappeared into his cabin. Elizabeth got up from the

table, went into the pantry, and refilled both of their mugs from the huge coffeepot still hot on the stove. She held the mugs up close to her face as she brought them back. She could feel the steam, moist and warm, seeping into her pores, and she could smell the strong, sharp odor.

Dowling reappeared in the doorway, filling it with his broad shoulders, stooping slightly as he crossed the threshold. He was carrying a small parcel, wrapped in velvet that was such a pure, jet black that it stood out even against his black sweater.

He set the parcel down between them, and untied the black ribbon that held it closed. He lifted back the flap of black velvet. Inside was a long, polished teakwood pipe, the size and shape of a flute. It was a hard, shiny black against the lustrous black of the velvet, and inlaid with exotic Oriental filigree work in silver. About two-thirds of the way down the pipe was a teakwood bowl, perhaps two inches high and four inches in diameter. Its covered wooden top was flat, and had a small hole at the center. It looked as beautiful and exotic as a rare-Eastern snake.

"Is that an opium pipe?" Elizabeth asked, in hushed tones.

"Yes," said Dowling.

"Do you . . . are you an opium addict?"

He laughed, a short, terse laugh. "Not everyone who's ever smoked opium is an opium addict."

"Then you have smoked opium?"

He did not answer, but Elizabeth took the answer to be yes, and moved along to the next question.

"What's it like?"

"I couldn't describe it. You'd have to experience it for yourself."

"Oh, well, I hardly think that's very likely. Besides, where would I get it. Oh, I know you can get laudanum in any pharmacy, but that's not really the same, is it?"

"You'd have to drink a lot of laudanum to get the same effect," he agreed.

"And one would feel like such a little old lady, not at all wicked or depraved like a real opium fiend," said Elizabeth. She hesitated for a moment, and then said casually, "Do you have any on board with you?"

204

"No," he said. "I never smoke opium on shipboard. Try me ashore."

She laughed nervously. "Oh, don't be silly," she said. "But why not, if I may ask? What would happen if you smoked opium on shipboard?"

"You're asking a lot of questions, for someone who's not taking a personal interest. Let's just say opium gives you a different attitude toward duty than the one a good mate needs on a crack ship."

"Oh." Elizabeth felt oddly chastened, and suddenly realized that she was very tired. She was about to excuse herself and go back to bed, but Dowling continued.

"It makes things happen in your body. It takes away all the reasons you have for not feeling good. They aren't important anymore, and all that matters is your senses. Do you know what I mean?"

"I . . . I don't think so," stammered Elizabeth.

"Oh?" Dowling's upper lip curled back in that sardonic smile again.

Elizabeth felt her body contract. She tried not to blush, and she tried not to appear nervous. Dowling's eyes held hers as though they were lashed together.

"Perhaps not," he said. "Well, I'm going to get back up on deck. A pleasure, Mrs. Rogers."

The log read:

Friday, April 9, 1875, ninety-nine days at sea.
Moderate breezes from NE. Ship running smoothly, all hands healthy. Sighted Punta Bonita lighthouse just before sundown, Alcatraz Island lighthouse just after. A good voyage.
Latitude 34° 04′ N
Longitude 126° 10′ W
Sailed 241 miles
Made 241 miles

Ninety-nine days at sea. Forty-three days since he had slept with his wife. Close to forty since he had talked to her. Wales did not spend much of his time thinking about it, anymore. The master of a deepwater ship had precious

205

little time for reflection, which was just as well. And Wales, during the past month, had thrown himself into his work, and the challenge and satisfaction of keeping the ship moving smartly and on course. That had occupied him completely. He had driven the *Wind* in fair winds till she practically flew across the water, riding the crests of the waves, skimming over the ocean. In the doldrums of the equator, he had tacked and maneuvered, he had beaten, he had nosed her this way and that, latching onto any scrap of wind in the rigging and riding it for all it was worth. He had even welcomed with relish the two sudden squalls they had passed through, the instant decisions he had been called upon to make, the crew—his crew—working as one man to carry them out: the triumph of riding out the storm.

Only at night, alone in the double bed in his captain's quarters, did his single-mindedness waver.

It was hard to think of the business of men while he lay on his back, in the darkness. It was impossible to feel the same way in a nightshirt that he felt in heavy boots, a bulky sweater, and rough trousers. He could not glory in the strength of his arms, his shoulders, his powerful grip, when under that loose nightshirt, slung across the center of his body like a frayed and useless hawser, lay his sex, limp and vulnerable and unused; or worse, hard and throbbing till it ached, and no one to offer relief to it.

He thought of the men who had thrown in their lot with him for this voyage. Some of the crewmen would disappear in San Francisco and have to be replaced, but not many, for Captain Rogers had a reputation as a fair master. His officers would stay with him. Young Harris, with his sea legs under him now. He was a good enough second mate. Soon, because of his family connections, he would be a captain, and he would never be a good captain. Wales had seen enough of him to know that, and he would put it in his report, but it would not matter. Harris would never be able to lead men, and he would never have that sixth sense for the sea that cannot be taught, only refined, and that comes only from a deep, abiding love for the sea.

Whiteurs had that sixth sense, but he lacked the education. And then, there was his race. Wales could think of no reason why a black man should not be captain of a full-

206

rigged ship, but he had never heard of one, either. Nevertheless, out on deck he felt a closer kindship to Whiteurs than any man he had ever sailed with, and he knew that he would trust the bosun with his life anytime.

Dowling was harder to figure. If one sailed with a man for over three months, dealt with him as closely, day to day, as a captain and first mate must deal with each other, one would expect to know him better than Wales knew Dowling. The man was a crack sailor, one of the best Wales had ever shipped with. Perhaps that was all he needed to know about him. Still, there was something about Dowling that made Wales uneasy.

After he had finished thinking about his crew, Wales still could not sleep. His body still felt useless in repose. And he still had a gnawing, aching, empty feeling in the pit of his stomach.

Elizabeth lay awake in her bed, too.

She had made no more midnight excursions to the pantry since the night she had talked to Dowling. That had been weeks ago.

But she had not been able to get him out of her system. She still heard phrases, little pieces from their conversation suddenly flooding her mind when she was supposed to be thinking of something else: *Try me ashore . . . the kind of warning a sensible woman would heed . . . what matters is your senses . . . try me ashore. . . .*

And when she lay in bed at night, all too often she found—as she did this night—that fantasies crowded her brain. Fantasies of Dowling looming over her, of herself powerless to resist him. Fantasies in which the handle of her cabin door turned slowly, with an agonized creak that sounded like a human moan. Then the door pushed open, sweeping in a slow, inexorable arc. . . .

Her eyes follow the door, in the fantasy, and then turn back to the open space it has left. But the doorway is not empty now. He is in it. And once his eyes meet hers, even from across the room in the dim light, she cannot look away.

By the time he reaches her bed, that bold, challenging stare has reduced her to quivering jelly. She has no voice to scream, no power in her limbs to resist. He throws back the covers and she is naked under them.

In her fantasy, she feels his hands on her, all over her. She squirms and sighs in her bed, and her own hands go to the places she has fantasized as feeling the strong, probing fingers of Thomas Dowling. She touches her breasts, and the nipples swell up and harden under her fingertips. Her hands trace a pattern down across her stomach and her hips, first light and teasing, with trailing fingertips, then kneading with her palms and the heels of her hands. She cups a hand, on each side, over the bones of her pelvis, with her fingers pointing inward. In her fantasy, he is holding her down now, pinned to the bed. His ice-blue eyes bore into her; they devour every inch of her body. Her hands begin moving now, her fingers working their way toward the center of her sex. Pulling back with her fingertips, she parts the lips slightly. She is wet, and growing wetter. Her face freezes, her breath stops. She moves her hand toward the heart of the sensation.

A sound outside in the dining room interrupted her; and, her concentration broken, she raised herself up on her elbows to listen.

There was somebody moving around out there. Probably Wales. Yes, almost certainly it was Wales: her intuition told her that. And this was their last night at sea, at least for a few weeks. He had brought the ship through. Perhaps he could have made better time, a safer passage, but he had brought the ship through. And it would be a fine gesture on her part to be civil to him on this one night, especially since she was far too wakeful and tense now to think of even trying to sleep.

She threw back the covers, and sat up in bed. She was naked, just as in her fantasy. She had taken to sleeping nude when they reached warm climates, now that she shared her cabin with no one and had no need of modesty. She kept her nightgown at the foot of the bed in case she were called upon for some sudden emergency.

She wondered if she needed to put on her nightgown now, along with her robe. She looked down at her chest, where her nipples had subsided, now that the passion of her fantasy was past. *No*, she thought. *I'll just be up for a*

*minute. And Wales and I are hardly on good enough terms
that we're likely to get so close that he'll notice.*

She sighed, tied the sash of the dressing gown around her
waist, and stepped out, the polite but distant smile with
which she planned to greet Wales already fixed on her face.

But the formal smile died on her face. The man who sat
at the table, facing her in the door, the man who stared
calmly at her as if he had been expecting her, was Dowling.

Her hand went to her throat, and she clutched the lapels
of her robe together.

"Oh, excuse me," she said. "I didn't know you were
here. I was just going to get something from the pantry . . .
don't pay me any mind. . . ."

She walked toward the pantry, edging sideways as if she
were trying to get past him in a narrow space. Her feet
shuffled, and the rest of her body was tense and contracted.

He followed her, like a cat. He stood in the entryway to
the pantry, his hand up against the door frame on one side,
his shoulder leaning against the other. She could smell his
male presence, like an animal. She was afraid that whatever was about to happen, she would have to let happen.

"We'll be in San Francisco tomorrow," he said. "That's
Tuesday."

"Y-yes?"

"Thursday morning, at ten o'clock, I'll be in the lobby of
the Palace Hotel."

"I don't understand what you mean."

He took her by the forearms and pulled her close against
him. She raised her head to look at him, and he caught her
mouth with his own, in a hard, demanding kiss.

She felt as if it were happening to someone else. Or as if
she had stepped out of her body for the moment, while this
thing was happening to it. So how could she resist? And
when the insistent pressure of his lips and tongue forced
her lips open, how could she hold them closed? His tongue
filled her mouth as it had never been filled before, and sensations shot through her that seemed to belong more to her
fantasies than her real life. Was it she, Elizabeth Rogers,
who was here half-standing, half-melting, in the overpowering arms of this man?

His hands pulled downward suddenly, and her robe
parted at the shoulders and chest. Her left breast was com-

pletely bare now, and pressed up against his rough shirt. It prickled and tickled her, and her nipple ached from the intensity of the feeling.

Her head swam; she was dizzy. She could no longer separate herself from what was happening; she could no longer resist him. Her arms went up around his neck; she clung to him tightly, and returned his kiss with all her pent-up passion.

After an interval that could not be measured, he stood back from her, and held her at arm's length. Her left breast still bare and heaving, she looked up at him with eyes glazed over.

"Thursday morning at ten o'clock, in the lobby of the Palace Hotel," he said. "And now you'd better get back to bed. Good night."

She could not speak, by only nod her head in stunned wonderment. She pulled her robe closed again, and walked out of the pantry and back to her room, closing the door behind her with an almost inaudible click.

Dowling was preparing to head back up on deck when Wales walked out into the saloon.

"Everything under control?" asked the captain.

"Everything under control, sir," said the mate.

"It's been a good voyage."

"Well, we shouldn't have any trouble from here on in," Dowling said coolly.

"We'll be taking on the harbor pilot in the morning. I want the yards squared, the ship trim and ready to pass anyone's inspection *before* he comes on. Is that clear?"

"Right, sir."

"Very good, Mr. Dowling."

The ship docked in San Francisco harbor shortly after noon, April 10, 1875. Elizabeth stood on deck, next to her husband, but not too close. They did not look at each other. Wales's eyes met Whiteurs' for an instant, and they shared again the satisfaction of a successful voyage completed. Wales was dressed in his shore clothes, the traditional captain's stovepipe hat on his head. He was aware of being the center of all eyes, as the captain of a full-rigged ship arriving in port always was—and he knew from the harbor pilot that the *Wind* had posted the best run of the season from New York to San Francisco.

Elizabeth stood straight and proud, too, looking neither to the right nor the left. Her husband was to her right. Thomas Dowling was to her left. She did not have to look at Dowling to know the hard, taut set of his muscles, or the cold, piercing, exciting glint in his eyes.

ᔧChapter Twenty-three

SAN FRANCISCO HAD GROWN TREMENDOUSLY
in the almost ten years since Elizabeth had last seen it. It
was a big, bustling city now, but still, for all the natural
beauty of its location, it could scracely be called a pretty or
picturesque town. It was street after street of two-story,
wood-frame buildings, with no skyline, no variation. The
city the sourdoughs built was still too new, too recently
removed from its mining-camp origins, to have gotten
around to the architectural distinction of commissioned
public buildings or monuments. The one major architectural project, the new city hall complex, had begun six
years earlier in a burst of civic fiscal optimism, before the
great panic and depression of 1873. Now it lay uncom-
pleted, and lichens grew on its walls.

Elizabeth had not noticed any of these urban shortcomings the last time she had been in San Francisco, but she
did now. Elizabeth had grown, too. She had been a little
girl under the watchful eye of her mother, or Mrs. Perkins.
Now she was a grown woman and a mother herself, and
with her husband tied up all day with the business of arranging cargoes and repairs for the *Wind*, she left little
Anne with Jennie and went out to do some shopping and
sightseeing.

But for all its vulgarity, Elizabeth loved San Francisco.

The city was exciting and full of life, like the West it was part of. When the sun finally broke through the morning fog, Elizabeth could see across the Golden Gate to Mount Tamalpais, rising above the wilds of Marin County. The air was cool and brisk and not too damp, and it made her feel good to be alive. And at ten o'clock, not having known she was heading there when she had started out an hour earlier, she found herself walking up the front steps of the huge, garish Palace Hotel.

Dowling was waiting for her in the lobby. He exuded the same rugged masculinity in his shore clothes as he had in his working garb—unlike so many ship's officers, who became stiff, wooden bores or effete dandies in their dress, once they got away from the ship. The sight of him took her breath away.

But she was determined to be cool, polite, and formal. As he crossed the lobby to meet her, she held out her gloved hand to him, and said, "How are you, Mr. Dowling? As you see, I am here promptly at ten. And what was it you wanted to see me about?"

Dowling took her hand, but not in a proper polite handshake. He clasped both of her hands, and looked deep into her eyes without speaking. He looked into her eyes for a full minute, and after that no more pretense was possible for Elizabeth.

They left the hotel together, and Dowling hailed a hansom cab. He gave the driver an address on Grant Street.

"Chinatown, huh?" said the driver, not looking around.

Dowling did not answer, and the driver prodded his horse into motion.

Elizabeth felt very much on edge. She half expected the driver to turn around and refuse to take them. It seemed to her that he must know she was a married woman, out with another man on the way to . . . God knew where. But nothing of the sort happened, and the cab continued on its route through the streets of San Francisco, down Sacramento Avenue toward Grant Street, and Chinatown.

The cab stopped in front of a small, neat house with a trim, lacquered front door. Dowling paid the driver, and the cab drove off.

"Where are we?" asked Elizabeth.

"Wu Ling's," Dowling said, knocking at the door.

"And what . . . what kind of place is Wu Ling's?"

"An interesting place."

No one came to answer the knock. Dowling waited patiently and did not knock again. Elizabeth's nerves were frayed almost beyond her tolerance. What if no one came? She would never be able to go through this again, if there had been a mistake. She would die if it turned out that Dowling proved to a poor guide, if he turned to her shame-facedly and said something had gone wrong, the address was wrong, they would have to go to the next block. If he told her the day was wrong and she would have to meet him again tomorrow, she would never do it.

There was a slow, shuffling sound behind the door, and then at last it opened. An ancient Chinese stood in the doorway, with a curiously unlined face, wispy white beard, and clear black eyes. He appeared to know Dowling, and bowed low to him. Dowling bowed in return.

Elizabeth stood back from the doorway, hidden behind Dowling. She had retreated unconsciously behind him at the sound of the door latch, and was now a little surprised to find herself there. He stepped aside to let her enter first. She took a deep breath, and stepped over the threshold and into the house.

The Chinaman led them down a corridor and into a wide, low-ceilinged, dimly lit room. The smoke hung in a heavy cloud, and Elizabeth fancied that she could feel its effect on her as soon as she entered.

And perhaps she could. Otherwise, why did the scene not seem more strange to her? Certainly, it was like nothing she had ever seen before. And as her eyes got used to the gloom and the smoke, so that she began to see the scene around her, she was curious, but accepting. She wanted, simply and with no urgency, to see it all.

There were perhaps twenty low couches in the room, spaced about three feet apart, their heads against the wall, their feet protruding out toward the center of the room. They were made of bare wood, dark and highly polished, and at the head of each was an ornate ceramic block, which seemed to take the place of a pillow.

"It looks so hard," she whispered to Dowling.

"Once you've had a pipe, it doesn't seem hard," Dowling

said. "You're the most comfortable you've ever been in your life."

She found this quite easy to believe, and thought no more about it.

The room was about two-thirds full, there being equal numbers of Westerners and Orientals. She could not tell very much about the social class of the Chinese, but the whites were clearly people of some status, by their dress and grooming. She saw two women on the couches. All of the other patrons were men. Both women were white; the only Oriental woman in the room were the silent, beautiful, silk-clad serving girls who glided silently and unobtrusively through the smoke, between the couches, preparing pipes for the opium smokers.

The smokers themselves lay languidly, separately, moving not at all or very slightly. There was no way of telling whether the two white women had come alone or accompanied, since everyone, men and women alike, seemed totally self-absorbed, with no eyes even for the flowerlike sensuality of the handmaidens.

Then Elizabeth noticed a couple of exceptions. A very young serving girl knelt beside the couch of a middle-aged man. She filled his pipe ceremoniously, and handed it to him, turning the bowl upside down and pointing it over the top of the glass chimeny on the lamp beside the couch. Then, with the same solemn, ceremonious pace, she stood up, removed the silk dress which was the only garment she wore, and lay down on the couch next to him.

Her body had the color of old ivory and the soft, smooth, vulnerable texture of a flower. She was as slim as a boy, and her breasts were like buds, with that breathtaking quality that comes just before full womanliness. She curled next to him, her head against the bottom of his rib cage.

"Is she under the influence, too?" Elizabeth breathed to Dowling.

"No," said Dowling. "He must be a regular customer, and she knows what he wants."

"But he's not doing anything to her," Elizabeth said, a little confused.

"It's enough for him that she's there. That's all his senses can handle right now, in the state he's in," Dowling told her.

216

One of the white women, too, had her own handmaiden. If anyone had described this scene to Elizabeth, she would have been shocked and unbelieving. But seeing it was somehow different. Elizabeth felt many things, but shock was not one of them. And she accepted it as though it were the sort of thing she had been accustomed to seeing all her life.

The woman's dress was open to the waist, and her shift had been pulled up to expose her breasts. It was not graceful or esthetic. The shift was bunched up around the woman's collarbone, and her breasts were heavy and sagged off to each side. But that only added to the voluptuousness of the image. This was not a work of art, it was a woman's naked breasts: naked to be touched. And a wide-eyed, serious-visaged Chinese girl knelt next to her, gently rubbing her index finger over one nipple.

There were two couches, together, with no one on them. The old Chinese gestured with his eyes toward them, but Dowling shook his head. The Chinese nodded, and continued on through the room. Dowling followed him, and Elizabeth came behind.

She was wondering why she was here.

She thought she knew, but there were things that she did not understand, and which were beginning to worry her. Was opium really such a sexual depressant? Did that mean he was not going to make love to her? Then what had that passionate kiss meant, back on shipboard?

The Chinese proprietor showed them into a small, candlelit room, and left them alone there. There was nothing in the room except the flickering candles in the corners, and a straw mat on the floor. Dowling saw the doubt and confusion in Elizabeth's eyes, and spoke to it.

"We're going to use the opium," he said. "Not ride it all the way to oblivion. I won't let you smoke too much."

"Hold me, Thomas," Elizabeth said.

He shook his head. "Wait," he said. "Everything in time. This will be unlike anything you've ever known before, so let me introduce you to it the right way."

"But I'm scared. I want you."

He shook his head again.

"Wait," he repeated.

The door opened and closed silently, and a Chinese girl

was standing inside. She bowed low, and walked over to them. She was carrying an opium pipe, and a lantern, and a small inlaid box that held the drug. She also carried two embroidered silk robes, one of which she gave to Dowling, the other to Elizabeth.

"Am I supposed to . . . ?"

Dowling nodded.

"But where . . . ?"

He nodded again, in the direction of the far wall. She looked, and saw in the dimness a bamboo screen leaning up against the wall. The girl went over and set it up for her. Dowling had just a trace of his sardonic smile on his lips, and Elizabeth did feel a little foolish. But the screen was there, so it must be allowed in the ritual. She went behind it, and changed into the robe. She did not need to be told to leave nothing on under it.

When she returned, Dowling was already in his silk robe, lying on his side on the mat. He had apparently changed in the middle of the room, in front of the Chinese girl. Elizabeth lay down on her side, facing him.

The Chinese girl sat between them, and prepared the pipe. Elizabeth was not sure she could read the Oriental features correctly, but she guessed that the girl could not be more than fifteen. She had a broad, flat face, with long black lashes framing her almond eyes, and a small, round mouth. She was cameo-beautiful, and in her dark, liquid eyes there was a look of wisdom, or of experience, that had nothing to do with her years, but rather with something that Elizabeth had never known and could only guess at.

The opium was black and gummy, and it bubbled in the pipe when the flame was put to it. It spread through Elizabeth's body like liquid, flowing thickly, bubbling and gushing, carrying the voluptuous sensations throughout her system, so that her forearms, her back, her toes all glowed and tingled with the same thrilling languor she felt in her thighs. Her body was in a state of pure bliss. It was as Dowling had said, the straw mat and the hard floor were all the comfort she needed.

She looked over at Dowling. The lines of his body flowed with the loose, billowing folds of the silk robe, and looking at him filled her with pleasure. She no longer felt the urgent, frantic, ragged edge of desire that had torn at her before. Her sexuality, his sexuality, were no longer prodded by the tension between need and guilt: no longer spurred by repression, she was somewhere beyond lust, into sheer sensuality. She could have floated toward him and been content; she could have glided over until her body was inside those flowing folds of silk, pressed against his.

As they shared the pipe, the Chinese girl passed it back and forth between them. As she leaned forward to take it from Elizabeth, Elizabeth saw her in the same way: beautiful, voluptuous. A creature with long, sensual fingers that wrapped, one by one, around the stem of the pipe. A creature of warm, soft flesh, ensheathed in silk that flowed and shimmered like water, or like the silken feeling inside Elizabeth. In a hazy vision, she saw the tips of two budding yellow breasts brushing thick, pink nipples, sinking down into pillowy, full white breasts.

She drew back. She was not ready for that vision, not even with the opium. She looked at Dowling's face, concentrated on it for erotic reassurance. She wanted more opium, and she waited for the pipe to come back to her.

But instead, Dowling handed it back to the girl, and dismissed her with a languid gesture of his hand. Silently, she she picked up the lantern and backed away from them.

Elizabeth assumed she would leave the room, but she did not. She retreated to the side of the room facing Elizabeth, and sat down cross-legged, her wrists resting on her knees, the thumb and forefinger of each hand arched and touching in a circle. She sat, motionless between two candles, like a slim, female Buddha.

Elizabeth could see everything, and nothing. Her eyes took in the whole room, and yet nothing was as it seemed to be; nor did anything need to be. So she could see the walls, and the glowing flame and melting wax of the candles, and the Oriental woman, and Thomas Dowling's face, with its half-smile softened by drugs and sensuality, and his hand, reaching over to her, undoing the sash of her silken robe. After that she could see all those things, plus the white, silk-framed strip that ran the length of her body, from her collarbone to her toes.

She could tell that the Chinese girl was looking straight at them, but she could not tell what she saw. The girl sat motionless, scarcely breathing. Her eyes were open, but there was no expression in them. And they seemed to be focused, if they were focused at all, directly on Elizabeth's sex.

So she was immutably part of whatever was to happen. Elizabeth assimilated that into her soul, and it passed out of her immediate consciousness.

Dowling's body was now, magically, only inches from hers. But it was still screened from her, behind a veil of silk. He had opened her robe and thrown it back so that the front of her body was naked; but he had not touched her yet.

He made no move to undress himself, and Elizabeth found her hand moving over to his waist. As delicately as he had performed the ritual on her, she undid his sash, lifted the edge of his robe, and tossed it back. And they still had not touched.

His penis lay quiescent, curled and nestled against the pocket of dark blond hair below his waist, hanging downward. It almost reached the straw mat, but not quite.

It grew thicker, first before it became either longer or straighter. And it twitched, once, twice, three times. Dowling's breathing grew deeper. Then, as the twitching became a steady, growing hardening ascent, he slid his hand down under the base of his penis, and the arc described by the head was outward, away from his body, until it swung up to butt against her thigh, the first time she had felt him.

His penis continued to swell, and it pressed harder into her thigh, which gave against the pressure, but still resisted the forward pushing force of his rising sexuality. The feeling amazed Elizabeth. It was still the only place that they were touching. Waves of sensation rippled out through her body from that spot, from the tip of his penis, and each wave was subtly different from the one before it.

She looked down along his body, the naked, sinewy male muscles so close to her, hers for the taking and touching and holding, hers to be press against the length of her own body, to flatten her breasts against, to mold her thighs around. She had never looked so frankly and openly at a man's body before, but she did not even think of that. It seemed the most natural thing in the world now, as her head bobbed slowly up and down, and her eyes traveled the path from his naked shoulders and chest down to the straight, white shaft that bridged the space between them and pushed a soft dent in the creamy smoothness of her thighs.

And then, finally, too insistent to be held back, it popped forward, and caught again at the confluence of three soft lines—the one between her thighs, and the two on either side of her triangle of Venus.

"Ohhh . . ." she said, and her voice floated on the hazy air. "Will it just stay there?"

He nodded without answering, and she sighed again. She had never known sex to be so languid, so voluptuous; she had never expected it would be this way with the forceful, direct Thomas Dowling of the *Western Flyer*. Her fantasies had been the violent, intense carnality of her earlier illicit encounters, with Dowling in the role of the most primitive, animalistic sailor of them all. She could barely remember those fantasies, that vision of the man anymore, but from far back in her subconscious, the memory gave a special overtone of surprise and wonder to her response.

She wanted to touch him, too, with the same delicate and concentrated sensuality with which he had touched her. She leaned forward slightly, and pushed her chest out toward him. She wanted to press her nipples against his chest, but even before she made contact with his flesh, she felt an otherwordly sensation, like touching and more than touching, swirling around her nipples. It was the red-gold hair on his chest, and it teased her like the snappings of electrical current between her body and his.

She could tell that he felt it, too. She did not move any closer; she breathed in and out, and her breathing and his provided all that was necessary to stir up the electric charge that passed between their two bodies.

Elizabeth never knew how long they stayed that way, joined only by the lightest of touches. She only knew that the very space between them was charged with more sexuality than she could have imagined in the most impassioned embrace. And that it seemed as if it could have lasted forever.

Then there were new sexual phases that lapped, one over the other, as two bodies touched more and more, in one delicious place after another, at the same lushly unhurried

221

tempo, until at last their bodies were intertwined. Dowling's knee parted Elizabeth's thighs, and slid between them; the inside of his thigh lay against the inside of hers.

Half of his body convered half of hers. One of her breasts was crushed flat against his hard chest, and the moisture of their perspiration squished between them. The other breast was dry and round in the open air, and his forearm leaned against it as he reached up to run two fingers feather-lightly across her eyelids, her cheeks, and her lips. Soon those same fingers would leave a trail of exquisite shudders down her neck, across her collarbone, along her chest, and up the soft incline to her nipple.

After that, his mouth would find that pink, sensitive special portion of flesh. His tongue would be wet, and match her nipple in texture. She would watch them together, and observe his geranium-pink tongue against the dusky, almost beige, rose color of her nipple, and the light cherry tint to his lips. His tongue would be subtle and probing and delicate at first, until with the passionate noise of sudden suction, half her breast would disappear into his mouth.

He lay perpendicular to her then, his mouth on her breast. She could see his lips stretched wide, to take in as much of her as he could, and she could feel his tongue working where she could not see.

She wanted to put her mouth on his body, too. She was not sure she could move, but the opium languor was receding, just a little, and when she tried her body swung around lightly and effortlessly. They faced in opposite directions now, and Dowling lay passively on his back.

She nuzzled with her face and lips against his chest, licking and nibbling at his nipples, though she was not sure that it felt the same to him as it did to her. She knew, dimly at first and then more than dimly, what she wanted to do. But she did not know, even in this debauched, opium-tinged world that she had drifted into, if it was all right. Her breeding stopped her, and snarled her impulses in confusion.

She slid her cheek a few inches down his chest, and then stopped. She looked, and there it was, now only half erect. Aching with desire and tenderness for that powerful and vulnerable root of his manhood, she rocked her cheek against his chest, and her body trembled.

For a moment Elizabeth's whole mood of sensual abandon hung in the balance, btu Dowling seemed to understand, and he took her head in his hands, and guided it gently to where she wanted it to be.

The tongue is the most delicate of all human sensors, and whatever one feels with it is experienced in such subtle details of shape, texture, surface, mass—yes, and taste— that it is known beyond doubt, and never forgotten. Elizabeth's sensory awareness was still enhanced by the opium. She learned about man's sex from the drug and from Thomas Dowling, that morning in San Francisco. She learned about the ridge, the thick, engorged vein that grew there under her lips and tongue, as she glided up and down the length of that shaft. She felt it become hotter, go from wrinkled to smooth, from soft to hard, a wonderful strange hardness unlike any she had ever known, not like wood, or bone, or china. She ran a wet line along it with the tip of her tongue, covered it with the flat of her tongue, took it inside her mouth. And gradually, the sense of exploration gave way to the intensity of pure lust, and she sucked on his penis as if the whole universe were concentrated there.

Dowling beckoned to the Chinese girl, and she came over to them again, filled the pipe, and handed it to him and Elizabeth in turn. Elizabeth had forgotten about her. She had not realized she was displaying herself so openly in front of another person, another woman.

Or perhaps she had realized it, all along. As the opium sensation flowed anew through her body, the girl once again seemed an organic part of everything she was experiencing. Elizabeth would have liked her to stay. She would have liked the girl to take off her silk sheath dress and lend her body, her sensuality, to theirs. But Dowling waved her away.

The girl went back over to the side of the room, and sat in the cross-legged position she had assumed before. Elizabeth's eyes met hers as she lay on her back, naked, her mound of Venus rising slightly over the outline of her thighs. She thought about the girl. She thought about being fifteen and seeing this open sexual drama played out in front of her, and not for the first time. She felt that she would have liked it. She imagined herself at fifteen, and lying on this mat, as Dowling rose slowly over her and she spread her legs wider to receive him. The reverie made her feel wonderful, and she kept her eyes steadily linked the gaze of the young girl, as the sailor's huge body descended on her.

Then the tip of his penis separated her flesh, and her eyes swam. There was nothing in the world but that round, knobby tip which she had explored with her tongue and now knew so well, going all the way up that moist passage deep into her body's core.

"Hey! Mistah Petahs!"

Whiteurs turned in the direction of the voice. He knew that he was the one being hailed—all black sailors on the Barbary Coast, for reasons no one remembered or cared about, were called "Mr. Peters."

"You likee Chinese girl, Mistah Petahs? Velly good plice—two bittee lookee, foh bittee feelee, six bittee doee."

Whiteurs always wondered how much of the Chinatown pidgin English was the way they really talked, and how much was for show, for the tourists. He had played enough shuffling and scraping Negro roles, when he had to—to keep a job, to stay out of a fight—so that he sympathized with anyone who had to play a role to get by. It was not like that with Captain Rogers. He had never had to act out a blackface minstrel show with the captain. They were two men together, and the captain had made it clear from the outset that he would respect Whiteurs, or any other seaman, for the job that he did and the kind of man he was.

The Chinese prostitute stood at the barred window that had been crudely cut out of the wooden door of her "crib," the cheap shack that was her workplace, home, and prison. She looked good enough to Whiteurs, and he sauntered over for a closer inspection.

"Nice Chinee girl, Mistah Petahs. Like bit black fella plenty much. Have plenty big black fella. Your father, he just left here."

That was part of the ritual, too—they all said it. A Chinese, so Whiteurs had been told, considered it an honor

224

to sleep with a woman who had been had by his father. *Some honor,* he thought. His father had been a white man on a plantation from which his mother had been sold away even before he was born. *Cut out the bullshit, bitch. You been in America long enough. You know the lingo. You just a slanty-eyed American, now. Same thing if I was to walk in your crib with a bone through my nose.*

But he said nothing out loud. It was all part of the show that Chinatown put on for the tourists, like the fake opium dens that thrill-seeking but fearful society white folks were led through. But it was none of Whiteurs' business to change it, nor to concern himself with what sort of act this Jackson Street doxy was putting on, if act it was. He wanted to get laid, and the cribs of Chinatown offered a good cheap lay.

The girl stood a few steps back from the window as Whiteurs approached, to give him a proper look at the merchandise. She was dressed in the traditional Chinese prostitute's garb of black silk blouse with a narrow band of turquoise, embroidered front and back with delicate, colorful flowers. Below the waist, she was naked. Her hips were slim, and the triangle between them was small, neat, and jet black. Her thighs were skinnier than Whiteurs liked, but they looked strong.

Behind her, on a faded horsehair couch, sat another prostitute. She was heftier, with a broad, impassive Mongolian face and heavy thighs. She was dressed identically to the other girl, and her belly drooped slightly, but not displeasingly, as she sat.

Anywhere from two to a half-dozen prostitutes might share one of these cribs, so Whiteurs suspected there might be a few already working in the back room which was separated from the room that he looked into by a heavy curtain. In the front room were a sofa, a couple of chairs, a worn but clean Oriental carpet, and a chest of drawers. Like all of Chinatown, even here in the Jackson Street slums, everything was clean. The girls were clean, too, and they smelled good. Whiteurs decided he liked the slim one. He nodded, and entered.

There were three prostitutes and their customers already occupying three of the six beds in the back. All of them were white—the Chinese, as Whiteurs knew, rarely if ever patronized the prostitutes who were used for the Occidental tourists. He heard a high-pitched, girlish scream of excitement from the bed next to where he and his girl lay down, and saw, without surprise a white boy of no more than twelve and a middle-aged prostitute arise. Boys under sixteen were a common sight in the cribs, and they were generally charged only half price—whether to encourage future patronage or because they came so quickly, Whiteurs never knew. He dropped his pants down to his knees, and rolled over heavily on top of the prostitute.

His lust sated, Whiteurs walked through the streets of Chinatown. He felt good. He was on his way to Kearney Street, to drink Pisco brandy until he passed out. He generally managed to stay on his feet until he had drunk his entire pay, which he considered a judicious method of budgeting, since he could fairly well count on being rolled for anything he had left, after he passed out.

He was crossing Grant Avenue when he saw the captain's wife and First Mate Dowling, coming out of a building which he knew to be an opium den—and not one of the tourist fakes, either, but a quality, high-priced opium palace.

Shit, thought Whiteur. *Why'd they have to go and do that? And Why'd I have to see it?* Whiteurs was angry, depressed, disconsolate. His loyalty was to the captain. He would have to tell him.

Neither Dowling nor Mrs. Rogers had seen him. He watched them walk down to the end of the block, get into a hansom, and drive off. He saw Dowling's hand on Mrs. Rogers' waist—hell, on her ass!—as he helped her up into the cab.

Whiteurs pictured Mrs. Rogers for a long time, as he continued his walk over toward Kearney Street. He pictured her as he had seen her that afternoon, leaving a house of debauchery in Chinatown with another man. And he pictured her as he had seen her on board the *Western Flyer*, coming up on deck with a page of calculations to lead a rescue party to a sailor lost at sea. He pictured her nursing a near-dead black man, whom she had saved from the sea and the sharks, back to health. He knew he would never tell a soul about what he had seen that afternoon.

⮠Chapter Twenty-four

OPIUM OR NO, ELIZABETH COULD NOT PRETEND
that she did not remember what had happened. And opium
or no, she could not pretend that she had not entered into
it willingly—eagerly, in fact. Nor could she pretend it did
not have a tremendous impact on her. She had felt things
with Dowling that were unlike anything she had ever felt
before. And now, a month out at sea, she still felt them, in
unexpected bursts: a glow, a shudder, and she could not
pretend she did not know where it came from.

She could not pretend. So she simply refused to think
about it at all.

And she could not pretend about Dowling, either. When
she saw him, she looked through his clothes and saw him
naked. She could not look at Wales, her own husband, and
picture his naked body. But she could picture Dowling's—
every muscle, every sinew, every organ. With her mouth,
she could remember the shape and taste and texture of his
penis. She did not know what Wales's penis was like. It had
been inside her, although she could scarcely even remember that, now. It had given her pleasure, and she had felt
close to him during those times. But she had never touched
it; she had never even looked at it.

So she stayed away from Dowling completely. She went
on having her meals in her stateroom. She never went up

227

on deck during Dowling's watch. And if, at night, she burned and shuddered and could not sleep, she tensed her body against the feelings, clutched her pillow, and sometimes cried.

She knew instinctively that she did not want to have anything more to do with Dowling. The sexual attraction had been too irresistible, the sex itself too wildly exciting, to be sustained without love. And she did not love Dowling. Nor, she knew, did he love her. He would not support her when she needed it, he would not give her kindness when she felt alone. All he could offer was sex so exciting and all-consuming that she would die for it, and that was not enough. She could expect nothing from him but that naked edge of excitement, and she shrank from it.

The feelings were still there; the sexual awareness of him and probably even the lust were still there. But without the anticipation, and challenge of the unknown, it was like being out in a cold wind. It was better to be alone.

Wales had waited until the third day out at sea, so the surprise would be complete. Then he paid a visit to the nursery.

He wore his heavy jacket. It seemed bulkier than usual, and his arms were folded awkwardly over his chest, but not so awkwardly that four-year-old Anne would notice anything unusual. He knelt down so that she could run over and hug him, but he did not unfold his arms to hug her back. She noticed that.

"Papa, what's wrong?" she scolded. "Don't you have a hug for me?"

"Of course I do, sweetheart. But first . . ." he paused dramatically.

"First what, Papa?"

"First you have to tell me something."

"What is it, Papa?"

"Who would you like to hug? Right here on this ship, that is."

"You, Papa."

"And who else?"

"Jennie."

"And who else?"

"Mama . . . ?" Anne was starting to become a little unsure of where this game was going.

"And who else?"

Now Anne looked puzzled and serious. "Nobody else."

"Are you sure?"

Wales looked past her at Jennie, a twinkle in his eye. Jennie could hardly keep from bursting out into a fit of giggles. "I think I can guess," she said, her eyes on his chest. "But I don't believe it."

"Of course I'm sure, Papa," she said. "But . . ."

She was interrupted by a curious but unmistakable sound, apparently from somewhere in the center of her father: it was the irritated meowing of a newly awakened kitten! Anne's eyes opened wide with disbelief, which almost immediately became exstasy.

"Well, I guess that let the cat out of the bag," said her father, as he pulled back the lapel of his coat to reveal a white, furry, curious head.

He set the kitten down on the floor.

"Oh, Papa!" squealed Anne. And even before she picked the kitten up, she leaped into her father's arms and hugged him tightly around the neck. This time he hugged her back, unrestrainedly.

"Oh, Captain Rogers!" cried Jennie, and she looked as if she, too, would have hugged the captain if decorum had not held her back.

The kitten was all white, with a pink nose, and in three days at sea, hidden away in the captain's cabin, it had already developed its sea legs. Now, nose to the ground, eyes alert, it had begun to examine its new surroundings, until it was snatched off its feet and cradled, undignified but content, in the loving arms of its new mistress.

"I thought you should have a playmate for the long days," Wales said. "It gets lonely for a young girl at sea, I know. You should have a companion." He knew, though, that he was talking to himself. Anne was completely absorbed in loving her new kitten.

"That is the sweetest, nicest thing, Captain Rogers," said Jennie. "And you're so right—that was just what Anne needed. I think you're wonderful. A wonderful father, that is. So thoughtful and . . . well, it's just the cutest kitten, anyway. Anne loves it. And I . . . I have laundry to do.

I'd better . . ." she backed out of the room, blushing and bumping into things.

"She's beautiful, Papa. I'm going to call her Legend—Jennie's been reading me beautiful legends out of my reading book, and she's just as beautiful as any of those legends."

"That's a pretty name, sweetheart. What legends does she read to you?"

"Oh, lots and lots. She read to me about the Frog Prince, last night. He was a handsome prince until a mean witch got mad at him and turned him into a frog. Then he was awfully lonely and sad for a long time, until a kind and beautiful princess loved him, and when she kissed him he turned back into a prince. Isn't my kitten beautiful? Jennie loves her too, I know it."

"She certainly is, sweetheart."

"Has Mama seen her?"

"No, she hasn't. You can show her to Mama when she comes in to see you."

Dowling encountered Jennie in the companionway.

He was going up, she was coming down. They stopped one step apart, and Jennie moved off to one side. Dowling did not. He stayed at the center of the step below her, and stared at her. They were at eye level.

"Excuse me," said Jennie nervously.

"And where are you off to in such a hurry?" asked Dowling.

"I have to get back to the baby . . . if you'll excuse me, please, I—"

"Don't you ever get lonely, all by yourself out here in the middle of the ocean?" asked Dowling. His bulk seemed to swell up in front of her, to block off the entire passage.

"No, Mr. Dowling, I don't. Now, will you please let me get by?"

"You don't?" He laid the side of his index finger along her cheek. She shuddered with distaste and pulled her head back. "A pretty little thing like you shouldn't be alone, night after night."

"Well, I'm not alone. I have Anne for company, and that suits me very well, thank you. And I'm not such a little thing, either."

"No . . ." he looked her up and down shamelessly, and she turned her body away from him, but whatever angle she presented to him, she felt as if she was showing him something that he should not see. "No, I guess you're not. And of course, there is little Anne, isn't there? Well, perhaps it's best to keep it in the family, after all."

The color drained from Jennie's face, and her fists clenched. "What do you mean by that?" she demanded.

"Don't get too lonely, pretty one," Dowling said with a leer, and before she could reply, or even react, he was past her and up the companionway.

There was no challenge in teasing Jennie, or in flirting with her. Even as he was doing it, Dowling was bored. If she wanted to fuck the captain, what business was it of his? Dowling was not much interested in who virgins wanted to fuck. Their timid sexuality made him restless.

Dowling was restless all the time, anyway. The Pacific Ocean was his home, his freedom, his natural element. Now he felt like a caged panther in it. The ship was too small for him. The ocean was too small for him, the world was too small for him. He felt chafed.

He was angry at himself. What a setup, and he had failed to take advantage of it! The captain's wife . . . the chink wench . . . she had been there in the corner of the room the whole time, waiting for his signal, and he had never called.

He hadn't been afraid to; that was not it. He knew, and had known then, that there was no chance of screwing up. He had the captain's wife hotter than a Chinese firecracker, and ready for whatever he wanted to do with her. A threesome would have been no problem. But he hadn't done it.

And worse, he found himself not liking the idea that she would have been receptive to it.

Jennie had never thought about having a romantic liaison with Captain Rogers. She would have been afraid even to dream such a thing, and she would have felt far too disloyal. Jennie was a warm, loyal, and conscientious girl. Jennie only thought that Captain Rogers was the most wonderful man she had ever met in her life, and she only hoped that someday she would meet a man who would be even a little bit like Captain Rogers.

Her fondest fantasy was that something would happen to Mr. Dowling—not an accident, she could not fantasize that, but maybe when they got to Manila he would be arrested for some bad thing he had done there before, or maybe he would leave the ship and go off to join a smuggling operation, or some other evil enterprise, so everyone would be glad he was gone and Captain Rogers would not try to get him back. Then Captain Rogers would have to find a new first mate.

And somewhere in Manila, there would be a wonderful ship's officer, stranded out without a ship. He would be tall and dark, like Captain Rogers, with the same wonderful, kind eyes that Captain Rogers had. And he would be down on his luck, lonely, and very, very grateful to Captain Rogers for signing him on as the *Western Wind*'s new first officer.

And he would be even more surprised, and pleased, when he met Jennie his first day at sea, and discovered that she was going to be on board for the whole voyage. But it would not take the whole voyage—he would fall in love with her at first sight, and she with him. And he would be so grateful to Captain Rogers for rescuing him from Manila, and letting him meet Jennie, that he would never want a ship of his own—he would never want to be anything but the first mate of the *Western Wind*, so that Jennie could marry him and go on sailing with the *Western Wind* and taking care of her love, little Anne.

Jennie could not understand how Mrs. Rogers could feel the way she did about Captain Rogers. She knew it made the captain feel very lonely and unhappy. She decided that Mrs. Rogers must be a very cold woman.

Mornings were the worst time for Wales. He woke up with a hollow, empty, dead feeling that was strongest in the pit of his stomach but sent its enervating waves throughout his body. Only duty drove him to swing his legs over the side of his bed, and put his feet on the floor. He did not taste his coffee in the morning. He did not know whether he drank it standing up or sitting down, whether it burned the inside of his mouth or was like lukewarm dishwater. He only knew that he drank it alone.

It had been this way every since Elizabeth had left his bed.

The feeling never left him, throughout the day. It receded into the background; it became less than his entire existence, the way it was in the morning, but it never left him. His work was demanding, and occupied his mind and at least part of his emotions. He was almost grateful for storms and emergencies that kept him up for twenty-four or forty-eight hours at a stretch, so that there would be no morning for one or two days. He drove himself so hard that he was exhausted at night, and could fall off to sleep without much trouble. But there was no answer to those mornings.

For Elizabeth, the middle of the day was the hardest to bear. The nights were awful, but she could handle them because she knew there was something she could do about her sexual frustration, though she had rejected that once and for all. She did not want to go to Dowling again. And if her body sometimes ached at night, still her soul did not want him, and she would not split the two. Not ever again.

She did not know what her soul wanted. But at high noon, when she would have gone up on deck with the big Dent sextant to shoot the sun, she felt an emptiness that was beyond measuring. She was cut off from Wales, and from feeling a part of the ship. And she could no longer hide behind scoffing at his seamanship, telling herself she did not care about sharing a ship with the likes of him. She knew it was a lie. Her husband's seamanship was steady and reliable day to day, brilliant and spontaneous when it had to be.

Elizabeth could not quite remember what had gone wrong, or whose fault it had been. All she knew for sure was that she could have had everything she had ever wanted. It was only at arm's length even now, but a door had been shut, and she was on the other side. And she had no idea how to open it again.

"Mr. Dowling," said Wales. "I want to know about it, if my officers are carrying guns on watch."

"It's a habit I picked up in the CHina Seas," said Dowling. "It's taken for granted there, so it didn't occur to me that it was necessary to mention. And, of course, I was a ship's master in the China Seas."

"Well, you're first officer here." Wales bit off the words. "And there'll be no carrying of firearms by my officers unless I specifically order it."

"It'll be a difficult habit to break," said Dowling.

"The only reason for carrying a gun aboard this ship, mister, is in case of a threat of mutiny."

Dowling shrugged.

"And if I found one of my officers bearing arms without authorization, after specifically being instructed to the contrary, I would take that as a threat of mutiny. Do I make myself clear?"

"Do you want to search me?" asked Dowling, curling his lip back insolently.

"I'd like your word that you will not carry a gun on watch again."

"My word?"

"Yes."

"As an officer and gentleman," said the first mate.

Wales stared hard at him. Dowling's face was a cold mask. Wales knew that he had either to accept the man's word, or not. He would get no further cooperation from Dowling.

"All right. I want a full report on what happened this morning between you and that sailor."

"There's nothing to report. He got out of line, and I disciplined him."

"That's all?"

"Yes, sir."

"That's not the kind of discipline we use aboard this ship, and you know it. That man's jaw is broken in three places. He may have lost the sight in one eye. What in hell did you do to him?"

Dowling did not reply. Wales decided to let it go as a rhetorical question. He continued:

"It's not to happen again, mister. You can consider this an official reprimand."

"Aye, aye, sir."

* * *

It was late, by the time Wales got down to the nursery. The winds had been baffling all day, and had finally come out dead ahead, so that they had to take in sail and beat for all of the late afternoon. They had sailed 150 miles, and made only 58 miles of forward progress. Calculating their current position and their new course had been arduous, tiring, and lonely work.

Wales did not miss sharing the work with Elizabeth in the same way that she missed it. He missed her in his bed. He missed her smile, and the music of her voice; he missed her company. But he was used to doing the work by himself, and he had gone back to doing it himself with no sense that he was put upon or asked to carry more than his share.

Still, some nights it was more tiring than others, and this was one of them. And most frustrating of all, by the time he got to the nursery, Anne was asleep. Jennie put her finger to her lips as she opened the door, and Wales tiptoed in. Legend was curled up at Anne's feet, a white ball of fluff. Anne's eyes were closed, her fist lay next to her face, and she was snoring lightly.

"Is she all right?" Wales whispered.

"Yes, of course she is, and don't worry—you don't need to whisper," said Jennie in a quiet voice that had a little merry laugh in it. "She's a good sound sleeper, that one—she sleeps the sleep of the innocent. She just got tired and couldn't wait up for you anymore. She fell asleep sitting up and playing with her kitten, poor dear. I had to carry her to bed."

"I hope she wasn't too disappointed," said Wales. "I just couldn't get down here any earlier."

"No, of course not, Captain—don't worry about that." Jennie looked up at the tired, crestfallen face of Captain Rogers, and added sympathetically, "I'm afraid you're the one who's really disappointed."

Wales hesitated, then smiled shyly, looking more like a little boy than a hard-bitten captain. "Yes, I suppose I am. I do look forward to relaxing with her at the end of the day."

"Well, why don't you come in and sit for a few moments, anyway?" said Jennie impulsively. "I know I'm not much company, but perhaps I'd be better than nothing?" She laughed nervously.

"Thank you, Jennie, you'd be wonderful company," said Wales. "I'd like that very much."

Afterwards—and he thought about it often afterwards—Wales could never quite remember the sequence of events, or what they talked about. He remembered Jennie's warmth, and her compassion. He remembered how he began to realize that he felt proud of being the man that he was; and in feeling that pride, he began to realize how long it had been that he had missed it. He remembered looking down at his hands and seeing them as strong, yet sensitive. He remembered feeling the muscles in his shoulders, the breadth of his back, the solidity of his chest; he remembered being aware that he moved with the easy, masculine grace of command.

And as he remembered it, when he took her in his arms, it was with those feelings of strength and protectiveness—those, and gratitude to her for reminding him of things that he had almost forgotten. He did not know what she felt as her arms went around his back, or when her pink lips parted slightly and met the gentle kiss that he placed on them. Perhaps it was more passion than he felt, but he did not really think so. Jennie was not responsible for what happened next. The passion was something that flamed between them, unexpectedly: but flame it did. Jennie's girlish figure was suddenly a woman's body pressed against his. He could feel its heat. He could feel her stomach, her breasts, her thighs. His kiss became passionate, open-mouthed; she opened her mouth to him in answer, and they sank to their knees, then to the floor of the cabin, kissing and touching each other greedily.

Their clothes were bunched together and bulky. Wales could feel her body through them, but not enough. He pushed her skirt up in the front, and lifted her waist to push it up in the back. His hand was on her bottom, separated from her flesh only by the thin muslin of her pantaloons; impatiently, he ripped at that, and held the two rounded cheeks in the hugeness of his hand, pressing her pelvis tightly against his. She gasped with wonderment.

But the mood was not to be sustained. Little Anne moaned in her sleep, and the two of them froze and looked up. The baby did not waken. Wales and Jennie looked at her for long moments, until they were satisfied that her

236

sleep was undisturbed, but when Wales looked back at Jennie, he could only see the round cheeks and innocent eyes of the girl in her teens who worked for his wife and took care of his daughter. He took her face in his hands and held her tenderly for an instant, before confusion took over.

"I . . . I am sorry, Jennie," he said. "I don't know what came over me."

He stood up, and brushed at his clothing to cover his embarrassment.

"No . . ." she said faintly, pushing the upper part of her body to arm's length off the floor, and looking up at him beseechingly.

Jennie felt the awe that she always felt when the captain came into the nursery. She had tried to keep the baby awake, knowing he would arrive eventually, and she felt personally responsible for the captain's disappointment when she told him that little Anne had gone to sleep—but even so, she was surprised to find herself asking him to come in and let her keep him company. But there was something in his eyes she had never seen before—vulnerability, terrible loneliness—and her compassion reached out to him on instinct.

When he took her in his arms, she clung to him, scarcely able to believe it. She began to feel things she had always dreamed about, without realizing what they were. And as his kisses became more passionate, as he held her and laid her down on the floor with him, she realized that she could give him what he wanted—that she, Jennie Speaker, could satisfy him.

Her arms clung to him tightly, and she let him do the rest—anything, everything he wanted. She thought that she would faint when she felt his hand on her naked flesh, and at the same time she felt stronger than she had ever felt before. She pressed hard with her pelvis in the direction his hand was guiding her, and she felt something hard pressing back.

And then he stopped. The baby moaned, and she froze, holding onto the feeling so that she would be right in the same place when he came back to her. But he never came back to her. She was left lying on the floor, at his feet. She

237

started to reach out to him, to plead with him, but she knew that would hurt him, or at least cause him discomfort. So she pulled her self together. She got to her knees, smoothed her skirt down over her legs, and folded her hands in her lap. Her eyes were lowered. She might have been saying her prayers.

"Good night, Jennie," said Captain Rogers. He started for the door.

Jennie knew that there was something more she had to say to him, and she leaped up and ran over to him as he stood in the doorway.

"Captain . . ." she began. She put her hand on his arm, left it there for a few seconds, and then removed it. "Captain Rogers, I just want to let you know that . . . if you want to forget this, I'll forget it too, and you can still come in and we'll just talk anytime you want to, if you're lonely or need a friend or anything. And if you don't want to forget it . . . sometime . . . if . . ." Her eyes wandered helplessly, as if trying to find a refuge from the tears that would soon be filling them.

Captain Rogers squeezed her hand. "Good night, Jennie," he said, and closed the door behind him.

◆Chapter Twenty-five

ELIZABETH DID NOT EVEN GET OFF THE *Western Wind* in Manila. She gave Jennie one day off, and suggested that Wales take her ashore and show her some of the exotic sights of the Pacific port. She stayed on board ship, took care of little Anne, and nursed her jealousy. The memory of San Francisco was fresh, yet repressed, in her mind. Instead of thinking about it as something that had happened to her, she made it into a fantasy of what Jennie and her husband were doing that afternoon in Manila.

When Jennie came back with stories of open-air markets and street magicians and beautiful teakwood carvings, Elizabeth was cold. The next day she was abusive, finding fault with everything the girl did, until little Anne cried, and Elizabeth felt ashamed of herself, and stopped.

They stayed in Manila for seven days. The crew was on duty the whole time, loading and unloading cargo, but the afterdeck was quiet. Wales was ashore most of the time. Harris went with him when he was off watch, to learn about business transactions in foreign ports. On the fourth day, Dowling appeared in Elizabeth's cabin.

He did not bother to knock. Elizabeth was in her shift, trying to get some relief from the tropical weather. When Dowling entered, she recoiled in shock. It was, literally, the last thing she had expected. She reached for her robe, but he moved too swiftly for her. He interposed himself between her and the robe, and stood there, daring her to try and get past him.

She did not try. She stayed where she was, sitting, uncomfortably aware of the outline of her nipples against the thin shift, but unwilling to give him the satisfaction of crossing her arms over her breasts, thereby admitting to him that he was making her ill at ease. She hoped that she would not get excited.

"I'll scream," she told him in a level voice.

"No, you won't."

"Try me."

He folded his arms, and stood at ease in front of her. He tried to look into her eyes, not at her breasts, but Elizabeth could see his lids flicker.

"We've still got a lot to talk about," he said.

"Not like this, we don't."

"And what's wrong with this? We've done it before."

"I felt differently then," said Elizabeth, the irritation breaking through in her voice. "Or maybe I didn't. Anyway, I acted differently."

"It doesn't have to be different."

"I think it does. A lot of time has passed since then."

Dowling allowed himself a slow sneer. "It didn't have to be that long," he said.

"What do you mean by that?"

"With proper handling, we would have made port five days sooner."

"Oh, you think so, do you?" Elizabeth flushed red with defensive rage, and her body felt hot and dry.

"Yes, I think so."

"And I suppose you think you could have done better if you were captain?"

"I've been a captain. I know what I'm doing."

"Well, you're not a captain anymore, so you must have been doing something wrong. And you don't have any business in this cabin, either."

"This isn't the captain's cabin."

"No, it's mine, and I see whom I want." But she was suddenly, and terribly, aware that allowing him to be there with her undressed, was an acceptance of intimacy between

240

them that she could not stand. She was about to end the conversation, to tell him to leave again, and really scream if he did not. Instead, she asked, with venom in her tone, "Why do you come skulking around now?"

He began to answer, but she cut him off. "You could have come to try and see me anytime. You knew where I was. Or were you afraid to take the chance when Wales was around?"

Dowling's face darkened. "I'll show you who's afraid!" he said. He grabbed her by the waist and jerked her to her feet, pressing her tight against him. She ducked her head down on her chest, but he pried her face up with his own, locking his mouth against hers in a hard and brutal kiss.

She reached back to try and pull his hand away, but he only caught her wrist and held her arm behind her back, pulling up on it so that she cried out with pain, her scream muffled by his kiss. She struggled, twisting his face this way and that until she finally wrenched her mouth free from his.

"Let me go, you . . . you animal!" she panted furiously.

His breath was coming short now, too, and he pushed his body against hers, giving another tug to her arm every time she backed away from him.

"Come on—you want it—don't you?—come on—" he repeated, with each panted breath, each step, each jerk of her arm; and she: "*No! . . . No! . . . No! . . .*" until finally she ducked and twisted and pulled away from him. She reached her robe and held it in front of her, glaring at him.

"Get out!" she hissed.

They faced each other, each tense, angry, suddenly exhausted.

"Why don't you go back to him?" Dowling asked, managing one last, weary sneer.

"Why don't you go to hell?" said Elizabeth.

"That's what you want. You don't fool me. You don't even do a good job of fooling yourself. Go on—you deserve each other. If it's not too late."

And he spun around and walked out.

❦Chapter Twenty-six

GO BACK TO WALES? NO, SHE HAD NEVER thought of it. Dowling was wrong, dead wrong.

She missed the life she had shared with Wales. That was true enough. And she had come to have a grudging, then less grudging, respect for him. But he had injured her too much for her ever to forgive, or forget.

And, for that matter, who could say what he felt? No doubt, Wales was as little interested in reconciliation with her as she was with him—and that had nothing to do with Jennie Speaker, either. Dowling may have thought himself clever; he may have thought that he knew just how to jab the needle into Elizabeth, but that was not necessarily true. Elizabeth was not going to fall for that sort of insinuation—not that she cared if anything had gone on between Wales and Jennie Speaker. If it had, well . . .

The point was that it had not. The idea was unthinkable. Jennie Speaker? Wales might as well go and have an affair with little Anne.

Elizabeth could not quite remember the enormity of Wales's injury to her. She knew that if she thought about it, she would remember, and she was sure that when she remembered, she would only reaffirm her conviction that it really was too much for her to forgive or forget. In any case, it was true, because it had been true for so long.

Elizabeth was lonely, and she would go on being lonely. It was cruel—perhaps it was unfair, perhaps not, but it was so. She would go on living with it.

She felt sorry for Wales, though, in one particular: Dowling. The mate's arrogance had grown into open contempt for Wales's seamanship and command, to the point where it was dangerously close to rank insubordination. Elizabeth was very much afraid that she was partly to blame for the situation. Dowling had been made bold by what he thought of as his conquest of the captain's wife; and after her rejection of him, he had been stung to even madder extremes of competition. Elizabeth would have liked to say something to Wales about it; but of course, there was nothing she could say. She shouldered her blame in isolation.

Jennie lived for the evening visits that Captain Rogers made to the nursery, and the pain she felt each time he came. They never touched again, after that night. She never told him how she felt about him, though sometimes she felt that he must know, and sometimes she was sure that he did not—and she thanked God, from the depths of her suffering, that he did not.

He came every night. Sometimes he just played with the baby, and sometimes he would stop and talk to her. There were days when Anne learned something new, or did something special, and then Jennie had a topic to start a conversation with—and he would always listen, with delighted interest. She was learning to construct things with building blocks that the ship's carpenter had made for her. They were special blocks, with tongue and groove edges, so they would hold together even under the constant rocking of the ship. Anne made houses with them, and cottages, and barns, never ships. She pretended that Legend was a farm animal, and made stalls and stables for her that were much smaller than the cat was, but served the game perfectly well anyway.

Anne was starting to learn her letters, too, and Jennie could show off that to her charge's papa, holding up the block-printed ABC's for Captain Rogers' approval.

Other evenings, the captain would sit and talk to Jennie about his day. That was the best of all. Jennie did not understand very much of what he said, but she knew that he had no one else to talk to, and that she could understand his feelings, even if the details did not make sense to her. She could tell when he was pleased, when worried, when frustrated, and she rejoiced with him, or suffered for him, with all the compassion that was in her soul.

Jennie could tell, also, about the strain that was growing between Captain Rogers and Mr. Dowling. Jennie's response to it was very simple. She was fiercely loyal to Captain Rogers, and she hated Mr. Dowling. She thought he was an evil, evil man. She avoided him whenever she could, and she glared at him with hatred when she did see him.

Jennie, of course, had no idea of what had transpired between Dowling and Elizabeth. No one on the ship did, in fact—no one except Whiteurs, and he kept it to himself.

But Whiteurs saw the rift between Dowling and the captain more clearly than anyone. He saw it clearly because he knew the root of it; and he saw it clearly because he, more than anyone, knew what was happening on the bridge and in the fo'c'sle.

The fo'c'sle was not a tranquil place. Elizabeth still maintained her status as a kind of mythic heroine, because of her rescue of the sailor Mapp, and the able seamen of the *Wind* resented the captain for Elizabeth's disappearance from her one-time regular routine of operating the sextant on the bridge each midday. Without knowing any of the details, they knew that something was wrong between the captain and his wife, and they were not about to blame their heroine.

They knew that something was wrong between the captain and the first mate, too. It was obvious that Dowling did not respect the captain's judgment or his authority. The crew waited to see how long the old man would put up with it. And as they waited, they began to take sides, with one faction of the crew declaring that Dowling was the man who really knew what he was talking about, the other faction supporting Captain Rogers.

Whiteurs knew where he stood. He did not know what was going on between Dowling and Mrs. Rogers, and he was not going to interfere between the captain and his wife.

He would not hurt Mrs. Rogers. But Dowling was another story. Whiteurs considered killing him. The idea did not frighten him in the least, and he gave it some long, dispassionate thought. It was not hard to kill a man at sea; Whiteurs had known it to happen to other mates. A belaying pin from behind, at night, and then over the side . . . Dowling was tough, one of the toughest men Whiteurs had ever seen. But Whiteurs was not convinced that the mate was tougher than he was.

Still, the ship would be in big trouble without Dowling. There was no third officer, and the second mate was a joke. Whiteurs decided against it. But he also resolved to keep a close eye on the mate, and to act if the balance were to tip in his mind. Whiteurs had never killed a man on shipboard before, certainly not an officer. And he had the innate conservatism of a seaman. But this was a special situation, because of what he knew. So he remained alert.

"Jennie, I want to speak to you."

"Yes, Mrs. Rogers?"

"I've decided that I want Anne to spend more time with me."

Jennie was shocked. Anne, playing with her blocks in a corner of the cabin, looked up at the sound of her name, and moved over a little, to be out of sight behind Jennie.

"Is something wrong, Mrs. Rogers? Have I done something wrong?"

"No, don't be silly," said Elizabeth impatiently. She was hoping there would not be a scene, because she would not know how to handle it. She had not thought beyond the impulse. She had frozen her mind at that point, as if the concentration of energy would pull all other wills and emotions into its orbit.

"What is it, then?" Jennie asked plaintively.

"Nothing," said Elizabeth. "I want my daughter to spend more time with her mother, that's all."

"Of course, ma'am," said Jennie. She was flustered and becoming more so, but she did not know why. "That's lovely. I'm sure that Anne will enjoy it."

"I want her to start sleeping with me, in my cabin."

"What?" Jennie took a step backward, and Anne moved closer to her. "Oh, but Mrs. Rogers, are you sure? She's got her own little bed in here, and all her little clothes and toys. And we have our own little routine, her and me, that she's used to at bedtime. It helps her to get to sleep, and—"

"I'm sure that she and I can establish our own routines," said Elizabeth.

Jennie stopped, at a loss for words, and no match for Elizabeth's strength. Elizabeth began to relax a little. It was not going to be difficult, after all—there would be no argument, and she could just glide through it. But suddenly, little Anne leaped up and ran over to Jennie, clasping her about the legs, burying her face in Jennie's dress, and hiding from her mother.

"No, Jennie, no!" she cried. "I don't want to leave you! I don't want to!"

"Now, you stop that this instant, young lady," said Jennie, stern and tender at the same time, stroking little Anne's hair. "You just stop. You have to show proper respect for your mother. How were you brought up, anyway?"

"But, Jennie . . ." sobbed little Anne.

"Not another word," said Jennie. She was down on her knees now, her arms around the baby, rocking and soothing her. "Not another word. Your mother loves you, and she wouldn't do anything that wasn't for the best, you'll see."

Elizabeth felt like an intruder. She wished she could just run away and be forgotten; but that could not be, so she stood in cold silence and waited for Jennie to finish the job of calming down little Anne. Jennie held Anne against her body, enfolding her with her arms and swaying back and forth gently, while Anne's little hands went around the governess's neck. Elizabeth had never noticed before how strong Jennie's arms were. But Anne clutched just as tightly. For a while, it was hard to tell who was comforting whom.

Anne stopped crying, and Jennie dried her eyes with a handkerchief.

"There, that's better, isn't it? Now, when did you want her to move into your cabin, Mrs. Rogers?"

"This evening, Jennie, thank you. I'm sure you'll be able to manage the details. Ritter will help you."

"Does this mean I won't be able to see Papa anymore?"

Anne had her tears under control, but her voice was still plaintive with sorrow, and it stopped both Elizabeth and Jennie short. They both turned to look at the little girl, and their eyes stayed on her. Neither of them could look at the other.

"Will I?"

Apologetically, Jennie said, "You know, Mrs. Rogers, the captain comes by here every evening to see the baby."

"Well, of course." Elizabeth had not thought about that aspect of her impetuous decision at all, but she was not going to admit it in front of Jennie. And she was determined to carry it through. "Of course, Captain Rogers can come and visit Jennie in my cabin anytime he wants to."

"Of course, Mrs. Rogers. Or—"

"I don't see any reason why the captain shouldn't be just as glad to visit his daughter in my cabin as in your cabin. Do you, Jennie?"

"Oh, no, ma'am. Oh, no."

"Well, then. Tell Ritter to set up a crib for Anne in my room, and start moving her belongings. I'll come by to pick her up this evening . . . er, after Captain Rogers makes his visit."

"Yes, ma'am."

"I believe that should be the simplest arrangement, don't you?"

"Whatever you say, ma'am."

Elizabeth turned to Anne. "All right, darling, I'll see you later. We'll have a wonderful time, you'll see."

"Y-yes, Mama."

"Good-bye, then."

"Good-bye, Mama."

Jennie came up to Elizabeth by the door, and spoke to her quietly.

"What will you be wanting me to do, then, Mrs. Rogers?" she asked.

"Well, I'm afraid there'll be a great deal less for you to do, Jennie. And, unfortunately, there isn't much else that you're qualified to do on shipboard, is there?"

"No, ma'am." Jennie turned away, fighting hard not to show Elizabeth her tears of humiliation. Elizabeth went out.

She wanted even more to hold back her tears when she

was alone with little Anne, but finally the emotions proved too strong; and the baby, having no motive for restraint on her own part, did not make things easier for her. They held onto each other, and both cried for a long time.

They had stopped by evening, when Captain Rogers came to visit the nursery, but their eyes were still red and swollen. Jennie found it impossible to talk to the captain, but Anne told him of her mother's plan. Captain Rogers frowned and turned to Jennie, who hastened to add:

"Oh, I'm sure that Anne will find it perfectly amiable, once she gets settled in. It will be a nice change for her, and I know she and her mama will have fine times together."

Wales looked closely and sympathetically at Jennie. "I'll speak to her," he said. "Perhaps I can reason with her. It's going to be hard for—well, it's not fair to you."

"Oh, no," Jennie said quickly. "Please don't do that. I think . . . I think . . ." she began, then she stepped so close to the captain that she might have touched his arm without even reaching, and continued in a whisper: "I think that Mrs. Rogers probably just wants to do this for a little while, and then things will get back to normal. I think it's best not to try and do anything about it."

Captain Rogers was persuaded. He could only stay a short time, because they were expecting bad weather and he had to be back up on the poop deck, so he kissed Anne goodnight and left.

Anne was moved over to Elizabeth's cabin. She brought Legend with her, which did not please Elizabeth overmuch. She was not a pet lover, nor was she excited about the prospect of having cat hair all over everything; but she permitted it. Jennie went to sleep alone.

ᴖChapter Twenty-seven

THE STORM HIT AT DUSK. IT BEGAN AS A
violent squall and within an hour had reached typhoon
proportions. Captain Rogers gave orders to lead all braces
to the poop deck and the topsides of the deckhouses and
secure them there, and that a line be run from the poop
deck to the fo'c'sle. Very soon it would be all but suicidal
for any hands to remain on deck.

Down below, Jennie cowered in her bunk. Storms terrified her; and she knew this one was worse than any she
had been through before, even the awful, infamous Cape
Horn passage. She was glad, now, that little Anne was with
Mrs. Rogers, who always kept her head in an emergency
and would take care that no harm came to the baby. She
wished that someone would come and take care of her. She
opened her mouth to scream for help, but all that came out
of it were prayers.

Anne woke up with the first explosion of the storm, and
cried out in fright. "I want Jennie!" she wailed. "I'm
scared. I want Jennie!"

"Jennie can't help you now," said Elizabeth. "You're
best off right here with me. Now be quiet. There's nothing
we can do except stay right here, and trust to Papa to keep
the ship afloat and save us."

"I want Jennie!" wailed Anne, unappeased.

"Jennie can't help you!" said Elizabeth sharply, angrily. Anne was startled into silence for a moment; and Elizabeth was startled too, by her own rage. "Here, darling," she said. She scooped up the cat, which was crouched in a corner, and gave it to Anne to hold. "You take care of Legend, now, and everything will be all right."

The gale howled to an unbearable crescendo, peaked by the awful crack of the mizzen-royal mast. It was directly above Wales, as he stood on the poop deck directing the two men who were battling the helm to keep the ship on course. The mast toppled sternward, and Wales looked up and saw it above him, like a huge tree felled the wrong way by a clumsy axeman. Its size made it appear to be moving slower than it really was, but Wales knew he had only a second to act. He shouted a warning to the helmsmen and dove for the side of the deck, clear of the mast's downward course, as the helmsmen did the same.

But the track was impossible to judge. The ship lurched wildly, as the wheel spun, unmanned. The falling mizzenmast caught the spanker, broke it loose, and bounced crazily off to one side. Wales saw it flying straight for him, as at the same moment a huge wave combed the poop deck and hit him from the back. The breath left his lungs and his feet jerked out from under him, and through no power of his own, he was pushed, sliding, across the deck and out of the path of the mizzen-royal. The mast crashed hard into the deck, knocking a huge hole in the timbering, through which water poured and from which Wales could hear issuing a sound unknown to the bridge of a ship, but chillingly familiar to him—the terrified scream of his daughter.

He got to his feet, coughing and sputtering. It only took him an instant to recover, but as he did, he looked up to see a thirty-foot wave of black water, marbled with white and crowned by a rolling, snapping, angry whitecap, towering over the stern of the ship. Wales clung to the fallen mast, the only thing within his reach, wrapping a rope around his wrist and praying that the rope was secure to the mast, and that the mast was jammed on the deck so it would not be washed overboard.

The wave hit. Wales's head was rattled against the mast, against the deck, against the mast again; he saw blinding

252

flashes of light that matched the magnitude of his pain. He threw all his will into maintaining consciousness, and somehow he managed it. But his strength was sapped; the water pried loose his fingers and picked up the arm that was wrapped around the mast, so that only the rope in his other hand, tied around his wrist, held him to the mast, and the ship.

But the rope held. The mast held; and his grip held, although his arm felt as though it must surely be ripped from its socket. His lungs held, although they were ready to burst when the wave finally passed.

He had, over the side of the rail, a momentary glimpse of an arm, a head, and then nothing but the implacable sea. So one of the helmsmen was gone, poor bastard. And what about the other?

A moan came from the deck, not far from Wales. Holding onto the mast, he made his way across the deck and found Braun, the other helmsman, lying trapped.

Alive. He had been caught by the spanker, not the mast, or he would have been crushed to death instantly.

"My shoulder, Cap'n," muttered the man. "Broken."

"Don't worry, Braun," said Wales. "It saved your life. Let me try to get this thing off you. . . ." He heaved, without success. There seemed no way to budge the heavy, tightly wedged beam, and then suddenly there was. Wales realized that someone else was beside him, lifting along with him, and he looked up to see Whiteurs. Another heave, and the sailor was free.

"Get forward, Braun," said Wales. "You'll have to make it yourself."

"Aye, aye, sir."

The wheel was jammed now by the debris from the fallen mast. Whiteurs and Wales worked feverishly to free it, and when it could move again, Whiteurs took his place behind it.

"You don't have much of a chance there," Wales said.

"One more wave like that over the stern, and none of us have a chance," said the bosun. "We're pooped." He tested the wheel. "Rudder still Okay."

"Lash yourself to the helm," said Wales. He looked at the hole in the decking which had never been far from his

253

thoughts, and tersely gave his sailing orders to Whiteurs. Then he headed below.

Elizabeth had no warning of the falling mast—just the cracking of the ceiling over her head, the rush of cold wind and seawater, and the tarred, splintered wooden cylinder, like the neck of some beheaded dragon bent on destroying her cabin in its death throes. Anne screamed, and her mother snatched her up in her arms and held her tightly. Anne burrowed close into Elizabeth for protection, and clasped her arms about her mother's neck. "Mama! Mama!" she cried over and over.

After the first shock, and her instinctive reaction to it, Elizabeth found herself just as instinctively taking stock of the situation. The cabin was too dangerous to stay in. Perhaps the whole after deckhouse would prove the same; but anyway, they had to get out of the cabin.

"Stay here while I get our foul-weather gear from the closet," she told Anne. "Then we'll go to Papa's cabin."

"No, don't leave me, Mama!" Anne wailed.

"It's just across the room, darling."

"Don't leave me!"

Elizabeth picked her up and carried her on one hip as she struggled to keep her footing on the wet, slippery, wildly pitching floor. Anne did not have the reckless courage that Elizabeth had possessed at the same age; and Elizabeth was glad of it. *I must have been crazy*, she thought. She no longer had that sort of courage, either. She was frightened to death. But she knew what had to be done from instinct and training, and she was grateful for that.

Halfway across the room, the wave hit them. It came crashing through the hole, taking a good quarter of the roof with it, and sending huge chunks of beam and planking down into the cabin. Elizabeth was caught hard in the side by something, and pulled down and buffeted by the swirling water. Her senses reeled, and for an instant she blacked out.

When she came to, she found that she was still holding Anne tightly, and she planted herself on one knee and held the child up high, so that her head would be clear of the water.

She struggled back to her feet, and found that she was

nearly waist deep in water, and that the ship was tilting astern. There was a dull pain in her side that all but immobilized her right leg, but she forced herself to walk. She still wanted to get their mackintoshes and hats, even though they were soaked through to the skin already. They'd need them if they had to leave the after deckhouse and go out on deck.

The closet door was held shut by the water pressure against it. Elizabeth set Anne down on a tabletop, took up a bar, and pried it open, bit by bit, until she could reach in.

Anne watched her, whimpering but trying to be brave, too. She was cold and frightened, but her mama's strength and determination gave her courage.

With a peevish hissing and sputtering, Legend swam across the room and scratched at the side of the table. Anne pulled her out of the water and held her, gratefully, as Elizabeth finally succeeded in squeezing her arm and shoulder into the closet and pulling out their foul-weather gear.

She turned her attention to the door of the cabin, but at that moment it opened, and much of the water that had been trapped in the cabin rushed out into the saloon, which was already awash but not as flooded as Elizabeth's cabin. Wales stood in the doorway.

"Papa!" cried Anne, and Elizabeth, too, was glad to relax some of her tension and vigilance, and turn to Wales for strength and leadership.

"Bring her about!"

Whiteurs looked at Dowling for the briefest moment, then turned back to the helm. "This course, sir," he replied. "Cap'n's orders."

"Goddamm it, you black ape!" Dowling screamed above the gale. "We can make it, if we do it now! We can outrun this storm. The captain's not on deck now—he doesn't know what's going on. He's downstairs taking care of his wife, not the ship. You can't give orders based on what conditions were twenty minutes ago. Come about and put the wind to our backs—that's an order."

"Cap'n's orders," Whiteurs said again.

Dowling stood about fifteen feet away from Whiteurs, holding onto the mizzen rigging. He was barely able to hear the bosun's voice, but he knew what Whiteurs was saying, and it made him livid. He advanced on the bosun, crouching to keep his balance on the treacherous deck.

"Are you going to obey my order, mister?"

"No, sir. Cap'n's orders," Whiteurs said stubbornly.

Whiteurs saw what was coming, but there was nothing he could do about it. Lashed to the wheel, he could not defend himself, and Dowling's punch caught him full in the jaw. His neck snapped back, and he slumped helplessly where he stood. Dowling tipped Whiteurs' jaw back, looked at his immobile face, and let it drop again. He took out his knife, and cut the black man loose.

No sooner did Whiteurs hit the deck than he spun like a snake and caught Dowling with a kick to the kneecap. Dowling fell backward, but he was on his feet, knife still in his hand, by the time Whiteurs regained his.

The two men faced each other, moving back and forth no more than six inches to the right or to the left. Both men knew that the fight would be short: if one of them did not end it quickly, the storm and the sea would. Dowling feinted with his knife once, twice; Whiteurs bobbed, gauging the feints. Then the mate saw an opening, and lunged.

He came in high, and fast. He launched himself like a bolt, and the footing was so bad there was no way Whiteurs could dodge him. The knife blade gleamed in the darkness.

At the last second, Whiteurs' right hand whipped out and grabbed the knife by the blade. He twisted it, and yanked it out of Dowling's hand, as the mate stumbled backward. Then he flung the knife away from him, over the side. Two of his fingers went with it.

Whiteurs leaped on top of Dowling, his knee catching him in the groin, his hands—the bloody one and the whole one—going around the mate's throat. He held on, and squeezed. He was still squeezing when he was struck behind the ear by a belaying pin and laid out.

"Are you all right, sir?" asked one of the sailors who had come up on deck with Harris as he leaned over Dowling.

Dowling shook his head from side to side, slowly. His fingers tested his throat. "I'm all right," he said. "Take the wheel."

"Aye, aye, sir."

Two sailors battled the wheel under control, and Harris

directed the third: "Put this man under arrest, and see that his wounds are taken care of."

Dowling was barking out orders to the new helsman as Whiteurs was led away.

"It doesn't look good, Mr. Dowling," shouted Harris.

"Don't worry about a thing, Mr. Harris," replied Dowling, with something like a grin on his face. "Back in the China Seas we used squalls like this for sailing practice."

"What is it?" asked Elizabeth. "Are we going to be hauled under from the stern?"

"I hope not," said Wales. "But we're going to ship a lot of water, and it could get to be too dangerous to stay here. Perhaps it is already. I want the stern quarters evacuated right now."

"What does that mean, Papa?" asked Anne.

"It means I'm going to take you, and Mama, and Jennie, and put you where you'll be safe, up in the fo'c'sle where the sailors live." He smiled, and touched her cheek, and turned to Elizabeth to include her in the smile too. "It'll be an adventure. Then, when we're safe from the storm, and we have your ceiling fixed up again, I'll take you back."

"All right, Papa. Take Legend too, please," said the little girl, and thrust the kitten into her father's hands. Surprised, Wales held onto the animal, looked down at it, and then dropped it into one of his large pockets. "She'll be safe there," he said. He turned to Elizabeth. "Are you ready?"

"Yes, Wales. But . . . should you be taking time to do this? They'll need you up on deck. I can take the responsibility down here, and get us out."

"I'll do it," said Wales. "It's going to be dangerous, and I don't want to take any chances."

"What do you mean?" Elizabeth, shocked at herself, nevertheless found her mood shifting from concern to defensive anger. "I don't care if it's dangerous! I've handled myself in dangerous positions before, and I can handle this."

"*Elizabeth.*" Wales's voice was level, but awesome in its purpose. "This will not happen again."

She was chastened. "No. You're right, Wales. Let me put on Anne's mackintosh, and . . . *good God!*"

The ship was acting crazy, rolling and pitching dangerously. It felt completely out of control, and great new quantities of water and debris were pouring in through the roof of the cabin. It felt as if the *Wind* had gone completely out of control. "What does it mean, Wales?" Elizabeth asked.

"I don't know." He took a step toward her; but movement was so difficult, and there was no time. "You'll have to take charge of the evacuation, Elizabeth. Find Ritter to help you. God be with you."

The *Wind* had righted herself when Wales came on deck. She was running with the wind, under Dowling's orders and his helmsman's execution. The great waves piled up at her stern, and raked the poop deck. The helmsman came near drowning more than once, just from the water that filled the air, but the ship sailed on, climbing from valley to peak along the ocean's surface, again and again.

Dowling and the helmsman were the only ones on deck now. Dowling felt himself, at that moment, master of a Yankee clipper, not some smuggler manned by a crew out of Singapore with prices on their heads worth almost as much as the cargo. He knew he could do it, and he was doing it—driving a crack Yankee ship through the fiercest of gales. He could even put out sail now, sail that Rogers had ordered taken in, and make it work. The *Wind* would carry it for him.

But Tom Dowling was no dreaming madman, either, and he knew he had signed on as first mate for this voyage. He'd have to answer to the captain for superceding his orders—and answer he would. He'd made the right decisions, and the *Western Wind* was answering for him.

Still, he felt the shock of confrontation when he saw Captain Rogers come out of the companionway, and for a split second, he wished himself someone else. Rogers moved toward him as if in a dream, slowly across the shattered, storm-lashed poop deck. Finally, they were close enough together to be heard over the wind.

"Who ordered this? Where's Whiteurs?" shouted Rogers.

"Below. I gave the order. It had to be done."

"Whiteurs was keeping course under my orders."

"Conditions changed. You weren't on the bridge. And it's working, goddamm it, Captain! We're licking the storm!"

"One more wave over the stern could swamp us!"

"We can stay ahead."

"And the passengers?"

"I assumed you were taking care of them—*Captain*."

The bitter sarcasm in Dowling's tone was plain even over the howl of the storm. The two men glared at each other with open hatred.

"Go below and place yourself under arrest, Mr. Dowling. That's an order."

"You're going to need me before this is out, Captain."

"I said that's an order, Mr. Dowling."

Dowling held the captain's eye a moment longer, then gave way. He still managed a slight curl of his lip.

"To my cabin, sir?" he asked.

"No. Forward," said Wales.

Dowling descended to the main deck, and went on, hand over hand, along the rope that stretched from the poop to the fo'c'sle. He went quickly, with an incongruous, almost carefree manner, down the length of the empty deck.

"Shall I alter the course, sir?" asked the helmsman.

At that moment, Wales could see another form on the main deck. It was Elizabeth, holding Anne, starting across the open deck.

"No . . . no. Steady as she goes," said Wales.

He wanted to go to his wife and daughter, to lead them across, but he could not. For better or worse, he was now the only responsible officer left on the *Wind*. There was no one to spell him, no one to help him. He would have to trust Elizabeth to herself, and little Anne to her.

They were tied together. The child clung to Elizabeth's chest, her arms around her neck, her legs around her waist; and a piece of rope encircled first Anne's waist, then Elizabeth's. Wales could see Anne's face, over Elizabeth's shoulder: bloodless white, eyes tight shut, mouth a thin line. She shook her head every few seconds to clear the water away from her nose, so she could breathe. She was terrified beyond terror, clinging to her mother and blotting out the rest of the world.

Of his wife, Wales could see only her back. And while they were still near the stern, her hands, small and pale. One would reach out ahead, and grasp the rope. Then, slowly, the yellow slicker would move along to cover it,

259

and the other hand would be left exposed to Wales's view. Then that hand would slide up and be absorbed again into the compactness of her body. And it would all start again. Wales fancied he could see, too, a dark stain on the rope as she passed along it, the imprint of hands rubbed raw and bleeding. He knew it was his fancy—his eyes could see nothing so minute at this distance.

But he knew that the stain was there.

She was doing it. With his daughter clinging to her, tied to her, she moved, step by step, along the rope. She stumbled once, and Wales's heart sank, but she got to her feet again and went on. And the ship went on, too, plowing through the seas that crashed around it and sent torrents of water sweeping across its decks, tugging and twisting at the feet of anyone trying to negotiate a passage. The ship went on, and Wales willed it with his skill and his prayers to keep to an even keel until they were safe across.

And then they had made it. Elizabeth had made it. With wild relief, Wales saw her reach the fo'c'sle and disappear inside. He felt a great lump of tension dissolve inside him and vanish in a rush. He put his hand to his forehead, and bent his head down.

He placed his other hand in his pocket, and felt something there that at first he could not identify. Then he remembered. It was Anne's kitten, still sopping wet, but warm and rumbling.

They gave Elizabeth and Anne the cabin normally shared by the bosun and the ship's carpenter. It was the only private space in the fo'c'sle. The cabin was covered with fresh blood—Whiteurs' blood, from his fight with Dowling. Whiteurs had been bandaged, and taken to the brig. Dowling was next door to Elizabeth in the carpenter's shop, but technically under cabin arrest and incommunicado.

Elizabeth was too tired, and too concerned about her child, to worry about either the blood or Dowling. She secured a blanket, and wrapped Anne up in it. Anne went to sleep promptly, and Elizabeth waited for Ritter to arrive with Jennie.

But they did not come. Elizabeth went back to the hatch to look aft. There was no one in sight.

I'll take the responsibility down here, she had told Wales. She had found Ritter, told him to get Jennie and follow. She had convinced him that it was, in fact, the captain's decision, since the after part of the ship was becoming dangerously flooded. So they should have been right behind her. Perhaps Ritter had not believed her after all . . . ? No, that could not be it. But Jennie was still back there, in danger. She jammed her sou'wester down tighter on her head, and started back.

The wind and the sea lashed at her yet again. Her hands were raw and bleeding, and the salt water scored them with pain. The way back seemed more tiring and arduous than the first crossing had been, even without Anne to carry. She only hoped that once she had Jennie, and could start for the fo'c'sle again, she would get a second wind. She would need it.

She did not know how she made it back to the after deckhouse. As she neared the hatch, she found that she was moving, and holding onto the rope, out of some sort of instinct she no longer understood or cared about. She did not care very much whether she made it or not, but she somehow understood that she was going to, anyway.

She saw no one in the saloon, and so she struggled on to Jennie's cabin. Jennie was there; she was crouched in a corner of her bed, paralyzed with fear. Ritter was there; he was on the floor, motionless.

His face was clear of the water. "Is he dead?" asked Elizabeth.

Jennie did not answer.

"Is he dead?" Elizabeth repeated. "Is he dead or alive?"

"I . . . I don't know," said Jennie.

"What happened?"

"He hit his head."

Elizabeth knelt down beside the steward. "He's breathing," she said. "That means he's alive."

She regretted the sarcasm. She felt sorry for Jennie, but she felt as if she were talking to herself. She bent down beside Ritter, shook him, slapped him, and gradually brought him back to a grudging consciousness. He moaned, and sat up slowly, holding his head in his hands.

"Are you all right?" she asked.

"I think so," he said. "In a few minutes."

"Right," said Elizabeth, and left him. Ritter was not the problem. He was no tough sailor, but he could take care of himself. Jennie could not. She was in no condition to do anything without being led.

Elizabeth went over to her, and took her by the hand. She spoke steadily to the girl, in a quiet, soothing but firm voice, and got Jennie to her feet.

Jennie stepped gingerly down into the water on the floor, as though she were testing the surf at a beach. Elizabeth held her hand and walked with her, out through the ruined saloon, up on deck. Gently and patiently, she explained to her about the rope, about where they had to go and what they had to do to get there safely.

Jennie spoke demurely, like a shy girl turning down an invitation to dance. "Oh, no, Mrs. Rogers. I'm afraid I couldn't do that."

"Of course you can, Jennie. Captain Rogers said you should. Captain Rogers said it would be all right."

Jennie nodded agreement, but she did not move. To show her that it was all right, Elizabeth took a couple of steps out along the rope, then turned back and extended her hand.

"See, Jennie? You can do it, too. Come along, now."

"I've no coat. . . ."

Elizabeth sighed. She returned to Jennie, took off her own oilskin slicker and sou'wester, and wrapped them around the girl. Then she clasped Jennie's hand firmly, once again, and still talking, still encouraging, began to lead her out. Finally, Jennie took the first step.

There was not much use in Elizabeth's talking to Jennie once they were out in the wind, but she kept it up, anyway, and she kept up the firm pressure of her hand, and brought the girl one step at a time, placing her hand on the rope, moving her along. Elizabeth walked facing backward, so that Jennie could see her face.

Wales caught sight of them when they were about half-way to the mainmast. He had not seen Elizabeth return, so he was shocked and confused at first. He quickly realized what must have happened, and for a moment he was angry—*why couldn't she have sent a sailor back?*—but then he stood transfixed, his heart scarcely beating, watching, powerless to help.

For a moment he was confused as to who was who; but the one out in front, leading, coaxing, had to be Elizabeth, and the other Jennie, wearing Elizabeth's slicker. Elizabeth moved even more slowly than she had when carrying the baby. She coaxed Jennie along, holding her hand the whole time, gradually getting her to move more surely. "We're going to make it, girl!" Elizabeth said warmly, although she knew Jennie could not hear.

A great crack came from up above them. They had lost the main-royal yardarm. It split from the mainmast and fell, only to catch in a tangle of ropes long before it reached the deck.

But it was enough to panic Jennie. She pulled away from Elizabeth, and started to back up in the direction she had come. She raced backward, and within three steps she had stumbled over her own feet, and fallen.

"Jennie!" shrieked Elizabeth. She lunged back after her. Ritter, who had just appeared on deck, tried to reach her from the other side. But neither of them was anywhere near close enough, or fast enough—not for the suddenness with which her body slid along the deck, propelled by undertow. They saw the glint of panic and effort in her eyes, as she tried to scramble back on all fours, and the water and the slant of the deck drove her along. Then another huge wave broke over the side of the ship, and when its waters had receded they no longer saw her at all.

❧Chapter Twenty-eight

WHEN THE AFTER DECKHOUSE WAS REBUILT, Elizabeth was moved back to her cabin. She had suffered from exposure and exhaustion, and her constitution was still shaky. Ritter helped her across the deck, now dry and sun-bleached. The decking above the cabin had been repaired, and the interior cleaned out and restored. Wales had ordered that as a first priority after the storm. Elizabeth was grateful. The fo'c'sle was no place for a woman, favorite though she was among the sailors. And it was certainly no place for a child. She was glad to be back in her own cabin.

But if Wales had come for Elizabeth himself, and taken her back to his cabin, she would have gone with him.

When she was settled, he came to visit her in her cabin. He played with little Anne. Then Elizabeth put her to bed, and she and Wales talked. After so long, it should have been tense and difficult for them to talk to each other. But after the experience of the last few days, which they had shared so intensely, it seemed natural.

They did not talk very much about Jennie. Wales praised Elizabeth for her bravery, and told her not to blame herself. She nodded, and thanked him, and he knew that she did blame herself. She wanted to know the damage to the ship, and the repairs that were being made, so they discussed that at length. He told her about Dowling's insubordination, and she listened intently.

"Will he be under arrest for the rest of the voyage?"

"Yes. That's beyond question. He won't be allowed to resume his duties."

"What will you do for a first officer?"

"It'll have to be Harris. I'll give Whiteurs the responsibility of acting second officer, and he'll be in charge of the other watch."

"Then there really isn't any qualified officer aboard the *Wind*, except you," Elizabeth said.

"Ron Whiteurs is one of the smartest, toughest men I've ever sailed with," said Wales. "But . . . no, there isn't."

"Wales, I'd like to help," said Elizabeth. "I'd like to do the navigating for you again. I mean . . . I'd really like to. If you want me to."

"Yes, I would," said Wales. "That would be a great help to me. I'd like that very much."

"Then I'll do it."

There was a long pause, during which Wales looked several times as if he were about to speak, and several times as if he were about to get up and leave. Finally, he said:

"Elizabeth . . . will you come back to my cabin?"

"Tonight?"

"To stay."

And it was Elizabeth's turn to be silent for a long time before she spoke.

"No, Wales. Not now. I don't know why. I should. Perhaps I even want to. But . . . no. I'm sorry."

Wales accepted it as he would accept a law of nature, with a seaman's fatalism. He smiled, said goodnight, and left without touching her. Elizabeth knew that he wanted to touch her.

Nothing in her life had ever affected Elizabeth as did Jennie's death. She could not stop thinking about it. She could not stop reliving it. Over and over again, she saw the expression on Jennie's face, as she slid across the deck. Over and over again, she saw her trying to scramble back. At the very end, Jennie had tried to save herself. When it was too late, she had fought for herself.

If Jennie had learned how to fight like that sooner, Elizabeth wondered, would she still be alive? And she could not help wondering, too: if Jennie had learned to fight like that sooner, could she have had Wales?

Elizabeth did not become sentimental over Jennie. She did not suddenly discover wonderful qualities in the girl that she had always somehow overlooked; nor did she suddenly discover how fond of the girl she had always been, without quite realizing it. It was the death that she focused on. She could not stop reliving the scene, and every time, she came to the same conclusion, the conclusion that everyone told her to put out of her mind: that it was her fault.

She could have found a sailor, and sent him in her place to rescue Jennie—a strong man, who would not have let the panicked girl pull away from him. She could have waited for Ritter. Together, the two of them could have saved her.

No one else blamed her. Even Ritter, who bore no love for Elizabeth, had praised her bravery and told her that she had done all that was humanly possible.

She had been too proud. She was no heroine, but she had fancied herself one. And now a weak, timid, frightened girl was dead.

She had been most afraid that Anne would blame her. She knew that Anne had not really wanted to leave Jennie to come and stay in her cabin, and she questioned her own motives for insisting on it. But even Anne seemed to be closer to her now. The girl did not want to leave her mother's side. She came up on deck when Elizabeth sighted the sun with her sextant, and played quietly next to her as she sat at her desk with her chronometers and her set of Bowditch tables, working out the difficult five-place logarithms.

And when Wales came to visit in the evening, Anne was shyer and quieter than she had been when he came to visit her in Jennie's cabin, but she seemed very happy. She would sit and listen quietly, or play contentedly with her kitten while her mother and father talked to each other.

They were coming to treat each other like old friends—comrades-in-arms who had been through a war together, or two doctors who had worked side by side trying to stave off an epidemic. Wales made no more mention of her returning to his bed. Elizabeth knew that if there were a next move, it would have to come from her.

They sat and talked every evening, either in her cabin or up on deck. At first they just talked about running the ship, but gradually they came to include other topics: the beauty of sunsets in the South Pacific, anecdotes of friends in common and tales heard and retold, health, family, childhood memories. There was still much that they did not talk about. Elizabeth thought—but was not sure—that Wales still wanted to touch her. But he never made any move to. And if he did feel longing, he became, to her sorrow, more and more comfortable with not expressing it.

Elizabeth never had sexual fantasies anymore. She never woke up in the night sweating, overcome with sexual longing, needing to touch herself.

She was afraid she would never feel it again. She was afraid that if she went back to Wales, nothing could be rekindled, and she would not take the chance of trying. That was for his sake. She could not bear the thought of coming to him, and then disappointing him.

But what she feared most was that if her sexuality were reawakened, she would remember the ecstasy of that afternoon in San Francisco.

✥Chapter Twenty-nine

WHITEURS LIVED AFT NOW. HE DID NOT WANT to. He would have preferred to stay in the bosun's quarters, but it was not possible. Captain Rogers had asked his advice in choosing a new bosun, and he had recommended Mapp.

"Very well, Mapp it is, then," said the captain.

"You don't think it's a bad idea to have two colored men in authority, sir?" asked Whiteurs.

"No, why should I?" said the captain. So that was agreed upon, and put into effect.

It had worked out as he had hoped. Whiteurs wanted to know what was going on in the foc's'le, and his racial link with Mapp gave them a bond that stretched farther than rank.

That same bond meant that Whiteurs talked to no one else about what passed between himself and Mapp. He only listened, and watched, and kept his own counsel.

The crew was divided. It had been divided before, and Dowling's arrest had only intensified that divisiveness between those who supported the captain and those who supported Dowling. Whiteurs did his part to dampen the effect of the tension with hard work and strict discipline, but it was a losing battle, because Harris would not, or could not, do the same with the men in his watch. Although Harris would never have described himself as such, he was becoming identified in the minds of the crew as Dowling's man, whereas Whiteurs was the captain's man.

"There's one thing that's helpin', though," Mapp told Whiteurs one evening, as they stood by the rail. "That's Mrs. Rogers. Ain't a man on this crew don't like her, an' her an' the cap'n gettin' together again sure makes ever'one feel better. If there's gwine be any peace on this ship, you kin thank her."

"Mm-hm." Whiteurs nodded agreement. He tapped the burnt ash from his clay pipe over the rail, refilled the bowl, and set a match to the tobacco. He was thinking about Mrs. Rogers and Dowling. He knew that Mapp was right about how much disharmony Mrs. Rogers had healed aboard the *Western Wind*. He wondered how much she had caused. "Good night, Mr. Mapp."

"Good night, sir."

Whiteurs walked very quickly. He knew that the men knew he and Mapp talked, but he did not want to flaunt it too obviously. And he was not yet, and would never be, quite comfortable with being called "sir."

"They's some men won't talk to me around the fo'c'sle, sir," said Mapp a few nights later. "Some as don't trust me, 'cause they know I talks to you, and some mebbe has somethin' to hide."

"Oh?" Whiteurs grunted, expressing just enough interest to encourage Mapp to go on.

"There's two seamen, Molinas and Brown."

"I know them."

"They's somethin' ain't right with them. I think they's mebbe crazy."

"Yeah."

"An' something else . . ."

"What is it?"

"I don' know. I think they mebbe got a gun."

"A gun!" Whiteurs' voice was like a pistol shot itself, so immediate was his shock.

"Yeah. They been talkin' about Mr. Dowling, an' how he oughter be cap'n o' this ship, but crazy-like, not jus' grumblin' an' carryin' on, like the others does. I don' think they care who be cap'n o' this ship. I think they jus' crazy, an' grabbin' onto the talk goin' around."

"But the gun?"

"I jus' gots a feelin'. Talkin' about they gonna fix somethin', they got somethin', then kinda whisperin' to each other. I tells you, I thinks they got a gun. I wouldn' take no chance with 'em, that's all."

Whiteurs grunted agreement. "I'll talk to the cap'n," he said. "Looks like we're gonna have to search the fo'c'sle."

You never knew, on board ship. There had been dissension, men taking sides, yes: but nowhere near as bad as he had seen on other ships. He had shipped out on a three-master once, where there had been a knife fight almost every day, till there was practically no one on the crew with both his ears intact when they reached Sydney. He'd been on hell ships, where the men talked mutiny every waking minute, but nothing had come of it. And now here . . . if there was any truth to Mapp's suspicions, if these lunatics had managed to smuggle a gun on board . . .

It was evening, and the captain would be in Mrs. Rogers' cabin with his daughter. Whiteurs looked for him there, and found him.

"Something urgent I have to talk to you about, sir," he said. "Can I see you in your cabin for a minute?"

Some sixth sense prompted Elizabeth to speak up. "I'd like to know, too, if there's any danger. You can speak here, Mr. Whiteurs."

Whiteurs looked at the captain.

"Go ahead, Mr. Whiteurs. You can speak freely in front of Mrs. Rogers."

Whiteurs nodded. "But the child . . ." he said.

"Let's go into my cabin," said Wales.

Elizabeth picked up Anne in her arms, put her in her bed, and kissed her forehead. "I'll be back in a minute, darling," she said, and followed the two men out.

She had not been inside Wales's cabin in months. She was amazed by how strange and how familiar it seemed, at the same time, and how exciting it felt to be there. But she only had an instant for that rush of feeling, because Whiteurs was talking then, and her attention was fixed on him.

He recapitulated briefly, for her benefit. "There's been some tension on the crew. You know that. Mr. Dowling . . . well, he had a lot o' the men thinkin' he was some kinda cock o' the walk, beggin' your pardon, ma'am, and . . ." He turned his eyes from Elizabeth, back to the captain.

He knows, Elizabeth thought with a sudden flash of intuition. "And you know the rest. But there's two sailors, Molinas and Brown, been talkin' a lot about Mr. Dowling. Been talking mutiny, maybe, but no one else took 'em seriously. The crew ain't thinkin' mutiny, they just ain't happy with each other. But Mapp says these two swabs might have a gun."

"Does he know for sure?"

"I think prob'ly if he says so, he's right."

"Right. Pipe all hands on deck, and we'll conduct a search. Let's not waste time."

"Aye, aye, sir."

Whiteurs turned to go, but before he reached the door, the night was ripped by three loud explosions. At any other time, there would have been a moment of shocked disbelief, but now the three of them knew instantly what it meant. They were too late. The mutiny had begun.

Wales went to the locked strongbox where he kept his weapons. He took out a pistol for himself and one for Whiteurs, and two boxes of ammunition. Each kept the pistol in his hand, and put the box of bullets inside his shirt-front.

"Get back to your cabin and bolt the door," said Wales. "Take care of the baby. I'll be back."

"Shouldn't I have a gun?"

"No. You don't know how to use it. It'd be more of a danger to you than to an attacker. Just don't open the door; don't let anyone in."

He put his gun down on the big desk next to where he stood, and held her forearms in his hands. They were wide and strong and warm. "All right?" he said.

"All right, Wales," she said. She slipped out of his grip and threw herself at his chest, wrapping her arms around his body. He gathered her in and held her tight, and if there had been time, they would both have sobbed unashamedly. "But please be careful!"

* * *

She did as he said. She ran back to her own cabin and bolted the door behind her. Anne was sitting up in bed, her eyes round and frightened.

"What's happening, Mama?"

"Nothing, dear." She sat down on the bed, and hugged her daughter with arms that were still warm and full from the feel of her husband's body. "Papa will take care of us."

"Will Papa be all right?"

"Oh, yes, darling, oh, yes," said Elizabeth, and then she was no longer able to hold back her tears. "He'll be all right. He has to be."

At that moment a volley of shots rang out on deck.

"Papa will be all right," Elizabeth repeated, holding Anne and rocking her back and forth. He had to be all right. Everything that mattered in her life depended on it, and she had only just realized it. "Papa will take care of us."

There came the sound of footsteps on the companion-way, and Elizabeth rushed to her door. She started to throw back the bolt to welcome him, but checked her hand. Wales's orders had been not to open it, and she would follow them, until she heard his voice outside the door.

In the next moment, the rapid scuffling of the footsteps and the inchoate shouting of unfamiliar voices told her the story: it was not Wales and Whiteurs returning below. It was the mutineers.

Elizabeth hung next to the door, scarcely daring to breathe, listening intently for any clue as to what had happened.

She heard them rattling around outside her door, and she picked up a heavy poker and stood guard, in case they should break it down. But they moved on.

She heard them next outside the door of Dowling's cabin, and this time she heard the door open.

"Mr. Dowling!" a voice shouted. "We got the captain. We're taking over the ship for you."

"What are you talking about? Put down those guns." That was Dowling's voice.

"We're taking over the ship! You're going to be our leader! Come on!"

"You men are stark raving mad. You're out of your minds. Put down those guns before you hurt someone."

"We've got the captain, I tell you!"

"I don't believe you."

"Well, it's true! Are you with us or against us? We did it for you."

"With you? You're insane, I tell you. I'm no part of this mutiny. Give me those guns."

Then yet another shot. A sharp cry of pain from Dowling. The more banging and shouting as they rampaged through the officers' quarters. She heard the sound of the captain's door being thrown open, some violent crashing and shouting, a couple of wild gunshots.

Her door was tried again, pounded on.

"Mr. Harris!" came the mutineer's voice through the door. "Mr. Harris, are you in there? We're taking over the ship! You can lead us! We've got the captain!"

We've got the captain. Elizabeth held her breath, and made no reply.

Another shot. It splintered through the door, and sped past her so close that she could feel the disturbance in the air. She jumped back, grabbed the baby, and lay down on the floor, shielding her with her body. But the mutineers had gone on. She heard them farther away, outside Harris's cabin, repeating their litany again: *We've got the captain!* There was no answer from Harris's cabin, either, and the mutineers went back up the companionway.

It was quiet again, except inside Elizabeth's head, where those ominous words echoed again and again: *We've got the captain.*

At length she could not stand it anymore. She told Anne to stay in bed, and not to worry. She was going to take care of Papa.

"What did those men mean, Mama?"

"I don't know, sweetheart. But I'm going to find Papa and take care of him. He'll be all right, and so will you. You get some sleep, now."

She was not crying now. She closed the door tightly, crossed to Wales's cabin, and found his medical bag. Then she ascended the companionway.

She put her head through the hatch cautiously, and withdrew it quickly as a shot rang out.

"Who goes there?" came Whiteurs' voice out of the darkness.

"Elizabeth Rogers, Mr. Whiteurs. Was it you who fired that shot?"

"No! Don't try to come out on deck."

"Where's my husband?"

"He's here here with me. He's hurt, but he's still alive."

"Then I'm coming out."

"Mrs. Rogers, no! It's too dangerous."

"You can't stop me, Mr. Whiteurs. I'm not trying to sound like a character in a melodrama. But I'm going to go to my husband."

"Wait!" Whiteurs shouted, in a different tone. Then lower,: "Can you hear me?"

"Yes," she answered, keeping her voice low also.

"All right, then don't come until you hear the signal. We're behind the binnacle. Run to the starboard side. Got that?"

"Binnacle . . . starboard side, yes."

"We've got two wounded men here. You have the medical kit?"

"Yes."

"Water?"

"No."

"Get some. Then come back and let me know when you're ready. Got that?"

"Yes."

She turned, and went back down the companionway. Below decks, she looked fleetingly at the two closed doors. No use to call Harris—if he were man enough to be of any use, he would be out by now. Dowling? Perhaps dead. No time to stop and find out now. She filled a canteen, and went above again.

"Mr. Whiteurs."

"Mrs. Rogers? All right . . . ready . . . *now*!"

He leaped out from behind the binnacle, to the port side, guns blazing. Elizabeth ran, crouched low, to the starboard side. She heard a bullet fly past her, very nearby, and she dived the last few yards, clutching bag and canteen, and rolled in to safety as Whiteurs dived back from the other direction.

Her elbow hurt from where she had landed on it, but she

blinked back the pain, and looked up. Wales was lying no more than a foot away from her. His face was pale in the moonlight, and made paler by pain. It was drawn and contorted, but his eyes were open, and when they met hers, he managed something like a smile.

"Where are you hurt?" she asked, bringing the canteen up in front of her and uncorking the top.

"Him first," said Wales, his voice a hoarse croak. "He needs it more."

He gestured with his head toward the sailor beside him, and Elizabeth looked over. She recognized the man. It was Mapp, and she could see, with a sinking heart, that he was very badly wounded. His chest was a dark, wet stain. Still, she turned back to Wales, irresolute.

"Wales . . ."

"Take care of Mapp first."

Elizabeth obeyed. She crawled past Wales, and propped the sailor's head up on her lap.

"Seems like you's always savin' my life Miz Rogers," Mapp said. "Too late this time, though."

"Don't be silly, Alexander. You'll pull through. Drink this." She put the canteen up and moistened his lips.

"Thank you, Miz Rogers," he said with great effort. "You done saved my life once. Cain't be expected to do it twice. You take care o' the cap'n. God bless you."

It took Elizabeth a moment to realize, and then a bit longer to accept the fact that Mapp had died in her arms.

Numb, she did not know what to do with him. It seemed unthinkable to put him down. Finally, she did it without thinking, and turned back to Wales.

"Where are you hurt?" she asked, holding up his head and putting the canteen to his lips.

"Side. Bullet passed clear through, I think."

She cut away his shirt, cleaned the wound, and bandaged him tightly. He was right: the bullet had gone clear through; there was a bullet hole front and back. She had to fight back an almost overpowering wave of nausea when she saw the second one, but she knew that it was good that there was no bullet to remove.

"Are you comfortable?" she asked.

"Couldn't ask for better," he said. He tried to lift his hand, and she saw him wince with the pain.

"Don't," she said.

He did, anyway. He lifted his hand and touched her cheek. She leaned over and kissed him, long but gently.

"What happened below?" he asked her.

"Anne's all right. I left her alone, but she's safe. I hope she'll be able to sleep. Harris . . . I guess he was afraid to come out of his cabin. There was a lot of shooting down there. Ritter, too."

"Dowling?"

"I don't know. They broke into Dowling's cabin. I think they shot him."

"Is he dead?"

"I don't know. I didn't look."

"We have to find out. Mr. Whiteurs . . ."

Whiteurs shook his head. "I'm stayin' with you, Cap'n. Let him die, for all I care."

"You're going to go down and tend to him. That's an order."

"Aye, aye, sir."

"Take the medical bag. And do the best you can. Forget about your personal feelings. Is that clear?"

"Aye, aye, sir."

"Give me my gun back."

Whiteurs handed one of the two weapons to Wales. Wales pulled himself up on one knee, and sighted the gun over the top of the binnacle.

"Wales, don't . . . !" protested Elizabeth, but Wales waved it aside.

"Go!" he hissed.

Whiteurs broke in a zigzag course for the hatch. Wales kept up a barrage of gunfire. There were no answering shots from the darkness, but Whiteurs kept going. He made it safely to the companionway, but Elizabeth did not see him arrive there. She was too absorbed in the look of strain on Wales's face at every recoil of the revolver.

"Please," she said. "Please, Wales. Rest." She knelt beside him, head tucked down for safety, and stroked his shoulders gently, taking care not to press against his injured side. He slid down to rest against the wooden case that housed the ship's compass, now shattered by gunfire.

Elizabeth noticed for the first time that there was another body on the deck. It was the helsman, lying dead where he had fallen, beside the wheel, just a few yards away. He was lying face down, and there was a puddle of blood under his head. Elizabeth guessed that he had been shot in the face, and she was grateful that she did not have to see it. One more dead body. It made her cringe. So much death! And how much more would there be, before this nightmare was over? She recoiled from the sight of the corpse, and her shoulder blade brushed up against Wales. She wanted to shrink close to him to nestle in against his chest for protection, but she was afraid of injuring him.

She began to realize that she was cold. A chilly night breeze was blowing, and she knew that it would be much colder before morning.

But if she was cold, what about Wales? Yes, he was shivering. His shirt was in tatters, where it had been cut away to treat his wound. He was weak and probably feverish. She took off her jacket, and covered him with it as best she could.

"Cap'n . . ." Whiteurs' voice came in a soft hiss from the top of the companionway. Wales painfully raised himself back up, and propped his revolver over the top of the binnacle. With an effort, he steadied his hand, holding his wrist firmly with the other hand for support.

"Come on!" he croaked.

Whiteurs ran and dived, as Wales fired into the night.

"He's alive," said Whiteurs. "I'll give you a full report. But first . . ."

He had a blanket under his arm, and he began to unfold it, and spread it over Wales.

"Bless you, Mr. Whiteurs," said Elizabeth.

"Mm," said Whiteurs, averting his eyes from her shift and her bare shoulders. "You'd better get under here, too. You're going to need it as much as he does."

"I'm all right," said Elizabeth.

"Do as I say," said Whiteurs. "You sit down next to the cap'n, like so . . ." He guided her into position, and tucked the blanket around both of them.

"All right," said Whiteurs. "Feel all right, Cap'n?"

"Aye," said Wales.

"Mrs. Rogers?"

Elizabeth's bare arm and shoulder were touching Wales,

and the heat from their bodies was mingling under the blanket. She felt an all but forgotten, or perhaps never before experienced, electricity that she could not concentrate on because of the dire extremity of the situation, but which made it very difficult for her to concentrate on anything else.

"Mrs. Rogers?"

"Yes, I'm much better," she said. "Thank you, Mr. Whiteurs."

"All right, then. Mr. Dowling was shot, right enough. He's alive. Lost some blood, but not hurt real bad. Shot in the leg. Can't walk worth a damn, though. Bone's broke. He'd took care o' himself pretty much, even dug out the bullet." Whiteurs winced at the thought. "He's a tough one, all right. I cleaned the wound and put on a proper bandage, and left him down there. Like I said, he can't walk too good, wouldn'ta done us no good. Ritter's in your cabin, ma'am, takin' care o' the baby. She's okay, too, mite scared, but Ritter's calmin' her down. Wanted to know about her mammy and pappy, I told her you 'uz both fine, takin' care o' the ship. Harris . . . I coulda ordered him up, even though he outranks me, but . . ." Whiteurs shrugged. "What the hell. He just ain't man enough to be much use against a couple o' loons with guns. Well, he ain't the only one, is he. Got a whole fo'c'sle full o' the same thing."

Elizabeth listened fitfully. She paid attention to the part about her daughter. She was glad Ritter was there to keep her company. But for those few moments, it was hard to think of anything else—danger, death, the fate of the ship and everyone on it—anything else but the physical closeness, the touching and the warmth of huddling together under this rough blanket with the only man she had ever loved.

"Cap'n . . ."

"Yes, Mr. Whiteurs?"

"I been thinkin' . . . did you hear any shots when I run back before, 'ceptin' yours?"

Wales thought about it. "No," he said. "I don't think so. No, I didn't."

"No," said Elizabeth. "There weren't any others. Wales

fired four times, and that was all the gunshots there were."
She remembered, vividly, each one of the four stabs of pain
on his face.

"Could be they're out of ammunition, then," said Wales.
"They had to run out, sooner or later. We should go after
them, now, before they slip away."

"They ain't moved since I been back up on deck," said
Whiteurs.

"Nor when you were below," said Wales.

"Where are they?" asked Elizabeth. She was suddenly
ashamed that she did not know. "I guess I haven't been
very observant. I'm not much use in an emergency, I'm
afraid."

"You had plenty enough on your mind," said Whiteurs
kindly. "They're on one of the low yards of the mizzenmast, good spot as long as they got guns, but if they're out
o' bullets we got 'em treed like a couple o' bear cubs."

"If they're out of bullets," said Wales grimly.

"Well, I'll tell you somethin' about those two," said Whiteurs. "It's my feelin' that they ain't too 'specially bright.
And if they had any bullets left, I don't think they'd think
o' not usin' em."

"Could be," agreed Wales.

"Let's try somethin'," said Whiteurs. He raised himself to
his knees, and shouted into the darkness: "All right, you
swabs! We know you're out of ammunition! You better
come down and give yourselves up now, 'fore we come up
after you!"

Only silence greeted his challenge.

"Well, now," said Whiteurs.

"That doesn't probe anything," said Elizabeth.

"No, but it might give some indication," said Whiteurs.
"Like I 'splained before, I don't think them two boys is all
that bright. I kinda 'spect that if they had any bullets left,
they would fired off one or two just to prove I was wrong."

"Well," said Wales, "let's go, then."

"Not you," said Whiteurs. "You're in no shape to go
climbin' no riggin'. I'm goin'."

Elizabeth held Wales's arm. He shrugged off her hand,
and Whiteurs' objections, and got to his feet.

"Let's go, then," he said.

* * *

Whiteurs, faster afoot, walked a step ahead, keeping his bulk in front of his injured captain. Wales, shuffling as he walked, kept pace, and held his gun ready. Elizabeth, knowing she could be of no help, stayed back behind the binnacle, standing. She could not bring herself—or it never occurred to her—to crouch back down out of sight.

No shots were fired. Whiteurs and Wales reached the base of the mizzenmast, and peered up into the rigging.

"Come down!" ordered Wales.

An object was hurled down from the lowest yardarm, right next to the mast. It missed Whiteurs' head by inches, and clattered on the deck. It was an empty revolver.

"I'm going up," Whiteurs said, and swung into the rigging without waiting for a reply. He fired a couple of warning shots as he climbed.

As the mutineers jumped to escape from Whiteurs, they became visible in the moonlight. They split up, one climbing higher up the mast, the other going out along the yardarm. Whiteurs chose the one going up, and climbed after him. Wales followed the other one with his gun, and took two shots, but missed on each. On the third, the gun clicked empty.

"Elizabeth!" he called. "The bullets—where I was sitting."

She bent down, and found the box of ammunition.

"I've got it, Wales," she said. "I'll bring it to you."

She started across the deck, but in that moment, she heard a flurry from the yardarm, and looked up, to see a dark, bulky shape drop from it, and the glint of a knife blade in the moonlight.

"Wales!" she shouted, and Wales stepped back, so that the sailor missed hitting him directly, but struck him a blow with his forearm as he landed. Wales was sent heavily to his knees, the gun flying out of his hand.

It landed at Elizabeth's feet, and she picked it up, but she was not quite sure how to load the bullets into it. She felt worse than useless.

The mutineer advanced on Wales in a rush, but he was on his feet, somehow, to meet the charge, his own knife drawn. It caught the sailor off guard. He had not expected that the injured man would be capable of such quick reflexes, and his rush was clumsy and ill-timed. Wales side-stepped, and braced himself, catching the sailor with his shoulder and knocking him off balance.

The sailor fell, and Wales leaped after him like a cat. His knife flashed once in the air, and then it was over.

Wales got to his feet. He had not the strength to pull his knife out of the mutineer's body, and it remained there, handle sticking up in the air. Elizabeth rushed to Wales, and caught him in her arms as he collapsed.

She eased him gently to the deck. He was bleeding again, and his eyes were glazed over. He looked at her face. For a moment, there was love in his eyes, but in the next moment, she knew that he could not see her anymore.

☙Chapter Thirty

ELIZABETH PUT HER EAR TO WALES'S CHEST,
and her fingers on his pulse. He was not dead, anyway. But
he had lost consciousness, and had reinjured himself badly.
He needed immediate attention, and a lot of it, if there was
to be even a chance of his pulling through.

Elizabeth felt an anguished wail welling up from deep
inside her. But before it passed her lips, the night air was
split by another scream, from high above the deck. She
looked up to see a body fly through the air, and fall into
the ocean.

She did not know who it was. If it was Whiteurs, they
were not safe yet. She tried again to put bullets into the
revolver, and this time, she was able to get the knack of it.
She stuffed them in, one at a time, until all six chambers
were filled, then clicked the cylinder back into place.

At that moment, Second Mate Harris stepped out of the
companionway, holding a revolver of his own. Elizabeth
did not waste time getting angry at him for his cowardice.
She turned back again to Wales, laying him as comfortably
as she could on the deck. Tending to his wound once again,
she left Harris to stand guard.

She only had one thing to say to him, over her shoulder,
with a vehemence that communicated all the things she
was not saying:

"For God's sake, wait until you're sure who it is before you shoot anyone!"

Then Whiteurs joined them on the deck. The mutiny was over.

Whiteurs and Harris took Wales below on a stretcher, and laid him down in his bed. He had not recovered consciousness.

Elizabeth could not bear to leave him, even for a minute. But there was Anne to be tended to, also, so she went across to her cabin.

Her cabin. It seemed so odd to think of it that way, now; so odd to think of her space as separate from Wales's. His cabin was hers, of course. The last few months—up until just a few hours ago—seemed a dim and incomprehensible memory.

Ritter met her at the door.

"She's asleep," he said. "She finally went off to sleep." He stood aside to let Elizabeth see into the room, over to the sleeping face of her child. She crossed to her, and bent over her. She could see Wales's features in the tranquil, sleeping face: his nose, his wide, smooth brow. Anne would wake up in the morning, though. And Wales . . .

"How is the captain, ma'am?" asked Ritter, his brow furrowed with concern.

"I don't know, Ritter," she said, unable to hold back any of her concern, or the gravity of the situation.

Ritter nodded his head.

"We'll just have to pray for him," said Elizabeth, suddenly full of compassion for the fat German who had been so loyal to her husband, and disliked her so much.

"Yes, ma'am," said Ritter.

Elizabeth turned to go.

"Mrs. Rogers . . ." Ritter began.

"Yes, Ritter?"

"Don't . . . don't worry about little Anne. I will stay with her as long as . . . well, what I mean is . . . I will take Miss Jennie's place. You'll be needing me more now than these officers will."

"Thank you, Ritter," Elizabeth said. "Thank you very much."

Elizabeth returned to Wales's cabin.

"He's still unconscious," said Whiteurs. "And you'd best get some sleep, too. I've fixed a cot for you."

"Thank you, Mr. Whiteurs, but I . . ."

She stopped, suddenly realizing how tired she was.

"Don't worry about the ship. I'll keep watch, the rest of the night. And there's nothing more we can do about the cap'n, 'cept wait. You get some sleep. You need it. You've sure as hell earned it. You're the best damn wife any ship's captain ever had."

He left without waiting for a reply.

Elizabeth lay down in her clothes. She felt warmed and undeserving. She felt buoyed by her love, and close to hopeless. She felt her strength and her fear and confusion. Within moments, she was asleep.

⊗Chapter Thirty-one

BY MORNING WALES'S CONDITION WAS
unchanged. He was still alive, still unconscious, and there
was nothing that they could do for him but wait.

But decisions had to be made about the ship, right away.
With no helmsman, it had drifted for hours, aback to its
canvas. Now it was miles off course—and leaderless.

Ben Harris was the senior officer now, and even he knew
that was a mockery. Nevertheless, it was true. Whiteurs
had taken care of those matters that needed immediate decisions and action—assigning a sailor to the helm, and a
detail to tend to the dead. Now it was Harris's turn to make
decisions. He and Whiteurs held a meeting before dawn, to
determine what was to be done. It seemed right that Elizabeth should be in attendance too, and she was.

Harris was nervous and ashamed. He did not quite know
how to face the other two. He stammered, began to apologize and make excuses, but Whiteurs cut him short.

"What course do we take now, sir?"

"Well, we . . . er, we have to make for the nearest
port."

"And what port would that be, sir?"

"Er . . . Valparaiso, I guess. I'm not sure."

"I think we're too far south of Valparaiso to make that a
workable idea," said Elizabeth.

"Where are we?" asked Harris.

"I don't know," said Elizabeth. "I won't know for sure until I see the instruments."

"But you can guess," said Harris. "You can guess well enough to plot a course for Valparaiso."

There was a plaintive whine to his voice that irritated Elizabeth. "Don't talk about things you don't understand!" she snapped.

"I'm sorry," said Harris, chastened and obsequious. "I just thought—"

"Oh, for God's sake, man," said Elizabeth. "All right, I guess we're on about the 53rd parallel—let's say somewhere below the 50th. I'd guess we've been blown out to sea, away from the coast of South America, but Lord knows how far out. Valparaiso is a long way north of us—call it the 32nd parallel, leaving out the fractions for the sake of simplicity—and I would guess that it would be a waste of time to try to get back to Valparaiso. Mr. Whiteurs?"

Whiteurs agreed. "Be slow going, too, if the weather's what I'd guess it would be."

"Well, then . . ." began Harris officiously, but he trailed off, at a loss for a way to continue. Elizabeth spoke again, impatient with the void.

"So I would guess that our best bet is to go on to Buenos Aires."

Harris gulped. "Around the Horn, you mean?"

"I say we should keep going," Elizabeth said. "We're still a good three or four days away from Cape Horn, and Captain Rogers will be recovered, and up and about by then."

"But suppose he isn't?" Harris burst out. "You can't know that. Suppose he doesn't get better? Suppose he dies?" Harris blinked. He knew he was in dangerous territory, but he had no choice but to go on. "Forgive me—I don't mean to be heartless, but you know it could happen. And then what? Mrs. Rogers—do you really want to go around Cape Horn with me in command of the *Western Wind*?"

Elizabeth was not going to back down either. "He is going to recover. He's too strong. He'll be on the bridge when we hit the Cape waters. And I don't see that we have any choice, anyway. Whiteurs will help you."

288

"Mrs. Rogers, I don't know the first thing about running a ship! I don't know the first thing about navigation. Even if you were to do all the sightings, and all the charts, and all the—damnit, I don't even know what it is that you do for the captain! I wouldn't even be able to understand the data you brought me. I wouldn't be able to make a sailing plan through the middle of the ocean, much less approaching the Cape. And if we have to go around the Cape with me in command, we might as well give up the ship and all of us for dead. Dead! Let me try to get the ship back to Valparaiso. That's all I can do."

Elizabeth and Whiteurs looked at each other. Elizabeth began to feel that Harris might be right. The thought of him in command around the treacherous and deadly Cape Stiff, where the wrong judgment of an instant could mean the end of a ship and certain death for everyone in it, was frightening to contemplate. But what was the alternative? All they could do was pray for Wales's recovery. Everything depended on him.

"I'll tell you what I think we ought to do," said Harris. "I thing we ought to get Mr. Dowling to take over the ship from here on."

He could not miss the shocked expressions on the faces of Elizabeth and Whiteurs, but he was too relieved at having found a solution to his dilemma to concern himself with anything else. He plowed straight ahead.

"Yes, I think that would be best," he said. "Circumstances being what they are, I think it is definitely time to reconsider Mr. Dowling's case. We really need him now, and after all, what he did wasn't really so bad, when you think about it, was it? Just a misunderstanding."

"No," said Elizabeth. "It's not possible. Captain Rogers' orders were that he be kept under arrest until we reach New York, and that is how it will be."

Harris flushed a deep red. Elizabeth glanced over at Whiteurs, but he was impassive. She knew that he agreed with her. *But he's going to let me fight the battle over Dowling on my own.*

She accepted that as just. She faced Harris levelly, not backing down. He averted his eyes first.

"Now, see here," he spluttered. "I'm in command of this ship, am I not? And that's my order—we release Dowling,

289

and he'll take over—I'll turn the authority over to him, until such time as Captain Rogers is fit to resume command. It's the best way, really."

"I won't let you do it," said Elizabeth.

"Oh?" said Harris. "And just how are you going to stop me?"

"I'm telling you that you can't do it," said Elizabeth. Her voice was hard and taut; her eyes never left Harris. There was no question who was the stronger of the two, and Harris crumbled. He was practically in tears as he spoke again.

"Well, then, how do you think we're going to go anywhere?" he demanded. "I'm telling you I can't do it! I can't run a ship! I never wanted to be out here at all—it was my uncle's idea! Who's going to take charge? Whiteurs?"

He turned to Whiteurs, who did not answer him. But Elizabeth could tell that Whiteurs, tough and dedicated as he was, was shrinking from the prospect.

"What does he know about being an officer?" Harris demanded of Elizabeth.

"He's a good sailor."

"That's not the same thing. Even I know that. The man couldn't even keep a log! And anyway, I'm still senior officer on this ship, and I say we. . . ."

"I'll run the ship, damn it!" exploded Elizabeth.

Could she have shouted it as loudly as it now seemed to her she had shouted? She heard her voice reverberating throughout the ship, to the room in which Ritter worried and her daughter tried to play, above decks to where the helmsman steered a course due east, a compromise course while he awaited further orders. She imagined it carrying, too, into the cabin where she could picture Dowling hearing, and chuckling sardonically to himself.

Well, for whatever wild reason, it had been said, and Harris and Whiteurs had heard it, even if no one else had. She could not unsay it; nor could she appear to hesitate, even for an instant. Fortunately for her, Harris was too scared to notice how scared she was. He opened his mouth and closed it again, twice. Elizabeth went on, before he could recover enough to find his voice.

"We'll set a southeasterly direction. I'll have to estimate our position and our course now; I'll plot the exact course

290

today and give the sailing orders. I'll let you know what sail we'll need—we've got to make up for lost time, but we can't crowd her until I'm sure we know exactly where we're going. Any questions?"

Harris had none. Humiliation and relief battled in his face, but they were not such strangers to each other in that place as to make the battle a hard-fought one. The decision was out of his hands now, and that was ultimately all he cared about.

"What are we going to tell the crew?" asked Whiteurs.

"Why tell them anything?" Elizabeth said. "After all . . . after all, we don't want to make the problem seem any worse than it really is, do we? Captain Rogers' fever will probably break by this evening, and he'll be back on his feet tomorrow."

"Have to tell them something."

"Not this morning, we don't. Mr. Harris will give them their sailing orders, and we'll leave it at that."

During the morning Wales recovered consciousness and tried to talk, but lapsed into a delirium. Elizabeth stayed with him. She spent very little time on deck, except for taking the noon sighting with her sextant.

She did not want to be on deck overmuch. There would be less question from the crew, if the orders came from Harris alone. And there was so much for her to do below.

There was the complicated business of figuring out how far off course they had drifted, and how to compensate for it. She set herself up at Wales's desk in his cabin so she could be near him if he needed anything, but his nearness occupied her mind, and his illness and delirium filled her heart. She had to fight to concentrate.

And she could not neglect little Anne, either. She made numerous trips into the nursery to sit with the baby. She made sure that she had one meal with Anne that day, although she herself had to struggle even to sit still and look at food. "Don't forget, you have to take care of yourself, too," Ritter advised her kindly, and Elizabeth nodded . . . but what else could she do? She felt pulled into three pieces: the ship, her child, her sick husband, all needing her so much.

She knew that even Wales had never had to take so

much responsibility. When he ran the ship, he ran the ship, and that was all. Was it because she was a woman—or just because there was no one else? Well, it did not matter. It all had to be done, and she would not sacrifice any of it.

She spent most of her time with Wales, tending his fever, sitting close to him as he tossed and turned and made incoherent sounds. She waw not sure if he knew that she was there—there was no sense to any of the sounds he made, nothing that was quite a word, although several times he seemed to be forming a slurred approximation of her name.

In the afternoon, she made a brief turn on deck. She brought little Anne along with her, partly to give the child an outing, mostly as camouflage for herself. She discreetly checked the helmsman's course, and what sail was out, and quietly gave orders to Harris. Then she went below again, before he relayed them to the crew. To her great relief, the weather held all that day, and there were no emergency decisions to be made.

Wales had a restless night, and the fever did not break. She sat up next to him, taking little catnaps and never allowing herself to sleep too heavily. In the morning she felt stiff and sore, but rested enough.

Around the middle of the next day, he came out of his delirium and recognized her.

"How long have I been out?" he asked her.

"Two days and two nights."

"Who's been in charge of the ship?"

She was seized with a great feeling of trepidation, and did not know how to answer him. But she kept her voice calm and level.

"I have," she said.

He reached out and took her hand. He squeezed it, and smiled at her.

"The captain's daughter, eh?" he said through dry lips.

"Wales, it's you and I together," she said, squeezing his hand in return. "It always has been, just as we said in the beginning. I didn't forget. It might have seemed as though I did for a while—yes, it even seemed that way to me. But I didn't."

He nodded to her. Then his eyes closed, and he fell back to sleep.

Elizabeth held his hand for a few moments longer, then

released it. And when she released it, she was crying. Tears flooded down her face, and little sounds bubbled up from inside her—not the great, wailing sobs that she felt, but little sounds that would not disturb her husband's sleep, or carry to any other ears on the ship. She kept that control, but she cried for a long time.

The next afternoon, they crossed the 60th parallel and prepared to head into the Cape Straits. Wales had still not recovered completely from his delirium.

"You won't be able to give orders the way you've been giving them," said Whiteurs. "You'll have to be up on the bridge, if we're going to do this."

"Of course we're going to do it," said Elizabeth. "What else can we do? But you're right. What is the mood of the crew?"

"The crew's been battered around a lot," said Whiteurs. "The mutiny, what happened to the cap'n, made 'em sober up fast. They'd slit their own throats before they'd make trouble for anybody."

"Good. Then we'll do it. Call all hands on deck, and I'll talk to them. Both of you will be with me. Oh, and I want you each to have a gun in your belt."

"I don't know how to use a gun, Mrs. Rogers," said Harris.

"You know how to stick it in your belt, don't you?" said Elizabeth. "Mr. Whiteurs, make sure he knows how to keep the safety on before he points it down his trouser leg. We don't want him to be the last of the Harrises, now, do we?"

∾Chapter Thirty-two

THE MASTS AND TIMBERS OF THE *WESTERN Wind* creaked as they had every day, sails flapped and ropes scraped across the rails and the yards. But this morning it all felt different to Elizabeth.

It was her ship now, and she was alive to it. It fitted around her as intimately as a kid glove to the soft fingers of a lady of fashion, and she could feel the effect of every puff of wind, every inch of sail, every fraction of a turn of the wheel. And she knew without shame that, much as she prayed and was still praying for Wales's recovery as quickly as possible, she had trembled all night with the thrill of the morning's challenge.

The weather was cold, but not cold for the Cape, and Elizabeth felt stuffy in her winter coat. The bottom of the Southern Hemisphere was undergoing an unusually warm spring, and the rocky islands they sailed past appeared to them as a dull green glow, with their burgeoning growth of lichens diffused through the patchy fog that was everywhere.

It was slow going through the fog: slow and frustrating. Elizabeth chafed at it. The sea was untroubled, the wind was baffling but fresh. She could have read it and used it to their advantage to set a smart pace. But there was no speed to be made with visibility so poor. And she knew that in the warm weather, the Antarctic ice mass could easily break up at the edges and send random icebergs floating out into the channel. It was not common for a big iceberg to find its way as far north as Cape Horn, but it was not unheard of either, so Elizabeth proceeded with great caution. A lookout was posted aloft, and another on the jib, so that eyes might have a chance to cut through the fog high or low.

Of all the demands on a commanding officer, surely this was the hardest: patience. To stand on the poop deck and feel the wind. To be able to recite, like a litany, the sails that should be deployed, the position of the yardarms to make the *Wind* live up to its name and take the Cape Horn passage with a speed and finesse that few, if any, had ever achieved before—and then not to do it. Surely nothing else—coaxing speed from the faintest puff of wind, battling a fierce gale—could be as taxing on the nerves, as stern a test of judgment.

And what, it struck her, *if Wales had faced this kind of weather on the outward passage? What would I have said to him, if he had crept along at this pace?*

She was afraid she could guess the answer all too readily. She would have told him, contemptuously, exactly how he could get more speed out of the ship, and jeered at him for not doing it. She would have behaved just as she had behaved, on the outward passage.

She shook her head, and walked quickly across the deck, as if moving away from the thought; but she certainly was not doing that. She carried it with her, clenched in her mind. There was a lot more to the responsibility of command than she had thought, and she wanted to be clear about it, so she would never forget it. *You never taught me that, Papa*, she thought.

Evening came, and then the next morning. They were well into the Cape Horn passage now, with no mishaps, no serious problems. Wales's delirium continued. Ritter divided his time between Anne and the captain, and Elizabeth came below as often as she could. She thought of sending a man aft to help out the steward, but decided against it. The crew's number had been badly depleted already, with the loss of Mapp, the helmsman, and, for that matter, the two mutineers.

Elizabeth was starting to feel the confidence of routine by the second day. She could read it in the swing in her step, the feeling of familiarity with her actions, the easy authority in her voice when she issued commands. They no longer echoed strangely in her ears and scared her a little, as they had done the first time. And along with these feelings came a renewed desire to put out more sail and fly.

There had been no sign of icebergs. But the fog was as dense as it had been the day before. Elizabeth bit her lip, and the *Wind* continued creeping forward.

That afternoon, they heard a cry from the crow's nest. "Shape dead ahead!"

"Is it an iceberg?" Whiteurs called out.

"Can't tell!" returned the lookout. "Reckon so. It's big enough . . . white . . ."

"No, wait!" shouted the sailor at the jib. "It's a ship! Sail ho!"

The *Wind* tacked to starboard and the two ships glided past each other. Elizabeth stayed at the far rail and let Whiteurs communicate with the captain of the other vessel.

"Who be ye?"

"The *Caitlin B.*, out of Baltimore, Mark Berlanga, captain. Who be ye?"

"The *Western Wind*, out of Stonington, Wales Rogers, captain. You be talking to Second Mate Whiteurs."

"I've heard of your ship. Where's your captain?"

"He's below, tending a sick man," said Whiteurs. Elizabeth nodded approval from the far rail. "What's the passage like?"

"Not bad. Weather should hold up, if you're smart about it. Just push through."

"Any ice?"

"Didn't see any. But don't rule it out—it's a crazy spring. How is it the other way?"

"It was clear for us. Good luck."

"Good luck to you. And give the regards of the *Caitlin B.* to Mrs. Rogers, the sailor's angel."

"Aye, aye!" managed Whiteurs, somewhat taken aback. And as he left the rail, he realized that he had almost forgotten. Mrs. Rogers was no longer, in his mind, the little lady who saved the sailor from drowning. She was his voice of authority—the captain of the *Western Wind*. *Shows how much a sailor needs that*, he thought. *It's the system that makes things run. And the system needs a captain on the bridge.*

By sunset, there was still no sign of ice, but the lookout reported a suspicious glow on the horizon. Elizabeth climbed the rigging, wrapping her skirts about her legs, to see for herself. She tried to use her telescope, but it was no use against the fog, and she had to rely on her naked eye.

There seemed to be a second sunset, to the south, but there was no color in it. It was a white glow, the ghost of a sunset, and as eerie as any specter.

Elizabeth had never seen anything like it before.

"Neither have I," said Whiteurs. "I can guess what it is, though."

Elizabeth nodded. "Ice, and a lot of it."

"What are your orders?"

"Maybe we can outrun it. By tomorrow we'll be center to the Horn and heading out. Reef the topsails, hold speed around nine knots, and keep on course, east-nor'east. If all goes well, if we hold to that speed and course, you'll reset the course to northeast at 0100 hours. If there's any variation, call me. Keep a double lookout all night. Call me at the first sighting of a berg."

She went below. There was nothing else she could do now, and she would be needed later. It was better to get some rest while she could.

She visited with Anne, and then lay down on the pallet beside Wales's bed. He seemed to be resting easier than he had been. Maybe it was a good sign. Maybe he would recover soon.

She pulled her blankets up over her shoulders. She imagined herself in a bed, not a makeshift pallet, and in a nightgown, not sleeping in her clothes so she could be up on deck at a moment's notice. And she imagined Wales not feverish and separate from her, but healthy and pressed close against her in the same bed. She burrowed down deeper under her blankets, and drifted off to sleep.

She was awakened by Harris at four o'clock in the morning, just before the first light of dawn, and she went back up on deck. The shadowy shapes of icebergs had been spotted nearby.

"We can't tell how big they are, Mrs. Rogers, but they're plenty big," said Harris.

Elizabeth's body was still sluggish from sleep, and she shivered with cold as she stood on the deck. "What's the temperature?" she asked.

"Thirty-eight degrees," said Harris.

"Wind?"

"Out of the northwest. We're holding to the northeasterly course since 0100 hours, ma'am."

"Right. Where has the ice been?"

"Off to the starboard side, ma'am. Hard to judge distance in the dark, but we figured—Mr. Whiteurs figured—that they weren't close enough to be any danger."

"Good." It was good, so far. The ice appeared to be to the south of them, and they were heading away from it. But there was turbulence in the air, and in the ocean, too. They were due for a squall. If the danger of the ice was really over, perhaps they ought to put on sail and get as much distance behind them as possible, while they could.

"Iceberg dead ahead!"

The cry came from the lookout aloft, and in the same instant Elizabeth saw it, not a hundred yards from the ship.

Elizabeth could not see the top of the berg. Her jaw dropped, and her senses froze in disbelief for an instant, but only for an instant.

"Near!" she commanded, and the sailors sprang to brace the yards, the helmsman brought the ship's prow close to the wind; the *Western Wind* moved in an even arc as it closed to within forty, then twenty yards of the berg. But by then the mountain of ice was to their starboard side, and they were slipping past it.

With the immediate danger over, Elizabeth looked up at the big iceberg as it passed them by. Her eye was well trained to judge, from her experience in the use of the sextant, so she knew that she must be right, but still, she could not believe it: the tower of ice rose close to 1,500 feet out of the ocean.

"Did you ever see anything like that before?" Elizabeth asked Whiteurs.

"Never anything close," he said. "Not half that size."

"Well, we're past it now," said Harris. "We're out of danger."

"Don't count on it," said Elizabeth. "I'm afraid we're just getting into it. We'll reduce speed to seven knots and try to feel our way through this."

Within half an hour, as the dawn began to break and their field of vision extended, they saw more icebergs to the windward side. All of them were immense. Although they were far enough away not to pose an immediate hazard, and therefore not worth contemplating, Elizabeth noted that some of them were, like the first monster, over a thousand feet in height.

Elizabeth pursued a northeast course, heading for the open sea. It would take her far away from her planned destination of Buenos Aires, but it was their only chance to escape the threat of ice.

By five o'clock, daylight was upon them, and the sky was clear. The fog had lifted. And they saw, arrayed before them, a sight which froze the blood of every sailor and officer aboard the *Western Wind*.

The entire horizon to the windward side of the ship was a block of immense icebergs. The rising sun glinted off them, creating such a blinding glare that it was almost impossible to look to the west. And the mass of ice was floating toward them.

Astern, another majestic, otherworldly wall of glaring ice rose, unbroken.

And to the leeward, also, great icebergs drifted by, like stray ships moving to catch up with some monstrous armada. The largest of these was over seven hundred feet high. The smallest was big enough to crush a ship.

There was nothing to be done but creep forward and wait for a break in the wall of ice, a chance to escape. All hands came out on deck, and remained there, waiting. They were silent, practically motionless. They stood and watched the inexorable drift of the icebergs. They listened to the sound of the wind rushing and waves lapping with a hollow echo that none of them had ever heard before.

Elizabeth sent Whiteurs aloft with a telescope, to try and find them a passage through the ice. He climbed to the main topgallant yard, from which vantage he could see for

300

miles ahead—and, if not over the tallest peaks, at least between them. After half an hour, he reported down to Elizabeth: there was no passage at all up ahead. The wall of ice continued in an unbroken arc to the north of them, and around to the east, so that the leeward side was rapidly becoming closed to them also. The ice ringed them in a horseshoe pattern, and the horseshoe was shrinking—and closing up.

"We're trapped!" croaked Harris.

"We're embayed," said Elizabeth. "I've read about it, but I never saw it happen, or knew anyone that it happened to. We'll have to tack about and sail southeast, out of this, before it closes in on us altogether and we really are trapped."

"We're going to have to turn this ship on a dime to do it," said Harris. "We can't do it! Look how close the ice is to us already."

"We'll do it," said Elizabeth. "We have to."

But she was not so sure he was wrong. She would practically have to stop her ship in midocean, and turn it back in the direction it had come, looking all the time for an opening that she could veer quickly into, and make a run for freedom in the open sea.

There was no time to be lost. The wind was coming up, strong and baffling, made even more erratic by the great cliffs and canyons of ice. It would be especially hard to come about smoothly. And the threat of sudden, squall-like gusts of wind precluded putting too much of a strain on the masts. But if they did not move quickly enough, it would be the end of them.

The crew was aloft now, in the rigging, along with Whiteurs, who kept watch for their escape passage.

Elizabeth tacked the ship, bringing its nose around in the ever-closing circle. At last it was heading in a southeasterly direction, but so close to the eastern wall of ice that they could feel the hull scrape against the ice that jutted out below the waterline.

They had to hold to a straight line now, parallel to the wall of ice, in spite of the wind which, though erratic, was still coming mostly out of the west. Closer and closer, the ship drifted toward the leeward ice.

"Swing in the yardarms!" Elizabeth had to order, at last.

301

They were so close to the iceberg, now, that in another moment the yards would have been snapped off against its sheer, hard face.

"How can I steer like that?" called the helmsman.

"You'll steer, dammit!" yelled Elizabeth at the top of her lungs. "Double reef all sails to windward! We'll keep her on course!"

If any man in the crew had questioned taking orders from a woman, that time was gone now. There was no time to do anything but react, and react as quickly as possible, to orders that changed from moment to moment, in response to the demands of a shifting wind that whirled around corners and ricocheted off walls of ice.

Even the prevailing wind shifted, as the gusts kept playing their tricks within the bay. It was coming around to the northeast, and blowing the horseshoe of ice in a circle. Cruelly, tantalizingly, the open channel stayed ahead of them.

All that Elizabeth could do was keep tacking, following the elusive open stretch of water. They were traveling almost due west now, but the wind and the surface current created by the moving ice were forcing them to drift southward, ever closer to the southern wall.

Elizabeth's eyes hurt from the blinding glare of the ice. Her body hurt from cold, and fatigue, and the constant tension in her muscles that came from urging the ship on to perform, as if she could show it by her own body's example how to make its timbers bend at the middle and curve around in a circle.

She was tired, and she might be beaten. The ship still drifted southward, to where the thousand-foot cliffs waited, with walls as sheer and smooth as the facets of a diamond, with the wind howling and eddying and blowing flurries of ice chips across the deck of the *Wind*. And if the wind did not change, or she could not stem the drift, the *Flyer* would be battered to destruction against that wall.

She leaned up against the side of the hatch for a moment and rested her head on the wooden bulkhead, knowing it was a dangerous thing to do. If her attention flagged even for a few moments, it would be hard to get it back, tired as she was. But she had to have that moment's rest.

And then, with her ear pressed against the bulkhead, she

heard a sound, over the gale, that made her heart leap. Footsteps on the companionway!

It was Wales! He was recovered, and up, and ready to take over for her. *Just in time*, she thought. *I couldn't have held out any longer.* The force of will that had held her up was permitted to slip away in a wave of relief, and she swung around in front of the hatch to greet the tall male figure who had just arrived at the top of the companionway.

It was not Wales. It was Dowling.

"It's all right—I'll take over now," he said. He was not really speaking to her, and she hardly heard his words over the gale. He was scanning the ice, and the sky, and the ship. When he turned his eyes straight ahead again, to continue out on deck, he seemed surprised to find her still standing in front of him.

She could not move. She was dazed and disbelieving as he faced her. He put his hand on her shoulder, and leaned down closer to her. "It's all right, little lady," he shouted. "You can go below now. I'll take over the ship."

She still did not move. "Go on, now," he said. "This is no job for a woman. Listen, you've done very well—I say, *you've done very well* up till now. Go on—we'll talk about it later."

It was tempting. In fact, it was almost irresistible. She did not have to do anything, just let Dowling move her out of the way.

Dowling put his free hand on her other shoulder. His hands felt strong and competent. If she fainted now, he would catch her; she could collapse into his arms. Her knees began to weaken.

But she did not give in. She stepped back, and twisted free from his grasp.

"No!" she shouted.

"What?"

She stepped closer to him, to be heard over the storm, but made it clear from her stance that she would not countenance being touched by him again.

"Mr. Dowling," she said, "you are still under arrest. That situation has not changed. I expect you to comport yourself as an American merchant officer and return to your cabin.

"What?" Dowling exploded. "You can't be serious."

"Is this a time not to be serious?"

"Elizabeth." He smiled at her in a way that was at once sexually provocative and patronizing—and desperate. "Let me . . ."

"Mrs. Rogers," she said. "Acting captain of the *Western Wind*. Mr. Dowling, we're in a state of emergency. I can't spare two sailors to take you below, so please don't force me to. I'm ordering you below—now."

"You damn stupid bitch!" said Dowling. "You're crazy! Look, my life is at stake! I don't have to take orders from you—you've got no status on this ship. I'd take them from Harris sooner than you—but this is crazy! The life of every man on this ship is at stake, and they're not going to take orders from you to lock up their only hope of getting out of here alive. Now let me pass!"

Elizabeth looked slight and frail next to Dowling. She gave way a step, then turned and yelled across the deck to the two nearest able seamen.

"Brawn! Felix! Come here."

The two men crossed the main deck, and climbed the steps to the poop.

"Take Mr. Dowling below. He's still under arrest. If he gives you any trouble, and you have to use force, take him to the brig."

"Don't be fools!" Dowling exhorted. "Braun, for God's sake? Do you want to live? Don't you realize—"

He broke off as the two men stepped toward him. Braun took his arm. Dowling shook it free.

"Get back to your posts," he snapped. Then he turned and went below.

Within seconds she had forgotten about him. She was calling up to Whiteurs on the mainmast for the position on their escape route. She was trying to bring the ship closer to the wind, to find those elusive gusts that would just fill the sails, and keep the *Wind* moving the way she wanted it to, not drifting out of control, southward toward the iceberg. It was a ceaseless struggle, and perhaps it would be a losing one, but she would not give up.

∾Chapter Thirty-three

At 1600 hours, we could finally look back at that trap of ice from the outside, as we sailed north. And just in time, too. We could see the walls of ice converging as we passed between them, and we were not a half-mile away when we saw the channel become closed off completely. Perhaps another crack occurred at a different part of the ice at the same time, but I am not aware of any such occurrence. In any case, I doubt very greatly whether we would have had a chance for survival, had we not breached the ice when we did. I can still see it on the horizon to the south of us, like the Jaws of Death.

This evening, Captain Rogers' fever broke at last, and he came out of his delirium. We exchanged a few words of conversation. He knew who I was, and who and where he was, things which he had not been able to remember during the time that he was delirious. He inquired about the ship, and I told him we were around Cape Horn and sailing well. I did not tell him about the danger of the ice floe, but will report in full tomorrow when he awakes. He is sleeping now, but peacefully. God willing, this will be the last entry I shall write in this log.

Eliz. Rogers,
for Benjamin Harris, Second Mate

"Mrs. Rogers . . ."

Elizabeth looked up to see Ritter standing in the doorway. She put the logbook aside, and turned to face him. "What is it, Ritter?"

"How is the captain now?"

Ritter closed the door silently behind himself, and tiptoed over to stand about six feet away from Wales's bed. Elizabeth stood up and joined him, and together they watched Wales's peaceful face, and listened to his regular breathing.

"He's still doing well," said Elizabeth. "The danger's over. He's going to pull through."

"Of course he is, Mrs. Rogers," said Ritter. "And how are you?"

Ritter's question ended on a sudden, upward note of concern. Even as he spoke, Elizabeth had begun shaking uncontrollably.

"I-I-I'm all right, Ritter, hon-hon-honestly I am," said Elizabeth. She put her hand on Ritter's arm to steady herself. "It's j-j-just that . . . well, I never allowed myself to even th-think that he wouldn't pull through . . . until just now."

Elizabeth was sobbing by this time, her face in her hands, tears rolling down her cheeks and gathering between her fingers. She felt foolish and vulnerable, letting down like this in front of Ritter, but there was no way she could hold back. Wales might have died. But he had not. The ship might have been crushed by ice, and Wales, and the baby, and herself, and everyone on board might have been killed. But they had come through.

Ritter put his arms around her, and she let herself be comforted by him. She let him hold her up, and she let his shoulder muffle her sobs, until they finally diminished. Even then, she rested against him for a moment longer. She felt dizzy, and it was hard for her to stand up.

"Mrs. Rogers, are you all right?" Ritter asked anxiously.

"Yes . . . yes, Ritter, I'm all right."

"Here . . . sit down," said Ritter, leading her over toward the desk chair.

"No, let me stand for a moment and clear my head . . . I'll be fine."

"Mrs. Rogers," said Ritter, "I misjudged you very badly. I owe you an apology. I was wrong about you."

"No, Ritter. You were right about me," said Elizabeth.

Ritter either did not hear, or chose not to respond. He went on. "I was wrong. I thought you were spoiled and irresponsible. But·you came through when it counted."

"You weren't wrong," Elizabeth said again. "You weren't wrong."

Elizabeth put a hand on the desktop to steady herself. Ritter continued to regard her with a worried expression.

"Mrs. Rogers, you've been driving yourself hard these past few days."

"No harder than any other sailor on this ship." But the dizziness was still there, and it was hard for her to argue.

"Yes, harder," said Ritter. "You are a strong woman, but even strength has its limits."

"You've done the work of three yourself," said Elizabeth, trying not to slur her words.

"Mrs. Rogers, please. You have to rest, and not on a pallet on the floor. You must sleep in a bed tonight, in the nursery. I will stay with the captain."

"I can't leave him," said Elizabeth.

"He is out of danger now," said Ritter. "He spoke with you before he fell asleep; he knows you have been here. He'll want you to be taken care of, too—he'll have my skin, if he hears that I did not see to you tonight."

"Ritter, you're being ridiculous. I'm perfectly all right, and . . ."

She still ached when she woke up in the morning. There was a mattress and a sheet under her, and a sheet over her, and a blanket. There was a pillow beneath her head, and very near her head was the solemn, staring, worried face of her daughter.

It only took Elizabeth a moment to realize where she was. Then she smiled warmly at Anne, and the worried look left the little girl's face. She threw her arms around her mother's neck, and hugged her.

Elizabeth tried to lift Anne up into bed with her, but she did not have the strength. That presented no problem, though—Anne took care of it herself. She clambered up

307

and sat on the pillow next to her mother's head. Elizabeth drew herself up on one elbow and kissed her. Then she sat up, too. She was in her shift, but her dressing gown was laid out at the foot of the bed, and she put it around her shoulders.

"Ritter said I must be ever so quiet, and not wake you, so I didn't," said Anne. "I played like a little mouse all morning, and all afternoon, and—"

"All afternoon!" said Elizabeth. "Goodness gracious, what time is it?"

"It's almost suppertime," said Anne. "But Ritter said I should wait until you got up, and then tell you—" She stopped, and frowned, as if trying to make sure that she remembered everything right.

"Tell me what, for goodness' sake?" asked Elizabeth.

"That Papa woke up this morning feeling all fine and well again," said Anne. "And Ritter made him rest for part of the morning, but then he got up, and got dressed, and went up on deck, and started taking care of the ship again, so you won't have to anymore, Mama. And I know he's all well again, 'cause I saw him." Anne's voice swelled with pride. "I saw him this morning, and he was walking and talking and everything. He picked me up. And I know something else, too."

"What else do you know, you little monkey?" said Elizabeth, hugging her daughter again. Anne slipped away, the better to concentrate on her gossip.

"I know that Ritter told Papa all about the icebergs, and everything that happened, and so did Mr. Whiteurs and Mr. Harris, and they all said that you saved the ship and everybody's lives. Is that true, Mama?"

"Oh . . . oh, no, I'm not going to cry again," said Elizabeth. But by the time she had gotten the words out, she was already giving them the lie.

"Don't cry, Mama," said Anne. "Papa's not angry at you. He thinks it's fine that you saved the ship."

"I'm all right, darling. I'm really happy. See?"

She pointed to her mouth. And sure enough, she was smiling. The smile quivered and trembled, and the tears still rolled down her cheeks, but it was the happiest smile that her face had formed in months.

* * *

She was not so happy a few minutes later, when she looked at herself in the mirror for the first time in over a week. In fact, she could hardly believe what she saw. Heavy dark circles under her eyes, chapped lips, raw, windburned skin, stringy hair. She almost cried again, just to look at herself.

Ritter had prepared her a bath, and she stepped into it now, putting the looking glass down near the tub, where she could reach it again. She let her body sink into the hot, soapy water, and for a moment forgot about everything except the way she felt, warm and relaxed and almost luxurious.

Her breasts floated on the surface of the water, and as she became aware of them, her eyes widened and her mouth opened slightly. She regarded them with the mixture of awe and familiarity that an amnesiac might feel on experiencing a sudden return of memory.

She brought her hands up, cupping hot water in each palm, then letting it trickle down over her nipples. Then she slid her hands down over the top of her breasts, across the nipples, and to the undercurve. Her hands were rough and callused from work, but the soap and water made them smoothly slippery. She did it again. She let the little finger on each hand experience the exact point at which the bone of her upper chest gave to the soft woman flesh of her breasts. She drew one finger at a time up over her nipple and then slapped it down on the far side. She did this twice, then cupped all her fingers under her breasts and pushed them up.

She ran her hands along her ribs, and across her stomach, in a slow, swirling motion. She could feel the outline of her ribs more distinctly than she remembered, and her stomach was hard and flat, too. But, amazingly, none of the feelings in her body were gone, or even dulled, though she had neglected them for so long. Her thighs were still wide, and firm, and round. And it still felt the same when she slipped a soapy hand between them. . . .

But what did it mean? She finished bathing quickly, toweled herself dry, and dressed. She found herself gravitating to the most feminine dress in her wardrobe; then, when it was on, she removed it. She could not quite bring herself to feel that she belonged in it, yet. She put on a more subdued dress, one which did not contrast so embarrassingly with her weather-beaten cheeks and sunburned nose.

She wished she had been with Wales when he had awakened that morning. That would have made it easier. This way, she felt nervous—as if it were she who had just recovered from illness, as if she were the disoriented one.

That was ridiculous. She had to go and meet Wales, now—not to take care of him, but to face him as his wife. And she no longer knew exactly what that meant. Had they really gotten closer to each other, in those anxious minutes before the two crazed mutineers had opened fire, wounding Wales and sending him into fever and delirium? And would he remember it? Or, perhaps—had it never happened? Had she only loved him later, when he was helpless?

The night of the mutiny seemed very long ago. She remembered other things more clearly. She remembered setting out to sea with Wales more clearly as if it were yesterday. She remembered the night he had saved her life, on the New York waterfront, and never mentioned it again. She had been just a child, then. Younger than when she had gone after the *Flying Cloud*'s record with her father? No, older. And she had never gone after the *Flying Cloud*'s record with her father. It had only seemed that way, the same way that it had only seemed as if she were grown up then. Her father had always done things his own way; she had been his mascot, until he suddenly had to recognize that she was a woman, and a person. After that, he had not been able to have anything to do with her. And she had never really had anything to do with him, or his ships.

She remembered the young officer who had courted her—the one who told her the story about her mother playing the piano during a storm, and she smiled at the memory. She could not remember his name, though she could picture the scene perfectly. She wondered where he was, now. Her father and mother were in their silly little inland farmhouse in Washington, Connecticut, and perhaps she and Wales would visit them there, after this voyage was over, among their treasures and mementoes from exotic ports. They were old now, and would be peevish and impatient with an active four-year-old granddaughter.

She thought about her mother playing the piano on

the *Spirit of the Waves*. The *Western Wind* had no piano. And her hands were hardly suited for such a gentle pursuit now, even if she could play. Their nails were cracked, and their skin was rough. She rubbed lotion into them, to try to smooth them. They would never be a lady's hands again. They were not much good for anything but clutching a rope.

Wales would want her to tell him about the ship, anyway, not show him her hands. After all, what did he care about how she looked? And why should he care?

She was glad that they had gotten to be friends again, at least. It meant that if nothing else, he would talk to her. He would be glad to see her again. He would appreciate that she had stood up for him, in not allowing Dowling to take over the ship. If anyone had told him about that, he might have some words of praise for the way she had handled the crisis—and some criticisms, too. And she would listen to his criticisms, because she knew that she would learn from them, even though she never expected to find herself in that position again.

She wondered if she would ever sail with Wales again.

She called Ritter. "Can you tell Captain Rogers that I'm awake now, and I'd like to see him—when it's convenient?"

"Oh, he knows you're awake, Mrs. Rogers. I took the liberty of telling him as soon as you woke up. Actually, he instructed me to. And he's been waiting to see you. You can go right ahead." Ritter smiled at her, and repeated the last words over again, so as to make sure there would be no possibility of her misunderstanding. "You can just go on—go right ahead."

Wale's face was pale, and his hands were thin and bony, but he looked healthy. He stood up when Elizabeth came into the room, and she resisted the temptation to tell him to sit down and not overexert himself. She closed the door, and stood near it, somehow afraid to come any farther into the room. Her heart fluttered.

"Hello," she said.

"Hello," said Wales.

"It's—it's good to see you yourself again."

"Yes, it feels good. I've already been up on deck. If

we're lucky enough to get a couple of days of easy going now, I'll be able to handle anything after that. But you've already taken care of the hard part for me."

She stiffened, and her voice grew formal. She cleared her throat. "I want to give you a full report on that, Wales." She cleared her throat again. It was hard to maintain the formality of voice that she felt was appropriate for giving a report to one's captain. And, in fact, she was not doing it very well. "I know it was unorthodox . . ." she continued, "and I guess you might have reason to think I was being arrogant and acting out of line again, but that wasn't it, really. I only thought that—"

"Please. I don't need a report."

"You don't?"

"No. I've read the ship's log, and I've talked about it with Whiteurs. You saved all our lives, and that's no exaggeration. No one else on board could have done it."

"Dowling . . ."

"Could he? Maybe, and maybe not. He certainly couldn't have done better than you did. And he'd forfeited his right by his actions."

"But Wales, so did I! I was just as arrogant as he was, I didn't understand anything about what it meant to take responsibility. I thought I knew it all, and I didn't know anything! I thought I was so clever, and I wasn't clever at all. Wales—Thomas Dowling didn't do anything that I didn't do."

"Elizabeth, listen to me!" said Wales. "Do you know what it's like to be in a delirium?"

"No . . ."

"It's not like being awake, and it's not like being asleep. Things happen to you that aren't real—but you know they're not a dream, either, because you're awake, and you can see the blankets across your chest and feel the sweat on your hands and the pain in your back from lying in one place too long. Yes, and you can feel it when someone is putting a cold compress on your forehead, and see the person sitting beside you, even if you can't make too much sense out of it—not the kind of sense you make when you're normal, anyway. Hallucinations, I guess they call them, but they're really just a different way of looking at the world. Yes, that's it—you see things in a different light, and different things are important, or they're important in a different way. And you don't remember very much, afterward, but some things stay so clear in your mind that you'll never forget them."

He paused, but she stayed silent, waiting for him to go on. She looked troubled. She felt frightened, but frightened of what she could not have said. Her eyes were cast down, looking at her feet.

"Dammit, this is a long way around saying something that I've been much too long in saying anyway. I love you, Elizabeth. Nothing else is more important to me than that, and I'm not going to put up with anything short of it. I mean to have you!"

There was a note of decisiveness in his voice that she had heard him use on deck, but never to her—not even the time he had ordered her off the deck. She felt as if she were hearing him speak for the first time. Sht started to raise her eyes to look at him, and make some reply—she did not know what—but she found it was too late. She was already in his arms.

She found herself in bed just as suddenly. All the buttons, ties, hooks, bows—all the fumbling, the awkward parts where one is forced to stop and think, *Wait! Is this really the right thing? What if . . . ?*—all never seemed to have happened. All she was aware of was his touch, and thinking that she had never wanted anything so much.

There was no time to think. It would only have gotten in the way of the feelings, and she wanted all of them. She reached for them, and gathered them to her. Wales brought them to her, again and again; and when there was no more strength left to make love, their love had a strength of its own, and that kept on going between them as they lay naked, close to each other, touching each other's bodies in familiar places and secret ones.

᭡Chapter Thirty-four

THEY WERE TWO DAYS OUT OF BUENOS AIRES.
The sea was choppy, and the ship was crank, but the
barometer promised no more than annoyance, and Whiteurs
was on watch, so Wales allowed himself the luxury of a
second cup of coffee with Elizabeth before going out on
deck.

They were interrupted by a knock on the door. It was
Ritter.

"Your pardon, sir . . . ma'am," said the steward. "Mr.
Dowling asked me to carry a message for him when I
brought him his breakfast this morning. He would like to
see the captain before we land at Buenos Aires, whenever
it's convenient for you, sir. Oh, and Captain, I did not tell
him we were putting in at Buenos Aires. I do not make a
point of discussing the ship's plans with Mr. Dowling."

"It's all right, Ritter," said Wales. "Mr. Dowling's
guesses are pretty sound. He's an experienced seaman, and
he knows the ship's situation as well as anyone. We're
short-handed, and we've lost supplies."

"And you're going to see a doctor, and make sure you're
all right," said Elizabeth.

"Isn't that always the way it is?" said Wales, his eyes
twinkling. "You let a woman on board ship, and you get
soft. Not like the old days when men were men, is it?"

"No, sir," replied Ritter, straightening his shoulders and trying to look dignified.

"Oh, go along with the both of you!" said Elizabeth.

"Tell Mr. Dowling he can come in and see me now," said Wales, and Ritter left to deliver the message.

"Do you want me to leave?" asked Elizabeth.

"No, stay," said Wales. "We're still partners, aren't we?"

Dowling looked different from the way Elizabeth remembered him. He was subdued, less secure. He looked like a man who had gotten lost, and was just beginning to realize he would never find his way back home. Later, Elizabeth was to find that she would never remember Dowling any other way than this. She thought he was surprised to see her there, but he did not say anything, and he avoided looking at her.

"I've done a lot of thinking, these past weeks," he said. "Even if it's your own cabin, jail's a jail, and it changes a man. Oh, I don't mean I've never been in jail before. I've spent a few nights here and there . . . Kowloon, Hong Kong . . . always able to bribe my way out. Couldn't do that here, though, no way. And perhaps I'll be in jail again, someday. But this is different. Maybe it's being on board ship, maybe it's . . . I don't know, just thinking about what happened. It ain't like going to jail for smuggling, or killing a man in a fight."

He paused, and ran his hand through his hair.

"Get to the point, man," said Wales. "You were never one to beat about the bush—don't start now."

"I'll never get another commission on an American merchant ship," said Dowling.

Wales said nothing.

"It's all down in the log, in black and white. Insubordination . . . relieved of duties . . . cabin arrest . . . and whatever you want to call that other episode."

His eyes flickered sullenly to Elizabeth, but did not stay on her.

"It wasn't called anyting," Wales said. "It's not in the log."

"It's not?" said Dowling. He looked at Elizabeth again. She met his eyes for an instant, then turned to Wales. It was like coming in out of a cold rain.

"I didn't think it was necessary, Wales. I know one has to put down everything, but—"

"It's all right, dear. Some things are just as well not set down, even in a world as small as a merchant ship." He turned back to Dowling. "But I know the story. It's not exactly a secret aboard the *Wind*, even if it never leaves here."

"Never leaves here officially, you mean," said Dowling. "Everyone in every port where there are American merchant ships will know it. But it doesn't matter, anyway. All it'll take will be what's in the log, and I'm washed up. And I'm not saying it's not just."

"What are you saying?"

"Let me off at Buenos Aires. There's no point in my going back to New York. What good is it going to do you or anyone else if I go before a maritime board? Let me off at Buenos Aires, and I'll get a ship back to the Orient. That's where I belong. A man can get lost there, if he needs to—or make a fresh start. People don't ask questions."

Wales did not say anything right away. He sat and studied Dowling's face, never turning his eyes away from it.

"Let him go, Wales," Elizabeth blurted out.

Both men turned to look at her. Elizabeth's urge was to apologize, and try to take back her words, or explain them, or soften them, but she quelled the urge. Dowling had spoken his piece. She had spoken her piece. It was up to the captain to decide, and she, like Dowling, waited quietly for his decision.

"You'll be permitted to leave this ship at Buenos Aires," he said.

"Thank you, sir," said Dowling. He turned and walked out. He did not look at Elizabeth again before he left.

"I've got to get up on deck," said Wales.

"Make love to me before you go," said Elizabeth, touching his foot with hers.

He put his hand over hers. "I can't," he said. "The ship."

"Of course."

"This evening, though."

"This afternoon?"

"What if there's a hurricane?"

"If there's a hurricane . . ." she smiled at him provocatively, "this one will be your turn."

"Right, Captain Rogers," said Wales. "And if not—expect me this afternoon."